The Murder Next Door

Sarah Bell

A catalogue record of this book is available from the British Library.

First paperback edition June 2021

ISBN 978-1-5272-8779-2

sarahbellwrites.com

This book is written in British English and therefore uses British spelling, punctuation and grammar.

Chapter One

Murder Most Cliched

Leeds, West Riding of Yorkshire
July 1912

Murder was not a topic Louisa had expected to discuss at the breakfast table. She tried to summon some horror at the tale emerging from her maid's lips but failed. The whole sorry story was just one long cliché, ripped straight from the pages of a ha'penny novel. It was hard to connect it with reality, though a dead man lay on his study floor in the neighbouring house.

The maid's story was interrupted by the creak of the door opening. The sharp tang of paint and turpentine heralded Ada's arrival, and Louisa wrinkled her nose even as a smile tugged at the corner of her lips. Stepping into the darkness of the dining room with its Victorian mahogany furniture and russet wallpaper, Ada was a compelling beacon of colour. She wore her painting clothes, a faded men's shirt and trousers splattered with a rainbow of splodges. The sleeves and legs were rolled to fit her short frame; Louisa liked to tease her about it but, truthfully, she found the look rather adorable. An old ribbon tied at the nape attempted to control Ada's copper curls – a source of endless frustration for her and envy for mousy-haired Louisa.

Worry furrowed Ada's brow. 'Did you know the police are next door? I saw them from my window.'

'Yes, Sophie was over there earlier.' Louisa turned back to the maid, but she was no longer there. She must have returned to the kitchen to give them some privacy. 'She said she heard the Pearces' maid screaming when she stepped out to fetch the milk.'

'Why, what's happened?' As Ada sat, a smudge of indigo paint on her left cheek became visible. The dark splash contrasted with her pale skin and made the birthmark below less dramatic than usual in comparison. Two red blotches, each the size of a farthing coin, spread from cheek to hairline. Louisa yearned to reach over and wipe the offending blot away ever so gently.

But now was not an appropriate time, so, instead, she passed Ada a napkin. 'You have paint on your cheek.'

'Thank you.' Ada took the napkin with a soft smile and scrubbed at the smear until it was stained. She threw it aside and reached for the willow pattern teapot. 'No one's been round asking for me, have they?'

Louisa considered her answer before deciding on the stark truth. There was no way to dress it up. 'No, I doubt the police will require your services as a sketch artist. Mr Pearce is dead, and his wife is missing, which makes her the prime suspect, and they strike me as the type to have a family photograph.'

Husband, wife and son frozen forever in a happy tableau. A family now destroyed. The boy would be an orphan once the police caught his mother and hanged her. The first stirrings of a proper reaction welled within Louisa, but the heavy clunk of Ada dropping the teapot interrupted.

Louisa's heart seized – it was one of few items belonging to the mother she had never met – but it was unscathed by the fall. A splash spurted from the spout and spotted the white lace tablecloth with its carefully stitched daisies.

'That's why she ran away!' Ada jumped from her seat, and her chair flew backwards.

Louisa steadied the wobbling chair. Her mind raced to catch up with this unexpected response. 'You saw Mrs Pearce leave?'

Ada nodded vehemently. 'With her son. I was in my studio. I'd gone over t' window to smoke and was staring at their front door mindlessly when it opened, and there they both were.'

'When was this?' Such information might be of use to the police when they came asking questions.

'Just after dawn.' Ada pulled her seat back and sat down again. She turned her half-poured cup of tea in her hands and jiggled her leg under the table. Her nervous energy infected Louisa even as she did not understand it. When Ada spoke again, she was still staring into the swirling tea. 'She looked scared. Not like a murderess.'

The plea in her words unsettled Louisa further. Wasn't Ada's attitude towards Mr and Mrs Pearce in–line with hers? She had never particularly liked either of them. The husband had a discomforting habit of unwanted commentary and the wife a distracted air that made one feel insignificant. Yet the soft earnestness in Ada's voice made it clear she wanted Louisa to agree.

Louisa made her reply as gentle as possible. 'A murderess might be scared by what she had done.'

She was unable to study the effect of her words as Ada turned away to stare out the window. Louisa followed the direction of her gaze, but all there was to see was their small back garden awash with vibrant summer flowers.

'It may have been a terrible mistake.' Ada did not sound convinced by her own muttered statement.

'One does not mistakenly put poison in a man's drink.'

Ada's head whipped round. 'Is that how it happened?'

'An assumption.' One the police had already made, according to Sophie. A man dead, presumed poisoned. A missing wife. The obvious explanation.

Ada tilted her head. 'You hate assumptions. You're always telling me not to jump to conclusions.'

'True, but fleeing the scene is not the act of an innocent woman.'

The little 'hmmm' she received in response was anything but agreement. Louisa awaited a further response, but instead, Ada reached over and took a slice of toast from the rack. Not even pausing to butter it, she took a too-large mouthful. The resulting grimace told Louisa it was cold, and Ada pushed the plate away with a sigh.

Her disquiet clutched at Louisa's heart, and she shuffled her chair closer. Using the table as cover, she placed a hand on Ada's knee, which stilled its jig. The heat of her leg scorched Louisa through the rough cotton trousers. Ada's hand moved to rest on top of hers, their fingers intertwining, and Louisa squeezed them, trying to tell her all would be right.

Sophie's return defused the moment, but Louisa left her

hand where it was. She trusted the maid with her secrets.

'Are you finished, ma'am?' Louisa had long given up reminding the maid she was a 'miss' not a 'ma'am'.

'Yes, thank you.'

'And you, miss?'

Ada did not answer, her eyes somewhere else.

Louisa separated their hands and gave her knee the slightest shake. 'Ada?'

Her head jerked, and she gasped like Louisa had awoken her from a nightmare.

'Are you finished, miss?' Sophie hovered by Ada's shoulder.

'Oh, yes. Thank you.'

The maid kept glancing at Ada as she collected the used plates. When Louisa caught her eye, she gave a subtle shake of her head to tell Sophie not to ask questions. She must have understood, for she gathered the last of the cutlery and walked away until Ada's call stopped her in the kitchen doorway.

'Sophie? Have you heard anything else?'

The maid shook her head, blonde hair slipping from under her cap. A short girl of sixteen, her terror when addressed made her look even smaller. Louisa often pictured her as a cowering puppy, but left to her work she was competent, and that was all Louisa required.

'No, miss. Only what I heard from the Pearce's maid, Mrs Mills, and that I've already told Miss Knight. I've 'eard nowt – nothing – else.' The correction was for Louisa's benefit.

'There's always been rumours, though,' Ada said.

'Yes. It's a strange household, miss. Or so everyone says.'

'Everyone?' Louisa seized upon the word.

Sophie turned to face her. 'I mean Mrs Mills. And Miss Harrison and Miss Layton, two doors up, on t'other side. They all say no good happens there. That Mr Pearce was a wrong'un. Oh!' She raised a hand to cover her mouth, and the plates rattled precariously. 'I shouldn't say that now, should I? Now he's dead.'

'You are safe to speak your mind with us,' Louisa reassured her. She, too, had heard the rumours about Mr Pearce. Her disinterest in gossip was not enough to stop their local busybody, Mrs Martins, from pulling her over whenever she had a story to tell. Mr Pearce and his wandering eye had been a frequent source of speculation. Even then, Louisa suspected the collective knowledge of her neighbours was more sanitised than the tales Sophie's fellow servants had to tell.

Ada downed the last of her tea and dropped the cup back onto the saucer with a clatter. She stood in one swift movement and, with some regret for her remaining tea, Louisa followed her into the sitting room.

The contrast between the two rooms still surprised Louisa even though it had been several months since she suggested Ada re-decorate. She had been eager to remove all traces of the house she once rattled around in alone, the one she had feared becoming her dusty mausoleum.

The dining room had not been transformed yet, but the sitting room had been Ada's first project, and the difference to the space, how much lighter and more spacious it felt, awed Louisa. Ada had banished the old darker furniture and Louisa's father's clutter to the attic and stripped the bold geometrical print from the walls. She replaced it with a honeysuckle pattern up to the dado rail, followed by plain cream wallpaper above. Dominating the centre of the room was a pale-yellow damask sofa and chair, gathered around a wicker coffee table and a marble fireplace that sat cold this summer's morning. Lemon-coloured curtains completed the effect.

It was behind those curtains that Ada stood. The fabric engulfed her head and torso, leaving only her trouser-clad legs visible like she was trying to challenge the duck-billed platypus for the title of most bizarre hybrid.

'You do realise you are currently embodying every nosy neighbour stereotype there is?' Louisa said to her back.

If Ada heard her comment, she paid it no heed. 'A police constable's guarding the gate.'

'Well, that is to be expected.'

'I'm not sure who it is, though. It's definitely not Davey.' Hearing Ada refer to a police constable by a child's nickname never got less odd, but since David Wilkinson never corrected her, Louisa also refrained from doing so.

The curtain fell crookedly back into place as Ada reappeared. 'I'm going to go speak to whomever it is. See what I can learn.' She held out a hand. 'Come with me?'

Louisa took the proffered hand and held it tight even as she replied, 'Is that a wise plan?'

'We're concerned neighbours,' Ada spoke with faked earnest.

'Inspector Lambert's orders were clear. No more interfering.' Louisa's next sentence went unsaid: *Remember what happened last time.* A familiar unease crept up her spine.

'We're not interfering. Merely seeing if we can help.'

'No doubt they will knock on doors later, searching for information. You can ask them then.' Louisa led her further into the room, away from the window.

Ada halted them. 'But sooner is better than later. It would only be proper for us to inquire.' The last sentence was said in a mock-serious tone as she pulled Louisa towards the door.

Now, it was Louisa's turn to stand her ground. 'Would it? I doubt it is police protocol to have their sketch artist at a crime scene.' It certainly would win Ada no favours.

'I can still ask. We're next door, after all. It'd be stranger if we didn't go. Even the inspector can't disagree.'

Won't he be pleased to learn that fact? Louisa had no desire to be confronted with his stern frown again.

The police tolerated Ada's presence for her skill with a pencil and ability to turn even the vaguest description into a useable sketch. However, they had little patience for Louisa since the Mary Fellowes incident.

'Begging your pardon, ma'am.' Sophie hovered in the doorway. 'But Mrs Mills was in a bad way earlier. Having coppers stomping around the place for hours won't have helped.'

'And the neighbourly thing to do would be to go check on her.' Ada smiled at the girl.

Louisa bit back a sigh. She was outnumbered in her own home. Though she told Ada this was her home now, too, and she had told Sophie she wanted her to be comfortable here.

Their faces stared at her expectantly, and Louisa pushed down her concerns and conceded defeat. 'All right.' She squeezed Ada's hand, who rewarded her with a slight smile. 'Though you need to get changed first.'

Ada peered down at her tatty clothes as if she had forgotten about them. 'Good point. I'll be quick.' She disappeared upstairs.

'Thank you, ma'am,' Sophie said. 'I've been worrying about Mrs Mills. Can't be easy to see a sight like that.'

Sophie went back to her chores, leaving Louisa to consider how she would react if she found a dead body. Calmly, she would like to believe, though it was one of those questions without a certain answer until a person found themselves in that particular situation.

Ada's return in a pink cotton day dress and with her rowdy curls forced into a simple twist broke Louisa's morbid pondering. Now she was the dowdy one in her blue-stocking uniform of a white blouse and long, stiff black skirt.

'Shall we?' Ada stood at the bottom of the stairs, offering her hand again. They would have to separate before they went outside. Whatever excuses they could give for their living situation – patron, companion, dear friend – explaining away the pair of them leaving the house hand-in-hand would be far harder. Their hands separated anyway for the ritual of donning hats and gloves, though they forwent coats.

A warm breeze engulfed them as they stepped out onto the quiet street. There was a distant rumble of trams and carts from the main road, but here, all was still. There was no sign of movement along the row of detached houses. If her neighbours were copying Ada in spying out their windows, they were doing a good job of hiding it.

The sun beat down from a cloudless sky, a welcome change after a rainy June, and a promise this summer might just live up to the highs of its predecessor. It was the weather for a walk round Waterloo Lake and a picnic in Roundhay Park, not a day that spoke of murder and other matters most foul.

'Oh, it's Constable Goodwin.' Ada did not sound best-pleased. 'I might be able to convince him to let us in. It would have been easier if it had been Davey or Smith, though.'

Louisa made no comment, bowing to Ada's superior acquaintance with the Leeds Constabulary.

Constable Goodwin turned towards them as they approached, and sunlight glinted off the metal badge on his black helmet. Up-close, he was already red-faced and sweating, his post by the white picket gate far from any offer of shade. Mere misfortune, or had he irritated a superior? Louisa refrained from asking.

As predicted, he did not look pleased by their presence. 'Miss Knight, Miss Chapman, I heard that was your house and wondered when you'd show your faces. No doubt you've come to tell us all how to do our jobs.'

You do not look in need of instructions on how to roast in the sun.

Thankfully, Ada answered before any of Louisa's sarcastic replies could fully form. 'Now, when have I ever told you how to do your job, Constable? Our maid says Mrs Mills is quite shaken. We thought we might be able to offer her some comfort.'

Constable Goodwin's stern look faded slightly. 'Your maid's not wrong. A sweet little old woman like that shouldn't have had to see such a thing. We calmed her down enough to get a story from her, but last I saw, she was sobbing in the kitchen.' He wiped beads of sweat from his shiny forehead.

Louisa glanced at the sun, still only beginning its journey across the sky. He would be truly suffering come noon. 'Ada, did we finish that jug of lemonade yesterday?'

'Lemonade? No, I think we covered it and put it back in the icebox. Why?'

'Would you like a drink, Constable? We would not want you growing parched in this heat. Though I suppose this is preferable to last week's rain?'

'Indeed. They're saying it could turn into another swelter yet. But a drink would be much welcome, thanking you, miss.'

'No bother. I will fetch it now and meet you inside, Ada?'

'If I may?' she asked the constable.

'Just to see to the old maid?'

Ada nodded and, after a few seconds of further hesitation, Constable Goodwin stepped aside. He shouted a belated warning to not touch anything at her retreating back.

'I'll be right back,' Louisa told him. It did not take long to locate the leftover lemonade and a glass she did not mind entrusting to clumsy constable fingers.

'Thank you, Miss Knight.' Constable Goodwin seized the drink and took a large gulp. 'You'll be wanting to go inside as well, I suppose? None of your nosing now.'

Ah, so forgiveness cannot be bought as cheaply as a glass of lemonade.

Still, he stood aside once more, and she walked the short path to Mr and Mrs Pearce's front door and whatever secrets might lay within.

Chapter Two

Behind Closed Doors

Ada seized her chance. She stepped round the constable and down the footpath. She paused at the front door, turning to watch Louisa head back towards their own home. She would've preferred to have her partner by her side, but no doubt Louisa would convince Constable Goodwin to let her pass soon. With that reassurance, Ada twisted the knob and stepped through the doorway.

Even though she had lived next door for more than a year, Ada had never set foot inside this house before. Mr and Mrs Pearce were always faultlessly polite when they spoke on the street, but Ada reckoned they had their suspicions she was more than a 'companion' and didn't want the stain of any closer association. Though Louisa said they'd also never associated with her before Ada moved in, back when she was their odd spinster neighbour. Ada had joked about which would make the most unreputable acquaintance, the spinster or the Sapphic couple?

She paused in the hallway, searching for anything that told her a little more about its inhabitants. The most noticeable aspect was its blandness. With its cream walls and light brown trim, the only colour came from a standard landscape watercolour – green hills, blue sky, serene river. So predictable, it blended into its uninspired surroundings.

Shoes laid in neat rows in their rack: men's Oxfords, women's Gibsons and a schoolboy's boots. Two gaps showed where shoes had been taken, unlikely to return – the only things in the hallway that looked out of place. Everything else was perfectly in line; even the umbrellas stood tidy in their stand. Ada resisted the urge to pull one out and leave it discarded at the side or to mix the shoes up, anything to make the space look alive.

She turned back to the front door. The mottled glass made Constable Goodwin a blurred navy outline. Assuming his vision was equally impaired, she tiptoed to the nearest door and edged it open. If the layout was the same as Louisa's house, it would open into the sitting room.

The room laid in darkness, its curtains drawn tight, dulling the interior as if in mourning for its fallen master. Though the walls and carpets appeared to be more cream and brown, she would sketch this room in shades of grey and black. Grieving colours.

Like the hallway, it provided little insight into its owners. Expensive furniture imitating a well-known designer told her only that they liked to keep up appearances. She imagined similar pieces were in sitting rooms across the country. The one personal touch was a row of framed photographs on the marble mantelpiece. A gap suggested the police had taken one, as Louisa had said.

Ada took two steps into the room. She itched to study those photographs. Reason brought her to a stop; there would be no explaining it away if Constable Goodwin checked on her. The last thing she needed was him reporting her sneaking around a victim's house.

The smell of Sunlight soap led her to a spotless kitchen. Mrs Mills stood at the sink, scrubbing a large brass pan. Ada called her name, and she dropped it into the water with a splash, soaking the front of her apron. She swore, the word out of place from the lips of a placid-looking middle-aged maid. Ada guessed she was about five years older than her mother, who had just passed fifty last month.

White streaks stood out against her dark brown hair, more visible than usual as she wasn't wearing a cap. She must've taken it off during the morning's stress and never replaced it. There was no longer master nor mistress to scold her for slovenly ways. Her face was lined, with grooves at the mouth, but despite the crow's feet at either side, her blue eyes were lively. They would be Ada's focus if she ever painted this woman's portrait. The rest of her looked defeated by time and circumstance, but the eyes declared her not broken yet.

'I'm sorry to have startled you. I'm Miss Chapman; I live next door with Miss Knight. Our maid, Sophie, was worried about you.'

'Ah, she's a good lass, that Sophie. I'm doing all right, miss. Trying to get these pans clean, though I don't know why.' She scrubbed the pan with more force than necessary as she spoke. 'No one's here to cook for anymore. I needed something to do, I suppose, to take my mind off matters. Off Mr Pearce.' Her voice shook.

Ada wanted to jump straight onto the mention of Mr Pearce, but the clear upset in the maid's demeanour stalled her.

'Understandable.' Ada pointed at the pan in Mrs Mills'

hands. 'Falling back on old routines at a time like this, I mean.' She searched her mind for more to say. Usually, her conversational skills were a source of pride, but in that moment, she drew a blank. Everything sounded trivial compared to the enormity of what happened here this morning.

'You've done a good job here.' She gestured at the gleaming kitchen. 'It's spotless.'

Mrs Mills gave a weak smile. Ada's compliment appeared to calm her, despite its banality.

They turned at the click of heels on the tiled floor. Mrs Mills tensed, glancing at the doorway, but Ada relaxed. Louisa was here, and Ada's hand twitched to hold hers once more. Instead, she clasped them behind her back, like Inspector Lambert did when he had his serious talks with the officers.

She allowed herself the luxury of moving a bit closer to her partner, though. Louisa stood several inches taller than her, and though other women found her height intimidating, it made Ada feel safer at Louisa's side, like women who had tall husbands. She was best never asking any Sigmund Freud types what the reasoning behind that was.

'Miss Knight.' Mrs Mills bobbed her head in a manner people rarely did for Ada. They knew who owned the house she lived in.

'How are you, Mrs Mills? We heard you were the one who found Mr Pearce.' Louisa said the words gently, but the maid still flinched.

'Yes, miss. I got up as usual to light the fires, and there he was in his study.' Mrs Mills' hands trembled.

Ada lightly clasped them until their shaking stilled. She guided the maid away from the sink to a small table and chairs in the corner meant for the servants' meals. 'Would you like some tea?' Her mother's standard response to any upset; Ada copied her for lack of a better idea.

Mrs Mills welcomed the offer. Louisa refused but still took the seat opposite the maid at the table. Meaningless chatter about locating the tea bags and kettle was the only conversation, and Ada tried to keep her voice light, telling herself she had to be patient. They were supposed to be here to support Mrs Mills, after all. A barrage of questions she was too distraught to answer would serve no purpose. Still, she wished Louisa would say more, find some clever way of asking questions without asking them.

Mrs Mills received the teacup and saucer with a grateful smile. Louisa remained quiet; her sculpted face serene and her hazel eyes calm as she watched Mrs Mills sip her drink.

Ada debated whether she should take the initiative. Yes, the tea had been her idea, Mrs Mills had clearly needed something comforting, but how long was she expected to stand there in silence and ignorance?

Her mind drifted as she waited, inevitably returning to the scene that'd haunted her since dawn. Mrs Pearce at her front door with the boy. She'd hurried him down the path, glancing all around her. The brief moment when their eyes had met and the fear shining back at Ada compelled her to run down the stairs and outside. Not that it mattered; they were gone by the time she reached the street. She had returned to her painting room and tried to laugh at herself. What a silly thing to have done. Why would she do that? If she concentrated on her easel and pretended the answer was a mystery, perhaps it would erase the shadow she'd seen there. The flicker of a memory she would rather forget.

Mrs Mills cleared her throat, bringing Ada back to the present. 'Thank you for the tea. I needed it. It's been quite the morning. The police had all sorts of questions, as I'm sure you can imagine. I answered them as best I could, for all the difference it'll make.'

Her bitter words melted the last of Ada's refrain. 'What do you mean?'

'They've made their minds up already. Here, I'll tell you what I told them, see what you make of it.' Finishing the last of her tea, she turned to Louisa. 'People say you're a clever sort of woman.' She took a moment to steady herself and continued, 'I found him face down at his desk. At first, I thought him sleeping. He does that sometimes, sleep in his office, if him and wife have been having one of their rows, and they'd a belter yesterday evening. I heard them clear as if I was stood int' room with them.' She paused and chewed her lip. 'This is the bit that'll interest you, miss. She said there was something in her drink. Accused *him* of poisoning *her*.'

Ada gasped.

Louisa's next question, though, was calm. 'And you told the police this?'

Mrs Mills nodded. 'They didn't appear to think much of it. Guilty conscience, they called it, whatever that means. It'd make more sense to me, though. Mrs Pearce hadn't been all that well in some time. Always some complaint. She kept losing weight and became quite forgetful at times. She'd give me an order in the morning, and then in the afternoon, she'd give it again and not remember saying it earlier. And every time she seemed to get better, she got worse again not long after.'

Ada agreed. 'She did look ill when I passed her on the street a few days ago.' They'd swapped the obligatory polite greetings, and Mrs Pearce had given the standard 'I'm fine, thank you', but she hadn't looked fine. More like a sickly child dressed in her mother's clothing. Skin unnaturally pale, face hollow, and even thinner than usual. Malnourished like the poorest kids growing up, the ones who never knew when their next meal was coming. An odd look for a middle-class housewife whose husband prospered.

'Yes, miss. She's been worse these last few weeks, and doctors weren't much use. Everything they gave her didn't make no difference.'

'Was she eating?' Ada asked.

'Best she could.'

Louisa took over. 'Did you ever see either Mr or Mrs Pearce acting suspiciously? Tampering with the other's food or drink, perhaps?'

'Nothing stranger than usual.'

Ada and Louisa traded glances.

'Stranger than usual?' Louisa repeated. 'What was normal then? For here?'

'They argued. A lot. More than I'd think normal. I wouldn't expect spinsters like yourselves to know much on the subject, but me and my Harry – God rest his soul – we had our arguments, but never like that. They properly went at each other. Screaming and bawling, accusing each other of all manner of dreadful things, but it always ended the same way, with Mrs Pearce on her knees, crying, begging for forgiveness. And him talking to her like she was a naughty puppy he was trying to train. I even saw them once in the hallway. He was stroking her hair like you'd pet a dog, whispering that he forgave her. And she'd thank him, say she wasn't worthy of his forgiveness.'

Ada pictured the scene too easily, and horror rose from her stomach and seized her throat. What manipulative words had made Mrs Pearce so submissive? So broken? And what sort of man was Mr Pearce that he did such things?

Mrs Mills looked away from them, studying her wringing hands. 'I didn't tell no one. At the time, I mean. I'm no saint when it comes to gossip, I'll admit it, but those arguments, her begging to be forgiven...that weren't for the gossipmongers to know.'

'Did he ever hurt her?' Louisa's face was never easy to read, but even she couldn't hide her disgust. 'Physically, I mean?'

Mrs Mills shook her head. 'I worried he would, I won't lie. And always questioned what I'd do if he did. Servants, we're not meant to see, but we do. Think it comes as a shock to some of your sort. Your Miss Dawson, she says you're good people. That you got her out of a fix, Miss Knight. Though she never said what.'

'And neither will I.'

'I weren't going to ask, miss. I only say because the police think she did it, the missus. I told them about the arguments. It's just further proof in their eyes. But they never saw her grovelling on her knees. Didn't see how frail she was this last month.'

'Poisoning is not a murder that takes much physical strength. That is why it is called a woman's weapon.' Sarcasm oozed from Louisa's reply.

If Mrs Mills noticed, she didn't react. 'She didn't have the strength of character for it, miss. She learnt to lie in her bed a long time ago if you know what I mean. Strongest display of will I ever saw her show was insisting they hire me.'

'How so?' Louisa asked.

'I'm old. Men like Mr Pearce show no interest in old widows like me. And even if he did, I've got a lifetime of experience avoiding the hands of so-called gentlemen. Not so the poor girl before me.'

Beautiful girl, Miss Clarke. All three members of their Sapphic household had noticed. Though Ada had merely wanted to paint her, and Louisa never looked other than to appreciate beauty, such was her nature. As for Sophie, it was too personal a question for Ada to ask, but the girl kept her distance from her attractive counterpart, even once going so far as to dive back through the front door upon sighting Miss Clarke on the street outside. Ada assumed she'd learnt from her previous experiences when it came to pretty fellow maids.

The confused tilt of Louisa's head implied maybe she didn't remember Miss Clarke after all.

'He was having an affair with her,' Ada told Louisa, putting her and Mrs Mills out of their misery. 'You must remember. Shortly after I moved in?'

'Ah, yes. I remember hearing about it now.' She turned back to Mrs Mills. 'Was this a common occurrence?'

'Not with me, miss.'

'No, I mean, affairs in general.'

'Yes. Couldn't keep it to himself that one. Lot of their arguments were about that.'

'Why was she the one apologising then?' Ada asked.

'From what I overheard, miss, he always said they were her fault – his affairs. She drove him to it. I think she had an affair of her own many years ago, long before my time here, and he's been using it against her ever since. But that's only my guess based on what I heard. I did try not to overhear, best I could, and other times, I was too busy distracting their son.'

'Did he hear these arguments?' Ada couldn't shake the image of his small frame illuminated by the gas lights as his mother ushered him away from their home. Inquisitive lot, ten-year-olds. How much did he know of what had happened in this house? Of the fights, affairs, and now murder?

Possible murder. Though Ada had to admit, the more Mrs Mills talked, the more the police's presumption sounded correct. Louisa often told her the most obvious answer was usually the correct one. Even the notion that Mrs Pearce herself had been poisoned added weight to the idea she had chosen to retaliate.

'We tried to stop him from overhearing, myself and Miss Davis, the nursemaid. Still, his parents' fights weren't quiet. Don't get me wrong, they both loved their son, but when they fought, it was like all else stopped mattering.'

Again, Ada pictured this with ease. Forgetting everything else when the blood was up. She stole a look at Louisa, whose face remained passive. Ada had never heard her shout. The only sign of a temper was when her sarcasm came with more bite.

Louisa continued, 'What happened to Miss Davis? She

was let go a little while back, I recall. Why? Not...the same reasons?'

'No, she got her full references, unlike poor Miss Clarke. Mrs Pearce said her son was too old for a nursemaid, but we all knew she was worried. And why. She was worrying over nothing, though. Miss Davis weren't that stupid, and I think he knew it.'

'But she was still too pretty for Mrs Pearce's liking?' Ada vaguely remembered the woman, though not as vividly as she recalled Miss Clarke.

'That's right, miss.'

A beat of silence. Then, in her softest voice, Louisa said, 'You don't believe Mrs Pearce did this, do you?'

Mrs Mills shook her head. 'I'd believe Mrs Pearce's accusation more – that the poison was in her glass. I can't see the missus as a killer. I told police that, too, when they asked. They were all very polite about it, but they weren't listening. What'll happen to her? To the missus? If the coppers find her? Will she...will she hang?'

Mrs Mills' words stabbed Ada in the chest. Her fists clenched so tight, her nails dug painful grooves into her palm, and her ears rang with the frenzied roaring of the mob all those years ago. Calling for death. For a hanging.

She tried to silence them, focusing on Louisa's muted response to Mrs Mills' question.

'If she's found guilty, then yes. She will be hung.'

Ada tried to push away the image of Mrs Pearce's skinny neck in a noose. She only succeeded in replacing it with the image of a different woman, her body hanging limply from the rope.

She didn't hang, Ada reminded herself. *Mabel's still alive.* The image that had tortured her for months had thankfully never come to pass. Perhaps Mrs Pearce would be given the same reprieve.

'Ada?' Louisa's delicate eyebrows furrowed.

Ada unclenched her hands and muttered an apology. She took a deep breath, trying to calm her racing heart and rid herself of the falling sensation in the pit of her stomach.

Louisa's concerned expression didn't change.

Ada continued the previous conversation before she asked any questions. 'There's the possibility a judge could be merciful,' Ada told Mrs Mills, putting all her effort into speaking calmly. 'Reduce the sentence to life imprisonment. They might be more lenient because she's a woman.' Mrs Mills nodded along with her words, though when Ada dared a glance at Louisa, her frown had deepened. That frown only made Ada's stomach drop more.

Mrs Mills provided a welcome distraction when she asked, 'And what of Master Gallant?'

Ada stifled an inappropriate snort of laughter. She'd forgotten about the boy's ridiculous name.

Louisa must have managed to refrain from rolling her eyes as she answered the maid's question seriously. 'To family would be the usual arrangement.' She still spoke with her softest voice, like she was handling the maid with care. 'An aunt and uncle, perhaps, if he has them. Or grandparents.'

Mrs Mills shook her head. 'I don't think he's any grandparents still living. There's lots of aunts, uncles and cousins, though. Mr Pearce's people mostly. They'll all consider themselves proven right by all this. From what I've heard, they never liked her.'

Poor boy. Hopefully, his family would love him for his father's sake. If not, there was a small chance of a happy home for him.

Ada asked, 'Where do you think Mrs Pearce might go?'

'I don't know, miss. What I do know is she left the bedrooms in a fine mess when she fled. I wonder how I managed to sleep through the noise. The police had a good search through and told me not to move anything. If someone wanted to know where Mrs Pearce might have gone, they'd be best starting there.'

Ada began to say that of course they'd look, but Louisa answered before her. 'Thank you, Mrs Mills.' She stood. 'But I think we had best leave this to the proper authorities. We should be off now. Unless there is anything else we can do to help?'

Mrs Mills shook her head, eyes fixed on the scratches marking the table.

Ada didn't move, even as Louisa was halfway across the kitchen.

'There's no harm in looking,' Ada called after her. Was she really going to leave without bothering to help?

'Please, miss?' Mrs Mills pleaded.

Louisa stopped, glancing between the two women. Ada's eyes met hers. She wished she could see herself then through Louisa's eyes, for whatever Louisa saw, it made her give a reluctant nod.

Mrs Mills seized her advantage. 'Their room is first on the left. Master Gallant's is the one after. Thank you, misses.'

Ada set off upstairs before Louisa changed her mind.

What if the police were wrong? What if Mr Pearce had set his wife up? One last chance to manipulate her from beyond the grave? If this was his final cruel trick upon his wife, at least it could be stopped. All they needed was evidence, and perhaps that lie within the confides of their bedroom.

Chapter Three

Bedroom Secrets

M r and Mrs Pearce's bedroom was as stated – a fine mess. The only furniture not covered in clothes was the wardrobe, its contents spread across the double bed, vanity table, bedside cabinets and floor. Ada waded into the disarray, unsure where to start. What were they even looking for?

Louisa hovered in the doorway as if the room were contagious.

At least there was life here. Finally, Ada began to sense the character of this woman so missing in the blandness of downstairs. She shifted through the dresses piled on the bed. All were of the latest fashion in bold colours and designs. Keeping with trends could be a way to avoid attention as much as garner it, but the boldness of her choices spoke of a woman not afraid to draw the world's eye.

Smoke clung to several of the dresses. Lord above, a cigarette would be grand right about now! Ada hadn't smoked since being interrupted at dawn.

Trying to ignore her craving, she studied the dresses in her hands. Had Mrs Pearce removed these dresses from the laundry? Why? Ada moved on to the next one and sniffed it, pulling back in disgust at the smell of sour alcohol.

Scrutinising it more closely, Ada spotted a stain obscured by the darkness of the magenta fabric.

'Would you be able to test a drink stain?' she asked.

'Test how?' Louisa's reply oozed caution.

'For poison.' Ada threw the dress at Louisa, who fumbled the catch. The beading clattered against the floor.

'Ada! Mrs Mills said the police told her not to move anything. Even if I could test a stain – which is unlikely – I do not think the police will appreciate us removing potential evidence.' With a scoff, she picked the dress up from the floor and tossed it – with significantly less force – back onto the pile on the bed. 'Perhaps you could tell Constable Wilkinson. He could have it processed as evidence.'

'Davey,' Ada corrected. 'It sounds ridiculously formal when you call him Constable Wilkinson.' An old argument. Louisa and Davey had never managed to be more than uneasy acquaintances.

Ada snatched the stained dress from the pile to study it once more. Louisa had presumed the poison was in Mr Pearce's drink. Had Mrs Pearce's hand shaken as she poured the wine that killed her husband? Or had she been the one to spit out poison? Or was it all utterly unrelated? An accident at teatime, no more?

No matter how much she stared at it, the stain gave Ada no answers, and so she hurled it back onto the bed, turning her attention to the vanity table.

A large array of pots and powders peeked out from beneath a discarded corset, showing a woman who cared for her appearance and herself. Ada flung the corset aside and searched them, finding complexion powders and blotting papers, and rouge in one of those tiny pots. The ones designed to be so small they could be carried in a handbag whilst hiding the truth that a woman's rosy cheeks weren't natural. Ada recognised some of the names. Coty and Rubinstein. Most likely purchased in London and not cheap. But Mrs Pearce had left them all behind. Deemed them non-essential.

Ada twisted the lid off a pot of lip rouge. Scarlet. And unused. She ran a finger along its smooth top, turning her fingertip red. Had Mrs Pearce had second thoughts about the attention such a bright shade would bring? Or had she purchased it before she became ill? It would not have improved her gaunt look, nor would many of her clothes. Is that why she left them behind?

Ada's finger continued to trace a groove into the smooth surface. The red built up under her fingernail until it looked infected.

'It is just lip rouge, Ada.' Louisa's voice was soft. Now Ada was the one being handled with care.

Frustrated, she tried to jam the lid back on the jar. Her violent movements sent the black disc careening across the vanity table until it hit a green perfume bottle with a loud ding. Ada slammed the now lidless jar down and turned her attention to the row of perfumes in the right-hand corner of the vanity table. More well-known names. Coty again and Guerlain from France. Ada picked up the nearest bottle, a thin purple glass cuboid filled with a pale liquid. A lilac atomiser attached to its spray suggested this was what Mrs Pearce wore last.

'Do not...' Louisa began as Ada spritzed herself with the

scent. '...spray that.'

Ada instantly wished she'd listened, coughing and spluttering as a pungent floral smell invaded her nostrils and tickled the back of her throat.

'Did you learn anything?' Louisa asked.

Ada much preferred her dry wit when she aimed it at other people. 'Her taste in perfume leaves something to be desired.'

'Yes, I can smell that for myself.' Louisa wrinkled her nose, wafting her hand in front of her face. 'Foul-smelling though it is, I doubt it was that which poisoned her husband.'

And what of the husband? This was their room, yet where was he? Where was his mark on this shared space? Was it merely the recent explosion of feminine clothing that buried him? Or had he lived surrounded by her things? An invader in a space she claimed for herself?

Now that she searched for them, Ada spotted the odd thing here and there. A pair of trousers thrown in a corner, the shaver on the washstand, and cologne on a bedside table. Easy to miss amongst the chaos Mrs Pearce had left in her wake.

'A hasty escape.' Louisa also examined the mess. 'She had not packed a bag to leave by the looks of it, which implies his death was not planned. Or at least not planned for last night.' She checked her wristwatch. 'We should leave, Ada. No good will come of us being caught here.'

Louisa was right. Of course, she was right. If Constable Goodwin caught them, he would go straight to Inspector Lambert. At best, Ada would get another caution. At worst, she'd lose her job with the police and be under suspicion herself.

She wrung the atomiser in her hands, staining it with the rouge still on her finger. Mrs Pearce was a vivacious woman, judging by her bold clothing choices, yet her brightest cosmetic was unworn. And, according to her maid, she spent her days on her knees, begging forgiveness for past sins. Had she had enough? Was this as clichéd and simple as Louisa said it was?

Whatever the answer, it wasn't to be found in this room. Or, at least, Ada wasn't the person to find it.

Disappointment squeezed Ada's heart. Louisa was saying something, but it was no more than white noise, overpowered by the screams and yells of that fateful day.

Despite the intervening five years, Ada was there all over again. Fighting her way through that baying crowd, ploughing onwards regardless of who she shoved out of the way. Repeating the same mantra to the rhythm of the blood beating in her ears: *It's not Mabel. It's not Mabel. It's not Mabel.*

At last, she had pushed her way to the front, and with only a constable blocking her path, she finally had a clear view of the woman they were dragging to the cart. Her whole world crumbled around her.

Mabel was frantic, clawing and kicking at the police officers, screaming that she was innocent. Her blonde hair fell all over the place, her hat half off her head as she threw herself this way and that, trying to escape the policemen's grasping hands. Her sapphire eyes, whose sparkle Ada had so enjoyed, were wild with terror. Ada yelled her name, trying to force her way past the constable. Over his shoulder, Mabel's gaze locked onto hers, just like Mrs Pearce's.

'I didn't do it, Ada! I didn't. Please! You have to believe me! I didn't do it!'

Ada believed her then, but her certainty had been slowly chipped away. Not that what she thought mattered. Judge and jury had found Mabel guilty.

She'd looked so tiny on the defendant's box. So helpless. Mrs Pearce would be the same.

Ada yelled, raising her arm to throw the perfume bottle across the room. A satisfying image – it smashing against a wall. Louisa prevented this, prising the bottle from her hand.

'I don't understand,' Ada spat the words out, struggling to speak, both past and present strangling her. 'What did Mrs Mills think we'd find here? It tells us nothing. Except she didn't pack her evening wear to go on the run.'

'I think Mrs Mills hoped we would learn something here, which does not mean there is necessarily something to be learnt.' That soft voice again. Ada would've preferred if Louisa shouted and told her to stop acting like a fool, even though she never would.

Louisa pulled a handkerchief from her skirt pocket and pressed it into Ada's stained hand. Once the mess was wiped away, Ada surveyed the room once more, trying to find what she'd missed. What clue had the police officers overlooked that a fellow woman's eyes might spot? A woman who had not already decided Mrs Pearce's guilt.

Yet what proof did Ada have of Mrs Pearce's innocence? A quick glimpse of fearful eyes had been compelling enough to send Ada hurtling downstairs and outside, wanting to help. Compelling enough to risk her job searching a murder victim's bedroom. But not compelling enough to convince a jury.

'I keep seeing her leave,' she whispered to Louisa, who pulled her into a hug. Ada clung to her, breathing in Louisa's favourite orange blossom scent. She wanted to stay there, forgetting about murder and poison and terrified eyes.

'I know,' Louisa muttered in Ada's ear, stroking her arm. 'I know. But there is nothing we can do.'

It'd be easy to agree. To give up. This was not their responsibility.

But there was a scared woman and a little boy out there somewhere.

Ada broke their hug. 'Let's look in the boy's room. Then we'll go.'

She didn't give Louisa time to disagree, striding past her to the next door down. Here, too, chaos reigned. Clothes were strewn all over. A toy box sat emptied of its contents. Trains, soldiers and boats littered the floor.

She picked up a few items at random, but they told her little. Woollen trousers and tin soldiers – the artefacts of schoolboys everywhere.

Where do children hide their secrets?

She was lying on her stomach under Gallant Pearce's bed when Louisa's voice rang out above her. 'Ada? What are you doing?'

'Looking for clues.'

A huffing sound illustrated Louisa's disgruntlement.

There were no boxes or toys under his bed. The room was carpeted, so no loose floorboard like Ada's favoured hiding spot as a child. She craned her head back as far as was possible, searching for anything hidden between the underside of the mattress and the wooden slats. As teens, her older brothers had gotten hold of a couple of erotic photographs and hid them in such a way. Not that she expected Gallant to possess such items, but still, it was best to check every possibility.

Finding nothing, she started to crawl backwards out of the confined space, muttering expletives under her breath – and out of Louisa's hearing – as her hair caught on the bed frame and pulled at her scalp. A short fight with the tangled strands freed her. She caught Louisa trying not to smile as she stood up and attempted to flatten her fly-away curls.

When Louisa spoke, though, her voice was sardonic. 'Find any clues?'

Ada ignored the question. She turned around on the spot, scanning the room. 'Where else would a child hide things?' she murmured as much to herself as to Louisa, not expecting an answer.

'Who says he had anything to hide?'

'All children keep secrets from their parents. Not always exciting secrets, admittedly. You're telling me you didn't have a spot where you hid things you didn't want your father to know about?'

Louisa frowned, but she proved Ada right by answering immediately. 'Yes, I did. Behind my bookcase.'

Ada wanted to ask what she had kept there – Louisa didn't talk about her father or her childhood often – but she pushed it aside to return to at a later date.

Both women turned to the pine bookcase stood in the corner. 'Worth a try,' Ada announced.

She grabbed a side and started dragging it forward, smiling at Louisa, who held up the other side to help. Curiosity always got the better of her.

Their efforts yielded a small gap. With a yelp of victory, Ada reached into it and seized a wooden box and raft of papers. The first page was dominated by an image everyone in the country recognised: the doomed RMS *Titanic* before its sinking. An advertisement clipped from a magazine invited passengers on the ship's glorious maiden voyage.

The next sheet had been clipped from a newspaper, its headline declaring, 'DISASTER TO THE TITANIC.'

A familiar headline. Three months ago, Louisa murmured 'My God' as she stared at the front page. Ada's teasing, that it was an odd choice of exclamation for a committed atheist, died in her throat as she leaned over to read the harrowing article. In one tragic night, fifteen-hundred souls had entered the icy Atlantic Ocean's cruel embrace. The news had only gotten worse as the days and weeks went by, and more stories appeared about the dead and missing. Many of them were passengers from the ship's lower decks, working-class people like Ada and her family who went on board with hopes of a new life.

People had believed such a marvel couldn't sink. That they were safe. They were wrong, and now they were dead. Such was the unpredictability of life. Death always hid around the corner – ask Mr Pearce. Ada planned to make the most of living whilst she was still alive, and such shocking news only cemented her belief.

Louisa peered over her shoulder. 'Strange thing for a little boy to keep.'

Why had young Gallant kept them? He was hardly the only person fascinated with the doomed ocean liner, but what in particular had so grabbed the attention of a young boy? Sheer morbidness? Little boys could be cruel. Fascinated by the notions of pain and death. A boy who lived two streets back from Ada growing up had strangled his neighbour's cat. And there were the boys who loved to torment the girls at school. Pig-tail pulling and pinches. Her brothers used to tease her, saying it meant the boys liked her. Even as a child, she found that an odd notion, and now as an adult, she found it even odder.

'Little boys are strange,' Ada replied.

Some boys never grew out of that mindset. They just learnt different and crueller ways of supposedly showing their affections. Like Mr Pearce, stroking his wife's hair and forgiving her for driving him to his affairs.

Ada touched her hand to her cheek, where the red blotches marked her skin. It had been both boys and girls who'd found cruel words for that.

Louisa lowered Ada's hand, briefly caressing her marred cheek. She held it loosely but said nothing, both returning their attention to the clippings. She must have known where Ada's mind had gone, even if she was no doubt questioning why the *Titanic* made her think about it.

It was unlikely the clippings had any bearing on Gallant's father's death, but the boy's obvious obsession with the tragedy was fascinating in its own right. Ada returned her focus to them, shuffling through them until a stern voice made her jump, sending the wooden box clattering to the floor and the papers flying into the air.

'And what do you think you're doing here?'

Chapter Four

The Art of Remembering

Ada yanked her hand away from Louisa's. Excuses flew through her mind as her stomach twisted.

Her panic was squashed as quickly as it had flared. It was only Davey. He grinned at her, flashing teeth that were not quite white and set in an unremarkable face. The most noteworthy aspect of his appearance was that – despite summer so far consisting of only two days of sun – he already sported a golden tan.

No one would call him ugly, but he was not a handsome man either. When Ada wanted to tease him, she said he possessed 'the most boring face I've ever seen.' When she tried to be kind, she called it 'distinguished.'

The most accurate way to describe him, though, was tall. If Louisa made Ada feel small, then Davey made them both tiny.

'Not funny,' she admonished him. Her smile undercut her statement.

'Quite funny. From where I'm standing, anyway. So, what you doing moving furniture at an active crime scene?' The question was jovial, but Ada doubted he would appreciate the honest answer.

Davey bent down towards the mess scattered across the

floor. Mixed amongst the *Titanic* clippings was a collection of toy boats. They must have spilled out of the wooden box she'd dropped.

When Davey stood up again, he had a sheaf of paper in one hand and a toy in the other. Ada gestured towards the boat, and he passed it to her. It was wooden, intricately carved and decorated, the details picked out in shiny red and yellow paint. Expensive, Ada would bet. On the bottom, Gallant had stencilled his initials in pencil.

'So, I'm sensing a theme 'ere.' Davey waved the clippings at her.

'Excellent police work, Constable.' Ada smirked.

His eyes narrowed into a glare, but the smile pulling at the corners of his mouth betrayed him.

'Why hide them?' Louisa, too, held a toy boat.

'He didn't want his parents to know?' Davey suggested. 'It's a slightly odd obsession.'

Ada bent down and grabbed the fallen wooden box to collect the boats. They were all variants of the same colour scheme. 'Boys have all sorts of obsessions, though. You went through a stage where you dreamed of being an actor if I remember correctly.'

Somewhere above her head, Louisa stifled a giggle.

Ada finished collecting the toys and straightened up.

She'd wiped the grin from Davey's face, but he recovered quickly, smiling at her once more. 'Never going t' let me forget that, are you?'

'Of course not.'

'This is somewhat different, though. Why is a ten-year-old boy obsessing over a national tragedy?'

Ada rattled the box. 'And why would he hide expensive toys?' She held it out to Louisa, who placed the toy in her hands with its fellows but remained quiet.

'Stolen?' Davey suggested.

Ada turned back to him, eyebrows raised.

He shrugged. 'It'd surprise you how many supposedly well-bred boys and girls get caught shoplifting.'

'Maybe,' Ada said. 'But I'm not sure any of this is relevant to his dad's death.'

'No. Probably not. We found the drug we think did his dad in, though. In the wine cellar – perfect for slipping into a drink.'

'What was it?' Louisa asked the question before Ada.

I knew her curiosity would win out.

'Hyoscine,' Davey answered.

Ada searched both their faces for a clue as to what that signified, but neither gave anything away.

Davey continued, 'They'll do the autopsy this evening, which should confirm if that's what killed him. Beyond that, it's a clear-cut case. The wife is the obvious suspect. The only hard part will be finding her and the boy.' He gestured at the messy room. 'You find anything in this lot that could help? Or in the master bedroom?'

Ada shook her head, not bothering to deny she'd also searched Mr and Mrs Pearce's bedroom.

'She packed in a hurry,' Louisa said. 'Not a planned escape.'

'We'd figured as much already.'

'Did you find the dress?' Ada pointed to the next room. 'The one that smells like sour wine.'

Davey's brow furrowed. 'I wasn't on shift this morning when they searched the place. Is it still there? I'll bag it and take it t' station. It might count as evidence, given where we found the poison.'

Guilt curdled in Ada's stomach. Had she given them another bit of the rope with which they'd hang Mrs Pearce? Ada had never witnessed a hanging, but she'd imagined one so often that the thud of the trapdoor and the creak of the rope echoed in her mind.

Not privy to her dark imaginings, Davey continued, 'You realise I'll have to take credit for this?'

Louisa gave a most unladylike snort. It brought Ada back into the room, and her mind raced to catch up with Davey's words. She shrugged; she could hardly demand recognition considering she shouldn't even be there. 'Fine. We should put this back and get off anyway.'

'No.' Davey took the box from her. 'I should bag this lot, too. It's probably just a childish obsession, but if the boy felt the need to hide them, we can't overlook it. Leave the bookcase; I'll deal with it. Oh, and go out the back door.' Davey jabbed a thumb in its general direction. 'The vultures are gathering outside.'

'You think this will make the headlines?' Ada asked.

'Here in Leeds, it will.' Davey rolled his eyes. 'I've already had our friend, Mr Smith, from Yorkshire Post badgering me. We're hoping it doesn't go national.'

Ada's face scrunched up. 'Couldn't that help with finding her?'

'Possibly...or spook her.' Davey returned his attention to the clippings in his hand, shuffling through them. 'And as best we know, she has the boy.'

'She does. I saw them leaving through my studio window.'

His head snapped up, eyes boring into her. He was Constable Wilkinson now. 'You saw them leave?'

Ada reiterated what she had told Louisa earlier, emphasising once more how scared and uncertain Mrs Pearce had looked.

She left out the part where she went running to help her, but Davey's first response was still, 'You don't think the wife did this.' A calmly stated fact.

Like Louisa, Davey read her like an open book. Most days, it didn't bother her, lying was too exhausting anyway, but today she would've liked her face to reveal less.

'I don't.'

'And you, Miss Knight?'

'I think it is plausible. But there is a lot that does not add up.'

'Such as?'

'You finding the poison for a start. She may have packed hastily, but is that not the one thing she would have remembered to either dispose of or take with her? And then there is her accusation against her husband – that he was poisoning her.'

'The maid tell you that? It's odd, no denying it. But she's not the one who wound up dead.'

'No, she is not.'

Their agreement led to mutual silence, Mrs Pearce's probable guilt an acknowledged fact between them. Ada wanted to break it, to disagree, but what argument could she make?

Davey offered to show them out. At the side entrance, he let Ada leave first and hung back to say a few words in Louisa's ear.

'What was that about?' Ada asked when Louisa caught up with her and they entered the house.

'He was worried about you.' Louisa bent down to unfasten her shoe buckles.

'Well, he doesn't need to be. Is that all he said? I can't think why he'd say that to you and not me.'

'Because we are both people who care about you?'

Ada smiled even though the answer didn't sit right with her.

In the kitchen, Sophie waited for them, intensely polishing Louisa's boots in an obvious attempt to feign disinterest.

'Mrs Mills will be all right,' Louisa told her. It was doubtful that was Sophie's only interest, but what else was there to tell her?

Ada didn't dally downstairs, escaping to the peace of her painting studio. A spare bedroom when she first moved in, Louisa had been eager for her to alter the room for her purposes. There was still a small single bed, hidden beneath piles of canvases. They'd decided the bed was necessary in case some nosy guest should ever question their sleeping arrangement.

Gathered on every available shelf and tabletop were paints in a wide variety of colours, brushes, sketchpads, and jars of dirty water. In the centre stood her easel, the half-finished painting from earlier that morning waiting for her return.

It appeared dull now. She had been experimenting with different brush strokes, trying to evoke the wind and rain of a grim evening in town. People rushed to and fro whilst trams and carts rattled along the roads. Everyone's heads down, focused on their own business, on getting home. She'd hoped to capture their isolation and urgency, but it was stagnant on the canvas, and she placed it with all the other work gathering dust on the bed.

Ada threw the window open to bring some air into the stuffy room and took a packet of cigarettes and matches from the windowsill. She lit one and breathed deeply, letting it calm her jittery nerves. She studied the scene outside as she blew smoke out the window. Constable Goodwin was still stood by the gate to the Pearce house, a few bored journalists gathered around him. A couple of them had dispensed with their jackets and hats in the heat, though the constable still sweated in his uniform.

A previously discarded sketch pad sat on the windowsill, and Ada flicked through it. All the drawings were insipid. Boring. Silly sketches of flowers and landscapes. Some original designs for the sitting room which looked nothing like how it had eventually ended up. She found a blank page, threw her cigarette end into a jar of dirty water, and reached for a pencil, but the view outside provided no inspiration. Instead, all she saw was the scene from that morning.

Maybe getting it down on paper would help exorcise it from her memory.

Mrs Pearce began to take shape on the page, the moment when she looked towards the window and their eyes met. Soon, Ada had drawn all but her face. That expression. If she got it right and showed Louisa, perhaps she would finally understand what compelled Ada.

Her pencil hovered over the blank space, but she dared not draw, tracing shapes in the air above the paper.

Instead, she moved on, drawing Mrs Pearce's son stood next to her. The one with his mind fixated on the cruel, icy deaths of the *Titanic*'s passengers. Yet the boy she drew was small and scared, hunched over in his coat.

Ada's pencil hovered once more over his mother's face. She made the softest indent where her eyes should be, barely visible on the page. They already looked wrong.

She swapped her pencil for another cigarette and turned back to the window. Outside, the journalists had dispersed. A few houses down, their local busybody – what was her name, Mrs Martins? – talked to one of them with great animation. What story was she weaving for them? No doubt Ada would find out in tomorrow's Post.

A warm breeze ruffled her hair as she blew the smoke out the window. It did little to cool her, and she sweated in the sun. Constable Goodwin had finally given in and removed his helmet. Davey must still be inside gathering evidence, or perhaps he had left when she was distracted.

What had he said to Louisa? Maybe it was just concern, like Louisa said, but why would he say that to Louisa and not her?

She shook the thought away, throwing the cigarette butt into the jar with its fellow, and concentrated on her sketch once more. The pencil was sticky in her clammy hand as she sketched in the surrounding details: the gravel path, the short picket fence and gate, the flowers on either side of the door.

The flowers were amiss. Too much detail. Too intricate for such a tiny space on the page. She was only putting off what was to come.

There was nothing left to draw but Mrs Pearce's face. The fear and horror and guilt.

Guilt. Ada hadn't considered it guilt before. Was her memory playing tricks on her? Trying to calm her conscience, convince her Mrs Pearce was guilty. So she could leave well enough alone without reprimanding herself?

Just like I did with Mabel.

A torrent of anger and shame overtook her until she feared she would be sick with the force of it. She unleashed her emotions on the picture, slashing across it with heavy pencil lines. They turned into large spirals spreading across the paper until all the detail was obstructed. The page was black, like the pictures she'd ruined as a kid. Yet she kept scribbling, pressing harder and harder until she ripped through to the next page. She pulled both pages out in disgust, leaving a ragged edge. The wad of balled-up paper missed the bin and skidded across the floor.

'Ridiculous!' she shouted. 'Absolutely ridiculous. You need to stop this. Stop it now. Before you ruin everything.'

She paced the short length of the room, but the limitations on her movement only made her feel more trapped. She wanted to walk far away, to start in any direction and never stop. Go where there were no dead neighbours. No former lovers in prison. No current lovers questioning her sanity.

Her pacing halted, and she closed her eyes as the memory played once more. The screams. The anger. And Mabel's frenzied fear.

Ada strode to the stacks of paintings piled on the bed and flung the topmost canvases aside with little care for her work.

Hidden at the bottom was a portrait of a woman. Blonde waves spilled down her back, and she grinned back at Ada. A cheeky promise in her eyes, a smile, and a chemise were all she wore. It hung ever so slightly off her shoulders. A tantalising suggestion of what waited beneath.

Ada's fingertips softly traced the wobbly paint strokes, where she had been unable to hold her brush properly from laughing. Mabel hadn't been able to stay still for long without giggling. Her laughter was infectious. Even now, it brought a grin to Ada's face.

It'd been one of her most treasured moments. Before that day. Before the murder. Before Mabel's imprisonment. When they were two young women in love and Ada day-dreamed of the nights to come through long, dull days at the mill. They believed they could take on the world and win.

They'd been wrong.

Mabel always maintained she didn't murder Mr Shaw. The judge agreed but only to the extent that he downgraded it to manslaughter and gave her life imprisonment instead of the noose.

Ada used to visit, back when she believed her innocent. The more evidence came out, the harder she found it to believe. It had been Davey – newly minted as a police constable – who convinced her in the end. They had the shoes Mabel tried to scrub clean and hide, a match for the bloody footprints found near the body. The witnesses who saw her fleeing the scene. She had been open about her dislike of Mr Shaw and disparaging of his treatment of the female mill workers.

Eventually, Ada was no longer so sure. She begged Mabel

for the truth, but she had no explanation, just her repeated refrain of 'I didn't do it.'

Ada's visits dwindled, then stopped.

A year later, she met Louisa. She was only curious at first. Louisa was closed-off, a mystery. But the more Ada made an effort to know her, the more she saw the person hiding behind the mask. The witty humour that took Ada by surprise at first but helped her to laugh again. During long walks when they would talk about anything and everything, Ada revelled in Louisa's enthusiastic answers, in drawing out the passion that lurked within her and the genuine interest Louisa showed in her in return.

What was Louisa doing now? Was she contemplating Ada and her odd behaviour? Was she thinking of Mrs Pearce? Or had she already written off the day's events? Like Ada should.

Ada hid the painting back underneath the other canvases.

With forced determination, she returned the morning's painting to the easel. She would complete it. Forget about Mrs Pearce. It was a matter for Davey and his colleagues. Despite their disagreements with Inspector Lambert, he was a clever man. Thorough. Not the sort to make an arrest for the sake of making an arrest.

Ada made her mind go back to last week as she mixed her paints. A June day so cold and wet it felt like February. As if the entire city had heard the phrase 'It's grim up north' and taken it as a personal challenge. She'd stood at the tram stop on her way home from the police station, shivering in her light summer coat, and wished the tram would arrive. Her attempt to kill time by doodling in her small sketchpad had been foiled by the wind, but she'd pulled it out again in the shelter of the tram, committing the miserable day to paper as best she could with another passenger at her elbow.

She planned to mockingly call the completed painting *A Summer's Day*. Nothing appealed to an English audience more than a collective grumble about the weather. She purposely used winter colours: smoky greys, dirt browns, and midnight blues. It was these that sat on her palette again, waiting for her.

Ada wet her brush, dipped it into the grey paint, and began.

Chapter Five

'Dinner' and a Dance

The painting was nearly finished when a knock on the door pulled her from her work.

'Ada? Dinner is almost ready.'

She kept painting as she called back, 'Since when do you call it dinner?'

Louisa always insisted dinner was the evening meal, unlike Ada, who had grown up with 'breakfast, dinner and tea.'

The door clicked open. 'It's six o'clock. You missed lunch; I didn't want to disturb you.'

'Have I really been in here that long?'

Louisa gave a small chuckle. 'You know what you get like when you paint.' She stepped closer, looking over Ada's shoulder, so close her breath tickled the back of Ada's neck and sent a shiver down her spine. 'That's Vicar Lane, is it not? Looks even grimmer than it usually does.'

Ada studied the picture with a critical eye. Perhaps she had overdone the gloomy tone.

Louisa touched her arm. 'Is everything all right?'

'It's just a picture, Louisa. Don't read too much into it.'

Ada moved away to clean her brushes as Louisa said, 'You're the one who always tells me–' She gasped. 'Your lovely new dress.'

Ada glanced down. She'd forgotten to change when she came home. Her dress was ruined, the light pink fabric coated in dark smears. She tried to scrub some off with her fingers, but it was already dry.

Ada swore, and Louisa flinched. She was so prissy about swear words.

The dress had been a treat to herself; she'd only bought it two weeks ago. How bloody foolish of her!

'Maybe Sophie can get it clean. If we ask her to soak it straight away.' Louisa didn't sound convinced.

'No. It's ruined.' Ada marched past her partner and into their bedroom. How could she forget to change? What a waste of money.

The buttons refused to unfasten under her shaking fingers. 'Damned things!'

'Here.' Louisa's fingers were soft but determined. In another situation, Ada would have savoured the sensation of her partner undressing her, but now all she felt was embarrassment. More like a child who needed help than a lover.

Tears brimmed in her eyes, but she tried to hold them back. She wouldn't cry. Ridiculous! What did she have to cry about? She was not dead or in prison or on the run from the law.

What must Louisa think? She'd never let Louisa see her cry before. She never let anyone see her cry if she could help it. No one took a weeping woman seriously.

Her dress finally pooled at her feet as Louisa undid the last button. Stepping back, she passed Ada a handkerchief without comment.

Swiping at her eyes, Ada asked, 'What's for tea?'

Louisa didn't correct her as she'd hoped. 'I asked Sophie to fetch a joint of pork.'

'My favourite.' Ada gave a watery chuckle and turned away from Louisa towards her wardrobe. 'I should get changed. I'll meet you downstairs?' She needed a moment to compose herself.

'Sure.' She waited until the soft pad of Louisa's retreating footsteps faded away.

Ada stared at her clothes. If she allowed her thoughts to return to Mrs Pearce or Mabel or Louisa, she would never make it downstairs for tea. Which dress to wear was at least a simple choice.

She shifted through them, eventually coming to a mint evening dress she often wore at home. Simple but pretty with a small, beaded pattern at the chest. She put it on as quickly as possible. Louisa was waiting, and the food would be going cold in its pans.

Downstairs, Ada took her seat at the hideous dining table. Louisa had tried her best with the new tablecloth she'd bought in Kirkgate Market – the daisy pattern was pretty – but nothing could disguise the table's bulky ugliness. Ada relished the idea of getting rid of it when she refurbished.

The whole room, with its dark and rich look, was stuck in the last century. Russet wallpaper with a golden-yellow diamond pattern throughout and an intricately detailed leaf border graced the walls. The mahogany table and china dresser matched the doors and window frame, which had heavy burgundy curtains on either side.

Light, that was what the room needed. To banish the last ghosts of Louisa's miserable father. But Louisa was reluctant, and though the late Mr Knight didn't sound like a man worth mourning, he was her father, so Ada didn't push the issue.

Sophie brought in the food and gave Ada a tight smile when their eyes met. Had she heard what happened upstairs?

'How was the rest of your day?' Ada asked Louisa with false cheer. 'Did you get to read...' She drew a blank. What book was it Louisa mentioned yesterday evening? It felt so long ago. The interceding day a mountain between them. 'The, um, t'other book you said you wanted t' read.' Her accent bled out as she scrambled to remember. She tried not to speak too strongly nowadays. Away from the mills and factories, a strong accent drew attention. And not the good kind.

'The new Sarah Grand book? No, I have not got a copy yet. I have been reading one of father's textbooks.'

Ada tried to comprehend the science and theories which so fascinated Louisa, but she struggled to keep up. She reassured herself that Louisa couldn't pick up a pencil and start drawing. At least not with any skill.

'What about?'

'Chemistry.'

Ada gave her a puzzled look. Louisa always had to be reminded to talk in simple terms. Such a vague answer implied she didn't want to discuss it, and Ada returned her focus to the food on her plate. It was lukewarm at best, the pork overcooked and chewy. She forced herself to keep eating.

Louisa said no more. Not about chemical compounds nor Ada's earlier silliness nor anything else, though Ada wished she would. The silence hung awkwardly between them, the table stretching until it was a football field dividing them.

It was Ada who nearly always broke such silence, saying the first thing that came to mind. 'Do you think Mrs Pearce killed him?' No point beating around that particular bush.

'I think she is the most likely suspect – nay, the only suspect at this time. The maid's revelations made me more sympathetic, more able to understand why she would want him dead, but that does not stop it from being a crime. This is not our fight, and I see no benefit in fighting it.'

Ada pushed the last of her vegetables around her plate. 'You're right. I know you are. I need to forget about her. It's not our problem, and we shouldn't make it so. That's why I was painting, to try to take my mind off it.' She pushed her plate away, unable to stomach the last few scraps of cold meat.

Louisa hesitated a moment, then she, too, pushed her unfinished food away and held her hand out to Ada. 'Then let us take our mind off matters, shall we?' She smiled. A secretive smile. Ada's attention piqued at the sudden change of attitude, and she took the proffered hand. Louisa had the softest hands, like silk.

Ada allowed herself to be led into the sitting room. When Louisa started moving the furniture around, Ada let out a surprised laugh. Together they pushed the sofa to the wall to create an open space in the middle of the room. Louisa selected a record from her collection.

The opening bars of Peerless Quartet's *Let Me Call You Sweetheart* played from the gramophone. Ada smiled at the choice and the memory it brought. A hot day, both of them boiling in their dresses as the band's music mingled with the chatter of the crowd and the quacking of ducks. One of the few times she'd let Louisa watch her paint.

'Whose turn is it to lead?' Louisa asked. A long-standing joke. *Which of us is the man? Neither.*

'Yours, I think.'

Louisa took the man's position. Ada revelled in the gentle pressure of her lover's fingers against her dress. On her shoulder. On her hip. It was a slow song – good for standing close. They turned in small circles, and Ada focused on nothing but Louisa, letting the day and its horrors wash away.

She relaxed into the dance and rested her cheek against Louisa's chest. The muted thrum of her heartbeat blended in with the gentle music, and a calm overtook Ada. She could stay like this forever.

Too soon, the music came to a halt, and they stopped. Ada stood on her tiptoes to place a soft kiss on Louisa's lips. 'Thank you,' she whispered.

Louisa pulled her close and returned the kiss. Harder. Ada lost herself in the kiss, revelling in the sensation. Every touch spoke of how Louisa loved her.

Only the need to breathe made her stop.

Louisa gave the tiniest tilt of her head towards the staircase.

Ada shook her head. 'Not tonight.'

Louisa's face fell. 'Did I misread–'

'No. You didn't misread anything. But I can't...I want...I just...I need you to hold me. Just. Hold me.' The words sounded trite even as she said them, her whole body cringing, but Louisa understood. Of course, Louisa understood. The disappointment washed from her face, replaced by a soft smile.

Still holding hands, Ada led them both to the sofa. Louisa

sat first, so Ada could fit herself into her arms. She closed her eyes at the tender touch of Louisa's hands in her hair, carefully removing pins and clips until Ada's curls tumbled out. She loved it when Louisa did this, stroking and twisting her curls round her fingers.

'Remember when we first heard that song?' Ada asked.

'Last year. That band...I cannot remember their name, but they were playing at the stand in the park. We were there because you wanted to draw the lake if I recall correctly.'

'Again,' Ada added with a chuckle. 'I'll get it right one of these days.'

Though she had been teasing, Louisa's quiet reply was sincere. 'You will. I know you will. I believe you can bring anything to life, Ada.'

In a different moment, Ada would have made a Frankenstein joke, and Louisa would have scoffed at her, pretending to be annoyed.

This was not that moment.

'I know. It means everything to me. Your belief.' Ada kissed her, trying to pour all her thanks and affection and love into the kiss.

A crack of thunder made them both jump and spring apart.

Ada stood and rubbed her eyes. It was like being startled awake, ripped from her sleep mid-dream, though this particular one had started as a nightmare. The whole day had an illusory quality to it. Perhaps Ada would wake tomorrow and greet Mr and Mrs Pearce walking down the street.

Louisa stood and moved to the window. 'The sun didn't last long.' The banal sentence signified the end of heart-filled truths for the day. Rain hammered the glass, and wind howled around the house. The glorious summer's day was already nothing but a hazy memory. No one looking at the dark grey clouds and rain-splattered pavements would believe there had been gorgeous sunshine only a few hours before.

'I'm off to bed.' Ada's body had finally remembered her lack of sleep last night, and she ached to the core of her bones.

Louisa checked her wristwatch. 'It is only eight o'clock.'

'I'll have a last cig upstairs.'

Louisa's face was impressively passive. No amount of insisting it was healthy – approved by doctors even – would convince her it wasn't a disgusting habit.

'Call it an early night. I've got that meeting about a commission in Haworth tomorrow.'

'The one to paint the portraits for that exhibit on the Brontë sisters?'

'What else? It's Haworth.' Ada laughed.

Louisa didn't. Framed by the grey skies in the window, her face was half-hidden by the gloom, but Ada knew what it would look like. Eyes worried. Mouth downturned. That was an expression Ada could get onto paper without any issue.

'I'm just tired,' Ada reassured her. She moved to Louisa's side to give her one last gentle kiss on the cheek. 'Don't stay up too late.'

This time, Louisa laughed. Ada was the night owl, Louisa the morning lark.

When Louisa came to bed, Ada was still awake. Eyes shut, pretending to sleep, every one of her nerves was aware of Louisa's presence beside her. The rustle of the sheets shifting as she made herself comfortable and then the slow rhythm of her breathing as she fell asleep.

Ada laid frozen. She wanted to toss and turn, kick at the blankets, punch the cushions, anything to help get comfy, but she feared waking Louisa. Her mind wouldn't settle. Wouldn't shut off. Memories new and old chased each other round her head. Questions of what she should've done and didn't do and what would she do now? The constant taunt that, in her determination to keep the chapters of her life separate, she'd left it too late to confide in Louisa about Mabel. Now, when she wanted to explain, she couldn't. And if she tried, would she even be able to form the words?

The next morning, Ada was in Leeds train station trying to avoid equally soaked fellow passengers as they scurried between the platforms. Last night's rain had not abated, and Ada had left in such a hurry she forgot to pick up a brolly.

She made it to her platform to learn she needn't have rushed. The crowd of people muttering and checking watches were a sure sign of a delayed train.

She fished her flask of tea out of her handbag, yawning as she did so. Thank heavens for Sophie. There'd been no time for breakfast. Once she finally drifted off, she'd slept so late Louisa had to shake her awake, and still, it'd taken a while to rouse her.

'Ow!' A man rushing for his train knocked her elbow, spilling tea down her coat. He didn't even stop to apologise. The man next to her tutted but didn't offer any assistance.

She scrambled through the contents of her bag till she found a handkerchief. It wasn't a particularly pleasant handkerchief – how long had it been in there? – but it would have to do. She scrubbed at the tea with no luck. The powder blue of her coat was no use in hiding the stain. The last thing she needed was to show up to her meeting with the Brontë society with an obvious brown stain on her coat.

The head of the society, Mr Finney, was reputed to be a stickler. A believer in propriety. Either he'd bought the 'companion' fiction or her friend, Mr Nicholls, wisely hadn't mentioned her living situation when he suggested Ada as a possibility. Whatever the reason, she didn't want to push his sensibilities any further.

'Blast it,' she muttered, still swabbing the tea stain. She didn't dare to say anything stronger in this busy public space. Though it would be fun to watch these suited businessmen react to a swearing woman.

She stood on tiptoes and craned her neck. No sign of an approaching train. Dare she risk making a break to the ladies' room? Arriving with a tea-stained coat was better than showing up late.

But neither was even better.

The train was nowhere to be seen. She could make it.

Elbows at the ready, she fought her way back through the oncoming crowd. She was constantly turning back the way she came to check for the train's arrival, primed to make a dash back at the first sign of steam. So far, there was nothing. This was all going to work out fine.

The main concourse was within her sights when a shout stopped her dead in her tracks.

'Gallant!' A woman's voice. Desperate and keening. 'Gallant!'

A man bumped into her back, surprised by her sudden stop. He walked away, grumbling about bloody women.

She ignored him. Frozen in place. A solid obelisk surrounded by an ever-moving crowd.

Mrs Pearce. It had to be. How many children were called Gallant? She was right there, and Ada could find her and ask all her questions. Demand to know if she poisoned him. Help her if she needed it. Or take her to the police.

Ada pushed back the way she had come, unconcerned by the trail of tutting and grousing she left in her wake. She needed to follow those shouts.

'Gallant!' What was the child doing to make his mother's voice so wretched? 'Gallant! Come back!'

Ada rushed towards platform three, praying she'd heard right and the shouts had come from that direction.

A train screeched to a stop at the platform, and the crowd surged forward. Ada tried to force her way through but got nowhere. The woman in front of her stared determinedly at the train door, feet planted. A stance that said she would board this train and no one was stopping her.

'Excuse me?' Ada tried to walk round her. 'Excuse me, I need to get past.' The woman moved as the crowd surged again. Ada fought against them, not caring who she pushed or who pushed her in return. She finally made it through, only to pause. Where to head next? The shouting had stopped. Or at least, she could no longer hear it.

The train left the station in a screech of metal and a cloud of steam. Ada took a few quick steps backwards to avoid being blinded by the grey mass.

After the smoke cleared, she ran back down the platform,

checking faces as they flew by. No one gaunt or scared, just bored travellers starting their day. Tired. Grumpy. Bedraggled.

None were Mrs Pearce.

Ada came to a standstill, breathing heavily. She must get back to her platform. She had to be on that train. Mr Nicholls had done her a favour in getting her this meeting. It would be callous to throw it back in his face, and it would do her ambitions no good. For all the stereotypes about artists, unreliable wasn't a good reputation to have in any career unless there was a title or money to make it forgivable.

Even knowing all this to be true, Ada headed in the opposite direction. She scanned every face as she passed, but there was no sign of Mrs Pearce. Had she left on the train? The desperation in her scream told Ada no. Her son had been running away, and she would've followed. She was here. Or nearby.

Ada would find her.

Chapter Six

Wine Only Makes Matters Worse

Three dresses were laid out on the bed. Louisa contemplated each contraption of lace and frills in turn. 'What do you think, Sophie?'

The maid stood beside her. 'Me, ma'am? I don't know. Um...the purple, maybe. It's a pretty colour.'

Louisa lifted the dress up and held it against herself. It was one Ada helped her choose. She had also praised the colour but in more poetic prose, declaring it like a bed of violets.

As if Louisa's thoughts had summoned her, the slam of the front door heralded Ada's return.

'Could you go tell her I am up here, please?'

Ada took Sophie's place a couple of minutes later.

'Going somewhere?'

'Mrs Williams invited us to one of her little soirees, remember?'

'Oh yeah.' Ada's face scrunched up. 'I forgot that was tonight.'

'I thought you were looking forward to it?'

'I am, I am, course I am.' But her voice was distracted, not excited.

'Is something wrong? Did your meeting not go well?'

'No, no, I'm fine. The meeting was fine. A slight to-do

with the train, so I was a bit late, but other than that, everything was fine.' She pointed to the dress hanging limply from Louisa's hand. 'Is that what you're wearing? I do like that dress on you.' A cheeky smile lit up her face.

'I know you do.' Louisa tried to match the smile, though cheeky always sat better on Ada. 'Did you get it then?'

'Huh?'

'The commission?'

'Oh yeah, yeah.'

'But that's great news!' Louisa's enthusiasm rang hollow beside Ada's apathy.

'Yes.' Ada nodded a little too eagerly, and a stray curl bounced along with her movement. 'Yes, it is.' She gave Louisa a tight smile that did not meet her eyes. 'I guess I should be choosing my own outfit. Wouldn't want to deny Mrs Williams a chance to show that the North, too, can be cultured.' She turned away towards her wardrobe.

Louisa wanted to ask more questions, but Ada could not have made it clearer that she did not want to talk. So Louisa went to find Sophie; she would need help with the buttons on the purple dress.

Outside Mrs Williams' townhouse, Louisa and Ada hurried up the footpath to avoid the still-falling drizzle. A servant took their coats at the door and led them into the parlour, where about ten people were stood around.

Hopefully, there will not be many more.

'Miss Chapman, Miss Knight.' Mrs Williams walked over to greet them with exuberance. With her light blonde hair and pale skin, she could have been a ghost, but her bold emerald dress confirmed her as a member of the living and kept Louisa's scepticism intact. She kissed Ada's cheek. 'Miss Chapman, you will have to tell me all about your latest project over dinner. I am sure you must have one.'

Beside her, Mr Williams was a short man with salt-and-pepper hair and beard. He gave them his usual sardonic smile; this was always his approach to his wife's flamboyance. Such predictability helped to soothe Louisa's nerves. This would be good for Ada; company would help her flourish. Mrs Williams could always be relied upon to put on a good spread of both food and people.

Unfortunately, normality came to a crashing halt halfway through the second course of dinner, when a man opposite Louisa – whose name she was struggling to remember – said to Mr Williams, 'Did you read about that poisoning in the *Evening Post*?'

Louisa's head jerked up from her plate, and then her gaze flickered to Ada, who sat frozen with her fork halfway to her mouth.

'Terrible business,' Mr Williams agreed with his acquaintance.

Please let that be the end of it.

But he turned to address Louisa and Ada. 'Up your end of town, was it not?'

Mrs Williams gasped. 'It was your street! I knew I recognised that address from somewhere. Did I not say that, my dear, when we read it?'

'You did indeed.'

All eyes round the table turned towards them. Louisa sat up a little higher under the scrutiny. What reply would end this conversation as quickly as possible and get them all to look away again? 'It is, yes,' Louisa said. 'A terrible tragedy, of course, but we know no more than that, do we, Ada?'

'No. No, we barely knew them. They didn't want to know the likes of us.'

Her last comment produced a smattering of uncomfortable chuckling from their fellow guests.

'Perhaps we should talk of happier topics,' Mrs Williams said with a pointed look at her husband.

'I think that is for the best, my love,' her husband agreed. He resumed his conversation with the nameless acquaintance. A quiet swell of voices followed as other conversations recommenced and people turned away. The crawling sensation of eyes on her lessened, and Louisa relaxed.

Ada remained quiet, picking at her food. When she noticed Louisa's attention, she shook her head. 'I'm fine,' she whispered. 'Fine.' The statement was undercut by her downing the last of her glass of wine. She was already at least one ahead of Louisa.

'We can leave after dinner if you wish.' Mrs Williams would protest, but Louisa would not let that sway her.

'No, no, don't be silly. We're here to enjoy ourselves. Look, this kind man has brought us more wine.' She sent a dazzling smile at the footman, who blushed as he refilled her glass. 'Thank you.' Ada took a large gulp.

'And you, miss?' he asked Louisa.

It seemed churlish to say no in light of Ada's comment. 'Yes, please. Thank you.'

Ada held hers up. 'Cheers.' They clinked glasses.

After dinner, Mrs Williams demanded Ada's attention as

they returned to the parlour.

Louisa withdrew to the edge of the room. The second glass of wine had left her light-headed, and she declined the butler who offered her more from a tray of champagne. She would have no more drinks that night. She hated being drunk, the lack of control and the loss of her wits.

'Miss Knight, I am glad to see you here tonight.' Mrs Mason, an acquaintance from previous nights at Mrs Williams', joined her. She also refused a drink with a wave of her hand. Everything about Mrs Mason was best described as dainty, but her frailty was an illusion. Her hands may have been slight, but they spent their days caring for the sick. Bandages and bedpans were Mrs Mason's trade, though it was hard to imagine when she was out of uniform. That night, she wore a baby pink gown that would have washed out Louisa's pale skin but contrasted beautifully with Mrs Mason's ebony complexion.

'I am glad to see you, too,' Louisa said with a smile. Mrs Mason could always be counted on for an intelligent conversation that Louisa actually understood, for they were both the staid add-ons to their creative partners. Mr Mason was a writer and a poet. That his wife still worked because his writings did not bring in enough money was tactfully never mentioned. To ask why she had married a poor poet would be uncouth, and Louisa already had a notion anyway. She did not need anyone to explain how mesmerising it was to see someone create beauty from nothing, each new piece showing a little more of who they were.

The pair talked pleasantries for a while. Louisa dared a glance to where Ada now stood with another acquaintance of theirs, Mrs Cohen, engrossed in conversation. Suffrage, most likely. Mrs Cohen was a well-known suffragette with at least one prison stay under her belt.

The sight did little to ease Louisa's worry. Whenever Ada spoke of the protesting women with admiration, Louisa's mind flooded with imagined horrors: Ada being seized by policemen, hauled through a baying crowd, and thrown in the back of a police wagon. Her shivering in a prison cell, wasting away but still refusing food until she was held down by unyielding hands and doctors shoving a tube down her throat.

Louisa wanted the vote. She was not sure throwing stones at politicians was the way to achieve it. Or that such violence achieved anything other than further souring people against the idea, and if that were true, what were all those brave women suffering for?

'Miss Knight?' Mrs Mason broke through Louisa's distraction. She dropped her voice. 'Excuse the intrusion, but is all well with you and Miss Chapman?'

I do not know. A hard truth to swallow.

'Yes, we are fine.'

'It must have been a shock to learn about that poor man next door.'

'Indeed. I am sorry, but I would rather not talk about it.'

'Of course. Of course.' Mrs Mason changed the topic to a tale from her work – a boy with smallpox. This led them onto vaccines and the utter folly of them no longer being mandatory in England.

Louisa kept up her end of the discussion. Easy enough when they both had strong, matching opinions on the matter. The entire time she stayed attuned to Ada, laughing and talking in the distance.

Mrs Mason moved onto a new story from her work. 'A boy I know was brought into the infirmary two days ago with a broken arm. He said he'd fallen from a tree, though I'm not sure I believe it. He's a bit of a tearaway.'

'How so?'

In her corner, Ada's laugh grew higher. Louisa suspected she had not waved away the tray of drinks. She dared another glance. Ada now talked to a short man who looked swamped in his formal attire. Mr Tallant was a local musician who knew everything there was to know about classical music but little else.

Mrs Mason still spoke of the boy with the broken arm. 'I think he's just acting up. He lost his dad last year and his mum when he was only a babe.'

The familiar ache of grief stirred within Louisa, the words hitting a little too close to home. At least she had faced such a situation as an adult. How would she have coped as a little girl?

She had no need for sympathetic glances, though, so she kept the similarities to herself. 'Whose care is he in then?'

'He lives with his father's eldest brother and his wife. The problem is they have a large family already and can barely cope with their own kids. So, he spends a lot of his time with a different aunt, who is a friend of mine. She's the one who brought him to the hospital with his arm and paid for the doctor and the pot.'

'Pot?'

'A plaster cast, sorry.' Mrs Mason sighed. 'And now he's-'

'I like the new style of music, Mr Tallant. Better than all

that boring old stuff,' Ada declared from the other side of the room. Too loud. A dull hush fell over the gathering.

Mr Tallant stared at Ada, his colour rising. Her words might have been innocuous, but for him, they were a red rag to a bull.

She had not finished. 'Not everyone shares your preoppu - preocca - preoccup -pre - pre - huh, obsession, obsession, with what came before.'

How much has she drunk?

Several faces turned to Louisa expectantly. 'Excuse me,' she muttered to Mrs Mason. The other guests pretended not to look, though no doubt they were all inwardly laughing at Ada's little show. Louisa kept her head high as she crossed the room, refusing to show her embarrassment.

'Louisa!' Ada called as she approached, waving her arms wildly. 'Tell our dear Mr Tallant he needs to be less of a stick in the mud and try new things.' She turned back to him. 'Have you ever tried being less *self-controlled*?' She smirked at him. This was no longer about music.

Fear flickered across his face, and he turned pleading eyes to Louisa. That Mr Tallant shared their persuasion had been long suspected but never voiced. Anger uncurled itself within Louisa; Ada should know better than to throw such accusations around.

'Enough, Ada.' Louisa seized her wrist, saying a hasty apology to Mr Tallant as she pulled Ada away to the relative privacy of the hallway. 'What are you playing at?' she demanded.

'All I was doing was having a nice conversation about music.'

'You are drunk.'

'And you're sober. Boring!' Ada yanked her arm out of Louisa's hand.

'Why must you be so obnoxious when you drink?'

'Why must you be so obnoxious when you don't?'

'You showed me up in front of our friends.'

'Because I'm so low born and ill-mannered? Your mistress from the slums showing you up in front of all the fancy people?'

'You are not my... For pity's sake, Ada. Let's go home.'

'No. I'm staying. I have to finish...' Ada took a few wobbly steps back towards the parlour, and Louisa moved to block her path.

'What is going on, Ada?' Concern and frustration fought within her.

Ada stopped fighting, looking over Louisa's shoulder into the distance. 'Do you ever feel helpless? Like the world is turning around you, and you want it to stop – to freeze – but you know it never will. There's nothing you can do but let yourself be spun.'

Her words hit Louisa like she'd struck her. For a brief moment, she was overtaken once more by the chasm of grief after her father died and left her alone, so alone in the world.

'You are not helpless. Neither am I.' Louisa placed her hand gently on Ada's arm.

For a few seconds, their eyes met in mutual understanding. All the frustration and anger melted away as they stood in that single agreement.

Then Mrs Williams stepped into the hallway. 'There's a cab waiting. I sent one of the men for it.'

Louisa thanked their hostess and then tensed, waiting for Ada's response, but Ada said no more than a mumbled apology. After checking the driver had the right address, Louisa followed Ada into the cab. The horses set off, and the cab jolted. Louisa waited for Ada to continue, but she sat back without a word, leaning against the leather seat cushion and studying the cab's ceiling as though it held the secrets of the universe.

Louisa matched her silence. She turned away towards the windows and watched figures flit past on the street. Despite the gloom caused by the grey clouds, it was still too early on a summer night for the gas lamps to have been lit. Louisa opened the tiny window in search of fresh air, but the minuscule crack made little difference.

'I'm sorry,' Ada said as they turned onto Roundhay Road. She shuffled along the bench till she pressed close to Louisa, and her hand rested on Louisa's upper thigh.

In the privacy of their home, Louisa might have enjoyed it, but even the seat of a cab was too public. She pushed Ada's hand away.

'Is this revenge?' Ada asked. She moved away again, crossing her arms in a huff and glaring.

'Revenge for what?'

'Last night.'

Louisa sighed. 'I am not angry about that.'

'No. You wouldn't be.' Ada shook her head. 'Sorry. That was... Sorry.' She fumbled in her bag and pulled out a cigarette.

'Can you not wait until we get home? It's stuffy enough as it is.' Louisa cringed at her scolding tone.

Ada shoved the cigarette back in her bag, and silence fell once more.

Was that what had been bothering Ada? The moment last night? It was admittedly an unusual turn of events when Ada refused an advance, but Louisa assumed she had read the moment wrong. It was a constant and careful balancing act between the two of them.

Hard to know – without desire – what was and was not appropriate. She had only wanted to show Ada she cared.

When the hansom rattled to a stop, Ada jumped out quicker than Louisa would have expected possible for someone in her current state. Louisa paid and tipped the driver, then joined Ada, who sat smoking on the doorstep. Louisa resisted the urge to wave the foul-smelling smoke away, instead taking a seat beside her.

Ada stared upwards. Twilight had painted the sky a bright pink. 'One of the hardest things to capture on canvas.' Ada pointed with her cigarette. 'Look at all the colours.'

Louisa only saw pink.

'Did I tell you I was late to my meeting?' Ada's voice was far away. Louisa suspected the alcohol was driving the conversation.

'Yes,' Louisa answered. 'The train was delayed.'

'And then I missed it.' Ada almost sang the words. She had the strangest smile on her face, still staring up at the evening sky. A trail of smoke drifted upwards from the cigarette that burnt forgotten in her hands. 'Just missed it. Showed up late with a tea-stained coat and my head entirely elsewhere. I'm taking it as a compliment on my artistic ability that they hired me because I gave them no other reason to do so.'

'I am sure they loved your pictures.' What else was there to say?

'She was there.'

'Who?'

'At the station. She was there. I heard her.' Ada flung an arm out and flapped her hand in the vague direction of next door. 'She was there.'

'Mrs Pearce? Did you see her? Trying to catch a train? Why is she still in the city? I would have thought she'd be long gone by now. Did you tell the police? Or at least Davey?'

'Ha! You're interested. And you said Davey.' Ada poked her in the ribs.

'This is not a joke.' Louisa stood from the doorstep, distancing herself from both the cigarette smoke and the poking hand.

'She'd lost the boy. She was there, and I couldn't find her. I couldn't help her.'

'It is not your responsibility to help her.'

'So I stand aside?'

'Yes. She is more than likely guilty, Ada. Tell me, who else has a motive or the means? You are fighting the inevitable. Same as we did with Mary Fellowes.'

'We?' Ada laughed bitterly. 'That was me, Louisa. You just took the fall.'

'It was both of us. You were the first to make the suggestion, but I seized it with both hands. We wanted her to be innocent, and that made it easy for her to trick us, to take the money and run.'

Louisa had been so certain the police were wrong. Biased. That they had wanted a villain and so made themselves one in the form of a woman. How could they be trusted to uphold the law in such a situation?

But it was Louisa who was wrong. Mary Fellowes turned out to be exactly what the police thought she was, and it nearly cost a man his life and both Ada and Constable Wilkinson their jobs.

And here was Ada, willing to do it all again for a woman who had not even wanted to know them.

But Louisa would not follow her down that rabbit hole again. Her father used to say, 'If you must make mistakes, at least learn from them', and Louisa had promised herself after the Mary Fellowes incident she would.

Ada refused to meet Louisa's eyes. Some of her ginger curls had escaped their clips and tumbled down from her pompadour. They always did towards the end of the night. On a happier evening, Louisa would have reached down and twirled them, luxuriating in the silky feel of those curls between her fingertips.

Ada stubbed the cigarette out against the doorstep and then flicked it away into the dirt; Louisa pursed her lips but said nothing. She moved to help as Ada staggered to her feet, swaying. Once she was steady, she turned her head to look up at Louisa, and their gazes locked.

'You would have me walk away?' she demanded. 'Stand by and do nothing? Again?'

'Again?'

Chapter Seven

A Restless Night

Ada looked startled, eyes wide and fearful, like a rabbit's before the farmer pulls the trigger. 'I didn't mean to say that. Forget I said that.' She pulled her arm from Louisa's grasp and stumbled through the doorway. In the hallway, she stopped to fumble with the catch on her shoes.

Louisa held back from helping this time, busying herself with her own footwear.

What did 'again' mean? What was Ada not telling her?

Sophie appeared at the top of the stairs in her nightgown, looking half asleep. She stepped aside as Ada weaved her way up the stairs, muttering a semi-coherent good night.

There was no good night for Louisa, who let that fact go unremarked. She had no more energy for another argument.

Ada had left her shoes, hat and coat in a pile in the hallway, and Sophie came downstairs to tidy them up. 'Leave it,' Louisa ordered, sterner than she intended. 'Let her clean her own mess.'

Sophie dropped the items as though they had scalded her. They landed with a thump.

'Can I get you anything, ma'am?'

A partner who is less dramatic.

'Could you boil the kettle, please?'

'Of course.' Sophie scurried into the kitchen.

Louisa collapsed onto the sofa in the sitting room. The curtains were closed and the room bathed in darkness, masking Ada's redecoration. In such dim light, it could have been the room of Louisa's childhood. She stood to turn the lamps on but changed her mind. Instead, she moved to the familiarity of the dining room and lit a candle. The flickering light illuminated a space that was untouched by Ada's handiwork.

Sophie jumped when she entered the room, and the teacup and biscuits rattled in her hands. 'Sorry, ma'am. I thought you were in the sitting room. It's going to be fully dark soon; wouldn't you prefer to be in there with the better lamps?'

'No. Here is fine, thank you. Go get yourself a cup if you would like. Join me.'

When Sophie returned, Louisa pushed the biscuits towards her. She took one uncertainly. They had a more relaxed relationship than the average mistress and maid, but tea and biscuits in her nightdress was still not the norm.

Once Sophie had swallowed her first bite, Louisa asked how her day had been.

'I went to see Mrs Mills this evening. Once I'd finished my chores, of course, ma'am.'

'How is she?'

'She was packing to leave and didn't seem keen to talk. So different to how she was yesterday.'

'She found a body yesterday. I cannot imagine she was herself at the time.'

'No, but she was even less like herself today. She's always

been chatty. The sort to stop and talk for as long as she'd get away with. Used to tell me all sorts of things about her late husband and her sons. But I couldn't get a word out of her today. She wouldn't even tell me where she was going. I'd guess t' her younger son, Tommy his name is. The older one's wife is a piece of work, at least according to Mrs Mills, and–'

'So you do not know where she has gone?' Louisa rubbed her forehead. Her maid's volley of words was making her head pound, and she took another sip of her tea whilst she tried to organise her thoughts.

'No, ma'am. She didn't want to tell me. Just said she had a place to go. There was a woman waiting for her in the hallway, who I've seen leaving their house before.'

'It could have been the daughter-in-law.'

Sophie shook her head. 'I don't think so. Mrs Mills always calls her 'the blonde chit'. This lady – and I think she was an actual lady – had dark brown hair.'

'Maybe it was a sister or a cousin. A niece if she were younger. Given the circumstances, I imagine she reached out to her family for support. The most likely outcome is she's staying with one of her sons. If she did not mention that, I imagine it is only because her mind is still understandably scattered after yesterday's incident. I would not worry, Sophie. If it helps put your mind at ease, ring the police tomorrow; she will have had to tell them where she was going. Here, help yourself to another biscuit.'

The maid took one with less hesitancy this time. By all appearances, Sophie had taken Louisa's words at face value, as hoped. The last thing they needed in the household was another person obsessing.

Louisa asked an inconsequential question about the day's groceries to move the conversation on, but her attention drifted away from the answer.

Mrs Mills, who had shown loyalty to Mrs Pearce, considered her innocent and had every reason to believe Mr Pearce deserved what he got. Could she be helping her mistress?

And how did that tie in with Ada hearing Mrs Pearce shouting at the train station? The police must have sent her picture round to warn the ticket officers and conductors to be on the lookout. Had Mrs Mills helped sneak her and the boy onto a train? Or had Ada, so preoccupied, imagined the whole matter?

'Sophie.' Louisa cut across a diatribe against their local butcher. 'I need a favour from you.'

'Anything, ma'am.' Sophie's response was as enthusiastic as it was sincere.

Who said good deeds went unrewarded? If Louisa were to murder someone, sweet, quiet Sophie would help her bury the body; of that, she was certain. Thankfully, what she had to ask was less severe.

'I'm worried about Miss Chapman. Could you keep an eye on her? She is not herself at the moment.'

Sophie gasped. 'You want me to spy on her?'

Louisa laughed even as the thought settled uncomfortably. 'Not spy. Just make sure she is all right. I am quite busy for the next couple of days, and it would reassure me to know she is in safe hands. Perhaps you could ask her about that trip to the art gallery she mentioned? It might help keep her mind off things.'

Sophie nodded but still looked uncertain. She bit her lip and opened her mouth before closing it again.

'If you have something to say, please say it. I hope you do not feel the need to hold your tongue around me.'

'It seems...well, a lot. Could you not just speak to her? Find out what's upsetting her?'

Thank you for the excellent suggestion. Why did I not think of that? Louisa held back her sarcasm. She had told the girl to speak her mind.

'I have tried.' Louisa forced the words out.

'It must be hard for her. All this with Mrs Pearce. I know Mrs Mills didn't think her missus did it. That must have upset Miss Chapman, given what happened all them years ago.'

'What do you mean?'

Horror spread across Sophie's face. 'Don't you know, ma'am? I thought you'd know.'

'Know what?'

Sophie shook her head. 'It was just a rumour. I shouldn't have said anything. My ma always said never to repeat rumours.'

This only piqued Louisa's attention. Sophie had grown up near to Ada. 'What rumours?'

'I shouldn't say, ma'am. Miss Chapman won't like it.'

Louisa bit back her frustration. Sophie had a point. Whatever this was, she was better hearing it from Ada herself. 'You are right. But still, you will keep an eye on her for me? Please?'

Sophie agreed, looking relieved at the reprieve.

Louisa finished the last of her now-cold tea, grimacing at

the taste, and wished Sophie a good night as the maid began to collect the china. As she went upstairs, she debated whether to confront Ada now or later. Ada was unpredictable when she'd been drinking; liquor would either loosen her lips or make her more confrontational. Waiting risked her saying nothing, laughing it off and keeping it locked away.

The choice was made for her. Ada lay snoring on the bed, fully clothed, and her limbs spread out so she took up all the space. Louisa felt a tick of irritation. She gave Ada's shoulder a shake, but she might as well have tried to wake the dead from their graves.

'Ada! Oh, for–' Louisa prided herself on not swearing, but, even so, she only just stopped herself in time.

She stripped off her layers of clothing and debated her options. It was the sofa or the bed in Ada's painting room. She could hardly kick poor Sophie out of her room.

Louisa nearly fell over three times as she made her way through the tiny moonlit painting room, tripping over paints and brushes and who knows what. Ada had banned Sophie from tidying in here, and so Louisa resisted the urge whenever she visited. At least she avoided the water jars. Those blooming water jars. Was it so hard to throw a glass of water away and replace it afresh? Rather than having thousands of them dotted around the room, growing stagnant.

Louisa had forgotten about the canvases piled high on the small single bed. With an irritated huff, she fiddled with the gas lamp until it lit and then began to throw the pictures onto the cluttered floor with less care than she normally would.

Usually, she treasured Ada's art, amazed by the talent it took to create such beauty.

A series of paintings of herself made her pause. A similar portrait hung in their sitting room; these must have been the discarded early attempts. Louisa had not understood what was wrong with the earlier versions back then and still did not. They showed her in a way she never saw herself and were the closest she would ever come to seeing herself through Ada's eyes. The woman in the painting looked clever and caring and, most of all, loved.

Her heart clenched, and she regretted her earlier cross words. There had to be more behind Ada's attitude to the Pearce murder. It should not have taken Sophie's careless words to enlighten her.

'I am sorry,' she muttered, then shook her head. Apologising to a picture of herself – how foolish. She would apologise properly to Ada in the morning.

She handled the remaining pictures with more care. A portrait at the bottom of the pile made her stop once more. A pretty woman, drawn in a state of some undress. Not Ada's best work – even Louisa's non-artistic eye saw that – but it felt familiar.

She stared at it a little longer until a creeping realisation came over her. She picked up the earlier portrait of herself, comparing them. The other woman had little in common with her. Loose blonde hair compared to pinned-up brown. Blue eyes instead of hazel. Louisa wore her favourite green dress in her portrait whilst the other woman wore no dress at all. Woman was perhaps overstating it; she could not have been older than twenty.

But there was one similarity: both paintings were drawn with love. Louisa could not say what told her that – what brush stroke, what artistic choice, what design – but she knew it to be true.

Both portraits clattered onto the bed.

Who was this woman? When had Ada drawn her?

Did it matter? Ada was allowed to have a past.

Was it the past?

Louisa cursed herself for being an unkind fool. She would not believe that of Ada. She would go to sleep. And think nothing more of this portrait or dead men or rumours from years ago.

It was not to be. The bed was cold and musty from being unused for so long. Despite her resolve to apologise, Louisa damned Ada for taking up their bed, calling her all the swear words she would not say out loud.

Ada with her secrets from the past. With her impulsiveness and her habit of running headfirst into trouble. *But that's what I first liked about her*.

Louisa turned over with an exaggerated thump, nearly falling out of the tiny bed and cursing Ada once more. Maybe if she went to their room, Ada would have moved with all the tossing and turning she did.

Some stubborn part of Louisa refused to go and look, though. She would stay here. Cold and angry. And in the morning, she would have good reason for her irritation.

Shivering, she pulled the thin blanket up to her chin. It had rained all day, and the night was chill. Last summer, the heat had made it unbearable to lie together during the nights. She would have welcomed Ada's warmth now.

Would Ada welcome her? Or was she getting fed up with boring Louisa, who could never truly return her affections the way she wanted? Would she tire of her and leave?

Who was the woman in the portrait?

Ada would not betray her. Louisa knew that. She knew Ada. Or did she?

Louisa huffed with frustration and sat up. Usually, if she could not sleep, she would read, but her book was by her bed. Her actual bed.

Being in Ada's studio was not helping with her peace of mind. She tiptoed across the room and down the hallway towards her study. An old favourite book would help soothe her restless mind.

Louisa's study was a room caught between two periods in her life. As a little girl, she spent hours in there being taught by her father, and the same oak desk he once sat behind still held pride of place. But there were touches of the new, too. The wisteria curtains were chosen by Ada, and the painting of Roundhay Park on the wall was by her hand. Whilst the bookcases matched the desk, many of the books on the shelves were recent additions. Some of them Louisa's father would have been more likely to burn than read.

The book on the desk was one of his, though – an old medical textbook. Louisa inherited her interest in the scientific from him.

Accepting sleep as a lost cause, Louisa sat and turned to the page she'd read the previous afternoon. Hyoscine: the drug that killed Alexander Pearce. She had suspected its importance as soon as Constable Wilkinson said the name, and looking it up had only confirmed her suspicions. An anaphrodisiac – or at least some chemists claimed it was.

Two years ago, Louisa had followed the Crippen case closely. A man named Hawley Harvey Crippen murdered his wife with a hyoscine overdose. The story, and Crippen's dramatic trans-Atlantic arrest, had been perfect newspaper fodder. At the time, a leading defence barrister had wanted to argue that Crippen merely intended to temper his wife's lust, and the overdose was accidental. The more Louisa considered it, the more likely it appeared the situation with the Pearces was the same, only with the roles reversed.

She put the book aside and went to the shelves in search of one of her novels. Those books she'd once kept behind a bookcase instead of in one because her father did not approve of such frivolity as fiction. In a pointless act of rebellion, she had put them above the shelf of law books her prosecutor father had set such stock by.

She paused, however, by a different shelf altogether, another that never existed in her father's study. The provocative pose and smile of the mystery woman flashed into her mind uninvited, and Ada's terse words in the back of the cab echoed, taunting her: 'Is this revenge?'

Sexology texts. All the theories she'd gathered to try to understand her lack of sexual interest. A search that only intensified when she first met Ada and realised she was falling in love but still with none of the subsequent desire attached.

Her fingers rested on the spine of a thin pamphlet entitled *Sapphos and Socrates* written by a German named Hirschfield sixteen years ago. How many times had she re-read its text to re-confirm the words written within? The giddy excitement when she had first seen his scale for sexual desire because it included an option for 0. An option for people like her, which meant she was not the only one. She had been surprised by the strength of her reaction. Such a small thing, one solitary number on a scale, yet it had her crying in shock and delight.

It did not provide her with all the answers she wanted, though. The reason why remained a mystery. Sexologists could not even agree on what caused homosexuality, never mind provide a suitable hypothesis for a situation where love and desire were exclusive.

Louisa's first attempt at explaining this to Ada had been an awkward, stuttering mess. She had never tried to explain it to another person before, and the final words of her explanation, the ones that were the best summary she had ever managed, were still engrained in her memory. *'I have never wanted anyone – man nor woman – and thought myself incapable of love and desire. I was only half-wrong.'*

Ada had been taken back at first, but she had made an effort to understand. They had progressed a lot since then, taking small and careful steps as together they learnt each other's boundaries. It still surprised Louisa how much she enjoyed the many ways Ada had taught her to show her appreciation even whilst she maintained her disinterest in having the favour returned. What she struggled with most was gauging the appropriate moment.

That was the delicate tightrope of their relationship. Many long conversations had brought them to their current understanding. Where Ada enjoyed physical affection and would nearly always welcome it should Louisa offer but accepted her partner was not so inclined, and they both reserved the right to say no.

The issue yesterday was the *nearly*. Though Louisa always asked to make certain her attentions were welcome, she did not always read the situation right. This left her flustered and embarrassed – regardless of how many times Ada told her it did not matter, that these misunderstandings happened. Louisa could not squash her own annoyance at her inability to get it right, and yet she also did not want Ada to always have to make her own advances.

A constant balancing act.

'Is this revenge?' Ada took the words back almost as soon as she said them. But she had said them, and that caused the tightrope under their feet to wobble a bit more.

And that was without taking the Pearce situation into account.

Louisa shook her head. How long had she stood there, staring at her bookshelf? She grabbed a novel at random and settled down into the desk chair, determined to think no more of Ada's words or the mystery portrait or Mr Pearce's death.

Chapter Eight

The Problem with Resolve

Late the next morning, Louisa stood in the doorway to their bedroom. She tried to summon the previous night's anger and failed. Ada looked so vulnerable asleep, her ginger hair spilling behind her on the pillow. This would be a rough awakening - even Louisa's limited experience of overindulging was enough to know that - but the phone call from the police had sounded urgent. Constable Wilkinson had said they needed Ada as soon as possible.

He did not, however, say immediately.

Louisa returned armed with tea and toast. 'Ada?'

No movement.

She placed the plate and cup on the bedside cabinet and knelt beside the bed. Her back protested after a night spent in her desk chair, causing a fresh flicker of irritation, but she tempered it to shake Ada's shoulder gently.

Ada groaned.

'You need to wake up.'

'Louisa?' Ada rose with another groan, her eyes scrunched shut, and a palm pressed against her forehead. 'What happened last night? God, I feel awful. How much did I drink?'

'I am not sure. A lot.'

Ada collapsed back against the pillow and buried her face.

'I'm sorry to wake you, but Constable Wilkinson called. I brought you breakfast first, though.'

With what looked like some effort, Ada sat up again. She summoned a sleepy smile when she noticed the cup and plate on the bedside cabinet.

'Breakfast in bed?' Ada cradled the cup, and Louisa moved the tray to rest on her lap. 'We've never done this before.'

'Well, do not be getting used to it. And, technically, only you.'

'You could join me?' Her cheeky grin turned serious. 'For just food, I mean.'

Louisa smiled but shook her head. 'My breakfast is already waiting downstairs. I was halfway through eating when the phone rang. Another day maybe.' She kissed Ada's cheek, purposefully right next to the birthmark, as was her wont. Whatever Ada's complicated relationship with the blotches that marked her skin, Louisa could not imagine her without them. They were as much a part of her lover as the ginger curls or green eyes or artistic fingers. 'Enjoy your breakfast.'

Downstairs, Louisa found the dining table empty. Sophie was washing up in the kitchen. 'Sorry, ma'am. It'd gone cold, so I thought you'd finished. I can make more if you'd like?'

'No, it's fine. More tea would be lovely, though, thank you.'

Whilst Sophie made a fresh pot, Louisa resumed reading the morning's newspapers. Leeds City Police had not gotten their wish: Alexander Pearce's murder had made the national press. It was far from the lead story, though, granted half a page about a third of the way in. Even the *Yorkshire Post* had relegated it to page four with a local councillor's scandal dominating the front page.

Louisa had started on her second cup of tea when Ada walked in, fully dressed but not much more awake. 'Did Davey say what the case was?'

'No. Constable Wilkinson just said they needed you as soon as possible.'

'Davey. You called him Davey last night.' She winced. 'I think.'

'I did. Yes.'

Ada hovered in the doorway. 'What happened? I can't...my memories are a bit...blurry.'

'We had a slight disagreement.' Ada raised her eyebrows, and Louisa forced a smile. 'It has been known to happen.'

Ada's face scrunched up. 'A slight disagreement, that's all?'

'Yes.' Or at least Louisa hoped.

'I should be going.' But still, Ada hovered.

For the second time that morning, Louisa abandoned her breakfast and joined Ada. She tucked away an errant curl. 'Go. Do your job. There's nothing to worry about.'

Ada stood on her tiptoes and brushed her lips against Louisa's cheek, a soft feather-light touch. 'I'll see you later today.' She walked away towards the coat hooks, leaving Louisa in the doorway.

Only after the front door slammed closed did Louisa return to the table. The ghost of Ada's kiss tingled on her cheek, but she forced her mind towards the day ahead. She had various errands to run: a trip to the milliner and the art supplies shop for Ada, a visit to Mrs Paulson, and a lecture at the university. Ada and her unexplained obsession with Mr

Pearce's murder would have to wait till the evening.

Once Louisa finished, Sophie came in to collect her empty cup and saucer, but instead of returning them straight to the kitchen, she hesitated by Louisa's side.

'Is something the matter, Sophie?'

'I heard Miss Chapman leave. When she gets home, do you still want me to...'

Louisa's words from last night hung unspoken between them. In the cold light of day, they were ridiculous. An over-the-top reaction.

'Maybe try to keep her occupied. She has a lot on her mind at the moment.'

'Yes, ma'am. Did you tell her about Mrs Mills?'

Darn! She should have told Ada, so she would be forewarned if any of the officers mentioned Mrs Mills' disappearance. Sophie had reported it to them earlier.

'No, I forgot. I will talk to her when she gets home.'

Sophie nodded and left, and Louisa prepared for her day. Yet despite all her efforts, her words to Sophie kept tumbling around her mind.

There was something Ada was not telling her, yet Ada was so darn terrible at keeping secrets. Louisa had long fretted she would say the wrong word at the wrong time to the wrong person or react too honestly to an accusation and rip the delicate tapestry of their lives to pieces. And what would Louisa do when that happened? How could she be cross at Ada for being too honest?

But that was a potential future problem. And as for her partner's current preoccupation, Louisa would not get involved.

This was not their mystery to solve.

With that resolution, she stepped outside. She made it three steps down the street before turning back.

Sophie was dusting in the sitting room. 'Ma'am? I thought you'd gone out?'

'You said Mrs Mills talked to you about her sons. Do you know where they live?'

'Oh! Are you going to find her?'

'Maybe.'

'Her youngest, Tom, lives in rooms near the canal, not far out of town. A writer, Mrs Mills said he was. She always spoke of him proudly, but I don't think he's doing all that well for himself. It's not a nice area down there, you see, ma'am.' She paused before adding in a rush, 'I could come with you if you'd like?'

A swell of gratitude blossomed inside Louisa. She imagined there was nothing the timid girl would like less than poking around the rougher parts of the city. It was not high on Louisa's list of things to do either.

'No. No, we are best leaving it well alone. If Mrs Mills has gone to her son's, the police will find her. Thank you for your help, Sophie. I should be going.'

If Sophie found her behaviour erratic, she kept the thought to herself. Louisa, however, certainly questioned it as she once more left the house, striding away with new determination. No more of this. Milliners. Art shop. Mrs Paulson. Lecture.

'How are you?' Mrs Paulson asked as Louisa took a seat. She was the only one of Mother's friends who played a part in

Louisa's life through sheer force of will. Father had never been able to cow her.

Answering truthfully was dismissed as soon as it crossed Louisa's mind. The old woman may have known her longer than anyone else, but that did not mean she understood her. 'I am fine, thank you.'

'And how is Miss Chapman? She is not with you today?' The thinning of Mrs Paulson's lips at the mention of Ada reaffirmed Louisa's decision.

'No, she's working.'

'I thought her job was as your companion? Is that not why you house and feed her?'

No, that's just what we tell people. 'That does not mean she has to be at my beck and call every moment of the day.'

'Hmmm. Not all women would be so considerate, but you have chosen to run a strange household. That maid of yours is still causing you no trouble?'

She's never going to let that one go. 'I do not think it is in Sophie's nature to cause trouble.'

Mrs Paulson quirked an eyebrow. 'I think the Gotts would disagree with you there.'

Louisa had a lot of choice words for Sophie's former employers but kept them to herself. Instead, she opted for, 'I did not come here to re-hash that old argument.'

'I do regret ever informing you of that tale, but how was I to know your reaction to such a scandal would be to hire the depraved little chit?'

'Sophie is nothing of the sort.'

'Hmph. If you insist.'

Louisa clenched her fists. 'Are you done with your

fortnightly query of my choices?'

Mrs Paulson's eyes narrowed. 'There is no need for that attitude.'

I could say the same to you.

She kept the comment to herself, saving it to share with Ada later. Thankfully, her partner always found Mrs Paulson's antics amusing rather than insulting.

How Ada had laughed when she learnt it had been Mrs Paulson who forced Louisa to the dinner party where they met. A flush of satisfaction had flooded through Louisa at being the cause of that merry sound. She wished she could go back to that day. Walking around Waterloo Lake, a warm spring breeze tugging at her hat and skirts with all the promises of a new year – and a new understanding – ahead of them. Ada by her side, full of smiles and teases. The contentment of knowing that this was her future.

She had been wrong there. Believing the future could be only happiness was a fool's dream. That did not stop her from wanting Ada by her side, whether smiling or crying.

Yet I have not taken her side.

Whatever Ada's motivations, Louisa should be helping her. What was she doing here? She should be looking for Thomas Mills.

'Excuse me.' Louisa cut off whatever Mrs Paulson had been saying. 'I should be going.'

'You have not finished your tea. There is still cake to come.' Mrs Paulson twisted in her seat towards the waiting maid.

Louisa spoke before the order could be given. 'That is very kind, but I have just remembered I have another appointment.'

'It is not like you to forget such a thing. Is there something on your mind? You can tell me. You are all that is left of dearest Emma. If you are in some sort of trouble, let me help.' The worry in her eyes was sincere.

For an absurd moment, the compulsion to tell the truth overtook Louisa. Let her lay the bare facts at the feet of this woman who had known her since a babe and see what she made of it.

She will not approve. Remember how she spoke of Sophie. The disgraced maid caught kissing another girl.

It would be her only link to her mother, gone.

She stood and shook her head. 'I appreciate your concern, but I am fine.'

Mrs Paulson frowned, and Louisa waited for another tirade, but instead, she simply said, 'Good. I shall see you in a fortnight then?'

'I look forward to it.'

The maid helped her gather her hat and coat, and she was soon hurrying down the street. For all Mrs Paulson complained about the spread of houses towards the once-village of Chapel Allerton, it at least meant the tramways came out this far. She needed to head back towards town; Sophie had said Thomas Mills lived in rooms near the canal.

Ninety minutes later, Louisa regretted not accepting Sophie's help. The girl could not be further from an intimidating presence, but at least she would be able to ask people questions without her accent marking her out as not one of them.

Following some rather garbled instructions from a nervous young woman, Louisa arrived at a likely looking row of terrace houses. Halfway down, another woman leant against the wall. Her eyes tracked Louisa's movements in a lazy manner.

'Excuse me?' Louisa called.

The woman swayed slightly, a bottle dangling from her hand.

At one o'clock in the afternoon! Louisa tried to keep her horror from her face.

Still, she had nothing to lose. 'Do you know a man named Thomas Mills?'

'Thomas Mills?' the woman slurred. 'Whose 'e then? Your lover boy?'

Heat rushed to Louisa's cheeks. What an accusation! 'No! Of course not.'

The woman laughed – a cruel, high sound. 'Why ya blushing like a little schoolgirl, then?'

'I need to speak with him.'

'Sure ya do.'

The door to the house opened, and a teenage girl in a much-darned dress hurried out. 'Excuse 'er, she don't mean what she says. Come on, Mum, let's get you inside.' She tugged at her mother's arm.

The woman yanked it away and nearly sent herself sprawling to the ground. 'I'll come inside when I want, missy. Thinks she's the bloody boss of me. I can still backhand ya, girl!' She made a wild gesture that finally over balanced her and sent her into a heap on the floor. She cried out as the bottle smashed beside her. Alcoholic vapours stung the back of Louisa's nose.

The girl sighed wearily as she went to help. This was not

an uncommon occurrence then.

Louisa had no desire to lay hands on the drunk woman but watching her daughter struggle compelled her to speak. 'Do you need help?'

She shook her head. 'No, ta. I'm used t' it. Just tell us what you need and be off. This ain't the sorta place t' be hanging around.'

'I am looking for Thomas Mills.'

'He owe you money?' The girl hauled her now crying mother to her feet.

'No. His mother might be in trouble.'

The girl's forehead creased. 'He's at number four, upstairs.' She staggered under her mother's weight. 'Will 'is mum be alright? She seems a good 'un.'

'I hope so. I will leave you be now; thank you for your help.'

It felt wrong, leaving the girl struggling under her mother's dead weight, but what could Louisa do? Her help was not welcome.

She knocked on the door for number four.

———

Thomas Mills knew nothing. The only useful bit of information he possessed was the address of his older brother, Daniel, which made it a lot easier for Louisa to track him down. She stood opposite him, squashed into a tiny kitchen, away from the prying eyes and ears of his wife and children.

Daniel Mills had his mother's face, but that was all they shared. He clearly wanted to ask, 'what the hell are you doing here?' Quite likely with a stronger word than 'hell.' Louisa suspected it was only her status as a gentlewoman that stopped him.

'Do you have any idea where she might have gone?' she asked.

'I told you. Tom's.'

And I told you, she is not there. Louisa fought to keep her voice neutral and her words polite. 'I have already been to speak with your brother.'

'If she ain't there, then I don't know where she could be. I haven't spoken to the old lady in months. I even saw about that dead gentleman int' paper and didn't recognise his name. Can't believe it was Ma who found him.'

'Your mother was quite distressed when we spoke with her. You understand that is why it is of great importance we find her?'

'Aren't the police looking for her? They were here earlier, asking the same questions.'

'Indeed, she is a witness in a murder case. You realise disappearing like this implicates her?'

He scoffed. 'No way. Ma didn't have owt t' do with it. She ain't likely to risk prison for some murdering toff.'

Louisa nodded, buying herself time. How to word her next question? 'Did your mother ever talk to you about her work? Or the Pearces?'

'I just told you, we don't talk often. She told us when she got the job. Think it was a dig at me, her having to go out and get more work. Can't even look after my own ma. But I had another little one on the way. Money was tight. What were I to do? And her darling Tommy weren't much use. Won't mucky his hands in a factory that one. Too good for it.'

The dingy room Thomas Mills lived in had not suggested he was 'too good' for anything. His brother's house was small, but at least it was well maintained. The wife's doing, no doubt.

Louisa tried to get the conversation back to her main focus. 'Your brother mentioned an aunt? Your mother's sister?'

'Aunt Peggy?' He paused a moment too long before shaking his head. 'Can't see that husband of hers being too happy if Ma shows up. Why are you chasing Ma, anyway?'

Interesting topic change. 'I told you. She is a witness to a crime.'

'And? You ain't no copper. The peelers hiring ladies to do their dirty work now?'

'She was distressed. I am concerned she might not be thinking straight.'

He shrugged. 'And? What are you going to say if you do find her?'

'I only want to know she is safe.'

He considered a moment, fingers drumming against the gleaming metal of the kitchen counter. 'Listen, I'll pop by Aunt Peggy's, see if anyone knows owt. And I'll stop by Tom's, too. He's more likely to talk to me.'

It was the best she would get. She pulled a pen and journal out of her bag and scribbled her name, address and telephone number. He took the page from her with no resistance, yet she was sure it was destined for the fireplace.

The younger Mrs Mills rushed to her feet as Louisa entered the living room. The oldest child paused in her play to stare. The youngest two continued unconcerned.

'Lovely to meet you all.' A ridiculous thing to say - she had not met them - but it was polite. She waved goodbye, and

Mr Mills opened the door for her.

Cannot wait to get me out of his house.

Louisa strode down the narrow street, boxed in by the dirty brown rows of back-to-back houses. The rain had let up, and children played on the street, unbothered by the humid air and stench of smoke. Their laughter and chatter washed over her. Ada spoke of spending every possible evening playing out on the street as a child. Louisa's father would never have let her. He was not a fan of playing. Louisa had learnt facts and ideas few children knew, but she never learnt the rules of hopscotch.

Reaching Abbey Road was a relief as she left the oppressive streets behind. Though the main road was clogged with carts, trams, and even a motor car, opposite the ruined abbey stood in all its picturesque destruction, surrounded by open space.

Louisa always found it the strangest sight. This once-proud structure from the past penned in on all sides by the future. The busy main street and the rows of terrace houses stood on one side. The river was on the other, now a dirty brown with the progress of industry. Beyond, out of sight, there was the train line laid next to the canal it replaced. Proof of the quick march of technology, lying side-by-side.

Her father once brought her here to teach her about monks, Henry VIII and reformation. She and Ada had visited two years ago, not long after they met. Ada spoke of the beauty of the mouldering ruin, not its history. She knew nothing of dissolution, but she still recognised a place once loved and revered, now left to crumble. She saw it in the stones, in the grounds. Ada knew the story of what had happened here; Louisa just filled in the blanks of the when and how.

What would Ada make of it when she told her about Thomas and Daniel Mills? The latter's lack of concern over his mother suggested either a psychotic level of callousness or that he knew he need not worry.

Louisa was so lost in thought she nearly missed the tram, sticking her arm out at the last moment. The conductor reprimanded her curtly, and she accepted it as deserved.

The same question rattled across her brain as the tram carried her towards town. Had Mrs Mills helped her mistress kill her husband? It took a cool nerve to remain inside the house, summon the police, and answer their questions. She'd even pointed Louisa and Ada upstairs. Where they found no answers. Had she known? Sent them on a wild goose chase? Or was she exactly as she appeared? A kind-hearted maid concerned for a mistress she had seen broken, making a last-ditch effort to help her.

If so, why leave?

Louisa sighed so loudly, the man next to her gave her a dirty look.

She checked her wristwatch as she got off the tram in town. Too late for the lecture she had planned on attending. She would head straight home. Ada should be back too - they could talk. Louisa would admit her mind was full of this murder, too. They could decide together what it was best to do. Whether it was worth putting the police's nose out of joint.

She considered what she would say as the second tram

rattled to Roundhay.

An anxious Sophie greeted her the moment she opened the door. 'Ma'am, you're late home.' She peered over Louisa's shoulder. 'Is Miss Chapman not with you?'

'No. Is she not home?'

Sophie shook her head.

Louisa checked the grandfather clock. Seven o'clock. Ada had not mentioned plans tonight; she must have forgotten to say something. Louisa told herself to relax. It was too early to panic. How much trouble could Ada get into?

A lot if she has gone hunting for a potential murderess.

Louisa turned cold. But Ada would not be that silly.

Would she?

Louisa closed the door behind her, giving what she hoped was a reassuring smile.

'And there's a visitor, ma'am,' Sophie told Louisa as she removed her hat.

'A visitor? We were not expecting anyone. Who is it?'

Chapter Nine

Mrs Mason's Request

'Mrs Mason,' Sophie answered. 'She's been waiting an 'our. I did say I didn't know when anyone would be 'ome.' Like Ada, Sophie's accent became more noticeable when agitated. 'She said it was important she spoke to you and Miss Chapman.'

Louisa frowned. Mrs Mason was a friend, but Louisa would not have expected her to visit on a matter of any urgency. 'Is she in the sitting room?'

Sophie nodded.

'Could you bring us tea, please?'

'I already fetched some for Mrs Mason, but I can bring more for you if you want, ma'am.'

'Please.' The maid left, and Louisa removed her coat and hat.

When she entered the sitting room, Mrs Mason stood in a quick, fluid movement. 'Miss Knight, I'm sorry to intrude like this.'

'No need to apologise.' Louisa waved her back down and joined her at the opposite end of the sofa. 'What's the matter?'

'You remember the boy with the broken arm I was telling you about last night?'

'Yes. Somewhat.' The memory was vague, overshadowed by Ada and her drunken display. Louisa felt a fresh twinge of annoyance.

'He's missing.'

Louisa's stomach dropped. Another missing boy. Alone and unprotected, just like Gallant Pearce. Or, at least, like Ada believed Gallant to be.

'His uncle, Mr Cartwright, came to the infirmary to check on him. He thought Stephen was still there as he never came home, and he wasn't with Miss Armstrong either. She's the other aunt I mentioned, my friend; she's not really an aunt, but she is like family to him. She was a *close friend* of his uncle – a different uncle, not the one who brought him in.'

'Mary,' Louisa cut off her babbling. Mrs Mason was usually so composed. She had to be considering her job – no one wanted a nervous nurse.

'Sorry. Mr Cartwright reported his disappearance to the police but told Dr Hollings – my superior at the hospital – they didn't take it seriously. Oh, they dutifully wrote it down, but they'll never look at it again. A kid with a habit of wandering off goes missing...it's not going to be a top priority. It certainly won't make it into the newspapers like your neighbour's murder.'

Sophie entered with the tea, and Louisa welcomed the distraction, for it gave her extra time to consider her response. There was nothing for it but to speak bluntly and try not to be too dismissive given Mrs Mason's obvious distress. 'If he has a habit of wandering off, is it not possible he has done that again?'

'His uncle already checked all his usual haunts. No one

has seen him. It's like he's disappeared into thin air.'

The fear in her voice infected Louisa and made her scared for this boy she had never met. Still, she knew she must act calm. No good would come of inflaming Mrs Mason's concerns. Whoever this boy and his aunt were, they must be important to her.

'Is there any reason to suspect foul play?' Louisa hoped not. A murder next door was quite enough.

To Louisa's relief, Mrs Mason shook her head. 'No, nothing like that. My fellow nurses said another boy came to the hospital to see Stephen. Everyone assumed it was a brother or a cousin, but he doesn't have a brother, and the cousins all claim to know nothing. And then the next time someone checked on him, he'd gone, and no one's seen him since, and...' Mrs Mason sighed. 'You're probably wondering what any of this has to do with you. I came here to ask your advice, and I was hoping Miss Chapman could provide us with a sketch. Do you know when she'll be home?'

'I am not sure. She is...working.' The lie sounded obvious to Louisa, but Mrs Mason did not question it. 'No doubt she would be happy to help, though, if you are willing to wait and give her a description.'

'Of course, thank you.'

'If Ada does a few copies, you can give one to the police and show the others to people around the neighbourhood. He cannot have travelled too far while injured.'

Mrs Mason gave her a weak smile. 'You're probably right. Still, we would all feel better if we knew he was safe. The Cartwrights and Miss Armstrong have searched the neighbourhood. Myself and Mr Mason have tried to help –

we've grown fond of Stephen ourselves – but what we can do is limited. And the hospital administration isn't being much help. The last thing they want is to draw attention to the fact they lost a patient. So we'll get no help from them when it comes to pressuring the police. I think they'd all be happiest if the whole matter was forgotten.'

'One little orphan, happily forgotten,' Louisa muttered as much to herself as Mrs Mason. 'But his family must intend to keep looking?'

'Of course. That's why I was hoping for your advice. Yourself and Miss Chapman, you've worked with the police, you've seen their investigations. What would they do next?'

'I wish I could help, but I have never worked with the police.' Which was technically true. If anything, she had worked against them.

'You assisted with that robbery case last year. The one with the Fellowes woman. I remember you talking about it.'

Embarrassment squirmed through Louisa. The tea – which Sophie had made exactly as she liked – turned sour in her mouth. She had bragged, hadn't she? About helping the police. One of Ada's friends had started calling her 'Detective Knight' and another 'Miss Holmes.' All in jest, but she had not stopped them. She'd enjoyed it.

'That was my one and only foray into investigative work, and it did not end well.'

'Still, any advice you have – any help you could give – would be appreciated. His family are desperate and running out of ideas. Stephen and this other boy are out there, alone. They'll be easy prey for anyone with bad intentions.'

Louisa fought to push the Fellowes case and its aftermath

from her mind. Surely, there was no harm in helping return a missing orphan to the only family he had left. Mrs Mason only wanted advice, and so Louisa considered the options. 'The other boy. If you could learn more about him, it might help with figuring out where they went.'

'My colleagues at the hospital said he spoke with a strange accent like he was trying to talk rougher than he was.'

Louisa gave her a puzzled look.

'Yes, I know, that should have alerted everyone to the fact he wasn't a relative, but they were all busy. No time to think about it for long.'

'How would Stephen know a boy from outside his social circle? Was there anything else your colleagues noticed about his friend?'

'He was about Stephen's age. I tried asking them for a description, but all they could agree on was that he was white, same as Stephen, which hardly narrows it down. And no one managed to hear his name.' Mrs Mason inclined her head. 'I know. It's not much of a start.'

Louisa frowned. 'It is not. But it is something. Is it possible the boys ran away together?' They might not even want to be found. There could be a good reason they left, unknown to Mrs Mason.

'Maybe they did,' she conceded. 'But they still need to be found. They could be in danger. Stephen likes to think of himself as a street rat, wise to the ways of the world, but he's still just a child. A good kid underneath it all.' Mrs Mason said the last with heavy emphasis as if tone alone could make Louisa understand why this child needed to be found. 'A good kid dealt a bad hand by life. I...I had...' Mrs Mason's voice shook.

She dropped her gaze to her hands, where she twisted her thin gold wedding band. 'I had a friend like him as a girl. The first time I ever met Stephen, he reminded me so vividly of Joseph. It was striking. Not in looks but his mannerisms, his personality. The same glorious optimism, though life gave neither little to be optimistic about. Joseph used to talk about all the great things he'd do when he was older. We used to say we'd get married one day.'

Louisa wanted to ask what happened to him, but the sadness in her friend's voice stopped her.

Mrs Mason dabbed at her eyes. 'The last words Joseph said to me was that he was going to make his fortune. He was thirteen. I never saw or heard from him again.'

'I am sorry.' An inadequate response, but Louisa was taken aback by such a personal disclosure. What else was there to say?

Ada would know what to say if she were here.

Mrs Mason smoothed down her skirts, then sat up straight, her eyes focused on Louisa once more. 'It is the past.' How much effort had it taken her to say those words so calmly? 'Whatever happened to Joseph, I cannot change it. It might not be too late for Stephen, though. He deserves better than starving to death in some stinking alley or falling into the hands of someone with lecherous intentions.'

The string of horrific possibilities Mrs Mason's words conjured were interrupted by a timid knock on the door.

'Come in, Sophie.'

The maid wore the same anxious expression from earlier. 'Do you want me to start making dinner, ma'am? And for how many?'

'Would you care to stay?' Louisa asked Mrs Mason.

'Yes, thank you, if it's not a problem.' A polite response without any of her earlier shakiness. Good manners and etiquette were an excellent way to hide one's emotions, and it appeared Mrs Mason shared that ability.

'Of course not. Three then, Sophie. Miss Chapman should be home soon.' She gave her wristwatch another look. Half seven. *Where is Ada?*

Sophie bobbed her head and left the room.

'Sorry.' Pushing down her unease, Louisa turned back to Mrs Mason. 'You were telling me about Stephen?' Maybe she could discern something about him. Some small fact that might help point Mrs Mason in the right direction.

'He's a typical boy, really, always getting into trouble. Little scrapes, you know, often with the bigger kids, the bullies.'

'So, he likes to fight?' The question came out with more disdain than she'd intended.

'No, I...what I meant is... perhaps 'like' is too strong a word. Though I must confess, he is a little too keen on the exploits of soldiers for my taste. Miss Armstrong told me he sometimes joked about running away to join the army or the navy. It worried her for obvious reasons.'

'He is not old enough to join, is he? Or does not look old enough, at any rate, if he lied about his age?'

'No. He's only ten and looks it. Even the British Navy would take one look at him and turn him away. The days of sending children up the riggings are long gone, fortunately. We thought he might still try, so his uncle went to the recruitment office in town, but they assured him they'd had no children come by.'

It was not much to go off. How to find two children in a city full of hidey-holes and runaways?

More information. If she was going to help, she needed more information. 'What about his aunt? The one you are friends with. What did you say her name was?'

'Eliza Armstrong. She's an actress and a dancer who performs at the Varieties. They advertise her as one of the few Black actresses performing in the north of England. A rarity.' Mrs Mason said the last two words with heavy emphasis, though it was hard to tell if it was disapproval, bemusement, or both.

Mrs Mason fished a piece of paper out of her handbag and passed it over. A show bill with CITY PALACE OF VARIETIES stamped across the top. Beneath it, big block letters screamed names and dates at her. Miss Armstrong's was near the bottom in smaller letters.

Louisa placed the bill on the coffee table. An actress. Not the company she would have expected Mrs Mason to keep. 'How do you know her?'

'She hurt her foot last year during one of her performances and came to the hospital to have it tended. There were some, um, issues, so I ended up being the one to do her bandages. We got to talking – you know my views on the benefits of speaking with patients – and she told me a little about her job. I promised I would go see her show and convinced Arthur to take me to the Varieties not long afterwards. When she spotted us in the crowd, she came over after her performance and invited us backstage.

'We had a couple of drinks and talked some more. About work, mostly, and our kids, as Stephen was there too. Apparently, he often snuck backstage to see her. We've been a few times now, whenever we can get an evening to ourselves around my work and the children. It's a fun show, and we enjoyed Miss Armstrong and Stephen's company. He's been there nearly every time. Always underfoot, like children are.' Mrs Mason smiled fondly, even as she shook her head. 'He likes to ask me questions about surgeries and blood and guts. You know how boys can be.'

Louisa did not, her experiences around children were minimal, but she nodded anyway.

'Eliza may not truly be his aunt, but she cares for him. She's been the closest thing he has to a mother. I can't imagine what that's like, what I'd do if it were my Dottie or Charlie.' Mrs Mason's voice dropped to a whisper, and her hands clenched into fists, clutching the fabric of her skirt. 'I couldn't face it. The mere notion makes me frantic with fear. Yet Miss Armstrong has no choice. And she can't even be upset – not publicly – because she's not his actual mum or aunt. She has to go on with her life, performing on stage with a smile, like nothing happened. To have to face that on top of everything else that she's been through these last couple of years.'

'Everything else?' Louisa seized on the part she could question, uncertain how to otherwise respond to Mrs Mason's further emotional outpouring.

'She's had a bad time of it in recent years. The death of Stephen's uncle hit her hard. And then afterwards, she met someone new, started to recover from her loss and look to the future. This man, he made her all sorts of promises, then left her in the lurch. It turned out he was married with a child. The same old story.'

Mrs Mason spoke with gentle pity, but whatever sympathy Louisa had for Miss Armstrong did not stretch that far. She was just another woman who allowed herself to be played for a fool.

'She told you all this?' Louisa would not have told such details of her private life to anyone except Ada. She certainly did not blurt them out to acquaintances, no matter how close.

Mrs Mason shrugged. 'I think she was happy to have someone to talk with. She has no close family outside the late Mr Cartwright and Stephen.'

To be a woman alone was not easy. After her father's death and before Ada and Sophie, how many days – weeks even – did Louisa go without speaking to anyone? And even she, who in the schoolyard had always craved solitude, had dreamt of company. Miss Armstrong's eagerness to share with her new friends made more sense in such a light. Maybe that, too, was why she had fallen for a charming man's lies.

Shame pooled in Louisa's stomach at her earlier judgement. She was lucky, after all. It had been Ada she fell for. Sweet, brilliant Ada. *Who's still not home.*

Louisa checked her wristwatch again and glanced out the window as if Ada would suddenly materialise on their front lawn. There was nothing there but an empty path and a darkening sky. Ada risked being caught in another summer storm if she did not arrive soon.

'When is Miss Chapman due home?' Mrs Mason must

have noticed her preoccupation. 'You told your maid she would be back for dinner.'

'Problems with the tram most likely. The number three is never reliable.'

'Yes, I was fortunate on my way here.' Mrs Mason paused and fiddled with her sleeve. 'There is something else I wanted to mention. I was going to wait until Miss Chapman was here, but...well, one thing I do know is that Stephen goes to Armley Park School.'

'Same as Ada did.'

'And her brother and sister still do if I remember correctly. I recall her once saying there's a substantial age gap between her and her younger siblings.'

Louisa nodded. 'That's right. You think her brother and sister might know Stephen?'

'It's not a large school. There's certainly a chance they might, particularly her brother. Would it be possible for you to ask, just in case? They might be willing to share something with Ada that they wouldn't with strangers.'

'Of course.' Louisa could not summon any enthusiasm for the idea. Ada's family were not her greatest admirers, judging by the strange mixture of gratitude and resentment she received from them. Still, there was no harm in asking a few questions for Mrs Mason's sake.

The door opened again, and Sophie interrupted. 'Dinner's ready, ma'am. Shall I leave Miss Chapman's in the oven to keep warm?'

'That would be for the best. She should be home soon.' *Am I hoping if I say it enough times, it will become true?*

The pair made polite conversation as they ate, the topic of

missing boys shelved for the moment. Louisa had little appetite. The hollow feeling in her stomach continued to grow even as her food slowly diminished, for there was still no sign of Ada.

'Maybe I should come back tomorrow?' Mrs Mason said as they rose from the dining table. 'Though, I'm working during the day, so I won't be able to visit again till the evening. And...'

And that is another day with a little boy missing.

'I will ring the station to see if Ada has been kept there for some reason and when we should expect her home.'

Louisa's nerves jangled as she waited for the phone to connect to the exchange. Was it her, or was it taking longer than usual? She drummed her fingers against the stand until she heard the click at the other end.

'Good evening, can you put me through to Millgarth Police Station, please?'

Her trepidation grew as she waited again, listening to the static and rubbing her churning stomach. Food had only made it worse.

One of the young constables finally answered. 'Hello, Millgarth Police Station, Constable Smith speaking.'

Louisa tapped her foot, waiting for the polite moment to respond. 'Hello, it's Miss Knight. Do you know if Miss Chapman is there?'

'Miss Chapman? She left before lunch. Why? Is something the matter?'

'No. No. She must have gotten waylaid coming home.'

'For nine hours?' The constable's disbelief echoed her own. The hollow in her stomach was now a pit.

'She probably ran into a friend or some such. Thank you for your help, Constable. Goodbye.' Louisa ended the call before he could ask any more questions.

Too early to panic. Ada could be visiting her family; they did not have a telephone, so there was no way to check. Or maybe she had gone to the art gallery, as she did when she needed to calm her mind.

But the gallery will be shut by now.

Family then. Ada's mother would be able to soothe her restlessness.

When Louisa re-entered the sitting room, Mrs Mason gave her an expectant look. 'Any news?'

'Miss Chapman left the station around noon, so she probably went to visit her family. She should not be too late since her father likes an early night. You are welcome to stay and wait as I do think asking her to draw a sketch will be helpful.'

'Thank you.'

'Is there anything else you can tell me about Stephen whilst we wait? I will try to give what advice I can.'

'I'm not sure what else there is to say.'

'Tell me about his aunt and uncle. The ones he lives with.'

'I don't really know them, but from what I've been told, they're a normal couple. Hard-working people with good intentions regarding their orphaned nephew, but they can't control him, and they don't have the time. He feels in the way there, like an added burden. Not that I believe Mr and Mrs Cartwright ever said that to him. He asked them once, and they denied it, of course, but kids can be perceptive. And I don't think he's wrong, horrible though it is to say.'

'Why was he sent to live there then?'

'Closest family he has. His other uncle was a musician, and he didn't leave much behind when he passed. His father worked at the brickworks over in Hunslet. It paid for a roof over their heads and food but not a lot else. There certainly wasn't any money left for Stephen when he died.'

'And the other aunt, Miss Armstrong, she has no children of her own? Why not place him in her care then? Even if not officially – as you said, she and the uncle were not married – could a familial arrangement not have been made for the best interests of the child?'

'No, Mr and Mrs Cartwright don't get along with Miss Armstrong.'

'Why not?'

'She corrupted their brother, apparently.' Mrs Mason spat the last word out.

'Because she's an actress?' Louisa's voice rose in confusion.

'Yes, partly, but he was a musician. They were both part of that world. It was the difference in race that bothered his brother and sister-in-law.' She related the last in a manner-of-fact voice.

Of course. Louisa cursed her slowness and the stupidity of her earlier questions. There was no chance the Cartwrights would ever have let Miss Armstrong have unofficial custody. It was surprising the boy saw as much of her as he did, though that could be explained by the aunt and uncle having little control over him. It also explained why Miss Armstrong and the younger Mr Cartwright had never married. Whilst not illegal like in some countries, it certainly would not have been well received.

A voice in the back of her head – the one that sounded like her father – agreed with those who would have been horrified, saying that such a coupling was a disgrace and a scandal. She forced herself to ignore it.

Louisa had her own theory regarding scandal. One she had cobbled together over many years, influenced by her father's scorn for the entire world, Ada's relaxed attitude, and her own intrinsic lack of concern for worldly matters. If Society was horrified, and yet none of the actual people involved had done each other any harm – physical or emotional, then Louisa wrote the whole scandal off as the business of no one but those involved. From what Mrs Mason had told her, the late Mr Cartwright and Miss Armstrong firmly fell into the 'not her place to judge' category.

She should have understood earlier – so similar and yet so different to the way people spoke of her and Ada. For there was no equivalent to their 'companion' lie for Miss Armstrong. She could never hide her race.

Mrs Mason watched her, impressively passive. Louisa took pride in being able to hide her emotions, but even still, some of her thought process must have been written across her face. The difference of their races was not a matter they had ever discussed before – a topic shied away from in polite conversation.

'I see.' What else was there to say? Mrs Mason did not need to be told how horrible it all was, least of all by her.

Her friend gave a tight smile. 'Mr Cartwright was surprisingly co-operative earlier today, but I think that was the panic. I'm not sure how much he'll be willing to involve Eliza in the search from now on. Talking on such matters will not help us find Stephen, though.'

A clear end to the topic. Louisa cast her mind back to pick up the strands of their previous conversation. What could be done to find Stephen Cartwright and his mystery friend?

'I still think the other boy might be the key to all this. That would be your best chance if you can learn more about him. It is a shame the descriptions were not more cohesive, or you could have asked Ada to draw a sketch of him, too.' Louisa checked her wristwatch.

'Eliza said she'd visit the hospital again tomorrow if she hadn't heard anything. She's the person who knows Stephen best; maybe she will be able to work out who this other boy is even from such a scant description.'

'Is there any other way I can help?'

Mrs Mason considered a moment. 'Maybe the pair of you could go speak to Mrs Cartwright. She might be more likely to talk to you.'

Louisa nodded, though she doubted how much use that would be. If a stranger showed up at her door asking questions about her family, she certainly would not let them in. Mrs Mason was clutching at straws, and Louisa suspected she knew it. 'I will need an address for Mr and Mrs Cartwright. How do you think would be best to introduce–'

Louisa's head whipped round at the sound of the front door opening.

Ada was home. Louisa's heart skipped, followed by a rush of hot anger soaring through her body.

She did not let it show as she turned back to Mrs Mason.

'Would you mind waiting a moment? I need to speak with Miss Chapman privately.' She stood from her chair but made it no further. The door swung open, and Ada rushed in, still in her coat and hat, exuding energy.

'Louisa. I have so much to tell you!' Before Louisa could respond, Ada's eyes fell on the show bill on the table, and her brows furrowed. Her face changed from excited to confused, like someone had flicked a switch. She seized the bill, studying it like she could not believe the words printed there.

'Is something the matter, Miss Chapman?' Mrs Mason asked.

Ada did not appear to have noticed her. She turned to Louisa with a grin, holding up the show bill like it was a certificate of great achievement. 'You know.' Her voice was a mixture of awe and confusion. She laughed as she threw the bill back down and reached into her handbag, so full the clasp did not close. Ada pulled out handfuls of crumpled paper and dumped them onto the coffee table.

Louisa plucked a sheet from the mess and straightened it best she could, ignoring the waft of tobacco scent that clung to it. It was the same show bill. She grabbed more sheets from the pile. They were all identical, dozens of them, appearing like magic.

Her bag now empty, Ada beamed proudly next to her pile of confounding paper.

Louisa scrambled for words. How had Ada got hold of these? Where from? And why? What was she doing with so many? Where had she been all this time? What the hell was going on? These questions stuttered out as a simple 'Ada, what?'

Ada was still grinning. 'I'll tell you how I know if you tell me how you do.'

Chapter Ten

Perplexing Police

A da's head throbbed as she tried to concentrate on the sketch. Daydreams of a late awakening and a hearty breakfast still taunted her. Instead, she'd been summoned to the station and a distressed woman.

Mrs Tyler stuttered as she tried to describe her attacker and sat shrinking into herself like she was trying to disappear.

Sergeant Potter wasn't helping. Ada wanted to tell him to leave – and would have if it was Davey or one of the other friendly constables – but he was a testy old man at the best of times. His questions became snappier as Mrs Tyler grew more scared and less capable of answering, and he silenced Ada when she tried to calm the agitated woman. The sketch wasn't one of her best; she doubted it would be of much use. Another crime never solved. The thought left a bitter taste in her mouth.

Her dismissal was a relief, and yet she lingered in the room until Sergeant Potter's barked order made it clear her further presence wouldn't help Mrs Tyler. The electric lights were dim in this part of the station, away from the public eye, but still bright enough to make her squint in her current state. She was nearing the end of the corridor when Davey appeared, striding with purpose towards the interview rooms.

He nodded but didn't stop to talk.

Ada moved to block his path in the small space. 'What's happened?'

He tried to shuffle round her, but she refused to move. 'Davey? What's going on? I could feel the tension in the station when I arrived. You have the same anxious energy now, and I doubt it's to do with poor Mrs Tyler. Is it Mr Pearce? What have you learnt?' Her voice was overeager, but she couldn't bring herself to care.

Davey sighed. 'There's been a development, and that's all I can tell you.' His face set and tone grave, he was in police constable attitude without a sign of playfulness. The development must be serious, which lessened the chance he would share it with her.

Still, she stared him down a moment longer before stepping aside. He hurried past as though he feared she would change her mind.

In contrast to his determined stride, Ada walked with deliberate slowness, hoping to run into a chatty officer. It wasn't hard to convince them to take five minutes out of their day to chat with a young woman, even one with a marked face. It'd been two years since she'd started working for the police, yet many of them still treated her like a novelty.

She was out of luck. The few officers she encountered were on a mission: heads down, marching forwards, focused on their current task. She reached the foyer without anyone saying a word to her, but hope flickered at the sight of Constable Smith alone behind the front desk and no one in the waiting area.

The young constable looked like he should be in a

schoolboy's uniform, not a police officer's. And, more importantly for her current concern, he gossiped like a schoolgirl.

She put on her best smile and hoped her powder had done its job, so she didn't look as haggard as she felt. 'Morning, Constable.'

'Morning, Miss Chapman. They bring you in for the Tyler case?'

'Yes, though Mrs Tyler is fairly shaken and struggled to give a decent description. It didn't help that Sergeant Potter was breathing fire down her neck the entire time like the angry dragon I suspect he secretly is.'

With a shocked snort of laughter, he leaned in close to reply in a confidential whisper, 'He does have the temperament of a dragon. God help anyone who invades his lair.'

Ada giggled, then nodded at him. 'How did you get stuck on the front desk?'

'Everyone's running around with this Pearce case. It's turned out not to be as simple as we first thought.' Ada wanted to jump on that sentence immediately but instead held her tongue between her teeth – an old childhood misunderstanding turned habit – and let him keep talking. 'Is it true you live next door? And that you saw the wife leave?'

News travelled fast round the station. All the better for her. Curiosity radiated off him as he waited for her reply.

'Yes. Davey told me you all think Mrs Pearce killed her husband, but, if I may say, you don't sound so confident now?'

He shrugged. 'She's still the most likely suspect.' He looked both ways before whispering, 'We've discovered she's not the only one with motive, though.'

Ada leaned in a little bit more, eyes wide with interest. 'Oh? Who else?'

'Do you remember the Pearces' maid, the one before the old lady?'

Ada nodded. How could she possibly have forgotten Miss Clarke?

'Inspector Lambert and Sergeant Potter went to speak with her, but it turns out she's dead. Died only a month or so after they sacked her. Ill health, her sister told them. She was furious about it, according to Wilkinson, blames Pearce for Miss Clarke losing her job and says that's what killed her. It left her penniless, you see, and with no prospects, and she just...gave in.'

'And you think this sister wanted revenge?'

'Wouldn't you? It doesn't sound like the world will miss him much.'

'So, that's what's got everyone so riled up?'

'Nah. Not only that, anyway. I think they found something else to do with the poison bottle.'

'What about it?'

He nodded towards the depths of the station. 'You'd have to ask Inspector Lambert. All I know is he came away from the lab with a frown that could curdle milk.'

Ada's hope disappeared as quickly as it arrived. Inspector Lambert wouldn't tell her, nor would he appreciate her disturbing him to ask.

'Maybe it weren't poison?' she suggested.

'Goodwin and Wilkinson seemed pretty confident it was.' He shrugged. 'But who knows?'

'What about you? What do you think?'

Constable Smith didn't get to respond as a man in an expensive-looking suit stormed through the entrance and demanded his attention. He had the self-assured air of a man whose business interests prospered, and as such, he thought the whole world should bow down to his demands.

Ada stepped aside and waved goodbye to Constable Smith. He didn't wave back, caught in the crossfire of the man's tirade. Some issue with a stolen briefcase that was of the utmost importance to find. Ada winced as the man's harangue attacked her skull. The closing door silenced him, though the cacophony of the busy city centre – trams and horses and people – only made her wince harder. At least it was cloudy; her head couldn't have coped with brilliant sunshine.

A dozen steps down the street, she ran into a serious-faced Inspector Lambert talking to Constable Goodwin, who watched his superior with care. The inspector was tall, with a face dominated by thick mutton chops that had gone out of fashion the previous century. White hair stood out amongst dark brown, showing how long he had been in the job. His black suit and bowler hat were at least more modern, presumably his younger second wife's influence. Ada could only assume said influence didn't stretch to the ridiculous choice of facial hair.

She smiled a polite greeting at them both and would have kept walking, but Inspector Lambert called her name. 'Miss Chapman, I had hoped to speak with you before you left regarding the Pearce case.'

'Me, sir?' She used her best innocent voice even as her

chest tightened. She forced herself to smile, though she was sure her nervousness must be written all over her face.

'Yes, you, Miss Chapman.'

Had Constable Goodwin grassed on her? He wouldn't meet her eye as they walked back towards the station and peeled away from their group as soon as they got inside.

Ada followed Inspector Lambert to his office in silence, every nerve in her body tense.

Was today the day she lost her job? She wasn't reliant on employment to survive like so many people were – a lucky situation to be in – but it'd still be a blow. Her job meant she had her own money. She didn't want to be anyone's dependent, not even Louisa's.

'Sit, Miss Chapman. And do stop looking so scared; I'm not going to scold you.'

'You're not?' Ada said as she sat with the inspector's neatly organised desk between them.

He lifted a file from the top of a tidy stack and placed it in front of him, tapping on the brown paper cover. 'Alexander Pearce: you knew him?'

Ada's heart jolted, but she shook her head. 'Only in passing. I said good morning if I saw him on the street, but that's about it.'

'And his wife, Clara?'

'The same. We had the odd conversation, but it was only small talk. You know the kind of things. How are you? Terrible weather we're having. I went for a lovely walk round park today. She asked how the redecorating was going once; she'd seen us throwing out the old wallpaper and made some comment about how she had been so happy to rid herself of all that awful green wallpaper which was so popular twenty years ago. You know the stuff, that vivid green–'

'But you didn't know her? She wasn't a friend?'

'No, sir.'

'Yet upon learning her husband was dead, the first thing you did was force your way into a crime scene?'

So much for not scolding me. 'I wouldn't say forced.'

Inspector Lambert gave her a look that said exactly what he thought of her pedantry. She didn't argue the point. Getting Constable Goodwin in trouble would do her no favours.

But when he next spoke, it was not to scold her further. 'What did you find?'

'Excuse me?' Her voice was several octaves higher than she would have liked, and she cringed. It would hardly improve his views on asking women to help. Still, of all the things he could have said, that was the last question she expected.

'In the Pearces' house,' he expanded. She could hear him forcing himself to be patient. 'You spoke to the maid, and I'm going to go out on a limb here and say you looked round, so what did you find?'

It was such an unprecedented turn of events, Ada didn't know how to answer, and she scrambled to remember. 'The maid told us the Pearces argued the night he died.'

'Yes, she told us, too. Anything else? Anything we may have missed?'

Surprises after surprises. Ada froze.

'Miss Chapman?'

She scurried to answer. This was a test, she was sure, and she didn't intend to fail. 'There was a dress in Mrs Pearce's room with spilt wine on it. You found the poison in a wine cellar, didn't you?'

'I was told Constable Wilkinson found that dress.'

Shit. She had told Davey to take the credit, and now Inspector Lambert knew he had seen them there and not told him. She opened her mouth, but no answer came out.

He waved it away. 'Never mind the dress for now. Tell me, Miss Chapman, what do you think happened?'

Not knowing if she would ever be given such an opportunity again, Ada seized her chance. 'I don't think Mrs Pearce did it. She was sickly looking the last few times I saw her whilst he appeared in perfect health. In my eyes, what the maid said about him poisoning her would make more sense.'

'Then who killed him?'

She had no reply for that. 'I don't know, sir.'

'Mrs Mills has disappeared, too. I'm surprised you didn't mention it since it was your maid who called us.'

'What?' Ada's face scrunched up. 'I didn't know. Sophie didn't tell me.'

But she will have told Louisa, who didn't bloody well let me know. She asked the inspector, 'Where would she go?'

'I was going to ask you the same question. When you spoke with her, did she give any clue?'

Ada tried to remember, but nothing Mrs Mills said had implied she would leave or where she would go. Once again, she had no answer. She was failing this test, and there was nothing she could do about it. With great reluctance, she admitted, 'I don't know. She never said anything about leaving. Does she have family?'

'Two sons. We already checked with them.'

'Does it matter if she's gone? Surely she told you everything you need to know?' Let Mrs Mills get as far away as possible from that benign-looking house and its secret horrors.

'She's a witness – and a possible suspect – in a murder case, Miss Chapman. Yes, it matters. We have further questions for her.'

'About what?'

He raised his eyebrows; she'd crossed a line. With all his questions about her opinions, she'd forgotten to whom she was speaking. He wasn't some gossiping constable.

'Sorry.' Ada looked away, studying her hands. A knock at the door spared her from further scrutiny.

Sergeant Potter entered. 'You're needed up front, sir.'

'Wait here, Miss Chapman.' Inspector Lambert strode out of the room.

Ada fidgeted on the chair, glancing around the office. It reminded her of Louisa's house when she first moved in. A relic from the last century, heavy panelling and dark furniture. The desk even looked like Louisa's father's – right down to the obsessive tidiness. There was only that one file out of place, sitting there unopened.

Mr Pearce's file. I could look. I'd hear Inspector Lambert coming back.

A bad plan. A terrible plan. A leaving-herself-jobless plan. A getting-Davey-into-trouble-for-ever-suggesting-they-hire-her plan.

The longer I hesitate, the more likely I am to be caught.

In five hurried steps, she was out of her seat and around the desk.

Chapter Eleven

The Fruits of Impulsivity

The file was heavy in Ada's hands, and she opened it with care, trying to not disturb anything. The first piece of paper was an incident report. She scanned it but learnt little she didn't already know. The coroner's report also revealed little of interest. Or at least nothing Ada could understand. There was the drug Davey had mentioned, hyoscine, but the rest was gibberish. She needed Louisa's expertise, but Louisa would've advised against ever looking at the file.

Hearing no returning footsteps, she kept searching. The next page was covered by a set of photos. Bile rose in her throat, and she covered her mouth, fearing the sight would push her already delicate stomach over the edge. Yet, she didn't look away. Mr Pearce lay face-up on the floor, his eyes vacant and foam around his mouth. Even in the sepia photograph, she could tell his skin was discoloured and blotchy. She flipped past the rest of the photos, knowing she wouldn't be able to remove the image from her mind.

She gasped at her and Louisa's names on the next sheet. Potential witnesses, its title stated, and she breathed a shaky sigh of relief. Written besides their names, in the neat compact handwriting of Inspector Lambert, was: *Likely to involve themselves?* And then underneath: *What do they know? Speak to Miss Chapman.* Nothing she couldn't have guessed.

She moved to the next sheet, which was notes from various interviews conducted on the day of Mr Pearce's death and since. Mrs Mills came first as the person to find the body. Her statement contained information similar to what she'd told Ada and Louisa, although there were a few new facts within. Mr Pearce came home early from work the day prior to his death, citing an upset stomach. After finding the hyoscine in the cellar, the police had asked about the Pearces' wine choices: Mr Pearce preferred a red, whilst his wife always drank white. The cellar had been his domain, though, Mrs Mills admitted – with reluctance, the notes emphasised – that she had seen Mrs Pearce down there from time to time.

Beneath the constables' scribbled notes, the inspector had jotted that her statement didn't disprove their suspicions about Mrs Pearce nor Mrs Mills' accusation against Mr Pearce. A conclusion Ada accepted with a familiar sinking feeling.

Shouting sounded from within the depths of the station, and her head jerked up, but it was just some reprobate who didn't appreciate being arrested and taken to the cells. Hopefully, he would keep the inspector busy.

She read on. A scribbled note at the bottom of the page mentioned Mrs Mills' disappearance and Sophie's report.

Miss Clarke's name appeared next on the list of people of interest. Ada struggled to comprehend that the beautiful young girl was dead, withered away within a month of when Ada last saw her. An address was listed for her, too, though the police had obviously not found her there. It was, however, where they found the sister Constable Smith mentioned. Mrs Parks...the only other person with motive to kill Mr Pearce.

Ada re-read the address, an unfamiliar street in Holbeck, and repeated it one more time to store it in her memory.

The notes described Mrs Parks as angry yet informative. A possible suspect but an unlikely one. She willingly co-operated with the police, confirming the rumours regarding why Miss Clarke was fired and stating that she had died from health complications a month afterwards. When pressed on her sister's death, she thought it was from consumption, but there had been no money to spare for a doctor. The interview must have concluded there, for the notes stopped.

Not wanting to dwell on Miss Clarke's sad life and death any longer, Ada moved onto the next sheet – a fingerprint analysis. Prints had been taken from the hyoscine bottle, Mrs Pearce's hairbrush and Mr Pearce's shaving knife. Ada tensed as she scanned downwards for who'd matched.

Footsteps made her jump. They were far too close. She'd forgotten to listen for the inspector's return.

'Shit.' She scrambled to put the papers back and close the file, trying to recall exactly where it had been on the desk.

Ada made it back into her chair as the door opened. She plastered on a smile and hoped Inspector Lambert wouldn't notice her heart trying to escape her chest.

'Are you quite all right, Miss Chapman?' He scrutinised her with his policeman's suspicious gaze.

'I'm fine, thank you.' Her voice wavered a little. 'Is everything in order outside? I heard shouting.'

She kept her eyes focused on his face and not the file, even though she longed to check if it looked the same as when he left. If he caught her staring, it would only increase his suspicions.

'All is well,' he reassured her as he took his seat.

She forced a smile, still resisting the urge to let her eyes flicker downwards to the file.

It made no difference. He glanced at the file and then back to her, causing her already racing heart to quicken.

She was up to her neck in it.

He spoke in an even voice. 'You're a fine artist, Miss Chapman. Your sketches have helped us on many an occasion; it would be a shame if we could no longer retain your services.'

Ada was unsure how best to respond. 'Thank you,' was all she could think to say, though she was certain his words were more a threat than a compliment. 'May I go, sir?' She started to stand, the quicker to be away from those judgemental eyes.

'I have a few more questions if you don't mind.' She dropped back into the chair with a thump. 'You said you didn't know Alexander Pearce well, but you did talk to him in the street occasionally. When was the last time you saw him?'

'A week ago. We rode the same tram home and spotted each other as we exited at our stop.'

'And how did he seem? Was he happy or sad, for example?'

'Happy, I suppose.' She struggled to recall their conversation. Though the last time she saw Mrs Pearce was burnt into her memory, she'd given no thought to when she'd last seen the dead man alive. 'Chatty, though he always was.'

'Tell me exactly what he said.'

Luckily, it was coming back to her now. 'He said good evening and asked me where I'd been. When I said the police station, he made a joke about it.'

'What joke?'

'Just a silly joke. What trouble had I got into to find myself there? When I explained my job, he made some smart comment about lady police officers.'

'Lady police officers?' he echoed, sounding amused.

'I told him I was neither a lady nor a police officer. It was a silly thing to say, really, but I didn't know how else to react, and he found it funny.'

'Would you say he was flirting with you, Miss Chapman?'

'Possibly. I considered it at the time, which reminded me about Miss Clarke and her dismissal. That whilst he might come across as a harmless man who likes a flirt, I shouldn't be complacent around him. I said a hasty goodbye after that.'

'Understandable,' Inspector Lambert said gruffly. 'Clever even, I would say. By all accounts, he was not a man to be trusted around women, but that is not the issue I wish to discuss. When you saw him last week, you would say he was in good spirits then?'

Ada nodded. 'He always was. He gave the appearance of a jolly man, even if it was only an act. Despite the rumours about Miss Clarke, I never would've guessed his home life was how Mrs Mills described.'

'As is often the case.' Inspector Lambert sighed. 'We do need to speak with the maid again. At any sign of her in your neighbour's house, I expect you to be straight on the telephone, Miss Chapman.'

'Yes, sir.'

'That's all for now.' He waved her towards the door, and she hurried out of her chair. Her hand was on the doorknob when he called after her, 'Oh, and Miss Chapman, for future reference, no more sneaking around crime scenes. It truly would be a shame to have to let you go.'

Following those ominous last words, she made her escape. She was shaking as she walked back through the corridor, though she wasn't sure whether it was her nerves or hangover – or both – that caused it. The interview with the inspector had at least been a temporary distraction from the latter, which now returned with a vengeance.

She wanted to find Davey and ask what he made of the inspector interviewing her, but he was nowhere in sight, and she wouldn't risk wandering the police station. *Best just to get out of here.*

Constable Smith waved her over as she passed the front desk. 'What'd Inspector want with you?'

'Just my opinion on my neighbours.'

'Did he say anything about what they discovered on poison bottle that made him so cross?'

The poison bottle. That must have been the fingerprint analysis she didn't have the chance to finish reading. If only she'd been quicker, hadn't hesitated.

'No. Nothing. He wouldn't tell me, anyway. Begging your pardon, I should be off. Good day, Constable.' He looked flummoxed by her curt goodbye, but she'd worry about that later. She needed to get out of the station.

Outside didn't provide the relief she'd hoped for. The sun

had come out from behind the clouds, and she cursed it, holding her hand up to shield her eyes.

Her shoes clicked against the pavement stones as she hurried down the street. Where to go next? The address for Miss Clarke's sister sprang to the forefront of her mind, but she pushed it away. Inspector Lambert's warning had been clear enough. She'd be risking Davey's career and her own reputation if she got herself fired.

She could go to her parents' home in Armley. Mum would be there. Ada longed to be gathered into her arms like a child and told everything would be all right, but the last time that happened was when Mabel was arrested, and she'd been wrong. Everything didn't turn out all right in the end.

The art gallery, then. The beauty of its tiled display room was the perfect antithesis after Millgarth Police Station's grim architecture. She could lose a few hours there, push everything from her mind.

And then what? She'd be no closer to knowing the truth about Mrs Pearce. It'd be an escape. Another chance to run away.

And there was more to know, Ada was certain. Something had shaken the police's confidence in their initial deduction, judging by the constables' anxiety and Inspector Lambert's newfound interest in her opinions.

Mrs Parks' address floated across her mind once more. Was the information she sought there? Was it worth the risk of her job?

Is my job worth more than a woman's life?

She changed direction as she neared the town centre, heading south towards Holbeck. A tram line ran in that direction, but she felt queasy at the mere thought; the journey to the station had been bad enough. A walk would give her time to think.

What questions did she have for Mrs Parks? And how to word them so the other woman would answer? Louisa would know what to ask, but with no handy access to a telephone, Ada would have to go home first. And there was no guarantee Louisa would agree to come.

Ada kept walking. She would go alone. If she returned home with fresh information, Louisa would have to believe there was a possibility Mrs Pearce was innocent.

Questions nagged at her as she walked, though only half of them pertained to Miss Clarke and her sister. The other half was lost in the haze of the previous night's memories. What had happened after dinner? There'd been a cab and sitting on the step and talking, but what exactly did she say? Did she and Louisa argue? The answers were lost to the fog of alcohol, but she'd an uncomfortable suspicion they wouldn't bring her any pleasure if she did remember.

At least the sky had clouded over again, giving her a reprieve from the sun's unforgiving brightness, though the clouds' grey colouring gave her a different cause for concern. She'd forgotten her brolly again.

The rain held off for the half-hour it took her to reach the address from Inspector Lambert's file, a back-to-back house built from orange bricks turned brown by the city's industrial smog, similar to her parents'. The black paint on the front door was peeling, the windows grubby, and the curtains all closed.

Did someone actually live here, or was her visit a wasted

journey? At least she hadn't fetched Louisa and was spared from sarcasm, though a few comments would've been worth the reassurance of her partner by her side.

Still, I'm here now.

With nothing to lose, she walked down the cracked pavement and knocked on the faded door.

Chapter Twelve

Miss Clarke's Tragic Fate

No one answered. Ada knocked again, harder. The sound echoed along the quiet street. Miss Clarke's sister – or any other family she had – were likely to be working; Ada should've thought of that.

Still, she knocked one more time, hammering against the wood, on the off-chance someone was there and hadn't heard. The door opened with a screech, and she tumbled forward, jerking her arm away to prevent herself from smacking the old lady now stood in the doorway.

'Sorry! I'm sorry!' Ada righted herself.

'Quite the racket you were making there. Takes time for me to make it t' door nowadays; I don't move as fast as I used to.'

Ada guessed the woman was in her seventies, though she could believably be eighty or ninety. She was short – even Ada felt tall beside her – with a wizened face and tufts of white hair peppering her scalp. Despite the return of the sunshine, she'd wrapped herself in layers of woollen shawls, all in various states of tattiness. It was as if someone had taken Ada's childhood imaginings of the wicked old witch from a fairy tale and placed her in the doorway.

Yet, when the old woman spoke, her voice was kind. 'Now, young lady, how can I help you?' Her eyes did the inevitable quick flicker to Ada's cheek, but they didn't linger there, and she gave no other reaction. That was always a sign of good character; at least her birthmark was good for something.

Ada introduced herself and asked, 'Did you ever know a woman named Miss Clarke?'

'Aye, a fair good few of them – my own daughters and granddaughters. I suspect there's one in particular you're here asking about, though. I didn't know papers were hiring lady writers nowadays. But everything's changing, isn't it? Look at them women demanding the vote. I wish I was still young enough to join them. I'd have loved the chance to throw a brick at a politician's head. Though who can tell the difference between those two? Ha! A brick and a politician! Are you a suffragette?'

'I believe in suffrage.' Ada suspected Mrs Clarke would see her diplomatic avoidance of the question for what it was.

'But you ain't chaining yourself to no gates any time soon?'

Not if Louisa has a say in the matter.

'Maybe one day. If need be and the situation doesn't change.'

Mrs Clarke let loose her sudden bark of a laugh again. 'Ha! The situation won't change. If you're waiting for men to stop being stubborn and thinking they're right, you'll be waiting a long time.'

Ada laughed, and Mrs Clarke gave her an approving look, but she didn't get to revel in the approval for long. The old woman's face turned sombre. 'Still, you're here because that nasty piece of work got himself poisoned. Want all the sordid details of what he did to my Susie to print in your little paper?'

'I'm not from the papers, ma'am.'

'Ma'am! Ha! Funny how age commands respect. At least in that aspect. I'm left to rot in this house, but nicely dressed ladies call me ma'am. Not from the papers, you say? Then where you from? I know lady coppers are still a step too far, so you're not police. Besides, we already had that lot round, stirring up old matters best left alone.'

'I'm a sketch artist for the police.' Instinct told Ada if she said anything but the truth, this woman would know. 'But I'm not here because of my job. I live next door to the Pearces. I remember your granddaughter; she was a fine young woman.'

'She was,' Mrs Clarke agreed. 'Then she went to *that place* and met *that man*.'

The old lady spat, right out onto the cracked pavement flags beside the doorway. It landed close to Ada's feet – an ominous, shiny blob – and she stepped to the side. Her shoes had been a present from Louisa.

'I'm no friend of Alexander Pearce's. I doubt the world will mourn him much. About the only person who will is his son. That's why I'm here: Gallant is missing. And I've reason to believe he has run away from his mother.' Ada hadn't told the police her suspicions. Not Davey, not gossipy Constable Smith, and definitely not Inspector Lambert. She wouldn't hand them another piece of rope with which they could hang Mrs Pearce.

'I've no ill will for the boy,' Mrs Clarke said. 'But if you're concerned for him, shouldn't you be looking for him? He certainly isn't here.'

'I'm looking for information. Anything which could help find him or his mother. Did your granddaughter ever tell you anything about the Pearces?'

The old lady laughed bitterly. 'Couldn't stop her.' She gave Ada a long appraising look-over; it took all her willpower to remain still and not squirm under that gaze. Mrs Clarke must've found something she approved of, for she said, 'I suppose you should come in then,' and then turned and disappeared inside the house.

Closing the door behind her, Ada stepped inside a small room. It was the older, less sanitary style of back-to-back – the type now banned, even under Leeds Council's slack interpretation of the housing laws. There were no dividing walls or separate kitchen; the entire lower floor consisted of one room. Dim light travelled through the thin curtains. A narrow pallet bed and faded blankets were pushed against the far wall, a wooden table and chairs cramped into a back corner, and a rusty metal stove and sink in the other. The whole room was leeched of colour – all brown and grey and black. If Ada chose to paint a picture of this room, Louisa would definitely ask what was wrong if she saw it.

Damp lingered in the air, and Ada decided against offering to open the curtains. Sunlight would do the room no favours.

Mum would hate this house. Her parents' home wasn't fancy, nor was the furniture new, but it was always clean and tidy. Mrs Chapman hated nothing more than a woman who didn't take pride in her home, regardless of class or status.

The old lady waved her to one of the chairs, shuffling

across to the stove.

'Do you need any help?' Ada called.

'No, miss. I'm not completely useless yet.'

After a few minutes of clanking and the whistle of the kettle, Mrs Clarke joined Ada at the table and handed her a china mug with a small chip in the rim and no saucer. Mrs Clarke's cup, however, had an even bigger chip; she'd given her guest her best crockery.

Mum would approve.

Mrs Clarke pinned Ada with her sharp gaze. 'Well then, ask your questions, dear.'

Ada sipped her tea and tried not to grimace. Did cholera have a taste? As discreetly as she could, she spat the drink back into her cup and placed it on the table, visions of a horrible death overcoming any polite compunction.

If Mrs Clarke noticed, she made no reaction, and Ada hastened to do as ordered and ask her questions. 'What did your granddaughter have to say about the Pearces when she worked for them?'

'She was full of praise for him and scorn for his wife. Susie said cruel things about her. I can't say for myself whether Mrs Pearce earnt them or not. I think she was a little hard on my Susie. There was always some small complaint. Orders to do a job again even though Susie would come home and say she did it exactly as asked.'

'Did Susie not live there? Mrs Mills – the maid who came after her – did.'

'To begin with, yes. Then the wife told her she felt guilty for keeping a young girl from her family. Which struck us all as odd. It took her a couple of hours a day to get there and back. Travelling across town before dawn every day, that's worse for a girl than not seeing her family. She was a clever 'un though, that Mrs Pearce. She offered Susie extra money – instead of room and board – knowing she couldn't refuse it. We all questioned what that missus was up to, and then it became clear in the end when it all came out.' Mrs Clarke clicked her tongue.

The old woman took a big slurp of tea and continued, 'She worried us all, she did. Me and Betty, that's Susie's big sister, and even our Kate said something. Kate's the youngest, and she's not the sharpest needle in the sewing basket if you catch my drift. If Katie is the one warning you there's something fishy going on, then you're standing in the fish aisle up at market, and you should've already sussed it out yourself. But our Susie wouldn't listen to any of us. Said we were worrying over nowt. Well, we were right to worry, weren't we?'

Mrs Clarke shook her head. 'You young lasses, you won't listen to your elders. We've been dealing with men since before you were born, but what do we know? Do you have a mum still with us?'

'Yes,' Ada replied hesitantly. Where was she going with this change in topic? There were no answers in her unflinching stare, and Ada gazed into her still full cup of tea instead.

'Do you listen to her when she gives you advice about fellas? And courting? And all the matters us old women know more about than you young lasses?'

'No,' Ada admitted. Mum would never understand her apathy towards men; she'd told Ada to refuse Louisa's offer to move in as her 'companion' and try to convince Davey to marry her.

Mrs Clarke shook her head, smiling ruefully. 'Of course, you don't. I hope it ends better for you than Susie.' She let go of a deep, shuddering breath. 'My poor Susie. She was too pretty for this world. From the moment she blossomed, I knew it would be the ruin of her. *Men* would be the ruin of her.' Mrs Clarke slammed her cup down with more force than Ada would've expected from someone who looked so frail.

'Mr Pearce,' Ada said after recovering from her surprise.

'Aye, that swine. He had to have her. And she was young and stupid and believed every word of rubbish he whispered in her ear. About how his wife tricked him into marrying her and had an affair with some cousin of his. How he needed someone who understood him.'

What was the truth, and what was lies? Knowing what she did of Mr Pearce, Ada was more inclined to believe everything he said was a lie.

Still, she filed away the mention of the cousin as a possible lead.

'And she told you all this?' Ada couldn't keep the surprise from her voice. She certainly didn't talk to her mum about the sensitive matters in her relationship. Though perhaps if her relationship issues were more typical – more male – she would be more inclined to do so.

'It all came out after he kicked her t' kerb. No references. Nowt. Nowt at least 'cept the babe in her belly.'

Ada stared at Mrs Clarke for a few moments, comprehending her words. 'She was with child?'

Mrs Clarke nodded. 'My poor girl. She was so scared. She thought he'd divorce his wife and they'd have a family together. What she got was a bastard on the way, and no job, no money, no references.'

A horrible suspicion crept over Ada, chilling her veins and filling her stomach with lead. Miss Clarke died not long afterwards. Ada was worldly enough to know the most likely cause of death for a woman in her condition and situation was an abortion gone wrong.

'You know how this story ends now, don't you?' Mrs Clarke whispered. 'I see the horror in your eyes. Shamed by what poor Susie did.'

'Mr Pearce,' Ada corrected. Her voice turned to cold steel. 'Mr Pearce did it.'

'Yes, he did,' Mrs Clarke agreed with renewed fury. 'You see why I'd dance on that bastard's grave if I still had the strength?'

Ada reached over and placed a comforting hand on Mrs Clarke's arm. The shawls were greasy under her fingertips, but she kept her hand there nonetheless. 'I'm sorry. For what happened to your granddaughter, and for coming here and making you dredge all this up.'

And to what end? All she'd learnt was Mr Pearce deserved his cruel death even more than she already knew. She saw again the crime scene photo, his mottled face and foam around his mouth. The image of Mrs Pearce on her knees, begging for forgiveness. And a new picture: beautiful Miss Clarke sobbing, blood-soaked, as her life drained from her.

Poison was too good for him.

She didn't say it out loud, but Mrs Clarke must have read

it on her face. 'If the wife did him in, who can blame her?' She laughed bleakly. 'Give her a medal, I say. What's the fancy one they give? You know, for services t' King and country? Ah, yes, the Victoria Cross. Give her a Victoria Cross for her services. She deserves it, as far as I can see. But no, instead, they'll give her the noose.'

The slam of the trapdoor and the creak of the rope were so loud in Ada's head, she flinched. The old lady patted the back of Ada's hand, still resting on her shawls; her skin was dry and cold.

'It's not a happy thought,' Mrs Clarke continued. 'But what can we do? Throw stones at policemen as well as politicians? Or have they already started doing that? It wouldn't surprise me. But ah, that would cost you your fancy job, for a start.'

'Maybe I should anyway.' Ada spoke with bitter conviction, surprising herself. She'd always shrugged off questions – including from her suffragette acquaintances – in regards to her choice of job before. A job was a job, after all. Her sketches helped capture criminals, not force-feed political prisoners. Yet it would be forfeit should she dare to more publicly demand the vote.

'It'll do us no good, dear,' Mrs Clarke spoke with quiet resignation. 'Men always win. Take it from an old woman.' She pointed to the empty fireplace. 'Our Betty showed us the papers yesterday. They were demanding justice for Alexander Pearce. I'd say he's been served the justice he deserves, but women like Susie don't get justice.'

'Yet Mrs Pearce will have to face justice. Or at least what's called that.'

Mrs Clarke's mouth twisted into a tight sad smile, and a silent understanding passed between them. Then she shook her head and peered at Ada thoughtfully. 'But you said you came here about her boy. None of this helps you, listening to an old lady's regrets. I'm afraid I know little about the son. Susie mentioned there was a nursery maid who looked after him, though she didn't have much good to say about the woman. Though I think it's cause t'other maid tried to warn her about *that man*.'

For a brief moment, Ada expected her to spit again, right onto the brown carpet.

'Still, even Susie admitted the boy adored his maid. When she was angry in her final days, she said she should've known. Mr Pearce barely wanted anything to do with the son he had, left it all t' his wife and nursery maid. You should speak to her; she probably knows the boy better than his own parents. I can't remember her name, though, I'm afraid.'

Ada frowned. 'Miss Florence Davis. They fired her, too. Not long after Susie left. The gossip I heard said Mrs Pearce was worried about history repeating.'

Mrs Clarke didn't look surprised. She screwed her eyes up, straining to remember. 'She came from the same agency as Susie. Leeds Domestic Agency, I think it's called. They've got an office in town. On Bedford Street...or is it Greek Street? Round there, anyway. I'm sure a clever girl like you can find it. They should have a forwarding address for her. I'd say she'd know where the boy is likely to go. He may even have gone looking for her if he's scared and alone. I hope you find her and him. Good luck, dear.' Mrs Clarke started trying to stand from the chair, but Ada waved her down.

'I'll see myself out. Thank you for your help.'

The air outside the house carried the distinct tang of coal, but it was still a relief compared to the damp interior. She leaned against the wall to smoke a cigarette, processing all she'd learnt. She wouldn't have believed her opinion of Mr Pearce could get much lower, and yet it had. The only surprise was that someone hadn't murdered him sooner.

Though that's not an argument likely to sway the police. Or a jury.

Then let Mrs Pearce run. Let her run far away and never be caught. Who cared if she murdered the bastard or not? A punishment fit for his crime – one the police weren't able to dole out.

Where did that come from? Ada took another drag of her cigarette, disturbed by the dark turn her thoughts had taken. Even when Mabel was convicted, she eventually allowed herself to be convinced justice had been served.

Justice. She told herself she helped bring people to justice, and Louisa agreed.

Ada threw the spent cigarette butt to the pavement and stamped it out with more force than necessary.

Carelessly throwing away her job – and her independence – wasn't an option, but she wouldn't help the police find Clara Pearce.

Let her run.

But was she running? The shouting at the train station had been from a desperate woman who'd lost her son. Mrs Pearce wouldn't leave him alone on streets unkind to children without protection.

No harm would come from trying to find the former

nursery maid and Gallant. What to do after that was a decision for later if she even managed to find them.

Her head jerked round at the clack of heels on pavement flags. For one absurd moment, she thought it was Louisa, but, of course, it wasn't. A tall woman in a brown work dress approached, two small girls clinging to her skirts. As she got closer, Ada's hope flared. Though not quite as striking as her sister, the resemblance was still clear enough that Ada knew she must be Mrs Parks.

'Afternoon, miss. Can I help you?'

Before Ada had the chance to reply, one of the girls piped up, 'What happened to your face?'

She fought the instinct to lift her hand to cover her birthmark, clenching her fists.

'Cecilia!' Mrs Parks scolded. 'I'm sorry, miss.'

'It's fine. I'm used to it.' Ada relaxed her hands. She wasn't a schoolgirl anymore. People – especially children – stared. There was no changing that fact, and she shouldn't judge a child for being curious.

Mrs Parks regained a little composure. 'May I ask why you're outside my house?'

'I came here looking for you, though I ended up speaking with your nan instead.'

'Me?' Mrs Parks' brow furrowed. 'Who are you? What do you need to speak to me about?'

'Your sister.'

Mrs Parks' frown deepened. She opened the front door and hurried the two little girls inside, telling them to go see their nan. Once they were safely away, she turned to face Ada.

'What about my sister?' She held herself to her full height

– back straight, chin jutted out – as if daring Ada to say anything negative and see what happened.

'I wanted to learn more about her. I live next door to where she worked.'

'You're one of *his* friends?' Mrs Parks took a visible step back as though the mere presence of Ada might infect her.

Ada hurried to correct her, shaking her head. 'No. No, definitely not.'

Mrs Parks' scowl softened, though she still kept her distance, watching Ada warily.

Ada continued, 'I'm not sure he was the type of man to be mere friends with women.'

'No.' There was no mistaking the anger in Mrs Parks' voice. 'He wasn't.'

A silence followed as Ada frantically tried to think of what she wanted to ask. Mrs Parks' grandmother had answered Ada's questions regarding Miss Clarke's death, yet there must be something more to pursue with her sister.

'You spoke to the police,' was the best she could come up with.

'I did, yes.' A hesitant answer. Mrs Parks regarded Ada with renewed suspicion. 'How did you know that?'

Ada cursed her foolishness. Unable to admit she read it whilst snooping in a police file, she had no better explanation than telling Mrs Parks her job.

'Huh. So the police sent a woman to speak to me? I've got no more to say. I'm not gonna act sad that bastard's dead. If the wife did him in, then good on her, but it might have been any number of women, and I wouldn't blame them. That actress, for a start. She was spitting feathers when she learnt he was married.'

'Actress?' Interest shone through Ada's answer, and she cursed herself once more. Could she not be subtle for once in her life?

Mrs Parks raised her eyebrows, but then she leant in closer like they were co-conspirators. 'The pretty Black one from Varieties. She showed up at the house when Susie was there. Let him know exactly what she thought of him and his lies.'

Ada tried to keep her tone neutral this time. 'Do you know her name?'

'Eliza. I don't know her last name. But that's what Susie said Mr Pearce called her. I'm sure if you go t' music hall, there'll be posters up.'

Ada restrained herself from jumping with joy. Two leads. She had two leads now. Three, if she included the cousin.

She would find Gallant Pearce.

And if she happened to find Clara Pearce...she would help her run.

Chapter Thirteen

A Variety of Issues

A da chose where to sit with care, scanning the rows of seats that lined the Upper Circle of the Varieties Music Hall – or the City Palace of Varieties, as no one but the management called it. She plumped for a seat near the back and at the end of a row. The couple next to her were so wrapped up in each other they paid her no heed, exactly as she'd hoped. A young woman alone at the theatre always risked drawing attention, but tucked away in a rear-corner, Ada hoped she'd remain inconspicuous. Or, at least, as inconspicuous as she ever managed; her hair and face weren't designed for blending in.

She studied the music hall through the haze of smoke drifting through the air. The obvious downside of hiding in the upper reaches was the long space stretching between her and the stage. Heights had never bothered her – there wasn't a tree in Armley Park she hadn't tried to climb as a child – but it was still disorientating to watch the people below, like staring into a canyon. Would she even be able to see Eliza Armstrong?

How long till the show started? Ada wiggled in her seat and glanced at her wrist, but she'd forgotten her watch again. The clock on the town hall had said half six when she passed, so the seven o'clock show must be due to start soon.

This was the first time she'd stopped all day, and her impatience made her jittery. Even her food had been eaten on the go, a pork pie from a street seller she'd passed on her way to Miss Davis' domestic agency.

A wasted trip. They'd been no use, refusing to give her any information. She should've tried to do it sneakily, pretending she wanted to hire someone or a similar ploy, like the clever detectives in the novels Louisa read. The idea only occurred to her after she'd already failed. She doubted she would've had the nerve to pull it off, anyway.

The secretary had told her in no uncertain terms the agency only gave away client information to the police, and then, only with a warrant. It had surprised Ada her colleagues hadn't already served such a warrant, but she'd seen no mention of one in the file. Perhaps they didn't know which agency Miss Davis had come from. And Ada wouldn't tell them. After all, they didn't share with her.

That is childish logic. You are playing with fire – be careful. The voice in her head sounded eerily like Louisa.

She had trusted Davey and his colleagues about Mabel. How could she not trust them in this, which was so much less important to her?

Or do you trust them? Now the voice sounded like Mabel. Saying what she didn't dare to consider. For all she had outwardly accepted Mabel's guilt, the question had never truly gone away, still hissing in the recesses of her mind when she watched some of the police's arrests.

And look how that ended with Mary Fellowes.

No one would notice if she lit a cigarette. Her minor

contribution couldn't make the room any smokier.

She deeply inhaled the calming smoke before exhaling. It settled her nerves, and she determined to push both nursery maids and lovers, past and present, from her mind. She was here to learn about Eliza Armstrong.

She contemplated how she'd paint this scene. The stage was the obvious focal point, but at the moment, it was also the dullest part of the room, hidden by a plush velvet curtain. She could amp up the smokiness. A scene of darkness with flashes of red and gold hidden amongst the grey. Painted from her viewpoint now, looking downwards, showing tantalising glimpses of the people below amongst the smog. A picture full of mystery.

Ada let out a little huff of laughter. The last thing she needed was more mystery in her life. No doubt Louisa would agree. She'd also like a partner who didn't miss teatime without warning.

The familiar unease of guilt settled in Ada's stomach, and she tried to rid herself of it. She'd explain when she got home. Louisa would be enjoying the chance to hide in her study and read her books in peace. Judging by all Ada had learnt in the past few days, she wasn't such a terrible partner. Louisa should just be glad Ada wasn't a man.

A low bar to cross.

And if her biggest brag was being a better partner than Alexander Pearce, she should as well accept spinsterhood as her only acceptable fate.

The guilt in her stomach only squirmed more, and Ada took another deep pull on her cigarette. Life always looked better with nicotine and alcohol in her system. She couldn't drink though, not alone in public. Probably for the best after last night.

The lights dimmed, followed by a swell of music, and Ada focused on the stage. The compere, a handsome blonde man who had a dashing smile – and knew it – made a show of introducing himself and announcing the acts to follow. There were no well-known names; random Wednesday nights didn't bring in the big stars.

'And Miss Armstrong and Miss Jain are here to answer the question, what goes on inside the minds of beautiful, exotic ladies.'

What the hell does that even mean?

After the compere finished his theatricality, the first act took the stage. A small pale man in a tweed suit with a pencil moustache, he launched straight into his comedy routine with none of the compere's preamble.

Ada tried to relax and enjoy his jokes, but she was too highly strung. She crossed and uncrossed her legs in an attempt to stop her knee jigging and foot tapping.

The next performers were a female duet. Young and beautiful, in matching white thin silk dresses, from the heavenly heights of the Upper Circle, they had an almost ethereal appearance and voices to match. Ada's jerky movements stilled; her worries washed away in a wave of song and graceful motion.

Applause erupted, breaking the spell and jolting Ada back to her seat at the top of the music hall. She must try to paint them when she got home. Her hands were reaching into her bag for her miniature sketchbook when she stopped and scoffed at herself. How easily she allowed feminine beauty to distract her; she was as bad as any man.

The compere announced Miss Armstrong and Miss Jain, and Ada forgot all about enchantresses. Two more attractive women walked onto the stage, wearing intricately beaded dresses that glinted under the electric spotlights. A tall Black woman – who must be Miss Armstrong – wore a sparkling silver gown. Her acting partner had a lighter tawny brown complexion and wore a more reserved plum colour. Miss Jain was also noticeably shorter, similar to Ada compared to Louisa. Though perspective was one of Ada's artistic challenges, she wouldn't be surprised to learn that, up-close, Miss Jain had several inches on her.

Miss Armstrong was the leader, walking out and addressing the audience with a smile plastered on her ruby-painted lips. The act was similar to one Ada had seen years before. The women talked about what they searched for in a man, with plenty of double entendres to keep the audience laughing, and some slapstick and dancing thrown in for good measure. Both actresses spoke in foreign accents she assumed were exaggerated for comic effect.

The set might have been unoriginal, but they gave convincing performances, committing to the bit.

When it was over, Ada applauded with the rest of the audience. It soon died down, and the next performer took the stage. A male singer this time – singing one of the music hall classics about girls up north, which would always be a favourite in a northern city like Leeds. Ada listened with half-an-ear, indecision keeping her pinned to her seat.

She'd come here to talk to Eliza Armstrong, and yet a niggling doubt held her back. Not how she would get backstage – she would solve that problem when she got to it – but whether she should have come here to begin with. She'd already shown up at the Clarkes' house and stirred up old anger, and Miss Armstrong, too, had past hurts inflicted by Mr Pearce. Seeing her on the stage – in her element – only reminded Ada that any such conversation would only bring her pain.

What did she hope to gain from Miss Armstrong? The actress was no friend to Mrs Pearce and unlikely to have much information on either her or her son. If what Mrs Parks said was true, she hadn't even known they existed for the majority of her relationship with Mr Pearce.

She did, however, have a motive.

Did it matter? If Ada would let Mrs Pearce run, should she not, too, leave Miss Armstrong to her life?

Yet she wanted answers, needed to know how Mr Pearce had ended face-up on his study floor, no matter what she might then choose to do with the knowledge.

Ada moved so suddenly, she surprised the couple next to her, who appeared to register her existence for the first time. She hurried out the arched doorway and down the stairs, weaving round a pair of ladies and startling a bored-looking usher near the exit.

The entrance to the Varieties' circle levels was set back from Upperhead Row, accessed by a small side street cut into the shops and offices towering either side. Ada walked the short distance to the less oppressive space of the main footway but stuck to the shadows, fumbling for her cigarettes.

The street was relatively quiet; Ada had never seen it

entirely empty. The few passers-by ignored a boy who tried to hand them flyers, jabbering at them about the delights of the Palace of Varieties. Ada had just found a cigarette but dropped it to the bottom of her bag and, instead, fetched a few coins out of her purse.

She'd gone flyering with Mabel a few times; a local music hall owner had thought two pretty lasses might garner a little extra attention. It was a thankless job. They had often dumped the left-over leaflets in the canal with the other rubbish gathered there.

'Oi, kid!' She swapped her accent to its full-Yorkshire twang. 'You ain't gonna get rid of anymore of them, you know.'

His eyes strayed straight to her cheek, and she waited for the inevitable comment. Instead, he looked at her full-on with a cocky grin spreading across his face. 'Says who?' He turned to a man passing by, flapping the bill in his face. 'Want t' see a show you'll never forget? You may have missed the seven o'clock but can still make it t' nine. Even leaves you with time t' pop int' Horse and Trumpet for a pint first. I've seen show, sir. You won't regret it.' The man pushed the paper away and quickened his pace.

Ada kept quiet as the boy tried his pitch once more on a passing couple. Though he wisely left out the part about a pint, they responded the same.

'You might be right,' he admitted to Ada, still grinning. He held a flyer out to her. 'Want t' buy tickets t' show, miss?'

'I already have a ticket, but I'll take that.' She plucked the leaflet from his hand. 'And these.' She took the remaining flyers from his other hand.

'Miss, I need t' get rid of those.' He tried to grab the bundle as she shoved it into her handbag, stuffing the paper into the small space, his nails scrabbling at the back of her gloves. A couple of flyers fluttered to the dirty cobbles.

'And you 'ave.' She winked at him.

He burst out into a delighted cackle, then came to an abrupt stop, peering at her suspiciously. 'What do you want?'

'Can you get backstage?'

'Yes. But I'm not supposed t' take customers back there.' He wrinkled his nose. 'You're not 'ere t' swoon over Mr Clyde, are you?'

Mr Clyde was the top-billed act Ada hadn't even stayed to see. She held back a laugh at the boy's revolted expression. 'No,' she replied, as seriously as she could. 'I'm not.'

'Lots of girls think 'e's 'andsome. Urgh!' The boy stuck his tongue out.

A smile pulled at the corners of Ada's mouth despite her best efforts. 'I'm sure they do. But the questionable charms of Mr Clyde are not why I'm here.'

'Why you talking fancy?'

Damn Louisa and her proper speech!

'I have a fancy friend. She's a bad influence.'

He opened his mouth again, but Ada forestalled him by holding up one of the shillings she'd removed from her purse. 'Want t' earn some more money?'

'Depends 'ow?' He stared at the coin with undisguised longing.

'There's an actress here. Eliza Armstrong. It's important I speak with her.' She dropped her voice to a dramatic whisper. 'Someone's life might depend on it.'

The boy gasped. 'Is it Stephen? Is this about Stephen? Do you know where 'e is? Are you gonna 'urt 'im?' He took a step towards her, squaring up as if he wasn't a foot shorter and weighed all of five stone. It would've been comical if the boy's concern hadn't been so sincere.

'Stephen? Who's Stephen?' And what did he have to do with Miss Armstrong?

The boy deflated as quickly as he had blown up. 'No one. He's no one. Why do you wanna talk t' Miss Armstrong?'

'Listen, do you want the shilling or not? They'll be another waiting for you when you come back.'

The boy snatched the coin from her hand. 'I'll 'ave to go round t'other entrance.' He ran up the street and around the corner, leaving Ada to wait in the doorway of a closed-up scarf shop. She reached for her forgotten cigarette, fighting past the mass of flyers and sending a few more fluttering to join their fellows on the ground. A pair of men walked past and gave her inquisitive looks, but she refused to meet their eyes, and they kept walking. Ada breathed in a deep lungful of smoke to try to calm the anxiety their gaze had prickled in her nerves.

What was taking the boy so long? Had he decided one shilling was enough for him? She would finish her cigarette and give him another minute before she tried the backstage door herself.

She was crushing the stub under her heel when a voice shouted, 'Miss! Miss!' and the boy re-appeared, jogging towards her. 'She said you can come through. Follow me.' He led her to the Swan Street entrance. Despite its nice-sounding name, Swan Street was little more than a tightly packed, cobbled alley. The Varieties had strung electric lights along the side of their building in an attempt to make it more appealing, but they only served to highlight the liquid glistening on the cobblestones. Ada didn't want to think too hard about what it was, even as her nose provided the answer.

Her guide took her through the backstage entrance, which led to a maze of narrow passageways, stopping outside a brown wooden door that looked exactly like all the others. 'Here you are.' He held out his palm. She gave him his shilling, and he pocketed it so quickly she barely saw his arm move. 'Well, good luck.' He waved at her as he disappeared back into the labyrinth of corridors.

Ada took a deep breath to steady herself, though it did little to calm her beating heart, and knocked on the door. 'Miss Armstrong?'

Chapter Fourteen

The Actress' Act?

A da didn't have to wait long until the door swung open to reveal Eliza Armstrong, still in her show costume. Up-close, she was even taller than Louisa. Her eyes widened and there was a flicker of recognition, even though that wasn't possible, and then she quickly schooled her face into a more neutral expression.

'Little Jimmy says you want to speak with me. You were even willing to pay him two shillings for the privilege.' Off-stage, Miss Armstrong spoke with a soft Yorkshire accent similar to Ada's own.

'It seemed the quickest way.'

A short laugh sounded from inside the dressing room. Miss Jain, Ada presumed.

'So, what is so urgent, Miss...'

'Chapman. Ada Chapman.'

Miss Armstrong's eyebrows raised a fraction. There was definitely recognition there, however impossible it was.

'You've heard my name before?'

'I have. Yes.'

That left Ada askew. 'How?'

'A friend. He lived near you.'

'Mr Pearce?'

Miss Armstrong flinched.

Ada had meant to introduce the topic more gently. Still, why the hell would Mr Pearce have mentioned her name to his mistress?

Miss Jain appeared at Miss Armstrong's side, her face screwed up in rage. 'That scoundrel?'

She, too, spoke in a subtler accent off-stage, though not one Ada could place. Since her knowledge of accents only went as far as Yorkshire, not-Yorkshire and posh, that didn't narrow it down much.

'I warned her.' Miss Jain tilted her head at Miss Armstrong. 'I said he was no good. With his charming ways and his 'woe is me' act.'

Miss Armstrong turned to address her friend, 'Yes, Aisha. You warned me and you were right to do so. And I didn't listen.'

Ada didn't dare to interrupt whatever moment of understanding passed between the two friends. Miss Jain's face softened at Miss Armstrong's words, but when both women turned back to Ada, Miss Jain frowned and narrowed her eyes.

Miss Armstrong's voice was impressively impassive when she addressed Ada again. 'How can I help, Miss Chapman?'

In for a penny in for a pound.

'You know he's been murdered?'

She didn't flinch this time. Her face remained a smooth mask.

Miss Jain, though, gaped at her. 'You don't mince your words, do you? Who did you say you are again?'

Before Ada could answer, Miss Armstrong turned back to

her friend, 'Do you think you could give us a moment of privacy?'

Miss Jain conceded but gave Ada a final warning stare as she brushed past her.

'My apologies for Aisha. She has been most protective of me these last few months. But to answer your question, yes, I knew about his death. I saw the papers.' She continued to give nothing away. A poker face Ada could only dream of.

'I need to talk to you about him. May I come in?'

Miss Armstrong didn't move. 'Why? What is it to you?'

'The police think his wife did it.'

'And? She probably did, and I can't say I blame her.'

'Because he cheated on her?' Ada spoke before she could stop herself. *I won't win her confidence like this.*

'Yes.' Miss Armstrong's strained reply was as expected.

Since Ada was failing at sweet talk, she jumped straight to the crucial point. 'Did you want to kill him? When you found out about his wife?'

Ada waited for anger or denial; instead, Miss Armstrong smiled. Only the slightest upturning of her lips, but her amusement was clear to see. 'Aisha was right. You don't mince your words.' She didn't answer the question, though.

Ada was getting nowhere. Time for a change of her less than stellar tact. 'Listen, maybe you killed him, maybe the wife did, maybe some other mistress did, I don't really care at this point. Let the bastard rot in the ground where he belongs.'

Miss Armstrong's eyes sparkled with amusement at the last sentence. 'Maybe we do have something in common. Come in. Have a drink.'

She stepped back into the room, and Ada followed uncertainly, wary of the sudden change in attitude. Apparently calling Mr Pearce a bastard got her quite far with his former mistresses and their families.

Best to seize the opportunity.

The dressing room was a small, cluttered space with no windows. A weak light bulb hanging from the ceiling kept it from complete darkness. The Varieties had gone as far as connecting their dressing room to the electric grid but only to provide the bare minimum of light. A mirror and vanity table scattered with cosmetics took up most of the space, and a few chairs stacked high with dresses claimed what little was left. There was barely room for the pair of them to stand. It reminded her of Mrs Pearce's chaotic bedroom on a smaller, dimmer scale.

Miss Armstrong bundled a pile of clothes from one chair and placed them precariously on top of another. 'Please, sit.' She stepped backwards, and Ada squeezed past. She sat, but Miss Armstrong remained stood. She turned to the vanity table, where she poured a healthy amount of gin into two smeared glasses.

Ada took one with a polite thanks, hoping it at least wouldn't taste diseased like Mrs Clarke's tea. The gin was coarse and tepid. It burned the back of her throat, like the cheap stuff they used to steal from Mabel's mum's not-so-secret stash, and she tried not to cough.

She took another sip. 'I liked your act.'

'Thank you.' The lack of enthusiasm implied Miss Armstrong didn't care for it herself.

But a job's still a job.

Miss Armstrong put her empty glass down – placed so perilously Ada wanted to lean over and push it back – and studied her. That intent gaze made Ada tense, even though she sensed curiosity rather than hostility there.

'You knew his wife.' Miss Armstrong spoke carefully, like she was giving every word great thought. 'You must have done, living next door.'

'I wouldn't say I knew her. We spoke occasionally. We were barely acquaintances, certainly not friends.'

'But you still knew about her.'

Ada tilted her head, confused. How much gin had Miss Armstrong drank? She'd just said she barely knew the woman. 'I don't understand what you mean.'

'Of course, you don't.' Miss Armstrong's soft, patronising tone implied Ada definitely did understand.

This wasn't going at all as she had planned.

Ada looked away from Miss Armstrong's expectant expression, trying to gather her thoughts. She walked her fingers along the chipped wooden edge of the vanity table.

Without looking up, she replied, 'I truly don't.' Her fingers reached the mirror frame, near a collection of perfumes. It was searching Mrs Pearce's vanity table all over again. The same sinking feeling that she was in over her head.

Even the perfume bottles looked the same.

Ada gasped. She seized a bottle and held it out to Miss Armstrong. 'This is Mrs Pearce's perfume.' The foul-smelling concoction Ada choked herself with.

'No, it's mine. It was a present.' Miss Armstrong snatched the bottle from her.

No need to ask who it was from. *How very unimaginative*

of the undearly departed.

'And you kept it?' She couldn't hide her scorn.

Miss Armstrong cradled the bottle protectively, like a treasure. A strange way to treat a gift from a cheating lover, particularly since she'd appeared glad of his death earlier.

Ada stared at her, robbed of words, unable to make sense of the other woman's actions.

The actress turned away, placing the bottle down with a lot more care than she'd taken with the empty glass.

'I'm sorry,' Ada said to her back. Sorry he cheated? That he died? Or that Ada was here and saying hateful words? She couldn't guess which bothered Miss Armstrong most.

When she faced Ada again, her expression was no help in deciphering an answer. Whatever her inner turmoil, her face was inscrutable.

'You came here with a purpose, Miss Chapman?'

'I wanted to meet you. I was curious.'

She had so many more questions, but how to ask them without being kicked out?

'And now you've met me.'

'And now I have.'

'Good night, Miss Chapman. It was lovely to meet you.' Miss Armstrong opened the door and stood aside.

Ada didn't move. She'd come for answers; she couldn't leave with nothing.

'Please, Miss Chapman. I have another show soon, and I must go find Aisha before we are due back on.'

With a reluctant nod, Ada stood. She stopped when she reached Miss Armstrong, only inches apart. So close Ada could smell her perfume. A sweet lavender, thankfully, not the foul one Mr Pearce had gifted her. Ada jutted her chin up, refusing to be cowered by the other woman's superior height, and looked her square in the eye. 'You never answered my question.'

'What question was that?' A calm reply. A reminder that Ada wasn't intimidating.

Still, she was determined not to look away. 'Did you want to kill him?'

The smallest flicker of Miss Armstrong's eyelid showed some reaction – fear or nerves or hurt – but her answer was composed. 'When I first found out about his wife, yes. It doesn't mean I did it. Did you?'

'Did I what?'

'Want to kill him?'

'What? Why would I want to kill him?' Maybe the actress really was drunk. She certainly wasn't talking sense.

'We both know why.' Miss Armstrong laughed and shook her head. 'Goodbye, Miss Chapman.'

Irritated by her amusement, Ada marched out the door and down the corridor.

Why would she ask that? What reason did Ada have to want him dead? Was Miss Armstrong just trying to deflect blame?

Ada stopped suddenly and changed direction – back towards Miss Armstrong's dressing room. She wasn't going to just walk away from that insinuation.

She barged in without knocking, but her angry demands died on her lips. Miss Armstrong faced away from the door, but her shoulders shook, and her sobbing was muffled but still audible.

Ada took a tentative step forward. 'Miss Armstrong? What's the matter?'

The actress whirled round, eyes blazing behind the tears gathered there. 'Are you still here?' she demanded, wiping her face with the back of her hand. She clutched an object tightly in her fist. Ada couldn't tell what exactly, though it definitely wasn't the perfume bottle.

Why was she upset? Did Mr Pearce's memory still affect her so badly? He was not a man worth crying over.

Surely, she didn't still love him?

Love makes fools of us all.

'I didn't mean to upset you.'

'No. You just came here to accuse me of murder. Well, am I wrong?'

She wasn't.

There was no tea to hand, so Ada went for the only available option. Gin. Just as good for drowning sorrows. Miss Armstrong didn't stop her as she poured out two more generous servings and pressed a glass onto her host.

Miss Armstrong downed her drink in one swallow. 'I didn't kill Alexander.'

Ada copied her and immediately regretted it. Her eyes watered, blurring her vision, as she tried not to cough and splutter. 'Neither did I.'

Glass clunking heavily on wood and the glug of a bottle pouring told Ada that Miss Armstrong was helping herself to another even whilst Ada still recovered from the last.

'Mother's ruin.' Miss Armstrong held her glass up in a mock toast.

'But we're not mothers.' Ada meant it as a joke, but Miss

Armstrong's face fell. Tears pooled in her eyes again.

Too late, Ada remembered Miss Clarke and her abortion. Had Miss Armstrong had a similar situation?

She no longer looked at Ada, studying the object still in her hand. A toy boat of all things.

With a sudden jolt to her chest, Ada grabbed the other woman's hand. 'Can I see that?'

Miss Armstrong's hand clenched around the boat, and she jerked it away. 'Why?'

'I think I've seen similar before.'

Miss Armstrong frowned, reluctant to hand it over. Ada waited, not saying another word. The moment stretched, until Miss Armstrong handed her the boat with great care.

It looked exactly like the ones hidden behind Gallant Pearce's bookcase. Red and yellow paint. Exquisite detail. It could join Gallant's fleet on their tiny ocean.

And on the bottom of the boat were two letters pencilled in by a schoolboy hand: *GP.*

Chapter Fifteen

Legality versus Morality

Louisa listened to the tale of Ada's day with increasing disbelief and horror – both at the risks Ada had taken and the events she had uncovered.

'And then Miss Armstrong grabbed the boat back and very politely asked me to leave. In a manner that told me I needed to get the fu...get out.'

Louisa barely registered the changed ending. She'd had so many facts and stories thrown at her that they chased each other round her mind, and it was impossible to process any of them. What she needed was her notebook. Writing it down would help her make sense of it.

Mrs Mason had remained quiet throughout Ada's regaling of her day but broke the silence that followed the end of the story. 'Why would Miss Armstrong have Gallant Pearce's toy boat?'

An obvious question. One Louisa should have asked. She had to think about this sensibly.

'He had to have been there at some point,' Ada said. 'Now or in the past. How else would Miss Armstrong have it? Surely even Mr Pearce would draw the line at giving his mistress his son's toys? Who does that?'

'Who introduces their mistress to their son, though?'

Louisa added. A knot of frustration built within her.

'You're sure it was Mr Pearce she had the affair with?' Mrs Mason asked Ada.

'She flinched at the sound of his name.'

'But that would mean...' Mrs Mason trailed off; her face twisted in confusion.

'Mean what?' Louisa prompted. 'What did Miss Armstrong tell you about this married man of hers?'

'You know Miss Armstrong?' Ada sounded confused.

Mrs Mason shook her head, as if to shake away whatever she was thinking. 'Nothing. Nothing. And yes, I do. She spoke little of him. Her acting partner – Miss Jain – had more to say on the matter, but it was mostly in the form of insults. But even if Miss Armstrong is Mr Pearce's former mistress, you're right, Louisa, how could she know his son?'

Louisa had no answer. The only sound was Ada fiddling with the fabric of her dress, those restless fingers tracing the cotton lines of her skirt. Louisa fought the urge to clasp them within her own – a way of telling Ada that, whatever this was, they would face it together. But she did not know how much Mrs Mason suspected about their relationship. It was always best to not test the waters.

Louisa seized a coherent idea from the jumble. 'Do you think it is possible Gallant Pearce and Stephen Cartwright knew each other?'

'Who's Stephen Cartwright?' Ada asked. 'The boy outside Varieties was looking for a Stephen.'

'Miss Armstrong's nephew. Sort of nephew; he is related to her late partner,' Louisa explained. 'And he has gone missing.'

'So, we have two missing boys who might know each other?' Ada asked.

'But how?' Mrs Mason asked. 'The only link between them is Mr Pearce and Miss Armstrong, and surely they can't have met through those two – not given the circumstances of their relationship. Miss Armstrong is linked to your murder victim, I'll concede that, but I can't see how Stephen could be.'

A piece of the puzzle fell into place. 'The boy in the hospital,' Louisa exclaimed. 'The one who tried to hide a posh accent. What if he was Gallant Pearce?'

'I still think it's a stretch.' Mrs Mason said.

Louisa was not completely convinced either. However, whilst it did not make much sense, it was unlikely to be a mere coincidence. How many boys with posh accents could a working-class child such as Stephen be linked to?

'We need to speak with Miss Armstrong again,' Louisa said. 'Ask if it is possible the boys knew each other.'

Mrs Mason agreed. 'I'll ask her when she comes to the hospital tomorrow.' She turned to Ada. 'Did you tell the police any of this?'

'No. Do you think I should? Will it help find these boys?'

'I'd ask you not to, if you can keep it to yourself without risking your job. It may be the police will learn about Miss Armstrong's connection to Mr Pearce anyway, especially if they do pay any notice to Mr Cartwright's report, but I don't think it would be wise to draw attention to it. If they can't find the wife, there's always a chance they'll try to pin it on Miss Armstrong. I know she gave you little reason to protect her but...'

'She didn't come across as a murderess either. I'll hold my tongue.'

Anxiety prickled underneath Louisa's skin. She didn't like the idea of Ada keeping secrets. However, there was unfortunate sense behind the request.

After a brief pause, Mrs Mason spoke to Ada. 'Miss Knight suggested you could sketch a likeness of Stephen.'

Ada jumped from her seat. 'Yes! Of course. Why didn't I think of that? Let me go grab my stuff from upstairs!' She rushed out of the room.

Louisa, too, stood and left the room to fetch her tools. Her bag was hanging from a hook in a hallway, and after a brief rummage, she found her notebook and pen.

After returning to her seat, she searched till she found a blank page and wrote Stephen's name at the top. She needed facts, and so she addressed Mrs Mason, 'When did Stephen disappear?'

'Yesterday morning.'

Louisa made a note. 'What time?'

'No one knows exactly. He was already gone when Nurse Simmons brought his lunch.'

'So, before midday?'

'Before one o'clock. Luncheon can take a while to serve.'

Ada returned with her artistic implements and sat on the floor with her pad and pencils spread across the coffee table.

'Wouldn't you be more comfortable in the dining room?' Louisa asked.

Ada smiled but shook her head. 'The light's better in here.' She turned to Mrs Mason. 'I'm going to ask you a series of questions. I need you to answer as honestly and in as much detail as you can.'

Louisa returned to her notebook, though she found herself listening to their conversation.

'Can you remember the last time you saw Stephen, or think of the strongest memory you have?'

'Is this relevant?'

'It helps to get the clearest possible picture in your mind.'

'It was in Miss Armstrong's dressing room. Mr Mason was with me, and both Miss Jain and Stephen were, too.'

'I bet that was quite squished.'

A short laugh. 'Yes. Stephen sat on the floor, his head in some book, and we were all talking. I can't remember how but the conversation turned to the two late Mr Cartwrights, Stephen's dad and uncle. He looked up at the mention of their names and joined his aunt in her reminiscing. I remember he looked so young – so vulnerable – when he spoke about his dad.'

'What was it about him that made him look that way?'

'His eyes.'

'Can you describe them?'

Louisa looked up from her notebook as Mrs Mason described, with some prompting from Ada, Stephen Cartwright's eyes and other facial features. She had never seen Ada at her sketching before, and stirrings of pride rose within her. The delicate way Ada asked questions, how she slowly teased the descriptions out of Mrs Mason. Ada was good at what she did, and Louisa was smugly unsurprised.

She turned back to her own work: a list of known dates and times for Stephen Cartwright and Gallant Pearce. It was despairingly thin and a few of the timings – Stephen's departure from the hospital, Ada overhearing Gallant's name at the train station – were questionable.

If Gallant Pearce had been the boy at the hospital, it could be assumed he had run away from his mother. Mrs Pearce was a wanted woman; she would not turn around for the nephew of her late husband's mistress. She would, however, turn around to find her son, which meant she was most likely still in Leeds. Finding Mrs Pearce, however, was not what Louisa was supposed to be doing. Better to concentrate on the missing boys.

She drafted a list of people to speak to regarding them. At the top were Miss Armstrong, Mr and Mrs Cartwright, and their children. Next came Ada's younger siblings, who attended the same school as Stephen.

There were also those involved with Gallant. Finding Miss Davis, the nursery maid, took on a new importance. She might know more about what had been going on in the household at the time of Mr Pearce's affair with Miss Armstrong. Learning more about Gallant Pearce became a priority, too, but who could she ask?

She tapped the end of her pen against the notebook. His school was the obvious starting point. She'd check with their local one, though there was every possibility he went to a public school further afield.

The list of things to do grew, but the list of where the boys could be remained short. Not because the options were limited, but because there were too many to name them all. The entire city was a possibility. They could also have snuck aboard a train, and if they had made it to a port like Hull or Liverpool, maybe even a boat. The image of them as stowaways was even more unsettling than them being alone in the city.

But this was all speculation. Nothing was certain. Not even whether the boys were together.

An idea came to Louisa. 'Sorry to interrupt. Mrs Mason, I know you said their descriptions were not ideal, but do you think your colleagues could tell us if the boy they saw was Gallant, if Ada could draw a sketch from memory?'

'I can ask,' Mrs Mason said.

'I should be able to,' Ada said, 'though it won't be my best work. I'll try once we've finished this.' She flashed Louisa a smile. 'Good idea.'

Louisa returned it, basking in the warm glow of praise, then contemplated her notes once more. So many questions, and at the centre of it all was Mr Pearce. Did his death relate to Stephen's disappearance? If the two were linked, solving one mystery could help solve another.

Louisa turned the page and started a new list: suspects. Who wanted Mr Pearce dead?

Mrs Pearce was the obvious first entry. Underneath her name, Mrs Mills. Louisa hesitated before adding Gallant Pearce to the list. So far everyone had dismissed him as a child, but children love their mothers, or so Louisa was told. Father had never liked to speak of hers.

Would Gallant Pearce have been willing to kill his father for his mother's sake? Far-fetched, but she must consider all options.

Next, she jotted Mrs Parks and her grandmother, Mrs Clarke. Like Gallant, the old lady was a long shot, but she had as much motive as her granddaughter.

Louisa glanced at Mrs Mason, still deep in discussion with Ada, before adding her final name: Miss Armstrong.

Of them all, Mrs Pearce was still the most plausible option. Mrs Parks and Miss Armstrong had strong motives but no opportunity. Of the Pearce household, Gallant was decidedly the least likely option, and would Mrs Mills have acted on her own accord? Doubtful.

The most conceivable scenario was still that Mrs Pearce had tried to drug her husband to stop his straying and misjudged it. She was indeed scared – as Ada said – when she left. And the more one learnt of Alexander Pearce, the more it was clear death could not have come to a more deserving man.

It was still manslaughter, though. Still a crime, even if it was an understandable one. Her father's lessons on the law had made that clear. She saw no need to ignore him on this. Mrs Pearce's actions had hurt others in the worst possible way.

'There. That'll have to do.' Ada held up her finished sketches for Louisa to see. One image vaguely resembled Gallant Pearce, the other must have been Stephen Cartwright. He had a narrow face and a slightly too large nose, but that was all that distinguished him. He could be any boy in a city of thousands.

We'll never find him. The sad conviction washed over Louisa.

But she had told Mrs Mason she would try. And better to have Ada searching for missing boys than a murderess. Or manslaughter-ess.

'Here. You can take this one to show at the hospital.' Ada passed the picture of Gallant to Mrs Mason, and then she waved the one of Stephen. 'And you're sure you don't want me to give this to the police?'

'Why would you not give it to the police?' Louisa asked. She must have missed a conversation whilst concentrating on her notebook.

'I know that was the whole point,' Mrs Mason said, 'but I've been thinking. If Ada takes the police this sketch or they recognise her work, then they will want to know how she knows about boys. Which would lead them to me and Miss Armstrong and the link to Mr Pearce, and we've already agreed that isn't the best idea.'

Again, Louisa nodded even as unease curdled in her stomach. Nothing good came of lying to the police. However, Mrs Mason was probably right in saying nothing good might come from telling them the truth either.

Besides, Ada had agreed to the secrecy, and she was the one risking her job.

Mrs Mason gestured to the sketch of Stephen. 'I do still hope it may be of some use to the pair of you though, if you're still willing to help look for him.'

'Of course, we are,' Louisa and Ada answered at the same time and then shared an amused smile.

Mrs Mason laughed briefly but when she spoke, she was somber. 'Thank you. I mean it, truly.'

'No need,' Ada said softly.

'None at all,' Louisa added.

Mrs Mason stood. 'Still, you have my thanks nonetheless, and now I need to be leaving. My husband will be wondering what's taking me so long.'

'We'll walk you to the tram stop.' Ada stood, and Louisa copied her.

'Thank you, but it's still light outside. I should be fine. I'll meet you both outside the hospital tomorrow? I finish at five – will that work?'

'That will be fine,' Louisa said. 'We will see you there.'

Once they had finished saying goodbye and closed the door, Ada mumbled something about necessities and disappeared upstairs, leaving Louisa to go back to the sitting room and her notebook.

'What you writing?' Ada asked upon her return. She had changed into a cotton nightdress and removed her hair pins, ginger curls now tumbling down her back.

'Notes. Trying to understand.'

'May I?' Ada sat on the sofa, and Louisa held the notebook out to her. Instead, Ada moved in close, resting her head against Louisa's shoulder, so they could look at it together. Louisa's spare arm settled on her waist, and she relished the closeness, especially when Ada responded by pressing nearer, her hand a delicate touch on Louisa's thigh. Before she met Ada, she had never known the comfort holding another person close could bring.

There were many things Louisa yearned to say, none of which were about poisoned men or runaway children, but Ada read her notes with an intense focus she did not want to disturb. Though Louisa was certain of the logic of what she had written there, it did not stop her nerves squirming as she waited for Ada's reaction.

Ada reached out to trace the words, her fingers following the pattern of Louisa's loopy handwriting. 'You put pen to paper and try to make sense of it all, like me and my art. Except words are your expertise.'

'I do not particularly feel an expert in anything right now. I cannot make heads or tails of any of this.'

Ada's finger stopped on a line. 'You still think Mrs Pearce the most likely suspect. And you're not wrong. But everyone I spoke to said the same thing: if the wife did it, good on her. And I...I agree with them.'

Despite her obvious hesitancy, her words did not come as a shock to Louisa. 'I do not disagree either.' From her current position, Louisa could not see her partner's reaction. Perhaps it was for the best given what she had to say next. 'But even if Mr Pearce deserved to die, it does not matter. The law is still the law.'

'Even when it's wrong? You must admit the law can be wrong. It denies us a voice as women. And look what it does to men like Mr Tallant, just for loving the same as we do.'

'There are cases when the law could be questioned.'

Louisa's father would be rolling in his grave. She had given him plenty of reasons to do that over the years – her relationship with Ada chief amongst them – but the knowledge never became any less discomforting. She had not completely disregarded everything he taught her, though, and that helped to settle her guilt. Her next sentences were those of the girl who had craved his approval. 'But this is not one of them. Whatever Mrs Pearce's motive, whether she intended to kill him or not, the fact is he is still dead, and she is the most likely cause of that.'

Ada tensed in her arms but did not move away, tapping another word on the page of the notebook. Manslaughter.

'It is still a crime. A person is dead, his family grieving; there must be repercussions. We cannot change those facts, no matter how much we might want to.'

Ada sighed deeply, her breath tickling Louisa. 'I know. I know. Yet I can't...I...' Ada's hands bunched up the skirt of her nightgown. 'There's something I have to tell you. Something I should tell you; should have told you a long time ago. I...'

Impatience prickled within Louisa, but she fought it down. This was clearly important. It would do no good to rush Ada, to force her to speak.

'I'm sorry. I should tell you. I really should.' Ada's voice shook, and she pulled away to the opposite end of the sofa. Tears gathered in her eyes, but she said no more.

What could Ada have kept hidden? Louisa normally considered her an open book, yet her behaviour these past few days had been disorientating. Did the reason why lie in whatever she was not saying?

Words died in Louisa's mouth. She did not trust any of them not to be the wrong ones. The words that would make it worse.

Instead, she held out her hand to Ada, an attempt to offer the support and love she was unable to voice. Ada laced their fingers together, and a heady rush of relief overtook Louisa. Ada's hand was a solid presence within her own, those hands which created beauty from nothing and whose simple touch melted away Louisa's anxiety. Perhaps if she held on tightly enough, they would not slip away.

But the choice ultimately had to be Ada's. Louisa never wanted her to stay because she felt she had to, either from obligation or dependency.

She met Ada's gaze, trying to decipher what was

happening behind those emerald eyes. There was sadness etched onto her face. A biting of her lip which indicated nerves.

'I know I've been acting strange these last few days.' Ada shook her head, smiling forlornly. 'That's an understatement – there, I said it for you.' Her voice was teasing, but it did not show in her eyes.

'You have, yes.' There was no point in denying it. 'But it has been a difficult few days. There, that's an understatement, too.'

Ada's laugh was weak, but it sounded genuine. Then she sighed. 'I don't know what to do.'

Here, at least, Louisa had an answer. 'Help me find the missing boys. We can do it together. Maybe the police will find Mrs Pearce and maybe they will not. We cannot control that. And I know it is not easy to walk away, but I also know how important your job is to you. We risked it once–'

'*I* risked it once.'

'We, Ada. We share the responsibility for Mary Fellowes. And that, too, is why we would be better staying far away from Mrs Pearce and the investigation involving her. You want to help, Ada? Then help Stephen Cartwright get back to his aunt and Gallant Pearce back to what family remains to him. They will not survive long on the streets; they need to be somewhere safe.'

'And if I'm wrong, and Gallant's mother is with him?'

Louisa hesitated. The obvious answer was that they would alert the police. It was not an action she would take any joy in, but it was the only available course. Her silence must have spoken for her.

'You think she should go to prison?' Ada's hand did not move but Louisa still had to fight the impulse to hold on a little tighter.

'If she is found guilty. The thought does not bring me any joy, but what other course is there?'

'Let her run.'

Three simple words. Uttered with complete sincerity. They chilled Louisa to her core. She slackened her grip on Ada's hand, and it was Ada who held on tighter.

'You heard what Mrs Mills said. She begged on her knees to be forgiven for his affairs. He as good as killed Miss Clarke and broke Miss Armstrong's heart and then he made his wife beg forgiveness for *his* sins. He deserved to die. If she put poison in his drink – whether she intended for it to kill him or not – she did the world a favour.' Ada's eyes were intense, and Louisa could see the longing there. She wanted Louisa to agree, to share her fury, and it would be easy to do so.

For Ada was right. She was gut-wrenchingly right. But she was also wrong. So terribly wrong.

Louisa fought to remain calm. To reach for the logic that was always her pillar. 'I am not denying his death was well deserved. But it is not up to us to decide whose murder goes unpunished. It is not to us to avenge Miss Clarke's death or decide if Mrs Pearce should walk away. You cannot be judge, jury, and saviour. This is why we have laws and courts. What would happen if every citizen took it upon themselves to kill those they deemed deserving of punishment?'

Ada deflated, her body slumping as if all her righteous anger was leaking out of her. It made Louisa want to take back her words, though she knew they were right.

'How is it fair?' Ada sounded lost.

'The world is not fair. We both know that.' How Louisa wished she had different words. Happier words. Instead, all she had to offer was cruel, hard facts.

To Louisa's surprise, tears pooled in her eyes.

'You're crying.' Ada sounded as shocked as Louisa.

Louisa swiped at her face with quick irritated motions. Why was she upset? Because the world was unfair? It was no new revelation to her.

'Here.' Ada grabbed her handkerchief from the mess on the coffee table and passed it to her. 'You're right if it makes you feel any better.'

'It does not.' Louisa gave a watery chuckle.

Ada moved closer once more and settled herself at Louisa's side, who drew comfort from the soothing warmth of her. Maybe the world was not fair, but it gave her Ada. Even if they had to hide, at least they had each other.

'I am sorry for being so contrary these last few days,' Louisa muttered.

Ada laughed, though there was a bitter undertone to it. 'I don't think you're the one who has been difficult. And I'm sorry I can't explain. I...'

'Shush. Whatever this is, you do not have to tell me tonight. Just tell me when you are ready.'

They lapsed into silence until Ada asked, 'Do you still want to try to find the boys?'

'I told Mrs Mason I would.'

'Then we'll try.' Ada sat up. Her eyes had that determined gleam which usually foretold some madcap idea. 'We'll try.' She squeezed Louisa's hand. 'Together. I want to be on the same side.'

'So do I.'

Ada leant forward and kissed her, and the world melted away for a moment. When they broke apart, Louisa rested her forehead against Ada's. 'We'll work together. With our different skills combined, we can do anything.' An old joke – and not a particularly funny one – but Ada giggled, anyway. 'I love you,' Louisa said. Because she was never good at saying it, always waiting for the right moment. Well, the moment felt right. 'And I know I do not say it enough. But please, never doubt it for a second. You brighten my life every day by being here and make my world a better place. Even when we disagree, when we see the world in different ways, there is no one I would rather *debate* with.'

Another old joke, and Ada laughed. They once had a *debate* about whether they were arguing or debating.

'Quite the romantic declaration from a woman who I distinctly remember telling me she doesn't make romantic declarations.'

'I guess that is just the effect you have.' This time Louisa kissed Ada, who returned it with a conviction that was dazzling. It told Louisa she was not going anywhere.

'I love you, too,' Ada whispered.

Louisa debated asking if she wished to go upstairs, but she had read the situation so wrongly last time that she did not want to ruin another moment. The tightrope of their relationship felt more stable, and she did not want to throw them off-balance again. So, she said nothing. Made no offer. Merely enjoyed Ada being pressed into her side, a thumb tracing lazy circles on her thigh, and those beloved raucous curls tickling her arm. Louisa twisted one gently through her fingers.

A gurgling noise interrupted their quiet contentment, and Ada's hand moved to her stomach.

'Sophie left you a plate in the oven. I am not sure how edible it will be now.'

'Might as well try it.' Ada stood up and moved away from Louisa, whose body protested the removal of her soothing presence. 'Come sit with me in the dining room?'

'Of course.'

Sophie had retired for the night, and so Ada fetched the leftover food and cutlery herself. She sat with Louisa and spoke of inconsequential matters, but Louisa was only half-concentrating. A nagging thought kept reminding her they had not decided what they would do if their search for Stephen and Gallant brought them to Clara Pearce.

It was a question with no right answer; a decision they should not have to make.

But her mind would not be silenced. Even once they had gone to bed, she found herself considering every possibility.

Louisa turned over, trying to be quiet. Was Ada still awake? What thoughts were rushing through her mind?

'Louisa?'

'Hmmm?'

'We'll find them – the boys – won't we?'

I don't know.

'Yes.' A stupid lie. Ada must have known it for a lie. But a necessary one. They couldn't give up before they had even started.

Ada's hand brushed against hers, and Louisa wrapped

their fingers together.

'We will.' Ada squeezed her hand. A little too tight.

Louisa returned the squeeze. 'Of course, we will.'

Chapter Sixteen

A Safe Hiding Place?

At least Ada had remembered her brolly this time. Well, Louisa had reminded her to take an *umbrella*. Unseasonably cold rain battered the oiled cotton canopy, and the constant drumming only fuelled Ada's frustration.

She marched through town with Davey at her side. He didn't even need to break stride to keep up with her furious pace, which only irritated her more.

She and Louisa had a plan: find the missing boys and let the police deal with Mrs Pearce. To that end, they had talked through how best to proceed over a companionable breakfast. The plan lasted until the shrill of the telephone brought Sophie scurrying into the dining room, telling them Constable Wilkinson was on the line. And so instead, Ada was storming through town and clinging to a brolly in a doomed attempt to remain dry.

'I thought you wanted to know more about this case?' Davey asked her. 'That's why you were sneaking around crime scenes and reading police files.'

That stopped Ada short, and she turned to stare up at him. 'You know about that?'

Rain ran in torrents down his helmet, and the navy blue of his constable's jacket was so wet it looked black, yet he stood there stoic as though he wasn't getting soaked through to the bone.

'Inspector Lambert told me and made it clear we're both on our last warning.'

'Both?'

'I saw you at a crime scene, and I didn't report it.'

'Goodwin did.'

Davey snorted. 'Yeah, we should have seen that coming.'

'If Inspector Lambert's so cross, why am I here?' *And not with Louisa like I should be.*

Davey mimicked Inspector Lambert's staid voice. 'We're chasing every possible lead by utilising all available resources.' He swapped back to his own voice to add, 'Or at least that's what he'll put in his report.'

'Well, look at that. He's finally found a use for women. Who knows, maybe we'll make a male suffragette out of him yet.'

Davey laughed deeply. 'Yeah, I don't think that'll happen.'

'No, but it's fun to imagine.'

The two shared a smile.

'Come on.' Davey set off again. 'I want to get the hell out of this rain.'

'I offered to share the brolly.'

'How would that work? Me under your brolly. Going to walk across town on my knees? That'd be a sight.'

Ada scowled as they crossed Centenary Street, narrowly avoiding a speeding motor car whose uniformed chauffeur sent them a rude hand gesture. Clearly, he didn't have a passenger.

The municipal buildings and the art gallery stood to their

right. A part of Ada wanted to give up this whole damn idea and walk the well-trodden halls of the gallery instead, dreaming of the day her work would be displayed there. But that wasn't an option.

They turned the corner onto Calverley Street, the town hall and its clock tower looming to their left. Davey continued to talk, but Ada grew more sober the closer they got to their destination.

The building they stopped at looked like any innocuous office. Anyone passing who didn't stop to examine the little metal plate fixed to the blue front door would walk past thinking it exactly that. Ada peered at the neatly etched lettering, blurred by the rain droplets gathered there:

Albion House

Home for women and children in need

Davey raised the metal knocker and rapped it against the wood.

The woman who opened the door took one look at Davey's uniform and frowned. She turned to Ada, and her expression softened. Was that pity in her eyes?

'How can I help, Officer?' Her voice was posh, like Louisa's. She also shared Louisa's sensible style, in her plain white blouse and a straight black skirt, but there the similarities ended. This woman was small and stout, dark brown hair pulled into a simple chignon and sharp blue eyes that scanned Ada. Louisa had never given her such a discerning hawk-like look.

'I'm Constable Wilkinson from Leeds City Police. Would you be Mrs Thornton?' He rubbed his hand on his soaked jacket, as though that would help, and then held it out.

She took it reluctantly, holding only the tips of his fingers, and confirmed her name. The house's manager.

Mrs Thornton's eyes slid over to Ada again as she dropped Davey's hand. 'What brings you here, miss?' Her gaze lingered on Ada's birthmark longer than most adults did. 'Are you hurt?'

'It's a birthmark.' It snapped out harsher than intended.

'My apologies. I thought it might be, but one cannot be too certain with the women who come to my door.'

'No, I'm not...'

'Miss Chapman is our sketch artist.'

Ada held her hand out, trying to balance the umbrella as she did and pouring cold water down the back of her coat. She fought to keep her face straight and her swearing to herself.

Mrs Thornton took the proffered hand. 'A sketch artist?'

Davey answered for Ada, 'There are two women we are searching for. They're witnesses to a crime, and it's of the utmost importance we find them. Miss Chapman has provided us with sketches.'

That was the official reason for her presence. Hopefully, Mrs Thornton wouldn't call them out on its flimsiness. The truth was, gaining access to a home for desperate women was the one element of policing where Inspector Lambert conceded a woman's assistance may be of use. Also, Davey had confided, the inspector thought he was sending them chasing after a red herring, since Mrs Pearce still being in the city made little sense.

Unless her son is missing. Ada had said nothing about that possibility. She'd promised Mrs Mason her silence. And she would only get herself in more trouble by mentioning the commotion at the train station two days after the fact.

Mrs Thornton made no move to let them inside. She held out a hand, and Davey passed her the sketches of Mrs Pearce and Mrs Mills. 'Witnesses' had been another slight fudge of the truth that sat ill with Ada. Mrs Thornton stepped away from the open door to study the pictures. Davey's pockets had done a surprisingly good job of keeping them dry.

Ada waited anxiously as the raindrops thumped against the top of her brolly, uncertain what she wanted to happen next. Mrs Thornton frowned, then handed the pictures back, shaking her head. 'No, sorry. I don't recognise them.'

Dismay washed over Ada, sudden and unexpected. She'd hoped there were answers here even as it warred with her desire for Mrs Pearce to run and never be found, and for her to play no part in it.

'Is there anything else I could do to help, Officer?' But Mrs Thornton's hand was already on the door, ready to close it in their faces.

Davey spoke before she could. 'May we come in, ma'am? We have reason to believe they may be linked to a woman in your establishment.'

'Why?' Her brow furrowed.

'Eyewitness reports. And there is another connection, though it is a delicate matter best not discussed in a doorway.'

She stepped aside, allowing them to enter a small, clean hallway with white-washed walls, the only decoration a plain wooden cross. The room was so lacking in warmth, Ada suppressed a shiver, despite being away from the damp air outside. Somewhere within the house, a baby cried, and Ada had an urge to join in. How nice, to be able to show all the anger and worry and upset built up inside.

'If you wouldn't mind removing your coats, hats and shoes.' She pointed to a row of coat hooks with shoes underneath – all women's. 'We are not usually so precious but, given the weather, I am sure you can appreciate there is enough work in this house without extra mopping to be done.'

Mrs Thornton led them into a compact office, with a paper-strewn desk and two chairs with worn cotton-padded seats, the floral pattern barely visible. A side table held a tea tray with mismatched cups and saucers. The clutter made Ada picture the stream of activity that must happen in the space. Constant paperwork, Mrs Thornton dashing to and fro, women in and out, pouring out their stories. Not an easy task. Over the last few days, Ada hadn't been able to listen to a small selection of such stories without wanting to step back and let the world burn.

Mrs Thornton took the seat behind the desk and Davey let Ada take the remaining one opposite. He stood beside her, an ominous male presence in this feminine space. He held up the sketch of Mrs Mills. 'A woman matching this description was seen leaving the premises yesterday.'

Mrs Thornton frowned once more, deep grooves creasing her forehead, like one of those wrinkly dogs. 'I can't think of anyone matching that description, though you must understand, Officer, we have women coming and going all the time. Try as I might, I do not remember every woman who passes through my door.'

Davey smiled at her. An 'I understand' smile. An 'it must

be hard' smile. For all his plain looks, Davey had always been able to charm. Though judging by Mrs Thornton's severe countenance, Ada doubted he'd have much success with her. 'I appreciate that, but this was a recent report. The woman's name is Mrs Mills.' He laid the sketch on the desk.

Mrs Thornton gave it a cursory glance and shook her head. Too quick. She was determined not to know, which meant she knew something. Or she was not in the habit of helping police officers.

Davey tapped the paper, forcing Mrs Thornton to look at it again. 'She was reportedly here yesterday and may have been considerably distressed.'

'Distressed women are commonplace for us, Officer.'

'Of course. You do vital work here for these women. Work that we – our hands tied by the law – cannot.'

Ada fought to keep a straight face. Davey was laying it on thick. Nothing else would have him openly disparaging the police department.

It did nothing to soften Mrs Thornton, and Ada's respect for her raised. 'A sad state of affairs, we can all agree. It is rare to meet a constable so honest about such matters. But the fact remains the same; I do not know this woman. Your reports must be wrong.' She stood, interview over

Ada moved to copy her, but Davey didn't. He pulled the other sketch from his pocket and placed it next to the one of Mrs Mills. Mrs Thornton studied this one more intently but said nothing.

'Mrs Mills worked for this woman, Mrs Pearce. Her husband, Alexander Pearce, was found dead four days ago. Poisoned. You know the name, I believe?'

Mrs Thornton shook her head again. 'I've never heard of anyone named Pearce. Mr or Mrs.'

'And Susan Clarke?'

Mrs Thornton flinched at the name – similar to Miss Armstrong with Mr Pearce's. No hiding the connection.

Ada, too, failed to keep her face smooth, jolting round to stare at Davey. No one mentioned Miss Clarke to her.

Mrs Thornton recovered enough to reply, 'I remember Miss Clarke, yes. Hard not to.'

'Why?' Ada insisted before Davey could continue. Mrs Thornton's gaze switched to her. 'Was she here?' Pregnant, abandoned, and desperate. It made sense.

'She was, yes. A man had gotten her in a bad way.' She kept her gaze on Ada, her tone heavy, searching for a feminine understanding Ada could only half appreciate.

'Mr Pearce,' Davey interceded.

'Was it, indeed? And you say he's dead? Well, whatever he did in this life, his soul is in God's hands now. May he bask in his eternal resting place.' All impeccably polite, but the implicate insult was clear: let him rot in Hell.

Davey paid no heed to her supposed piety. 'Miss Clarke died here, did she not?'

Again, Ada stared at him in shock. Mrs Thornton was answering the question, but Ada's mind had taken her to a different day, a year previous.

Miss Clarke must have sat on the same chair as Ada, explaining her predicament. She'd entered through that sterile hallway, not knowing she'd only ever leave to go to the undertaker's and a pauper's funeral.

Despite Mrs Thornton's efforts, the home must be a

miserable place for a woman to spend her last days. It was to that which Mr Pearce had condemned Miss Clarke, to satisfy his own greed and lust. Had he given it any thought? A single ounce of regret?

They'd never know.

If there is a Hell, let him rot there.

Ada wasn't sure if she believed in God or not. Louisa said there was no Heaven and no Hell. No God to judge mortals for their sins or to punish the pair of them for their perceived sin.

In that moment, Ada would take whatever punishment Satan had prepared for her, if Alexander Pearce were there screaming beside her.

A rush of anger flooded her veins. She shouldn't be here. If Mrs Pearce was hiding at Albion House, let her remain hidden. Ada stood, and Davey cut off talking to stare at her. She ignored him, fighting to control her voice to address Mrs Thornton evenly. 'Thank you for your time, ma'am. We should be leaving.'

'I'm not finished, Ada.' She wouldn't forget the look Davey gave her in a hurry. Confusion, yes, but also betrayal. They stared each other down for a few moments, a war of wills. Davey looked away first, back to Mrs Thornton, but his next words made it clear she hadn't won. Quite the opposite. 'Would it be possible for us to look around the facility?'

Mrs Thornton shook her head. 'I'm afraid not. A police officer's uniform is not always a comfort to the women under my care.'

'Miss Chapman, then?'

Mrs Thornton hesitated. Ada shared her uncertainty. A

chance to speak to Mrs Thornton alone intrigued her, and if she found evidence of Mrs Pearce's presence, she could always lie. Though Inspector Lambert wouldn't overlook that easily, should he learn the truth. Nor would Louisa, who'd been so understanding and yet spoke such damning sense last night.

Ada wished with new fervency she was with her partner, searching for the missing boys. Then, at least, if they'd found Mrs Pearce, they could have made a decision together.

Damn Davey and damn Inspector Lambert and damn Mrs Mills, if she was here, for being stupid enough to be seen. Damn Mrs Pearce and triple goddamn Alexander Pearce and his bloody, twisted ways.

'I assure you she'll be as unobtrusive as possible.' Davey gave Mrs Thornton a smile he must have thought reassuring. Ada found it fake. She'd bet Mrs Thornton did, too. 'We appreciate the work you do here. Don't we, Ada?'

'Yes, of course.'

Mrs Thornton studied her. 'It will have to be quick. It will be lunchtime soon.'

Ada nodded, and Davey voiced his agreement. The two women left him standing in the office.

'How long have you worked here?' Ada asked as they walked back through the bland hallway.

'Five years.' A curt answer.

Ada kept going anyway. 'It can't be easy work.' She remembered Mrs Tyler and her quivering fear. 'These women must come to you in great distress.'

'It's my Christian duty to help those in need. We help them find the salvation of the Lord.' There was no real conviction in her voice.

Another memory surfaced. Another woman. She'd been brought into the police station for solicitation and stood in the foyer shouting bloody murder at the constables about what choices did she have? It was the streets, the workhouse, or the contempt of those bloody pious shelter workers.

But Mrs Thornton's words struck Ada not as pious but rote. The way Louisa spoke to Sophie, when she was being polite, and nodding along to the maid's recitation about what she'd learnt in Church that Sunday.

Mrs Thornton led Ada through to another white-washed corridor lined with brown wooden doors on either side. There were no electrics, only a thin grey daylight trickling through the window at the end, providing little illumination. Her skin crawled at the clinical feel of the place.

Half-way down the corridor, a young woman in a brown pinafore crouched on her hands-and-knees with a bucket of water beside her, scrubbing the floor. When she noticed them, she struggled to her feet. The reason why became clear when her swollen belly became visible. Six months gone, Ada guessed. Anger twisted her heart as she looked at the girl's face. She couldn't be older than fifteen, if Ada were being generous, her round and child-like face at odds with her expanding body.

'Sorry, ma'am. I didn't know we'd a visitor.' Her accent surprised Ada. She'd expected something close to her own at its most common, but the girl spoke with the soft burr of rural Yorkshire. An accent that made Ada picture farms, sheep and fields. Things she only saw as the train chugged past.

'It was an unexpected visit,' Mrs Thornton replied.

The girl stared at Ada. 'Who hit you?'

'Excuse me?' Ada looked to Mrs Thornton for an explanation, but the older woman concentrated on the girl.

'Josephine! We don't ask questions like that. Besides, it's nought but a birthmark.'

Ah. At least, it's a different question than usual. For once, Ada gave silent thanks it was only a birthmark. The girl's question was a stark reminder that matters could be much worse.

'You mean you've had that since you were born?'

Ada nodded.

'Why?'

'It's just a mark. Plenty of people have them. It means nothing.' How many times had Mum told her that growing up?

'Why would God mark you out? He has a divine plan, don't you know?' The last was said with a sneaky smile at Mrs Thornton.

'Enough now, Josephine. Back to your chores with you.'

With some grumbling, the girl returned to scrubbing the floor, though it took some time for her to manoeuvre herself down again.

Ada nearly asked if it was appropriate in her condition, but she remembered her mother – even further gone than Josephine – still getting all her cleaning done. With the later pregnancies, Ada had tried to help, but her mother had never let a swollen belly stop her.

Better cleaning floors than out on the cold streets, which might be the girl's only other option.

Ada followed Mrs Thornton through the next doorway

with a growing sense of unease. She found herself in a long room full of beds with metal frames, like a hospital ward, with more white-washed walls adorned with another wooden cross. Most of the beds were neatly made, but a few contained nursing mothers, and a young girl of about five or six sat at the end of one. Her wide eyes followed Ada, who anticipated another question about her birthmark. The child's lips were a mess of scarlet rouge, the colourant more around her lips than on them. Clearly pilfered from her mother's make-up box.

Mrs Thornton sighed. 'Amelia! What have you done to your face?'

'Shiny red!' The girl sounded pleased with herself and oblivious to Mrs Thornton's stern tone. 'Like Mummy.' In her hand, she waved a pot of lip rouge, stained fingertips similar to Ada's when she searched Mrs Pearce's bedroom.

Mrs Thornton knelt next to the girl. She pulled out a handkerchief and attempted to wipe her face, but only spread it further. The girl didn't help, wriggling away and tossing her head side-to-side, screaming, 'No, no, no.' A nearby baby joined in her chorus with wordless cries.

Ada moved to help but Mrs Thornton shooed her off, so instead she examined the room. The other women all made a show of ignoring her, determinedly focused elsewhere, and there was nothing that hinted at Mrs Pearce or Mrs Mills having been there.

What did she expect? An 'X' to mark the spot? Like in those pirate books her brothers loved getting out of the library as children and, unbeknownst to them, Ada loved to borrow.

'Hey!' A woman careened into the room. 'What the hell are you doing to my daughter?' The newcomer was about the same age as Ada or slightly younger. She wore a red dress with signs of wear and a low-cut neckline – more appropriate to the evening than mid-morning. There was an unidentifiable stain on her left hip and mud on the hem.

The woman plucked her daughter from the bed and clutched her to her breast. She fussed over the girl's face. 'What happened? Is she hurt? Does she need a nurse?'

'It's only make-up.' Mrs Thornton held up the lip rouge. The girl reached pudgy hands out to steal it back, but Mrs Thornton kept it away from her grasp. 'Though I am intrigued to know where she got such a product?'

'Mine, ain't it?' The girl's mother also tried to seize it, and Mrs Thornton closed her hand, hiding it in her fist. 'Hey! I earnt that!'

'Through sin?'

'No. Got it from posh bint, didn't I? Gave it to me cheap. She can't wear it, anyway. She'd look like a clown.'

Ada's bemusement switched to interest. Making sure to speak in the accent she got from her parents, she asked, 'Posh bint?'

The woman turned narrowed eyes towards Ada, giving her a once over.

Mrs Thornton intervened. 'Take Amelia to the bathroom and clean her up, please, Miss Hartman. Then, I believe you are supposed to be on kitchen duty?'

'Yes, Mrs Thornton,' she replied like a scolded schoolgirl. She sloped off, her daughter howling her indignation at losing her new toy.

'Sorry about that. Miss Hartman is one of our regulars. She takes the bed and food for the night and pretends to repent but is back on the streets the next night. We'd turn her away but for the child.' Mrs Thornton frowned.

'Who's the posh lady she mentioned?'

Mrs Thornton shrugged. 'I could not say. Maybe someone she knows from the streets. A genteel lady fallen on hard times. I have known it to happen.' She clenched the pot in her hand.

Ada held out her hand. 'May I look?'

'I doubt it's of any relevance to your enquiries.' Mrs Thornton handed the rouge over. 'Speaking of which, is there somewhere in particular you would like to see? I would not want to keep your police colleague waiting too long.'

At the mention of the police, one of the nursing mothers flinched, her terrified eyes seeking Mrs Thornton, who moved to reassure her. 'Nothing related to you, my dear.'

Whilst Mrs Thornton was distracted, Ada studied the lip rouge. It was the same as Mrs Pearce's, she was sure. Same brand. Same label. Same design. But that didn't necessarily mean anything. Coty was a brand making a good name for itself. Still, it wasn't the type of product Ada would've expected to find in a place like this. The price alone would make these women wince.

Mrs Thornton returned to Ada's side, and she passed the pot back. The worried mother appeared a lot calmer, and Ada nodded towards her. 'Who is she?'

Mrs Thornton forced a tight smile. 'I think it would be prudent of me not to say.'

Having seen the woman's fear, Ada didn't push the issue.

'So, how can I help, Miss Chapman?'

'Are there any older women here? About fifty to fifty-five?' She had to ask. When Davey and Inspector Lambert asked what she had done during her time here, she had to have answers to give.

And if she found Mrs Mills? Or Mrs Pearce?

Let them run.

You cannot be judge, jury and saviour.

The snap of a trapdoor and the creak of a rope.

'A few,' Mrs Thornton answered. 'Though none by the name Mills.'

Ada forced herself to concentrate on the current conversation. 'May I meet them, anyway? She could've used a false name.'

Mrs Thornton led her to the refectory, a long rectangular room filled with mismatched tables and chairs.

Ada smiled at the non-uniformity. A woman about Mrs Mills' age was clearing away used plates and glasses, but when she turned towards them, her angular face was the complete opposite of the maid's roundness.

The next two women Mrs Thornton introduced were the same. The right age but the wrong faces. Ada suspected she was being led on a wild goose chase. Or Mrs Thornton truly had nothing to hide – one witness report and a pot of lip rouge weren't proof, after all.

'Will they be here long?' Ada asked, as they headed back towards Mrs Thornton's office and Davey.

'Most of the older women stay here permanently. They come here when they have nowhere else to go. Widows. Spinsters with no family left, or if there is family, no one willing or able to support them. This Mrs Mills...does she have a family?'

Ada said she did, and a silence fell. When they reached the corridor near the office, a compulsion to speak overtook Ada. Maybe Mrs Thornton – who saw so much female misery – could understand the quagmire in her mind. 'I don't blame her.'

Mrs Thornton stopped and turned to Ada with a puzzled expression. But beneath the mask of confusion, understanding blazed in her eyes.

'Mrs Pearce. Her husband wasn't a good man. Though you know that already, don't you, from poor Miss Clarke?' When had it become impossible to say Miss Clarke's name without adding the 'poor'? That was her legacy: pity.

'She died cursing him,' Mrs Thornton admitted. 'And he deserved it. He gave her those pills and left her to her fate.'

'He gave her the pills?' *If Hell exists, let it be extra torturous today.*

'The police do not know that?'

'They thought she died of consumption.'

'Who told them that?'

'Mrs Parks.' *Who'll now be in trouble for trying to keep her late sister's secrets from prying eyes.*

'I will pray for her. As I pray for her sister's soul.'

'Does God listen to non-believers?'

Mrs Thornton started, and Ada waited for a furious denial.

Instead, she calmly stated, 'The Church owns this place.' She said no more, but it was enough explanation. Perhaps that, too, was why Inspector Lambert had sent his female sketch artist to visit rather than the more official method of getting a warrant. Ada doubted that would be an easy task for Church-owned property.

It was a sensible place to hide. A Church-run women's home managed by a non-believer with reason to hate Mr Pearce. But how would Mrs Pearce have known about it? Or about Mrs Thornton and Miss Clarke's death?

The questions were half-way out her mouth when Ada stopped. She'd said the right words and asked the right queries. Now she'd walk away. Louisa would approve even if Davey and Inspector Lambert wouldn't.

Yes, walk away. It's what you're best at, after all. Mabel again.

'It was always a long shot,' Ada said to Mrs Thornton, determined to ignore the voice in her head. 'That she'd be here. Perhaps it is for the best we didn't find her.'

She expected Mrs Thornton to agree, but evidently that was a step too far when it came to truth-telling. 'If she killed her husband, she must face justice.' Her dry words were no more sincere than her earlier religious remarks. 'I would have thought you of all people would believe that, Miss Chapman, working for the police?'

'Taking a wage from them doesn't mean I always agree with their actions. The law isn't without its failures. As I'm sure the women in your dormitory could tell you.'

Mrs Thornton nodded without any further denial.

Ada had said enough. Too much. Time to walk away. 'We shouldn't keep Davey – Constable Wilkinson – waiting any longer.'

She turned to enter the office, but Mrs Thornton raised

an arm to stop her. 'Davey? That officer...you know him? On a personal level, I mean? When you spoke of the police not always being in the right...' She watched Ada with thoughtful eyes.

'Oh, that had nothing to do with Davey. I just...' Ada remembered her discussion with Louisa about the righteousness of the law, but she'd already skated too close to that topic with Mrs Thornton. She shook her head. 'I see things sometimes, and I question.' Like poor scared Mrs Tyler. And Mabel.

But you stopped questioning. Mabel's voice once more. It hadn't happened in so long and now twice in as many days.

Mrs Thornton surveyed Ada uncertainly. 'Then you are not...that is...you and the constable are not...'

It took Ada a few moments to realise what she was trying to say, but when she did, it wasn't a surprise. It was what people inevitably believed. That there had to be more to her friendship with Davey; the idea of a man and a woman being only friends was a foreign concept to many.

Ada shook her head, perhaps with a little too much vigour, as Mrs Thornton looked unconvinced.

'And his fellow officers?' she asked.

More head shaking.

'There has been no...untoward behaviour?'

'No.'

Davey told her Inspector Lambert had worried about that issue when Davey first suggested she work for them. But none of the officers had ever done or said anything more than the odd flirtatious comment. She suspected Inspector Lambert had marked her as out-of-bounds, and the other officers weren't stupid enough to challenge that at least within earshot of her or the inspector. It wouldn't surprise Ada to learn they wound Davey up when she wasn't there, but if they did, he never shared it with her.

Mrs Thornton still looked unconvinced, but she gave Ada a tight smile, her arm dropping back to her side, and the pair entered the office. Davey was reading through his notepad, but flicked it shut and jumped to his feet.

'Any luck?'

'Unfortunately, no,' Mrs Thornton replied.

'Then we thank you for your time, ma'am. We'll see ourselves out.' He dipped his head to Mrs Thornton.

'You're welcome. I hope you find your witness, officer. My regards, Miss Chapman.'

In the hallway, they stopped to wrap themselves back into their damp outerwear, and Davey asked her, 'You truly found nothing?'

The rain still thumped against the walls and window, and Ada allowed herself to concentrate on that and ignore Davey's question. 'If it's like this now, what will it be like come winter?'

They hesitated in the open doorway, watching the torrent of water rushing down the roads and pathways to the overflowing drains.

'You're ignoring the question. Which makes me wonder why?' Davey used his best policeman voice.

The young Miss Hartman and the blood-red smears on her face. The words 'posh bint.' Mrs Thornton and her fake piety and concerned face when she asked Ada about the possibility of men treating her wrongly. A woman who looked like Mrs Mills and had been sighted nearby but was definitely none of the women Ada met. Miss Clarke dying from pills Mr Pearce gave her. The fate of Mrs Pearce hanging like a spectre between her and Louisa, even as they spoke words of love and meant it.

'Nothing, Davey. Nothing.'

She put her brolly up and hurried down the footpath, trying to get away from Albion House – its secrets and female misery – as quickly as possible. Once she reached the road, she scurried down the kerb and straight into a puddle, soaking the hem of her dress.

'This blasted weather!' Ada marched on anyway. Davey caught up to her with ease, and they continued side-by-side. 'Do you remember how lovely it was last summer?'

'Considering how hot the interview room got, I'm not sure lovely is the word I'd use. And you're changing subject. Again. And you used the weather both times. Poor show, Ada. Now, what's going on?'

How to explain her tumultuous mind? More than anything she wanted to be rid of it, and yet, how to do that? The only idea she had was terrible, and Davey would hate it, too. But she needed to quiet all the doubts in her head, that battered against her skull like the raindrops hammering the ground.

'When does the inspector expect us back?'

'He didn't say. I can't imagine he'll expect us to be too long though. Why?' Davey said the last word with great uncertainty.

'If we're late, we could say we were following up a lead that went nowhere.'

'We could.' He sounded even less confident now. 'But where would we actually be going?'

She couldn't just come out and say it. She should at least try to explain. 'A woman may go to prison for killing a man who deserved it.'

'You mean Mrs Pearce? Yes, she will go to prison if we find her, no matter how much the bastard deserved it. She's still a killer.'

Huh, look at that. Davey and Louisa are in agreement for once. A stab of dull amusement, but Ada was too tense to truly appreciate the irony.

Davey sighed. 'And how does that relate... Oh, bloody hell, Ada!' He slammed to a sudden stop, turning to stare at her. 'Really? After all these years? You walked away. We walked away. No. No.' He stepped away from her, shaking his head, water flying off his helmet. 'No! Why?'

'I need the truth, Davey. Once and for all. And so do you.'

'We know the truth!' He forced the words out in an angry whisper.

'Please?' Ada hated the pathetic plea in her voice, but Davey's face crumpled, and she knew he would agree. He nodded, still frowning, and they changed course, back away from town, towards Armley Gaol.

Chapter Seventeen

Unbreakable Chains

The castle on the hill. The nickname had made Ada imagine it as like a medieval dungeon inside when she was a child, with prisoners chained to the walls whilst rats nibbled their feet.

Conditions weren't quite that squalor, Mabel told her years later, trying to joke and put a brave face on it, but it was still a dismal place, as expected of a gaol.

The prison warden led Ada and Davey down the dim corridor; there was no electricity, and the weak gas lamps did little to light the narrow space. *It's like someone purposely designed them to make the place that little bit drearier.* Ada expected horrors around every corner, fear twisting at her heart, though there was never anything except more bricks and stifling dampness. A sudden shout from within the depths of the building made her jump.

'You all right there, miss?' Polite words, but perverse amusement glinted in the warden's eyes.

'I'm fine, thank you.' The hitch in her breath surely gave her away, but the warden only grunted and kept walking. From only a short time in his company, Ada concluded he wasn't a sociable man.

It'd taken the pair's joint charm and Davey's warrant card

to grant them access. Ada hadn't considered minor matters such as visiting hours.

They halted outside a large imposing metal door. As the warden fiddled with his keys, Davey took a step closer to her. 'We can always turn around,' he whispered in her ear. 'You don't have to do this.'

Ada shook her head. She'd run away for too long. She needed to resolve this once and for all.

The door creaked open, and Ada stepped into a small room with a table and three chairs in the middle. The bars on the window split the dull grey light that filtered through, and the room lay in a gloom. Probably for the best. Bright sunlight would only make it more miserable, a taunt to anyone stuck in this dreary place.

'Wait here,' the warden ordered gruffly, pointing at the chairs. He locked the door behind him with a clunk, sending a shiver down Ada's spine. The room was already smaller, even though if she asked, she'd be back outside in the humid summer air within ten minutes. Not so for Mabel or the others imprisoned within these walls.

On the chair next to her, Davey looked no happier. 'Are you sure about this?'

'Not at all,' Ada admitted. 'But it's time to stop being a coward.'

'It wasn't cowardly to stop coming. We both stopped.'

'It was hardly the same.' *She wasn't your lover.* It was Ada she'd laid beneath and came undone. Ada who kissed her, drunk on stolen wine and life and love. Who drew her whilst she laughed and made love to her afterwards, painting her body with the colours.

'No,' Davey agreed as if he could hear her thoughts. 'Hardly the same.' His voice was soft, but Ada heard the unspoken words clear as day. Davey had loved Mabel, too. Silently and unrequited. That was why Ada had asked him to come instead of Louisa.

Besides, there was nothing she wanted less than Louisa and Mabel in the same room. Ada couldn't decide who would disapprove of the other more. And she'd have to tell Louisa first.

She needed to tell Louisa.

Tonight.

She'd said that the previous night, too. Louisa had clearly been trying her hardest to understand Ada's strange behaviour, but even her partner's logical mind couldn't solve a puzzle without the missing piece.

Tonight.

'Ada?' Davey pulled her from her thoughts. 'I think they're coming.'

Echoing footsteps heralded the return of the warden. Two sets. Two people. Gaoler and prisoner. The thud of shoes on stone grew louder with every step, surrounding Ada as the walls closed in further. There was no running from what she had set in motion. Her hands fisted in her skirts, and she wished Louisa were here to clasp her hand and never let go.

Ada gasped when the door opened and Mabel stood in front of her for the first time in two years. She wore a rough grey cotton dress, clean but threadbare. Mabel's wrists were cuffed, and Ada fixated on those callous silver hoops. The weight of the cold metal hung heavy on her own wrists as she sat and stared, restrained by invisible bonds.

'Sit,' the warden ordered, shoving Mabel onto a chair. He turned to Davey. 'You've fifteen minutes. I'll be right outside.' The door slammed behind him, and they were as alone as they were ever likely to be.

Ada forced herself to look up from the cuffs. Mabel used to take great pride in her reams of luscious blonde locks, the envy of every girl she knew. Someone had hacked them off, and not well, leaving thin, dirty strands that she'd attempted to plait. That unkempt plait stirred a tenderness in Ada's heart. Memories of quick hands smoothing down blonde hair – attempting to make herself look presentable, to hide what they'd just done – flashed into Ada's mind, unwelcome.

Those girls were gone. This was their new reality, and Ada wanted to run far away from it. Yet the unseen handcuffs grew chains, shackling her legs and feet, so she couldn't have moved if she tried.

Mabel's face was gaunt, prematurely lined, but worst of all were her eyes. The cheeky glint Ada immortalised on canvas was long gone, and Ada knew in her soul it would never return. Cruel hatred had made its home there now.

'What do you want?' Such fury didn't belong to the woman Ada had once loved.

Ada swallowed, wincing at her dry throat. Croakily, she answered, 'I wanted to see you.'

Mabel ignored that, turning to stare down Davey. 'And you? Pig.'

Davey's response sounded a lot more natural. 'Ada wanted someone to accompany her.'

'And what? This was the first time you were available in

the last two years?'

Had Ada made their whole affair up? It wasn't possible this woman glaring at her with such loathing had ever loved her.

But she did. And I loved her. And then I abandoned her. I did this. This is what I wrought. How much has she suffered, alone?

Guilt choked Ada. She tried to speak, but no words came, even as she sensed Davey willing her to talk. Eventually, she managed to stutter, 'I know it's been a while. I'm sorry.'

The words hung in the air, their inadequacy shaming Ada further.

'A *while*?' Mabel spat back. 'But at least you're *sorry*.'

Neither Ada nor Davey replied, and silence settled upon them like a condemnation. But who did it condemn? The prisoner, or the friends who'd let her down?

Mabel leaned back in the chair to survey them with dark, wry amusement. The smile that twisted at the corner of her mouth was an ugly, brutal thing. A cruel mimicry of the knowing smirk she wore in her portrait.

'So, what happened?' She spoke calmly now, though there was still a lingering mockery. 'Your mum finally convince you that you'd be better off as a copper's wife?'

'No.' Surely Mabel didn't believe that.

'No,' Mabel agreed, scanning her. 'You're far too well-dressed for a constable's wife. You've done well for yourself. Is that why you stopped coming? You no longer wanted to be associated with a scandalous past?'

'No.' That was true. Her visits to Mabel stopped months before she met Louisa. The two were separate chapters of her life. Yet, she was still there, brought to the prison because the past still dictated her present.

'Here to see the sights?' Mabel tried to gesture at the dingy room, but the handcuffs restrained her, the rattling chain echoing against the stone so loud, Ada wanted to cover her ears.

It was too late for that now. She'd brought herself to the prison for a purpose.

'Did you kill him?' The words stumbled out.

Mabel's reaction was instantaneous. Her face hardened, and her eyes narrowed, rage flooding them. 'You dare! You show up here after years with no word from you, in your fancy clothes, dragging along your lickspittle copper, then look me in the eye and ask me that?'

Davey's hand slammed against the table, and both women jumped. He was on his feet, towering over them both, and, for the first time, that intimidated Ada.

'Oh, drop the pretence, Mabel!' he shouted. 'You killed him! Maybe you didn't mean to, and maybe he deserved it. But neither of those things change the fact you stuck a knife in him then left him to bleed out. You know you nearly hung, right? It was only because the coroner couldn't say with certainty that Mr Shaw would've lived if you'd fetched help that the judge spared your life. You may not have intended to kill him, but by leaving him alone to die, you guaranteed it happened.'

Ada stared at Davey with growing horror. She'd heard some of this at the trial, struggling to comprehend what it meant beneath the legal jargon, but she'd never had it spelled out with such terrifying clarity.

'Huh!' Mabel made a sound that could've been mistaken for laughter if Ada hadn't heard her real laugh. 'You know everything, don't you, Davey? You knew enough to keep your distance. Our freshly minted police constable. What else do you know, Davey? Do you know about Rosie and Anna and Mary? Tell me that bastard didn't deserve to die.'

'Maybe he did. That didn't give you the right to kill him.'

And Ada was sitting on Louisa's sofa as they talked about who decided if a death was justified. When Louisa spoke sense in her calming voice, there was no denying the logic of what she said.

'No,' Mabel laughed bitterly. 'It's just men in fancy wigs who get to decide that. Though lucky me, they decided I get to live.'

Ada couldn't stand this any longer. 'Just tell me the truth.' A soft plea. 'It's all I ever wanted. Please, Mabel. I begged you so many times. I wanted to understand.'

Mabel stared at her. The silence stretched so long, Ada gave up and stepped away from the table. She would bang on the door and demand her release, flee from this dismal place and the woman she once loved. Then Mabel opened her mouth, and Ada froze, her entire world narrowed down to the small bow-shape of Mabel's lips moving.

'Yes. I killed him.'

The words echoed through Ada's mind. Davey's voice called her name as if from a great distance. She'd known the answer for so long, and yet to hear Mabel confess...it should've been a relief. Mabel belonged in prison, and Ada was right to call her a liar and walk away.

Dull shock faded, replaced with a growing chasm of grief

into which fury cascaded. A burning, righteous anger overtook Ada, and she found her voice. 'Did you mean to?'

Mabel shook her head. 'I panicked. I was scared. We all knew the rumours. He cornered me at leaving time. I'd left something behind – I forget what – and by the time I found it, everyone else was gone.'

'You told me to go on ahead because my mum needed me back straight away that day.' Ada didn't question her at the time, but how she regretted leaving afterwards.

Mabel nodded. 'He stood too close, whispering in my ear about how pretty I was. His hand rested on...' Her words caught, and Ada wanted to reach out and comfort her.

She took a deep breath and continued. 'On a place it shouldn't be, and I knew what would happen. I tried to run away, and I saw someone had left a knife out – one of the little ones we used for spare threads. I didn't think it'd kill him. I didn't mean for him to die. I thought he'd make it to a hospital, or someone would find him. He was screaming so loud; I was sure someone would hear.'

She cried now, great heaving sobs, not even attempting to wipe away her tears, and all possible words of comfort rang hollow to Ada.

How different Mabel's life would be if only Mr Shaw hadn't followed her that day. Ada allowed herself a moment to mourn all the days that would never be – stolen kisses, whispered confidences, shared smiles, nights of passion.

There was no possible happy ending for Mabel, not after Mr Shaw made his decision. For though Ada's world righted itself, had taken a different path to happiness, Mabel's never could.

A burning rage engulfed Ada. If he'd still been alive, she would've stabbed him herself. What a bitter irony. It could so easily have been the other way around if she'd been the one to stay behind that day.

Would Mabel have abandoned me like I did her?

'I understand,' Ada told her. More inadequate words. Nothing she said would change what happened or what Mabel's future was. No words could change Ada's past actions.

Because she should've known. She should've trusted Mabel. Yet it was the denial – the constant denial – that had sown doubt within her.

Davey cleared his throat. 'Why did you say you didn't do it?'

There was the crux of it all. Every nerve in Ada tensed as she awaited an answer.

Mabel shrugged, making the chain on her handcuffs rattle once more. 'I was terrified of what I'd done and couldn't face it. I didn't want it to be true, and so I found myself lying; it was easier than accepting that I'd killed him. And once I'd denied it, I couldn't stop. I lied to myself, and to you, and to a judge. I kept lying, even as I saw it pushing you away. Silly, really, looking at it now, but it wouldn't have made a difference if I'd told the truth.'

Ada's fury turned cold. 'It would to me.'

'Would it? I'd still be imprisoned for life. Maybe I should've told that judge I killed the bastard and was glad of it.'

Ada had no response to that. She wanted to tell her not to say that, not to cheapen her own life, but she knew the reply she would receive. What did Mabel have to live for?

Instead, Ada said, 'I should never have stopped visiting. I...'

Mabel smiled bitterly. 'Maybe it was for the best you stopped. Why should we both suffer?'

There were things Ada could say. Promises she could make. Would any of it make up for walking away? *Too late. Far too late.*

She said nothing.

'I think our fifteen minutes are nearly up.' Davey interrupted everything Ada wasn't saying.

'Well, it was lovely to see you,' Mabel said in a prim matron voice, a mockery of proper manners.

Still, no words would come.

Davey stood up and knocked on the door to get the warden's attention. There was a slight pause whilst they waited, the only sound the jingling of keys outside, then the door swung open, and her chance to say anything vanished.

She paused in the doorway, ignoring the warden's grumbling, and turned to look at Mabel once more. 'Goodbye.' *Say something else. Anything else.*

Mabel nodded. 'Goodbye.' There was a finality there.

The door slammed shut.

Outside, even the rain was a blessed release after the confinement of the prison, and Ada tilted her head to the sky and let it soak her face.

'Are you all right?' Davey asked her, quiet and concerned.

'No,' she admitted without looking at him, her eyes still closed against the rain. 'Are you?'

'No. Why did you want to come here, Ada? Just to hear

her say she killed him?'

'Yes.'

'Did it help?'

'No.'

'Do you want to talk about it?'

'No.'

She was being unamenable. She needed to talk. To unburden herself of the emotions that held her in their sway. Davey would try to understand, but Mabel had never been his to lose.

What she wanted was Louisa, for soothing fingers to muss her hair and tell her all would be well. She wanted the safety her partner's presence brought. But that'd have to wait.

'We should get back,' Davey said.

To the police station and Inspector Lambert and the question of what she found in Albion House.

The pair started walking. Ada didn't bother to open her brolly, letting the rain continue to soak her. Davey tried to start a conversation, but Ada's attention wandered, and he soon gave up. She hadn't been a good friend to him today, and she worried she'd be a worse friend by the time the week was over.

And a bad partner to Louisa, too. For they'd agreed it wasn't up to them to decide Mrs Pearce's fate. But who did get to make that decision?

Men in fancy wigs.

What would Clara Pearce's life have been if she never met a man who made her beg forgiveness for his sins?

If Mabel had come to Ada that night, she would have hidden her without question. Instead, Mabel rotted in prison because a man with lecherous intentions had put his hand where it shouldn't have been.

Was Clara Pearce at Albion House? Would she go to prison – and possibly hang – if Ada said she thought she was there?

Different choices...each leading to a different future.

Ada couldn't change the past. She couldn't hide Mabel or insist on staying with her at the mill. But could she save Mrs Pearce?

Should she?

You cannot be judge, jury and saviour.

What would she tell Inspector Lambert?

Chapter Eighteen

A Sharing of Events

L eeds General Infirmary was an imposing hive of activity on the outskirts of the city centre. The heavy rain had dulled the business of the commercial and financial quarters, but it made no difference to the work of medicine. People would always get sick, and the infirmary grew alongside Leeds' burgeoning population. Such growth meant that fifty years ago, the council moved it from the now improperly named Infirmary Street and commissioned the grand Victorian Gothic building Louisa looked upon now.

As always, she questioned why the architect, Sir George Gilbert Scott – famed for designing various structures in London – included blocky towers sticking out at the corners. Should a hospital building not consist of straight lines? Be clean and orderly to reflect the wards within? She once mentioned this to Ada, who found the whole conversation amusing and said such architecture would be boring. Louisa countered that boring was exactly what one hoped for in a hospital trip.

But Ada was not here, pulled away to the police station, and Louisa felt her absence once more. She could have done with Ada's softer human touch today and for someone to bounce ideas off. Ada and her often differing worldview were most illuminating in such situations, and Louisa needed illumination.

She reached the square outside the hospital entrance, where Mrs Mason stood beside a bench. A dark blue coat stood out against the bright white of her nurse's uniform, and she huddled under a black umbrella. She gave Louisa a weak smile, one that said she was not the bearer of good news and did nothing to improve Louisa's mood.

They exchanged the customary polite greetings, including the obligatory commentary on the dreadful summer rain. Then Louisa asked what Miss Armstrong had said in her scheduled visit to the hospital earlier that day.

'She was acting strange, telling me not to worry and apologising for having bothered me yesterday. That she overreacted and was sure Stephen was fine. When I said I'd asked for your help, she told me it was unnecessary. Said she hadn't meant to scare me so badly and to pass her apologies on to you.'

'Do you believe she just panicked yesterday?'

'Maybe, but her fear felt genuine. Her behaviour today didn't.'

It was another dull disappointment in a day of them. The thrum of the rain against her umbrella reflected her bleak mood. Miss Armstrong was the one person Louisa hoped could give them information. Instead, she was another dead end. *Though such a sudden change of heart could have meaning in and of itself.*

'Did you mention Ada's visit? Or Gallant Pearce and his father?'

'I mentioned Miss Chapman, which surprised her. She

said to tell her she's sorry.'

'Sorry? For what? Their conversation yesterday?' *Accusing Ada of murder?*

'I don't know. She said she had to go immediately after. The entire encounter was strange; I've never seen Eliza like that.'

'She must be under a lot of strain. Perhaps it is just that.'

'Maybe.' But Mrs Mason did not look convinced.

I can hardly blame her. Neither am I.

'I did not have much luck with my fellow nurses and the sketch of Gallant,' Mrs Mason added. 'The most certain answer I got was a maybe.' She shrugged, and the movement bounced water from her umbrella to the floor. 'How went your day?'

'I fared little better. The Cartwrights tried their best to be helpful – and push aside their confusion at my involvement – but they told me little of use. I only spoke with Mr Cartwright briefly in his lunch break, and the wife, whilst concerned, knows little of the boy she took into her home or her own children for that matter.'

A thin harried woman, she had never stopped moving the entire time Louisa was there. Talking with her, Louisa sensed intelligence and spirit buried underneath the domestic drudgery of chores, marriage and children. 'I returned after the schools finished to speak with the cousins. Like their parents, the older children tried to be helpful, but it's clear another little one underfoot had little impact on their lives or concerns. The younger spoke of ghosts.' Louisa said the last with disdain.

'Ghosts?' Mrs Mason repeated the word in a sceptical

tone that put even Louisa's to shame.

'Childish tales, no more. There was a boy in my year who swore blind he lived in a haunted house and used to try to scare us girls with tales of the ghost's antics.' The other girls had giggled and teased him; Louisa told him plainly there was no such thing as ghosts.

'And no help to us.' Mrs Mason sighed. 'Have I sent you on a wild goose chase? Eliza begged for my help yesterday, yet today she brushes it aside. The only reason I can think of is that she found Stephen without us, but why wouldn't she tell me that? So many questions, and no answers.'

'Or someone told her to stop looking.'

Mrs Mason's eyes widened in shock. 'Why would someone do that?'

'I could not say. I am just considering all options, however unlikely.'

Louisa may not believe in ghosts, but it still felt like she was chasing them. Stephen Cartwright, Gallant Pearce, and, however reluctantly, Clara Pearce.

'So, what next?' Mrs Mason asked.

'I am meeting Ada this evening to visit her parents.' She tried to sound encouraging, though she could not see what the Chapman children might know that the Cartwrights did not. 'And we said we would go to the Varieties tomorrow. Perhaps between us all, we can encourage Miss Armstrong to explain her change of mind.'

It was a meagre offering of hope, and the strain in Mrs Mason's voice showed she knew it. 'Yes, yes, you're right.'

Louisa had little else to say. The rest of her day had been as unproductive as her visit to the Cartwrights. A conversation with Sophie yielded little information on Miss Davis, the Pearces' former nursery maid, and a trip to their local school confirmed Gallant Pearce had attended there, with intentions to send him to a more exclusive public school when he was older. His teacher had a lot to say about the horrors of what happened to his father and little about where Gallant was likely to be.

Mrs Mason spoke into the silence. 'Maybe Miss Armstrong is right. Is it not possible she overreacted, and I followed her lead?' She sighed. 'But then there's the other boy – the one you think is Gallant Pearce – and that opens a whole new avenue of danger.'

'I will keep looking,' Louisa promised. 'As best I can.' That caveat felt more necessary than ever.

'Thank you. I know you will.' A frisson of understanding passed between the two women. Then Mrs Mason looked away, squinting through the grey sheet of rain at the clock atop the infirmary entrance. 'I should be going home. My family will be expecting me. I'll meet you at Varieties tomorrow; shall we say half six? That gives us time to speak with Miss Armstrong before she is due on stage.'

Louisa agreed, and the pair said their goodbyes, heading in opposite directions. Louisa was due to meet Ada outside Millgarth Police Station. A hastily thrown together arrangement and they had forgotten to take into account that the hospital and the police station were on opposite outskirts of the city centre.

She dodged puddles and umbrellas as she made her way past the store signs and advertisements of the city's central shopping district. Near the main entrance to Kirkgate

Market, a horse and cart dashed around the corner at a dangerous speed. Though Louisa stepped away from the pavement edge, she did not account for the ponding at the bend. An arched spray of muddy water soaked her skirts and the hem of her coat.

Sometimes, Louisa could see the appeal of swearing. The worst she could come up with was a muttered 'blast!' An also drenched labourer heading the other way more than made up for it with his more colourful expletive.

An elderly couple – she in a feathered picture hat, he in a top hat – glared at the labourer but stopped to enquire after Louisa. She insisted she was fine, trying to ignore the uncomfortable sensation of the damp fabric of her skirt and stockings gluing together.

The man gave a little 'tsk' of irritation. 'That rascal will get himself into trouble driving like a maniac.' He shook his head and made his tutting noise again. 'His kind always does.'

Louisa smiled and said a polite goodbye, relieved Ada was not here to hear a gentleman utter the phrase 'his kind' with such disgust.

The skirt plastered to her legs impeded the brisk pace of her walk, but eventually, she arrived at Millgarth, where Ada and Constable Wilkinson were waiting outside, huddled under an overhanging roof. Both looked like they had lost a battle with the day's incessant rain. Ada's coat and hat were soaked, despite the umbrella propped next to her. Had she forgotten to put it up at some point?

Ada gave her a tight smile as she approached. The tension of the day was clear in her face and in the crushed cigarette butts at her feet that Louisa pretended not to notice. Ada's enquiries must have been no more fruitful than Louisa's, and disappointment washed over her once more.

They had not found Mrs Pearce then. Ada finding her whilst officially helping the police might have been the best possible conclusion to this whole mess. It might even have helped find the boys, as Mrs Pearce could confirm if Gallant was also missing and direct the police in that direction.

'Good afternoon, miss,' Constable Wilkinson greeted her. 'What happened to your skirts?'

The amusement dancing in his eyes irritated her.

'A slight incident with a cart driver going too fast, nothing of import. I am guessing the pair of you had an unproductive day?'

'That's one word for it.'

Louisa tilted her head, waiting for him to explain, but instead, he shared a loaded look with Ada that only alighted Louisa's curiosity.

'We should go,' Ada said abruptly. 'You know how Mum hates it when people are late for tea. I'll see you later, Davey.'

She looped her arm through Louisa's and steered her away before she could even say goodbye. They retraced Louisa's steps back towards the city centre. There was fresh strain in Ada, evident in her silence where she would usually beguile Louisa with stories of her day.

'How went your morning?' Louisa asked.

'Hmmm?' Ada wrinkled her nose.

'At the women's home?'

'Oh, right, of course. I didn't find much of help. A little girl with rouge-smeared lips and a good Samaritan with about as much religious belief as you.'

Louisa furrowed her brow. Was Ada purposely speaking in riddles?

'So, no sign of Mrs Pearce?' Louisa prompted. 'Or her son?'

'The rouge was the same brand as the one on Mrs Pearce's vanity table. And I'm pretty certain Mrs Thornton - the house's manager - has her secrets.'

'What did Inspector Lambert have to say to that?'

'Errrrr...I may have down-played what I saw.'

'Ada-'

'I didn't lie!' She spoke with more force than necessary. 'We agreed to leave the police to their investigation, so I'm leaving them to it.'

'Ada-'

'And the police can't blame me for that. There was nothing concrete, anyway.'

'Ada, I am-'

'She probably isn't even there. It's not like I tricked him. I answered all his questions.'

If Louisa was not convinced, she suspected Ada was even less so. But what was done was done. Even if Mrs Pearce was at the women's home, Ada was right in saying what she saw was not evidence. Unless this display of guilty conscience was a sign that she had seen more than she let on.

'And that is all you saw?'

Ada came to a stop and looked her straight in the eye. 'Yes.'

Louisa believed her.

Ada started walking again, taking large strides that even the taller Louisa had to rush to keep up with. When they arrived at their tram stop, Ada flung herself down onto the bench with force. Louisa sat more sedately beside her, and Ada asked about her day.

Louisa was midway through the story of the day's various failures when the tram arrived, and she continued as they boarded and found seats. Whilst relaying her conversation with Mrs Mason, she recited Miss Armstrong's apology.

'Sorry for what?' Ada asked.

It was an excellent question. 'She did not say. Maybe she regrets some of the things she said to you. By Mrs Mason's account, she was acting out of character. Said she had overreacted to Stephen's disappearance.'

'And she didn't say anything about Gallant? Or the boat I saw?'

'No. The boat could possibly be Stephen's. That would explain how she had it.'

'You think Mr Pearce was giving his son's toys to his mistress' nephew? No wonder the boy hid them behind his bookcase.'

'And it would mean the two boys might not be together, might not even know each other. Why would they have been introduced?' Louisa sighed. 'We are going around in circles.'

'Speaking of going nowhere, the police spoke to the nursery maid today.' Ada sounded frustrated. 'Though I can't tell you where she is or what she said. That's not information to be shared with the likes of me.'

'The nursery maid Gallant was close with?'

'Yes. But that's all I know. Constable Goodwin is reluctant to be of any more help. He got an ear chewing about letting us near the crime scene. Davey, too.'

Louisa kept her 'I told you so' to herself. She was no

longer in any position to stand on a pedestal and tell Ada not to interfere.

'Mr Pearce's cousin was there, too,' Ada continued. 'Now, him, the constables were keen to gossip about.'

'Cousin?' How did he fit into it all?

'You know, the one...' Ada glanced around at their fellow passengers and dropped her voice to a whisper. 'The one Mr Pearce accused his wife of having an affair with.'

Another suspect for the list. 'And did she?'

Ada nodded. 'Quite the tragic love story to hear him tell it. Oh, we're here!' She jumped up to ring the bell just in time, and they hurried to grab their umbrellas and make their exit.

It had finally stopped raining, though the cobbles shone with a wet sheen, and puddles littered the pavement. Louisa took extra care to avoid them. Her skirt was nearly dry, and she wished to keep it that way. Thankfully, the dark navy fabric hid the worst of the mud stain.

The area of Armley where the Chapmans lived consisted of row after row of back-to-back terraces, of the style thrown up quickly and cheaply across the city to accommodate the influx of people in the last century. Over the years, public health acts and housing regulations were introduced to make them somewhat nicer and safer, though a parliamentary ban declaring that no more houses of this style were to be built said a lot about how far there was to go. Even still, Leeds Council ignored the ban and turned a blind eye to their continued construction because they were exactly what they were designed to be: a way to cram as many people into as small a space as possible, with little concern for minor issues such as sanitation. Louisa doubted she could live in one, though thousands - Ada's family included - did

Groups of children played out on the street. Boys in dirt-stained trousers kicked a tatty football in a circle. Marginally cleaner girls played a complicated-looking game that involved throwing stones and skipping to the location where they landed. It looked like they were trying to invent a new version of hopscotch without the chalk grid, so they could play on the wet ground.

A few children called 'hello' to Ada as they walked down the street, and she returned their greeting with equal cheer. A couple of them said a polite 'hello, miss,' to Louisa, but most did not bother. She had been to Mr and Mrs Chapman's home enough times that she was no longer a sight of interest to their neighbours.

'Anyone seen Pete or Rosie?' Ada called to the group of girls. She sounded at ease, and once more, Louisa wished she had her easy touch with children. But Ada grew up with siblings – both older and younger, surviving and not – where Louisa hadn't. An old pang of loneliness twanged within her.

The oldest girl – the leader of her little group – answered. 'Rosie's indoors with your ma, 'elping with tea. Peter was making trouble wit' Johnson lads and their lot last I saw 'im.'

'Johnson lads?' Ada frowned. Louisa looked at her curiously. Then she shook her head and with a 'cheers' to the girls, started walking again. After a few steps, she twisted back round. 'Hey! None of you know a boy named Stephen, do you? Stephen Cartwright. He goes t' Park school. New boy.'

'Aye. 'e's a cheeky bugger that one!'

Blood rushed to Louisa's cheeks – such language from the

mouth of a young girl. She would never have dared speak like that as a child. Thankfully, no one appeared to have noticed her reaction. She had enough of a reputation as Ada's posh – in less polite terms 'stuck-up' – friend as it was.

Ada asked the group, 'Any of you seen 'im recently?'

A solemn shaking of heads. One of the smaller girls scrunched up her face in concentration. 'Ain't 'e the boy who got took by ghosts?'

Not this again! Once more, Louisa saw the appeal of swearing.

The rest of the girls laughed. A chorus of voices told the speaker not to be silly and to shut up.

'Ain't no such thing as ghosts!' the oldest girl declared with all her youthful authority, which gained her Louisa's approval.

'There is at the mill.' The smaller girl crossed her arms.

The oldest girl tweaked one of her plaits gently – a tease, not a threat – and repeated that there wasn't.

Louisa glanced at Ada, waiting for her to say goodbye, but she didn't move, studying the girls. Louisa called her name softly, and she jerked around, shaking her head as if to clear it of whatever thoughts captivated her.

'Right, thanks, girls. We should head in and see if Mum needs any help. You see my brother, tell him to come in, will you?'

'He won't listen!' the eldest girl told her cheerfully.

Ada waved away the point and continued down the street, Louisa following. Outside her parents' house, she stopped to repeat the girl's word to Louisa. 'Ghosts?'

'The young Cartwrights said the same. Just childish tales.'

Ada hummed a non-committal response.

'What are you thinking?' Louisa asked.

'Just if it's a common tale, maybe there is more to it.'

Louisa raised her eyebrows.

'Not an actual ghost, obviously, but a reason everyone's saying it. A haunted – supposedly haunted – house. Or mill? That girl mentioned a mill. I'll ask Dad if any mills have shut recently. An abandoned building would make for a good hiding place.'

She was right. Louisa should have considered that. 'Good thinking.' Louisa wanted to kiss her but settled for a small, appreciative smile. Her reward was the adorable sight of a flushing Ada trying to hide her pride.

'Oh, it's nothing clever. Now, come on.' Ada reached for the handle on her parent's front door. 'Time to face the cavalry.' She flashed Louisa a cheeky grin over her shoulder as she opened the door.

Louisa shook her head fondly and replied in an undertone, 'And see if they can lead us to our ghosts?'

Chapter Nineteen

Family Affairs

The Chapman family home was spotless, as always. There was no disguising how cramped the main room was, leaving just enough space to squeeze between the sofa and the chairs around the dining table, but Mrs Chapman was winning her one-woman war on dirt. Louisa did not like to contemplate how many hours of cleaning it took her. The short period after her father's death, when their old maid retired and Louisa tried to survive without domestic help, was enough for her to know she had neither the patience nor the skill for it.

Mr Chapman lay on the sofa, his lanky legs stretched out before him. He cast a perfunctory glance over his newspaper, then smiled and put the paper down upon sighting his eldest daughter. 'Ada, my girl. I didn't know you were coming tonight.'

Ada leant to kiss her father's cheek.

Her mother appeared in the kitchen doorway. From her, Ada inherited her short stature, green eyes and round face. Not her hair, though – she was the only one with that flaming orange. Mrs Chapman was a dark blonde, whilst Mr Chapman and their other children were varying shades of brown. 'Ada, what a lovely surprise.'

Louisa stepped back to avoid Mrs Chapman as she crossed the small room to hug her daughter and ended up pressed against the wall. She had been here less than a minute and already felt out of place. The cog that did not fit the machine.

Once Mrs Chapman let Ada go, she addressed her other visitor. 'And Miss Knight, you're welcome as always.' She gave a bright, painted-on smile that reminded Louisa of a marionette doll. 'You will have to excuse me. I have to get back into the kitchen, or the pan will boil over. Will you be staying for tea, Ada?' She spoke in the careful formal manner she always used around Louisa.

'If that's all right, Mum?'

'Of course, of course. I'm always happy to have you at my table. To have you both. Please, Miss Knight, take a seat. Tom, move your legs so Miss Knight can sit down.'

'It's fine,' Louisa said, but Mr Chapman had already swung his legs out of the way.

Ada peered at the discarded newspaper. 'Racing odds? Never known you to bet on 'orses, Dad.'

Ada's sister, Rosie, skipped out of the kitchen, her twin plaits bouncing against her pinafore. At eight years old, she was the youngest. Rosie came to a stop at her sister's feet. 'It's 'cos of Mr Peterson down in number ten. He won big. 'is daughter, Sally, got a new dress and a new doll.'

Ada shared an amused glance with her father as she asked her sister, 'Did she really?'

'Uh, huh. Her new dress is pretty, too. Though yours is prettier. Did Miss Knight buy you that? I wish I 'ad a rich friend to buy me things.'

'Rosie,' her father scolded. 'I'm sorry, miss.'

'It's fine.' Louisa forced herself to smile.

Ada shot an apologetic grimace over Rosie's head, and Louisa gave her an understanding nod in return.

Rosie was unperturbed. 'I bet you 'ad lots of dolls when you were little, miss. Nicer than Sally's.'

'Um...' The honest reply would only make things awkward. Louisa's father had never given her toys; he deemed them a childish waste of time and energy.

Ada came to her rescue. 'Actually, Rosie, we're here t' speak with you.'

'Me? Why?'

'Rosie? Why?'

Daughter and father responded in unison.

'You and Pete,' Ada corrected herself.

Rosie wrinkled her nose. 'Why would you want t' speak t' Pete? He's so stupid. Do you know who 'e's been runnin' with? Skipping school and everything.'

Skipping school. That was bad news, both for their investigation and Ada's family. The one thing their parents had in common was a belief in the importance of education. Ada had told her how Mr and Mrs Chapman had to leave at age eleven and resented the disadvantage. It was not Louisa's place to comment on that, though.

Ada, however, did not hold back. 'Skipping school?' She turned to her father. 'And you're allowing this?'

'He's nearly thirteen, Ada. He can leave anyway in a couple of months. There's not much we can do.'

'Excuse me?' Ada was indignant. 'Do my other brothers know about this? You made us stay in school way past our thirteenth birthdays, even though we didn't have to and you needed the money we could get by working. And now what? You're just letting Pete skip? John got such a beating from you the one time he bunked. You confiscated all my colouring pencils for a month that time I went off because I wanted to draw instead, and now it's just *there's not much we can do?*'

Louisa remained quiet but internally cheered Ada's ferocity. *Not much we can do, indeed.*

'Yeah, Dad,' Rosie said smugly.

Ada did not look best pleased with this chime of sisterly support.

'It's more complicated than that,' their father insisted.

'Complicated? Are you hearing yourself? Are you hearing this, Louisa?'

The use of her name startled Louisa, but thankfully Ada did not require a response. 'This absolute steaming pile of horse–'

'Ada!' Mrs Chapman stood in the kitchen doorway, pointing a gravy-covered wooden spoon at her daughter. A single drop fell onto the grey carpet, but the usually house-conscious woman did not notice. 'That's no way to speak to your dad.'

'Unbelievable,' Ada huffed. She threw herself down on the sofa between Louisa and her father, into a too small gap, and ended up pressed closer than Louisa would have liked with Ada's family in the room.

'Unbelievable,' Rosie mimicked, crossing her arms exaggeratedly.

Their mother tutted and returned to the kitchen.

The heavy silence that followed was even more oppressive than the earlier noise. None of the Chapmans appeared inclined to speak, and so Louisa wracked her brain for something to say. 'The girls outside said Peter was at the park. Armley Park, I am presuming?'

'Yes, with some local lads,' Mr Chapman replied.

Louisa expected him to say more, and when he did not, she forced another smile. 'You are very fortunate to have a park so nearby. It's a bit of a walk for us to get to Roundhay Park, is it not, Ada?'

She was blabbering. How she hated small talk.

Ada's smile looked forced as she agreed.

'Rosie!' Mrs Chapman appeared once more. 'Tea'll be ready in ten. Go get your brother.'

'I ain't going nowhere near that lot.'

Louisa's eyes flickered between mother and daughter as they stared each other down. A creeping sense of unease crawled along her spine, and not just her usual discomfort at the strained welcome she was offered in this house.

'Would "that lot" be the Johnson lads?' Ada asked. 'What's Pete doing with them?'

'Just playing a bit of footy,' her father insisted. 'Nothing to worry about.' It was said in the exact tone of voice that said there was definitely something to worry about.

'Well consider me reassured.'

Louisa turned a laugh into a cough.

'Are you unwell, Miss Knight?' Mr Chapman's question had a sardonic edge. 'Nothing catching, I hope.'

'No, I am–'

'Rosie. Your brother. Now.'

'I ain't going!'

'I'll go.' Ada sprung to her feet. 'Coming, Louisa?'

'Sure, I–'

'Don't be silly, Ada. Sit down. I'm not sending Miss Knight chasing across the park after that ruffian. Rosie. Go. Before your tea spoils.'

This house was too small for so many loud people. Louisa pressed herself against the sofa as if that would help distance her.

Ada sat down on the floor at Louisa's feet. The softest of touches to the back of her leg startled her. Ada's hand, hidden by their combined skirts. It didn't move. There was no stroke of her thumb or tickle of her fingers. But still, it remained, a warm and soothing presence against Louisa's stocking that told her Ada was there. That she knew how much her family's raised voices rattled Louisa and apologised. Louisa tried to think of some covert way to reciprocate the touch, but there was nothing that would not attract attention.

Rosie stomped out of the house, whining the entire time. Her parting shot was, 'If I get murdered, I 'ope they arrest you for being bad parents.' The door rattled in its frame as she slammed it closed. How did such a little girl have so much force behind her?

'Murdered?' At Louisa's feet, Ada turned to look up at her father.

'She's being over-top. Like kids are. It was much easier with boys; I could just thrash them when they got like that. Your mum'll deal with her, same as she did you.'

'You're not thrashing Pete, though.'

'Drop it, Ada.'

Ada harrumphed but said no more.

Mr Chapman would not tell Louisa to shut up, though, and Ada clearly wanted answers about her brother's new friends, so let Mr Chapman be cross with her. 'Who did you say Peter was at the park with again, may I ask?'

'Some lads who used to go to his school. That's all.'

'Used to? Does that mean they are older than him?'

'A couple of years. No big deal. Anyway, speaking of murder, I saw in Post what happened up your end. Nasty business. She sounds like a right piece of work, that Mrs Pearce.'

Ada tensed against Louisa's legs. Louisa placed her hand on Ada's shoulder, never mind if her father saw.

'Oh, don't talk about that when we're about to eat, Tom.' Mrs Chapman entered the living room with a handful of cutlery.

Ada stood. 'Let me do that, Mum.' She took the cutlery and moved to the wooden table in the corner, setting the places.

'How are your studies going, Miss Knight?' Mr Chapman asked.

Louisa doubted he cared, but it was a polite attempt at conversation, and she answered with equal politeness.

The four adults were about to start eating when the door banged open. Peter Chapman marched into the house, flinging his coat and cap onto the sofa with wanton abandon. He was tall for his near-thirteen years – already taller than his mother and older sister – and like his father, he was all limbs, gangly arms and legs. Rosie came in after him, scowling.

'What's for tea, Mum?' Pete stopped short at the sight of

the full table and addressed Louisa. 'What you doing 'ere?' He had been a timid child when Louisa first met him only eighteen months ago, but with his new height had come new confidence.

'I am making a call with your sister.'

'Yours and Rosie's tea's in kitchen,' Mrs Chapman told him. 'You'll have to eat in there.'

'I'll eat on sofa.'

'You'll do no such thing.'

Peter looked like he would argue, but his swagger faded under his mother's stare, and he was a timid child once more. 'Yeah, Mum.'

Rosie snorted. 'Some gangster.'

The pair went into the kitchen.

'Gangster?' Ada hissed at her parents.

'Nowt as bad as that,' her dad replied.

What is going on with Ada's family? For all Louisa wished for siblings as a lonely little girl, right then, she was glad to be an only child.

'He's not fixing those horses you're betting on then?' Ada's joke sounded forced, but Mr Chapman still laughed. His wife frowned but said nothing, and Louisa focused once more on her food. A simple stew but delicious. Perfect for a miserable day like this one.

'Someone was hungry.' Mrs Chapman pointed at Ada's empty bowl.

'You not feeding my daughter, Miss Knight?' Mr Chapman asked.

'I try my best. When she lets me.' Her attempt at a joke failed to produce a laugh from Mr and Mrs Chapman.

Ada stood up and took her empty bowl into the kitchen, which did nothing to improve the atmosphere.

Louisa kept eating and tried to think of something to say.

'Ada's taking her time washing up,' her father muttered.

She was. Maybe she had gotten distracted by her siblings. *You fool. Of course she has.*

Peter and Rosie were the reason for their visit.

Louisa ate her last few mouthfuls with impolite haste and rushed to her feet, holding her bowl.

'Oh, Miss Knight, don't worry about that, I'll tidy it away. Why don't you take a seat on the sofa again? I'm sure Ada'll be back soon. No doubt the kids have waylaid her.'

'It's fine. Thank you, Mrs Chapman.' Before Ada's mother could protest further, Louisa strode the short distance to the kitchen.

She'd forgotten how tiny it was and nearly walked into where brother and sister stood toe-to-toe, if not quite eye-to-eye.

Peter not only looked down on his sister, he spoke down to her, too. 'Oh, spare me the lecture, Ada. We can't all paint pretty pictures and suck a rich woman's...what do you suck, if it's a woman?'

'Still a virgin then, brother?'

To hear her relationship described in such terms made Louisa's skin crawl, but she was no fonder of Ada's comeback. Why was that always the chosen insult? Virgin. Frigid. Because obviously, a disinterest towards sex indicated something was wrong. Even whilst people also said to remain untouched or be a whore.

Louisa cleared her throat.

Both siblings jumped. Ada looked shame-faced, but Peter was unfazed.

Rosie sat on a countertop, sucking her thumb. She spared Louisa the barest of glances before focusing back on her siblings. The young girl should not be in this room given the conversation, but sending her out would only draw her parents' attention.

Proving Louisa's point, Rosie asked, 'What's a virgin? And what do you 'ave for Ada t' suck on, Miss Knight? Is it a lollipop? Can I 'ave one? I've been good. I told Ada about the little girl who got 'er arm ripped off.'

Louisa was still trying to comprehend what that could mean when Peter snapped, 'She ain't got no lollipops, and no one wants to 'ear your stupid ghost stories.'

Louisa said a phrase she never thought she would. 'Actually, I would love to hear your ghost story.'

Ada might be right. There could be some fact to glean behind the fanciful tale.

Rosie jumped off the counter and led Louisa out of the kitchen.

'I'm going t' tell Miss Knight a story,' she told her parents, who still sat at the table.

Mr Chapman was leant in close to his wife, holding her hand, but sat up as they entered. 'I'm sure Miss Knight doesn't want to hear–'

'She said she did.' Rosie gave Louisa a look that clearly said, 'tell them.'

'I did,' she agreed.

This settled the matter, and the pair sat on the sofa, Rosie cross-legged on the seat cushion.

'Two 'undred years ago, there was a girl who worked in a woollen mill like Ada used to. She worked really, really hard every day, picking the stray pieces of wool from the floor. It was very scary work because the looms moved really fast, and sometimes kids would get stuck in 'em.' There had been no machine-based looms as early as 1712, but Louisa kept that thought to herself. 'An evil man named Mr Lived ran it. That's devil spelled backwards, that's 'ow evil he was, you see.'

She appeared to expect a response, so Louisa nodded. 'I see.'

'And he made all the children work for twenty hours a day.' Louisa doubted that, too, even in the days before the more recent labour laws. 'And he would whip them if they even paused for a break.'

'Dear Lord, where did you hear this, Rosie?' her father interrupted. 'I'm sure Miss Knight doesn't want to listen to this nonsense. Work can be grim in the mills and factories, miss, ain't no one saying otherwise, but pay no attention to Rosie's nonsense.'

'It used to be that bad,' the girl insisted. 'Still can be. What about that man Ada's friend killed?'

'Ada's friend?' Louisa asked, searching her memory for who she meant. Surely she would remember Ada mentioning a friend charged with murder.

Rosie nodded. 'She was really pretty. She used t' bring me sweets when I was little.'

'Who did she kill?'

'An evil man from the mill. Like Mr Lived.'

Louisa turned to Mr and Mrs Chapman, hoping they could give a more detailed explanation. Their faces were grave, and unease crept up her spine.

Mrs Chapman shook her head. 'That was a long time ago now.'

Louisa wanted to demand to know more but stopped herself. If she did not know, it was because Ada did not want her to.

There's something I should have told you. Was this what Ada had meant last night? Did this friend tie in with Ada's intense reaction to the Pearce murder? Was she merely a friend? Or was she a *friend* in the same way Ada was Louisa's *companion*?

'I haven't finished my story,' Rosie interrupted.

'Sorry.' Louisa turned back to face her.

'A girl named Sally got her arm caught in the machine. It was all bloody and disgusting. And Mr Lived, he refused to call for a doctor, and she just kept bleeding and bleeding and died. And he forced all the other children back to work and dumped her body in Leeds Liverpool canal.' Which also did not exist in 1712. 'And that night, he was counting his money in his office when he heard a noise on the work floor.'

'The girl had come back as a ghost,' Louisa cut in impatiently. Ada was wrong. There was no information to learn here.

'Where do you hear this stuff, Rosie?' Mrs Chapman rose from her chair and carefully tugged her daughter off the sofa. 'Think it's time you went to bed. Go on.' She gave her a gentle shove towards the stairs. 'I'll tidy up and come upstairs to tuck you in.' She gave the girl another nudge then returned to the table to clear up the remaining bowls and cutlery. 'What are Ada and Pete up to int' kitchen?' she asked her husband.

'Arguing.' Rosie had not moved. 'And it's not a silly story. Kids at school told me, and it's what Ada wanted to talk to me about. People 'ave heard Sally's ghost when they walk past.'

'Bed, Rosie.' Mr Chapman gestured up the stairs as his wife entered the kitchen.

'Like voices?' Louisa moved to join Rosie before she could follow her father's order, crouching at the bottom of the stairs. Mr Chapman's stare burnt into her back, but she ignored it, whispering, 'Do people hear voices at this mill?'

A nod.

'Do you know where it is?'

'Down near Canal. Not the big one.'

Louisa did not know where that meant, but Ada might.

'Go to bed now,' she muttered to the girl.

Rosie pouted, then made a show of stomping up the stairs.

When Louisa stood, Mr Chapman was still watching her. 'What was all that about?'

'Just a silly story, like you said.'

Mr Chapman frowned, and his eyes kept boring into her. 'You know I love my daughters.'

'Of course.' What an odd thing for him to tell her.

'What game are you playing, Miss Knight?'

'No game, sir.'

He snorted. 'Sir? As if the likes of you, fancy prosecutor's daughter that you are, need to call me sir. But it doesn't matter how much money you inherited, what clever games you–'

A riot of noise from the kitchen cut off whatever he had

been about to say, and three people spilled out of the tiny space.

'I told you what you wanted, Ada. Is that not enough t' shut you up?'

'Don't talk t' your sister that way!'

'Oh, I'm sure it'll be a great comfort when someone gives me a description and my sketch reveals your face.'

'You'd rag on your own brother?'

'I work for police. What? Did you think me and Davey are gonna step in and 'elp when you're inevitably caught?'

'ENOUGH!' Mr Chapman bellowed.

Louisa jumped, and both of his children fell silent.

A quiet squeak in the corner drew her eye to the stairs. Rosie's head peered around the quarter landing, but Louisa looked away before anyone else noticed. The last thing this family needed was another argument.

Ada stood opposite Peter with her hands clenched and eyes narrowed, her anger barely controlled. Louisa needed to get her out of here before she said something she would later regret. Or hit her brother.

'Ada, we need to go.' Louisa spoke in her bossiest voice.

'Oh, there's no need for that surely,' Mrs Chapman said. 'Just a silly little argument between brother and sister.'

'No. We need to go. Now.' Let Mrs Chapman hate her, and Mr Chapman wonder what game she was playing, and Peter scoff about rich women. None of that mattered as much as Ada.

Louisa rounded up coats and hats, and Ada took hers without a word. 'Thank you for the food, Mrs Chapman. Good night.' Louisa opened the door and bundled them both out.

She looked to Ada, hoping she had made the right choice, but her partner took off down the pavement, muttering under her breath. At the end of the street, Ada stopped and leant against the dirty orange brick of the last house in the row, eyes shut, her head tilted towards the sky.

'I can tell you want to smoke,' Louisa said. 'I promise not to judge too much if you explain what just happened.'

A brief flicker of a smile curled at the corners of Ada's mouth. She lit a cigarette and took a deep drag, blowing the smoke out above her and watching where it faded into the cloudy sky. 'They'll think you snobbier than ever now.'

'That is rather the bottom of my list of concerns for the moment. What is happening with your brother?'

'He's a fool. A fool who'll end up in prison or face down int' canal. But it turns out he's good for something, at least. I know where our missing boys might be.'

Louisa had so many more questions, but this was not the time to ask. 'So do I.'

And when their eyes met, Ada grinned.

Chapter Twenty

Ghosts, Past and Present

The information from Peter led Louisa and Ada to an abandoned factory rather than the mill of Rosie's ghost story, though the location was similar. A faded sign declared that it had once produced canned goods. Strewn rubbish collected in its doorway, a state of decay that indicated it had been abandoned for some time.

Foreboding seized Louisa. The dark, smashed windows and the door hanging off its hinges were not a welcoming facade. Every part of her wanted to turn around and go home to the comfort of her neat, clean house. This was not a place for her.

Or for young boys.

Stephen Cartwright might have considered himself 'a street rat,' but for Gallant Pearce, it would have been a shock.

'Shall we?' Ada asked.

Louisa's doubts were reflected on her partner's face. She gave Ada's arm a squeeze. Despite the situation, a wave of contentment rolled over her. It was good to be on the same team again.

Ada took a deep breath and glanced at either side of the deserted street. Louisa had just started to wonder what she was looking for when Ada leaned over and kissed her, a quick peck to the lips. Then she squared her shoulders, set her jaw, and marched forward.

She shimmied her lithe figure through the gap between the broken door and its frame and was nearly through when the lace trimming of her dress snagged on a rough edge of wood. She swore and pulled till it eventually ripped, freeing her.

Louisa's skirt was made of sterner stuff than Ada's flimsy summer gown, but neither of them had come dressed for breaking and entering, and that was exactly what they were doing. Louisa had not thought of it in such terms before. Her apprehension increased, but she could not walk away. If Stephen Cartwright and Gallant Pearce were inside the building, they could be safe in no time. All she needed was a little courage.

It was more of a struggle to fit her less trim figure through, and she winced as the splintered wood scraped against her back and stomach. She wriggled, and Ada pushed against the door frame until it suddenly gave way, and Louisa stumbled forward.

They were in a corridor, and the only object of interest was a machine that stood near the entrance. Its top section contained a clock, arms frozen at ten to four, and underneath, a series of metal slots. What had been its purpose?

Ada gave it a dirty look. 'I was forever late,' she told Louisa. 'Even with the knocker-uppers, I never made it on time.'

Louisa grinned at her. 'I can believe that.'

She followed Ada down the corridor to a wide-open space full of dust-covered machinery. Their metal cylinders and belts stood eerily still.

'It's so quiet.' Ada's awe-struck tone was similar to how Sophie spoke of her church.

In the distance, carts rattled by, people shouted, and dogs barked. It did not sound quiet to Louisa, and she said as much to Ada.

'But you can hear all that,' Ada countered. 'If these machines were going, you wouldn't hear a damn thing.' She gestured at the metal giants. 'It's strange. To be in a quiet factory.' Ada continued to scrutinize the room, fascinated, no doubt already drawing pictures in her mind.

Louisa, too, stared at the machines, but she could not imagine what it would have been like with them in operation, so she turned to the more pressing matter. 'Can you see any signs of life? Anything that might indicate someone has been living here?'

Ada shook her head, and the pair agreed to split up to search the vast factory floor. Once she looked for them, Louisa easily spotted the footprints in different sizes and shapes on the dusty floor. According to Peter, many people were rumoured to have used this abandoned building as a temporary refuge or as a hiding place for contraband.

Louisa bent down to study the prints further, trying to find any that looked smaller. Child-sized.

Ada called her name from across the building. A hitch in her voice caused Louisa to disregard the footprints immediately in favour of joining her. Ada was crouched down in the middle of what might have once been an office, pointing at the only two objects in the room. A pile of grey blankets and a small travelling case.

'Leeds General Infirmary.' Ada read from a label attached to the inner seam of the blanket. 'Smart boy took the blankets with him.'

'Stole,' Louisa corrected.

Ada stuck her tongue out. It was so delightfully *her* that Louisa laughed.

'There's food wrappers here, as well.' Ada continued her search.

Moving to the case and opening it, Louisa found boys clothes and two small toys – a metal soldier and a painted boat. The boat lacked the craftsmanship of the ones behind Gallant's bookcase, its artwork and carving not as intricate.

She pulled a shirt out next; it was of good quality, and the label belonged to a well-known tailor in Roundhay. Her father used to buy his clothes there. The chances of the shirt belonging to Stephen Cartwright were slim.

'Look at this.' Louisa showed the label to Ada, who seized the shirt with excitement. 'Gallant's. Has to be. I bet Mr Pearce used this shop and took his son with him.'

Louisa picked up the toy soldier. She flipped it over and showed the underside to Ada. On the bottom were pencilled initials: *GP.*

'Let's think this through.' Louisa pulled her notebook and pen from her bag, meaning to consider her notes again and how this latest development fit in.

Ada was smiling at her.

'What?' Louisa peered at her partner's grin suspiciously.

'You look like a constable. All ready to take your notes.'

'Am I supposed to take that as a compliment? You comparing me to Constable Wilkinson and his ilk?'

'I'm sorry. You look like a Sergeant. Better?'

Louisa gave a startled laugh. She had met the nasty crag-faced Sergeant Potter on several occasions – including when he had been threatening her over the Mary Fellowes incident.

'Charming.'

Ada flashed her another grin. 'Always. But are we going to do serious solving-a-mystery talk or not?'

Now it was Louisa's turn to stick her tongue out, which earned her a delighted giggle from Ada, as intended. Louisa wished they could keep doing this, teasing and joking, and forget all about murder and missing children.

That was not an option, though. They needed to concentrate. 'The boys are here. And there's no sign of Mrs Pearce.'

'So, Gallant left his mother at the train station. He goes looking for Stephen, learns he's in the hospital somehow, and goes to get him. They come here to hide. Where would they go next?'

'Back here.' Louisa gestured at the blankets and clothes. 'Wherever they have gone, it's a safe assumption they are planning to return.'

'So, we just wait?' Ada's voice did not quite hide her disgust.

'What else is there to do? We have no clue where the boys might have gone, but we know where they are returning to.'

'Fine. Fine.' Ada sat down on the dusty floor before Louisa could tell her to mind her dress. More conscious of the dirt, Louisa laid out Stephen's stolen blanket and joined her.

Louisa tried to speak of lighter matters to pass the time, but Ada's answers were distracted. Her eyes never stayed long on Louisa's face, roaming the walls and ceilings of the empty room, and her fingers drummed an increasingly irate rhythm on the floor. The fingertips of her gloves would be in a state when they left. At least Sophie would know better than to ask what had happened. Thinking of Sophie...she must be wondering where they were.

Louisa said as much to Ada, whose fingers stopped their tapping as she turned to give Louisa her full attention. 'You know, that was the first time I ever heard your name: the gossip about the strange lady who hired the disgraced maid. Must have been a good couple of months before Mrs Paulson introduced us.' A smile tugged at Ada's lips, and Louisa matched it. Old Mrs Paulson had had no idea what she was about to start. 'I've told you this before, haven't I?'

'You have, yes, but there are worse things than talking about how we met.'

Ada laughed. 'Janey, the girl from my school who replaced Sophie working for the Gotts, she was so scandalised. So keen to shock me. And she succeeded, if not for the reasons she thought.'

'Yes, two women being caught kissing...that would catch your attention for *all the wrong reasons.*' Louisa said the last with biting sarcasm. 'Though you were sceptical it was only kissing at the time, weren't you?'

'In my defence, poor Sophie had the worst luck, to be caught in the act of her first kiss and with a girl who blamed her for it.'

'I thought so, too. It was an impulsive idea, really, hiring her. A chance to do one good thing.' Louisa hesitated before adding, 'And I was so alone.' She had not included that confession the last time they spoke about this.

'Not anymore.' Ada caressed her knee, and Louisa cradled the comforting hand. 'Never again. I promise. I was...I was alone, too.'

The confession came as a shock. Louisa never thought of Ada – with her big family and all her friends – as lonely. Never considered they had that in common. Her heart panged, and she clutched Ada's hand tighter.

She repeated Ada's words back to her. 'Never again.'

Ada's face lit with the softest of smiles, and Louisa leant down to kiss her. To tell her she meant it. No matter what.

But her message must have failed, for when she pulled away, Ada was crying, and Louisa did not know what to say to right whatever wrong she had committed.

'I went to Armley Gaol today.' Ada spoke in a pain-laced whisper.

This was so unexpected Louisa had to ask her to repeat it. 'You went where? Armley Gaol? Why would you go there?'

Ada's words came tumbling out in such a torrent that Louisa could barely keep up. 'There's a woman there named Mabel, who I loved, and she killed a man – a bad man – and now she's doing time. Life. She'll spend the rest of her life in that place. The judge called it manslaughter, not murder, because he deserved to die. Well, the judge didn't say that, but he might as well. We all knew it. She said she didn't do it – promised me she didn't – but she did. And I loved her. But I still walked away. And now she's rotting away in that place, and how can that ever be right?'

Louisa's mind spun, trying to keep up with what Ada said and the implications.

Ada stuttered to a stop, and now more than ever, Louisa knew she needed the right words. The ones that would make everything better. Or at least not make it worse.

'Louisa, say something. Please. I'm sorry I never said anything. I wanted to put it behind me, for it to go away. We were new and different, and I didn't want to tarnish that with old horrors.'

Louisa had always known Ada had a past and accepted that because she was Ada's current choice. Was that still true if Ada's lover had been ripped from her? Was the choice still hers in that situation?

'Why did you go to visit her?' Facts. Facts were Louisa's friends. Cold plain facts.

'I wanted the truth. I wanted her to admit she had killed him.'

'And she did?'

Ada nodded. 'It didn't help, hearing her admit it. I thought if she did, I could tell myself she belonged there because she killed a man. But she killed a man whose own awful actions helped lead to his death, and I can't convince myself it's right.'

Sudden understanding flooded Louisa. A man like Mr Pearce. Ada watched Mrs Pearce flee her house and, in her face, she saw an echo of a woman she once loved.

Louisa did not get a chance to say any of that, though, as Ada's torrent of words continued. 'But he had a wife and kids. I'd say they're better off without him, but he brought them money and put food on their table. The wife struggled after he died, and she blames Mabel. Who else would she blame? So, Mabel suffers, and his family suffers, and it all could have been avoided if he was less of a...swine. The world isn't fair. You said that. And you're right. And I can't change what happened.'

'But if we find Mrs Pearce, you can change what happens to her.'

Ada sent her a pleading look. 'I meant to stick to the plan after we talked. To forget Mr and Mrs Pearce and find the boys. But...' She shook her head. 'He gave Miss Clarke the pills. That's what she told them at Albion Place. He knew of her predicament, and that was his *solution*.' She spat the last word out.

Louisa understood her anger and shared it, a low simmer in her gut. Miss Clarke had been naïve, but the punishment did not fit the crime.

But such thoughts would take them down a dangerous path.

'I thought if I knew Mabel was guilty, I could tell myself she deserved to be there and restore my faith in police and law. Tell them what I suspected about Albion House and how Mrs Pearce might be there, walk away like we said. But seeing her...she was so...different. And it could all have been avoided. All Mr Shaw had to do was stay away. I looked at Mabel, and I tried to tell myself it was justice, but...'

'But you do not believe that.'

There were many things Mr Shaw could have done to deserve his death, yet none of them changed the fact that Mabel killed him. Like Mrs Pearce killed her husband. And the law must punish killers, those that take another human life.

Louisa said none of that. The words tasted bitter in her own thoughts, never mind said out loud.

Tears streaked down Ada's face, and Louisa, not caring about her skirt, moved across the dusty floor to hold her close. It was all she could do.

There was no right answer. No logic. No clever solution.

'Thank you for telling me.'

'I thought you'd be angrier.' Ada's voice was muffled, her face still pressed into Louisa's shoulder, which was damp with tears.

Louisa would have thought so, too, but she could not muster any anger at Ada's secrecy. Only a deep sorrow that Ada had been afraid to say anything and Louisa knew why. She would not have received such news graciously in the early days of their relationship.

'No, no. I am not angry. Just sorry that you had to bear this alone.'

Ada tightened her arms around Louisa, and for a moment, they clung to each other. Whatever regrets lay in the past, they would move forward together.

Ada had loved Mabel, but people can love more than one person in their lives. Louisa had never believed in fairy tales. Real life was messy. Perhaps that was why she locked herself away from it for so long prior to meeting Ada. Even now, it could not all be picnics in the park and dancing in the living room.

'It changes nothing,' Ada told her. She sat up, her face close, looking into Louisa's eyes. 'Me and you. I lost hope in Mabel long before I met you. You gave me hope again. We are different, and I revel in different, you know that.' A slight, hopeful smile.

Louisa matched it. The words were a balm to her soul.

She had not realised how much she needed to hear them until she did.

'I do know,' she whispered. Her hand caressed Ada's face, her thumb stroking her cheek, tracing the red blotches of her birthmark. She leaned over and kissed her, right on the mark. More than ever, she hoped Ada understood the message she tried to convey.

I love you. Everything about you.

'I'm so glad I told you at last,' Ada murmured.

Louisa nodded. 'So am I. And I understand why you did not tell me until now.'

'It would have scared you off when we first met, admit it.'

There was a tease to Ada's voice, but Louisa answered seriously. 'It would have, yes. I am sorry.' It would have been the excuse she needed to bottle her feelings up and push Ada away.

'Don't be. The first few months of our, ahem, *acquaintance* were complicated.'

Memories flooded Louisa's mind. The months of uncertainty. Torn between her wish to know Ada, to spend time with her, and the need to rid herself of the pit of anxiety in her stomach when she thought about what Ada might want from her. The time Ada kissed her, taking her by surprise, and had shown up two days later, frozen on her doorstep, her tongue tripping with apologies. The shaky, hesitant first steps on the path to their current arrangement. The weeks of agitation, when she struggled to work up the courage to ask if Ada would consider moving in.

'Complicated is one way of wording it,' Louisa said drily.

'I like how it ended, though. Three cheers for Mrs

Paulson, the old harridan.'

Louisa laughed. Stubborn old Mrs Paulson. Her antics were a safe, well-trodden topic, and Louisa followed Ada's lead in moving away from painful discussions.

The hard floor numbing her buttocks and legs reminded her of where they were and the serious reason for their presence, but there was nothing else to do but wait. Might as well do that in happy reminiscence rather than silence or wallowing in bad memories.

'Did I ever tell you the irony of Mrs Paulson making me go to that dinner party?'

Ada smiled. 'Because there were rumours you were *that way inclined*. The same rumours I heard from Janey when she told me about you hiring Sophie. Wasn't Mrs Paulson the person who told you, as well? About Sophie and how she was fired.'

'Yes. Her tendency to gossip rather backfired in that case. She certainly never intended for me to hire her. Like you, I was outraged. I had not at all come to terms with my own sense of attraction at that point, as you can attest.' Ada's breathy laugh said she did not disagree. 'But the story stuck with me long after Mrs Paulson left. I went to seek her out, and you have met Sophie; how could I turn her away? I did not even consider the ramifications.'

'And I'm the impulsive one?'

'*Yes.*' Louisa said it with great emphasis, returning the tease, and Ada giggled. 'Anyway, I only went to that dinner to buy myself a break from Mrs Paulson's rather transparent talk about getting me out of the house and how my father would want me to socialise. You know, my father, the man who thought if it was not educational or professional, it was a waste of time.'

'When really,' Ada picked up the story with relish, 'she wanted to spend the entire evening whispering in your ear about eligible bachelors. And even had the decency to tailor her selections to...how did she word it again?'

'Men with a bit of intelligence about them, who are sensible enough to want more than a witless beauty for a wife,' Louisa recited in her poshest accent.

Ada snorted with laughter. 'And instead, she introduced you to me, not with any particular enthusiasm, but she still gets the credit for that. And to think, I nearly turned the invite down, but free food is free food.'

'I do recall Mr Davison being very proud of his generosity, having invited the 'nice girl doing his portrait' to stay for dinner.'

'Ha! He thought it made him appear cultured. He wouldn't know culture if it bit him on the...ahem, if it bit him.'

'On the arse,' Louisa finished for her, trying not to blush. Ada's gleeful laugh was worth it, though she quickly clamped her hands over her mouth, and Louisa shot her an inquisitive look.

'Too loud. I don't want to scare the boys off if they return.'

The realities of the present encroached on the rose-tinted past and pushed all Louisa's joy away. She stood up from the dusty floor, brushing herself down, and walked towards one of the cracked windows. The sky had been gloomy all day, but peering through the dirt, she saw it had turned to a grey twilight. 'It is getting dark.'

'Do you think the boys aren't coming?'

'I think we cannot wait here much longer.'

Ada joined her at the window, paying no heed to the dust covering her white dress. 'You're right. This neighbourhood is no place for us to be alone after dark.' Ada sighed. 'I really thought we'd found them, that we'd be the ones to take them home to their families.'

Louisa took her hand, sharing her disappointment. For a short while, she had allowed herself to hope this at least would have a happy ending. But there was no truth in fairy tales. Perhaps Father was right, and she wasted her time with the novels she once hid behind her bookcase. Real life did not turn out that way, as Ada's former lover would attest.

It was time to go home. They could always return tomorrow and hope for better luck.

They squeezed through the narrow opening in the doorway. On the street, Louisa linked their arms. The comfort of being close out-weighed any consequences. Hopefully, anyone who looked at them would think it was a simple act of protection – two women staying close.

They found a cab on Kirkstall Road. As soon as they stepped out onto their street, heavy footsteps caught Louisa's attention. Constable Goodwin marched in their direction. Their night was not over yet.

'Where have you two been all this time?' he demanded.

Affronted, Louisa retorted. 'Why are you here, Officer?'

'I'm asking the questions, Miss Knight.' He halted by their gate, blocking their entrance.

Louisa bristled. 'Is it a crime to return home late?'

'No, but it is suspicious, especially when you refuse to answer an officer's questions.'

Ada cut in. 'We visited my parents, and I got into an argument with my brother, so we ended up staying late.'

Constable Goodwin's face softened. 'I hear he's running with a bad crowd.'

'There are worse.'

'Not wrong. And your dad's a sensible man from all I've heard. He'll sort him out.'

'I hope so.'

'What brings you to Roundhay, Officer?' Louisa asked. 'Is it the Pearce murder? I cannot imagine what fresh clue would require you to come out at this time of night.'

'Someone broke in. They'll have been looking for money or valuables. Some ruffian kids.'

'Kids?' Ada demanded, her voice far too interested.

How has she got away with lying to the police so far?

The obvious answer was that she had not.

Constable Goodwin raised his eyebrows at her. 'Kids, yes. That's according to your neighbours on the other side of the Pearces. It was your maid who disturbed the robbers: go ask her. I'm not supposed to tell you anything.'

'Or you'll grass me up again,' Ada grumbled.

Constable Goodwin did not roll his eyes, but Louisa suspected he wanted to.

'I shouldn't have even let you in that day. That's on me. My apologies. You want some free advice to make up for it?' Ada gave a little tilt of her head that implied she was listening, and Louisa tensed in anticipation. 'If there's anything you're not saying, anything you're hiding, now's the time to talk.'

Ada said nothing.

'What do you mean?' Louisa asked. Was she imagining the threat inherent in his suggestion? The unspoken 'or else.'

'I mean, if Miss Chapman's keeping secrets, now is the time to share them before they catch up with her.'

That was definitely a threat. Worry prickled at Louisa. How much did the police know? Was Ada's job at risk?

'I've no secrets,' Ada said with force.

'All right. Don't say I didn't warn you.' He gave her a sad smile which implied he did not believe a word she said but stepped aside to let them pass.

Ada huffed. 'Come on, Louisa. Let's get inside.' Her hand encircled Louisa's wrist and tugged her down the footpath, and any chance to ask extra questions was lost.

'What was that about?' Louisa asked once the door had shut behind them.

Ada did not get the chance to answer as Sophie came careening into the hallway. 'Oh, ma'am! I'm so glad you're 'ome. I didn't know where you were, and there's been a break-in next door. I had t' call police, and they had all kinds of questions, and I couldn't say where you were. And a scary sergeant was 'ere, and he kept looking at me like I was dog muck dragged int' house, and he mentioned the Gotts, and them firing me and –'

'Sophie, Sophie,' Louisa spoke in her softest voice. 'Let us go into the sitting room, and you can tell us all that has happened. Calmly. And pay no attention to Sergeant Potter. By all accounts, he hates everyone equally.'

Ada snorted.

Sophie spoke in a quiet, shocked voice. 'He said the most

horrible things.'

'Because he's a horrible man,' Ada told her. 'I wouldn't spend a second worrying about him. Now, why don't you go with Louisa, and I'll make some cocoa?'

'Oh, I'll do it, miss,' Sophie said, but Ada waved the suggestion away.

Louisa led the maid into the sitting room and onto the sofa. 'Now. Tell me what happened.'

'I was doing some sewing here in the sitting room. Usually, I would do it upstairs, ma'am, but with no one being home, I thought it would be better to be downstairs. I know you always remember your key, but I wasn't sure if Miss Chapman had hers, she isn't always so good at remembering, or if you were together or not, and you can't always hear a knock on the door from my room.'

'That sounds perfectly logical to me.'

Sophie gave her a weak smile.

'Now about the break-in?'

'I heard shouting from next door. It sounded like someone was in pain. So, I went to the back door, and there were voices in the Pearces' garden.'

'What were they saying?'

'To hurry up and something about–'

She cut off as Ada entered, precariously carrying three cups of cocoa. Louisa took hers with a grateful smile.

'What've I missed?' Ada sat down on the chair opposite.

'Voices next door,' Louisa told her. 'What were they saying, Sophie?'

'Something about a pot. It didn't make a whole lot of sense. It sounded like a young boy, though he knew bad words I wouldn't expect a young boy to know. He kept swearing about this pot and how he wanted rid of it.'

Louisa and Ada shared a confused look.

'It couldn't be Gallant Pearce and his friend?' Sophie asked. 'Sorry, I heard some of your conversation at breakfast this morning, and I thought it might be possible. Though I didn't mention it to the police. I wasn't sure you'd want them to know.'

'Pot!' Ada shouted, her eyes gleaming with excitement. 'Stephen Cartwright had a pot on his arm. A cast from the hospital. Those things are bloody tough; chances are he won't have been able to remove it.' She laughed, shaking her head. 'The wrong place! We were in the wrong bloody place! Of all the rotten luck!'

It was not funny. It was the very opposite of funny, and yet, Louisa joined in with Ada's laughter. The irony of it all!

'Ma'am?' Sophie was looking bemused between the two of them, and Louisa pulled herself together.

'You are probably right, Sophie. Chances are it was Gallant Pearce and Stephen Cartwright.'

'So, what does that mean, ma'am?'

A good question. Why would the boys return to the Pearce house?

'Did the police mention if they took anything?' Louisa asked.

'A few trinkets. Do you think they'd try to pawn them? I doubt they'd get much if they did. Any pawnbroker would see two kids with obviously stolen goods and give them a pittance.'

'It won't last long,' Ada agreed. 'We have to go back to

the factory tomorrow.'

'But what if they notice we were there?' Louisa asked. 'They might already be spooked and move elsewhere.'

Ada sighed, and Louisa took that as a sign she was most likely right. She turned back to Sophie. 'Do they know you heard them?'

Sophie nodded. 'I shouted, 'who's there?' And then Miss Harrison, who works for the Saunders two doors up, shouted at them to clear off. She's got a set of lungs on her, that one. She rang the police, too, they said. I didn't think of that. I just panicked, and I knew it was a crime scene, so I rang them. Do you think the boys stole evidence? Something to save Gallant's mother?'

Louisa and Ada shared another glance. It was not outside the realm of possibility. Could Gallant Pearce have gone to remove some item that would see his mother prosecuted? Something the police might have overlooked?

Sophie finished the last of her cocoa and stood up, collecting their empty cups. Once all three were gathered, she hesitated for a moment.

Ada joined her. 'Let me take those.' She took the cups from the maid, nudging her back towards the sofa, and left the room.

Sophie would not meet Louisa's eyes. Instead, she studied her hands, twisting in her lap.

'Was there something else?' Louisa asked.

'That Sergeant,' Sophie whispered. 'He said the most terrible things about Miss Chapman. And I know she said to ignore him, but he was so scary, and I was trying to make sense of what he was saying, so I'd have something to tell you when you got home, but it was either nasty or nonsense.'

'Tell me anyway. Perhaps we can make sense of it together.'

'He called Miss Chapman all sorts of names. He asked if I knew my mistress' companion was a…was a…' Sophie lowered her voice even more as she spelled out the word she was unable to say. 'W. h. o. r. e.'

Anger flared in Louisa. 'He said *what*?'

Sophie flinched, and Louisa forced herself to be calm. Shouting at Sophie would not help. The maid was only doing as Louisa asked.

'He said all these awful things about Miss Chapman that I know aren't true, calling her that word, but I couldn't say why I knew they weren't true because, well, you know why. I don't understand why he was so mean.' Tears gathered at Sophie's eyes, and Louisa passed her a handkerchief. 'I just wanted to help. That's why I called the police.'

'I think Sergeant Potter is not fond of Ada, and he took it out on you. I am sorry you had to deal with that. You did the right thing by calling the police.' Sophie nodded behind the handkerchief, still sniffling. Louisa tried to think of the best way to help calm her. 'It is getting late. How about you go borrow one of my books from my study? You can read for a little; that should take your mind off things. It always helps me anyway. And then go to sleep.'

'That's a good idea. Thank you, ma'am. Good night.' She passed the soggy handkerchief back and left the room.

Louisa placed the handkerchief on the table and collapsed backwards onto the sofa. She wanted to push aside Sergeant Potter's insults as the angry words of an angry man, but

Constable Goodwin's warnings echoed in her mind. Ada had been playing with fire these last few days. Was she about to be burnt?

'Has Sophie calmed down?' Ada sat on the sofa beside her.

Louisa reached out and entwined their fingers. She would have to tell her what Sophie had said, and then they could figure out what this all meant and what to do. Together.

Chapter Twenty-One

An Unwelcome Surprise

A da flopped down onto the dining room chair. A second visit to the abandoned canned goods factory had turned up nothing but more disappointment. The boys and their possessions were gone. With them went Ada and Louisa's only lead and any hope of reuniting them with their families that day.

'I could try to find out what they stole?' Ada suggested as Sophie served ham sandwiches. 'If I get called into the police station.' A feeble idea, but the only one she had.

Louisa smiled weakly. 'And if you do not? And maybe – given Constable Goodwin's warning – it would be best if you are not seen poking around anymore.'

Ada squirmed. She'd tried to put aside the constable's words yesterday, but they kept needling at the back of her mind. Righteous anger had swallowed her fear of unemployment, but it came flying back with his warning. Perhaps it was for the best to stay away from the official police investigations. They would come to ask questions about the break-in, that couldn't be avoided. She was surprised they hadn't already. They must be chasing other leads.

'I am sorry I do not have more encouraging words.'

Louisa reached across the table and caressed Ada's hand.

'One of us must be the sensible one.'

Louisa chuckled but then turned serious. 'It may be we have done all we can for Masters Pearce and Cartwright. We can still go to the Varieties as promised tonight, but I doubt Miss Armstrong will be any more forthcoming.'

'And then what next? We walk away and forget about them?' Ada couldn't keep the disgust from her voice.

'When we have done all we can, yes. We go back to our lives. You have your work and your art to concentrate on, your designs for the house. Did you not have ideas about how to re-decorate this room?'

Louisa had been hesitant about stripping away this last part of what had been her father's home, and so the suggestion told Ada she was trying her hardest. Ada wanted to hug her close and not let go.

For the rest of dinner, they discussed potential colour schemes and furniture. Once Sophie had tidied their plates and glasses away, Ada enlisted her and Louisa's help in measuring the floors and walls of the room. She fetched her Chesterman measuring tape and a notebook from her studio. The tape had been a present from Louisa when they first decided to re-decorate, and she also volunteered one of her many notebooks to record the house's measurements.

The heavy wooden furniture proved an obstacle, but they were nearly done when a loud knock on the front door interrupted. Sophie excused herself whilst Ada and Louisa shared a questioning glance. It must be the milkman for his payment or some other tradesman selling his wares. Ada returned to showing Louisa the newly recorded figures.

'Ma'am?' Sophie stood in the doorway, twisting her apron with added zeal. That never boded well, and Ada tensed. Sophie's next sentence was so rushed, the only word Ada caught was her own name at the end, and she asked Sophie to repeat herself with growing trepidation.

The maid repeated the words slower. 'Inspector Lambert is here to see you, Miss Chapman.'

'Oh, it must be about the break-in.'

'Did he not ask to speak to me, as well?' Louisa asked, and the maid shook her head.

A jolt of cold spread down Ada's back like someone had poured ice shavings down her dress. Could Inspector Lambert know about her interfering?

Ada suppressed a shiver when Sophie added in a whisper as she passed, 'That nasty sergeant's here, too.'

Inspector Lambert and Sergeant Potter looked out of place in the airy hallway, like animals away from their natural habitat. The inspector's face was serious, and the sergeant gave her a disapproving look.

Nothing new there.

Yet why had Inspector Lambert brought Sergeant Potter – never her biggest fan – rather than Davey or one of the other constables? Whilst it might be considered usual for an inspector to have his sergeant as his right-hand man, Inspector Lambert didn't like Sergeant Potter any more than she did.

Ada gave what she hoped was a smile and not a grimace, and they swapped polite greetings.

'Is there somewhere we could speak privately?' Inspector Lambert asked.

'Yes, through here.' Ada led them into the sitting room.

'Please, Miss Chapman, take a seat.' Inspector Lambert gestured at the sofa, and Ada did as ordered, unsettled by being offered a seat in her own home. Neither of the men sat, leaving Ada looking up at them. It did nothing to dispel her nerves. Was this how it would feel to stand and stare up at the judge who pronounced her sentence?

At least whatever this is, it will not get that far.

'Are you here about the break-in, sir?'

'We will need to discuss that with you, but we have a more pressing matter we need to address first.'

Ada frowned. 'A more pressing matter?'

Inspector Lambert didn't answer immediately. The outline of his Adam's apple, just visible above his starched collar, shook as he gulped. Whatever he had to say made him uncomfortable, and this only increased Ada's discomfort.

He wasn't here to canvass her opinions again or give her more unusual orders, for both those matters he'd undertaken as if they were routine happenings. No, this was something else.

Inspector Lambert cleared his throat. 'Miss Chapman, do you recall we discussed your relationship with the Pearces?'

She nodded.

'You said you knew them both on neighbourly terms but were cautious around the husband given rumours about his infidelity?'

Another nod. She hid her hands under her legs to stop her anxious fingers from fidgeting. *Where the hell's he going with this?*

He cleared his throat again. 'Did you have reason to know from experience that the rumours of infidelity were true?'

She shook her head. How would she have known if they were true? She saw a little of the coming and goings of the house but not enough to know for certain what went on behind its doors.

'I heard the rumours,' she answered. 'I knew Miss Clarke had left and not happily. It made sense as a story.'

Inspector Lambert frowned, and Sergeant Potter let out a grunt that sounded involuntary. Ada got the distinct impression she was being slow, but what else did they want her to say? Whatever it was, she'd say it, if only to get the entire conversation over with. She wanted them out of her house as soon as possible.

Inspector Lambert's intense gaze scrutinised her as he continued in a voice laden with meaning, 'I was not referring to Miss Clarke.'

Who then? Miss Armstrong? They did not know about Miss Armstrong, and it had to stay that way. On that, Ada and Mrs Mason were in perfect agreement.

'I don't understand, sir.' Her voice came out squeaky and pathetic, and she cringed. She would make a terrible criminal.

Inspector Lambert coughed again and tugged at his collar.

'He means you,' Sergeant Potter said with his usual bluntness. 'You and Mr Pearce.'

'Me and Mr Pearce?' Ada's mind rushed to think what he meant. He didn't mean...he couldn't mean...they couldn't think she'd–

'Oh, stop playing stupid, woman!' Sergeant Potter snapped. He made a downwards swipe with his hand as though he wished he could slap some sense into her. The blow landed on his own thigh rather than her face, but it still made her flinch.

Ada refocused on the inspector, who met her eyes steadily, watching her reaction.

'Of course not,' she said. 'Where would you even get an idea like that from? It's quite the accusation.' The words rolled off her tongue, the words she thought a proper young lady should say in the circumstance. She couldn't react how she wanted, to laugh and point out exactly how badly they were barking up the wrong tree.

'We have a witness who claims you did.' Now he'd got his accusation out, Inspector Lambert's nervous energy had dispensed. His voice was even, his expression unreadable.

'A witness? Who exactly?'

'Mr Pearce liked to brag about his conquests.'

'I'm not his conquest!' Ada shouted. Her hands clutched the soft fabric of the sofa, grasping onto something real in the terrible dream she found herself trapped in. She'd fallen down the rabbit hole, except this wasn't Wonderland.

The two men continued to stare at her, stone-faced. This was no jest to them. No story from a make-believe world.

Inspector Lambert said his next words with measured care. 'By all accounts, he was a man who women found very beguiling, and he knew how to use that to his advantage. We're not here to judge; we just need the truth, Miss Chapman.'

Not here to judge! Ada smothered a hysterical laugh, hands clamped to her mouth. Did he really think she would believe him? That there would be no condemnation if she admitted to knowingly having an affair with a married man.

'We weren't lovers,' she insisted as if by putting enough

emphasis on the words, she could make them believe her. 'We weren't! You have to believe me! I mean, I...' The next words gathered in her throat, but she couldn't say them.

It was an unspoken truth. One she never said out loud to anyone but Louisa. There were subtle nods and innuendos and subterfuge, but the words were never plainly spoken. If she said it, she could never take it back. Never return to ambiguity.

Her feelings for other women were not illegal – as was the case for men – but that didn't make 'the love that cannot speak its name' any less true for them.

She would merely replace suspicion of one impropriety with confirmation of another.

And bring Louisa down with her.

'You what, Miss Chapman?'

She shook her head, defeated and cornered. 'I never would've slept with Mr Pearce.' Her voice was a whisper. A pathetic muttering.

Sergeant Potter grunted with annoyance. 'Not the way he told the story.'

His words set aflame all Ada's subdued anger. 'Oh, able to commune with the dead now are you, Sergeant?'

'Miss Chapman.' Inspector Lambert spoke her name evenly, but it was a clear warning. 'It was Miss Eliza Armstrong who told us. You've met her, I believe? Another woman who fell for Mr Pearce's charm.'

The fire of her anger froze into cold fear. For a few moments, she did nothing but stare at them, trying to process the implications. They'd questioned Miss Armstrong, and she'd told the police of their meeting and said Ada had an affair with Mr Pearce. Why would she say that? Did she want Ada to get in trouble? They were trying to help find her nephew, for God's sake!

'Well, she's lying!' Her petulant words made her sound like the liar.

'She's not the only one.' Sergeant Potter's words were a low growl. He stood way too close, an imposing presence above her. Ada pressed herself further back into the sofa cushion, wanting to be as far away as possible from him and his threatening words.

'Why did you visit Miss Armstrong?' Inspector Lambert continued in the same quiet manner, but he also didn't bring his sergeant to heel.

What answer could Ada give that didn't incriminate herself or Louisa or Mrs Mason or Mrs Parks?

'Miss Chapman?' Inspector Lambert prompted.

Ada's world receded to nothing more than the two faces staring down at her. She wanted to close her eyes and make this all go away. To cover her ears and shout 'la la la.' Wake up four days earlier, when she had never heard the name Eliza Armstrong, and Mr Pearce was just the neighbour she smiled politely at whilst maintaining a sensible distance.

'The inspector asked you a question.' Sergeant Potter stood so close, his hand nearly brushed her wrist where it rested in her lap. He could seize her in a second, like when the police dragged Mabel through the street. Ada had no idea who the officer had been that day, but in her mind, it was now Sergeant Potter.

An overwhelming urge overtook her to push him away and scream at him to get lost, but she forced it down, putting all her effort into remaining still. Why was he standing so bloody close? Had he never heard of manners?

She scrambled to remember what the question had been. Miss Armstrong, Ada's visit, why?

'I wanted to talk to her.' A pathetic response. One with an obvious follow-up question she'd no answer for.

Sergeant Potter didn't move, and she crossed her arms as if that would help. Her fingers flexed involuntarily, nails scratching her skin.

'About what?' Inspector Lambert asked the question she knew he would.

Well, I've always had an interest in the arts, sir. She kept her witticism to herself, though it was the only answer her mind supplied. It'd make Louisa laugh at least, when she told her afterwards, when this nightmare was over. *If it's ever over.*

Sergeant Potter rested his hand on the sofa's arm, leaning even closer to her, the sour coffee on his breath lingering in the air. 'Murder, perhaps?' His voice was quiet and dangerous in her ear. She wanted to shove him and make lewd suggestions about what he could go do to himself. Words that would shock Louisa so much that she wouldn't even scold, just stare in muted horror.

But those words didn't come. Instead, she repeated, 'Murder?' in a tiny mouse squeak of a voice.

'Enough, Potter.'

Sergeant Potter's threatening presence lingered a moment longer, then he followed his superior's order.

Ada sat up a little higher, appreciating the space.

'Did you discuss Mr Pearce's murder?' Inspector Lambert asked her.

'We did, yes. But she knew nothing. There was nothing to tell you.'

'She had this.' And from his pocket, he drew Gallant Pearce's toy boat.

Ada gasped and then realised in doing so, she'd lost all deniability. How would she explain this? What was she going to say? *Damn. Damn. Damn.*

'I would have thought this worth mentioning to me. Unless you have reason to keep Miss Armstrong's secret? A quid pro quo arrangement? Our being here tells you any such deal is already broken. You have no reason to protect her anymore.'

Panic seized Ada, squeezing her in its vice-like grasp, and there was no escape. Did he truly believe this? 'There is no deal! She didn't even like me. Or know me. She thinks I had an affair with *a man* for crying out loud!'

'With a man? What other option is there?' Sergeant Potter laughed to himself.

Ada's heart raced. Too much. Too much. She'd said too much. But silence would only damn her further.

She forced a giggle. As close to coquettish as she could, though it came out more deranged. 'I just meant the idea I would have an inappropriate liaison. I'm an unmarried woman, Sergeant. My expertise with men and affairs is limited.'

Sergeant Potter gave a disbelieving snort. He was a lost cause, and so Ada turned her focus to Inspector Lambert, who had resumed examining the boat.

'I've no doubt that is true, Miss Chapman.' Was she reading too much into the potential sarcasm there? 'But what other reason could there be that you saw something potentially linking a suspect to the scene of the crime and said not a word?'

'I didn't think it was t' do with murder!' Her words came out in a rushed slur, scurrying along, desperate for the officers to see sense, to stop staring at her with those hostile eyes. 'I thought it linked t' boys somehow, the ones Louisa's trying t' find.'

'Boys?'

Shit. She'd truly done it now. *Way to bloody go! Take Louisa down with me like a goddamn dimwit!*

How to fix this? She needed to fix this! But she'd said all the wrong things, and Sergeant Potter had moved too damn close again, and she wanted to disappear far, far away from them. Somewhere it was just her and Louisa, where she had kept her gob shut and stayed away from crime scenes, and they weren't both in trouble with the police.

'There were two boys broke in next door, sir.' Damn Sergeant Potter, did he really need to pick this moment to show some sense beyond his usual brutish behaviour?

'The same boys, judging by your face, Miss Chapman,' Inspector Lambert said. 'Who are they?'

Ada had thrown herself into the trap, and there was no way out. She opened her mouth, but no words came.

'Answer the question,' Sergeant Potter growled.

What choice did she have? There was no lie that'd make the situation go away. In a soft, defeated voice, she said, 'Gallant Pearce and Stephen Cartwright.'

Inspector Lambert's stoic mask finally broke. The anger glinting in his eyes was sharp enough to cut her as he repeated the boys' names with force. 'Gallant Pearce, our victim's son. And Stephen Cartwright, nephew of a potential suspect. And yet you told us none of this. Which leaves me with the question of why?'

For this, at least, she had a lie. One that might help keep Louisa out of trouble. Her job was a lost cause, but the 'dire consequences' Inspector Lambert had threatened Louisa with after the Mary Fellowes case might still be avoided.

'We only wanted to help. Nothing to do with Mrs Pearce. Just find the missing boys.'

'Miss Armstrong never mentioned you asking about her nephew. How did you know about him?'

Mrs Mason hadn't wanted her name given to the police, and she was guilty of nothing more than a kind heart and bad taste in friends. She also had two children and a husband with unstable income. Ada needed another lie.

'I saw the file.'

'That is your modus operandi.' Inspector Lambert's words were so dry the Sahara was jealous. 'And having read a police file without authorisation, you then used that information to gather evidence and withhold it from us.'

'I don't know anything, sir. There's nothing I withheld.'

He held up the toy boat.

'It's just a boat, sir.'

'It's evidence. Do you have anything else to say for yourself? Any defence?'

'I just wanted to help, sir.'

'Hmmm...I'm sure you did.' He paused and fixed her with his harshest policeman's stare. 'Where were you the night of Sunday 30th June?'

'Here. With Louisa. Why?' That was the night Mr Pearce died. The question they asked suspects. Her heartbeat raced against her rib cage so hard it physically hurt.

Did he really think her capable of murder? *He thinks me capable of having an affair with Alexander Pearce. Why not murder?*

A typhoon of hopelessness washed over her. At least, perhaps, her lies would prevent Louisa from drowning with her.

Inspector Lambert pocketed the toy boat and didn't answer her question of why. He moved to the window, his back to her. Ada looked to Sergeant Potter for an explanation and instantly regretted it. A malicious grin stretched across his face; whatever was about to happen, he was looking forward to it.

Ada turned back to the figure at the curtain. 'Sir?' The word came out as a croak.

He didn't turn from the window. 'Ada Chapman, you're under arrest for perverting the course of justice and on suspicion of murder.' His words were so placid, it took Ada a few moments to realise their ramifications.

'Murder?' Her earlier mouse squeak was back. Sergeant Potter grabbed her wrist and yanked her from the sofa, chuckling the entire time, and she tried to shake off his iron grip. 'Is this a joke, sir?' The words came out jolly, which only made her sound more deranged. 'I'm sorry I didn't tell you about the boat and the boys and Eliza Armstrong.'

'And Beatrice Parks?'

That stopped Ada short. So, they knew about her visit there, too. 'What of her?'

Sergeant Potter's hands dug a little deeper into the flesh of her arm, and Ada had to use all her self-control not to claw and screech at him. He muttered in her ear, 'You can ask her yourself.' The malevolent glee with which he said it chilled her. Fear tightened icy fingers around her heart.

'Sir? This isn't funny! I'm sorry. I'm sorry. Please, I'm sorry. Please, stop this. I didn't know anything. I didn't.'

'I didn't do it. Please, believe me, Ada. I didn't do it.'

Inspector Lambert remained at the window, not looking at her.

Sergeant Potter pulled her arm behind her back. 'Get off me!' she roared at him, her spare hand clawing at his fingers. His grasp only tightened, and then there was the metal clink of handcuffs.

No, he wouldn't. Those cruel restraints that held Mabel in their grip. Would he truly shackle her, too?

'What is going on in here?' Louisa demanded from the doorway, looking indignant. Ada wanted to run to her, but Sergeant Potter still held her in his unyielding grasp. 'You there, unhand Ada immediately. What is the meaning of this? You are guests in my home, and you are assaulting my companion, who is also your colleague. Pray tell, what is your explanation for this?'

Louisa had never put her righteous propriety to better effort. Sergeant Potter's hold on Ada's wrists loosened. He stepped back and muttered, 'Um, well, miss...'

Free at last, Ada stepped towards Louisa and the promise of safety. She would hug her and never let go.

Inspector Lambert quickly shattered her illusion. He, at last, turned from the window and politely nodded towards

Louisa. 'Miss Knight, good of you to join us. Tell me, what do you know of Stephen Cartwright and Eliza Armstrong?'

His words halted Ada, and she stood stranded in the middle of the room, awaiting Louisa's answer.

Her partner hesitated. Louisa's mind must be whirling, debating whether to lie and how much Ada had already said, what the situation unfolding in the sitting room meant.

Sergeant Potter regained confidence from Louisa's uncertainty. He followed Ada and stood behind her, ready to grab her again should she move. The gulf between her and Louisa was larger now than ever.

'I know the names, sir,' Louisa said.

'I'm sure you do. And to answer your questions, Miss Chapman is under arrest for perverting the course of justice and suspicion of murder.'

'Ada? Arrest? Murder?' Louisa turned to Ada, questions written all over her face, but she was merely confused, not horrified. 'There must be some mistake, sir.' She spoke with full confidence, a tone that wouldn't be challenged, and hope crept into Ada's heart. Louisa at her most sensible was impossible for anyone to argue with, even Inspector Lambert.

'Is that so? And tell me, Miss Knight, where is Mrs Mills?'

'I do not know. I thought you had men looking for her?' To anyone else, Louisa would appear impassive, but Ada saw the flicker of fear in her eye, and it enflamed her own once more.

'I do. So, your visits to Thomas and Daniel Mills were not fruitful then?'

'Visits?' It was Ada's turn to repeat words incomprehensibly.

'It's quite the twisted web you two have spun. No matter. We can straighten the whole debacle out at the station.' Inspector Lambert stepped towards Louisa. 'I warned you what would happen, Miss Knight, if you interfered in my cases again. Do I have to handcuff you, too, or will you come quietly?'

The heavy metal clicked into place on Ada's wrists, and she froze. This wasn't happening. This couldn't be happening.

Louisa didn't move. 'For what crimes?'

Sergeant Potter dragged Ada out of the room, so she didn't hear Inspector Lambert's reply.

Sophie hovered in the hallway, polishing the side table in a half-hearted manner which belied her real intentions for lingering. Her eyes widened at the sight of Ada in handcuffs. 'Miss?'

'Miss Chapman is under arrest for murder.' Unbridled joy rang in Sergeant Potter's voice.

Sophie stared at the pair, open-mouthed.

Sergeant Potter chuckled. 'Did I break the help? Never mind. Time to go, Miss Chapman.' His fingers stabbed into her shoulder and jerked her forward. The handcuffs rattled, cutting into her skin, and pain blossomed across her wrists. The cold metal restraints were real this time, and if she asked to be released, Sergeant Potter would laugh.

It was the police wagon that broke her. Its black paint and stamping horses were a sign of impending doom. Mabel was forced into a wagon like this one, struggling and screaming. Ada wouldn't go in there. She wouldn't. She tugged against the handcuffs as Sergeant Potter dragged her forward. It would do her no good, yet her only impulse was to fight and run. She wouldn't be Mabel. She couldn't be Mabel.

But the metal on her wrists was real, and there was no escape for her, any more than there had been for Mabel.

Sergeant Potter opened the wagon door as Sophie's voice sounded from the house. 'Ma'am? What's happening? This must be a mistake!'

Louisa's reply was a soft murmur, too quiet for Ada to catch.

A hand on her back told her to step up into the wagon.

'Don't I at least get to say goodbye?'

Sergeant Potter snorted. 'Goodbye? Your dear employer is coming with us.'

He shoved her, and Ada stumbled into the wagon's frame, pain exploding across her shins. 'No. No. You can't arrest Louisa.' She tried to twist to see behind her, but the sergeant's grip was too strong. He forced her inside with no care to prevent further injury.

Inspector Lambert arrived with Louisa – thankfully without handcuffs and looking unruffled – and stepped with her into the wagon. Sergeant Potter slammed the door behind them.

The inspector was staying then. Why would he do that?

Louisa sat beside her, closer than appropriate, given the inspector's presence. 'It will be all right,' she whispered in Ada's ear, her hand resting beside her leg, the gentlest of brushes.

Then there was only Ada's ragged breathing.

What more could they say with Inspector Lambert opposite them? Perhaps that was why he stayed.

The wagon jolted forward. The clop of the horses' hooves and the rattle of the undercarriage filled the silence.

Ada tried to draw comfort from Louisa's presence, but it only unsettled her further. Louisa shouldn't be there. This whole mess was her doing.

I've dragged her down with me.

She owed Louisa another apology, but this wasn't the time. Inspector Lambert would see it as an admission of guilt. Better to focus on getting her story straight. Louisa must be thinking the same, and Ada's irritation at Inspector Lambert's presence grew. They could have figured it out together, but the inspector had foreseen that possibility. He always was a clever little bastard.

Think. Think. Think.

She had nothing.

When the wagon came to a stop, her mind remained blank. She tried to gauge what was happening in Louisa's head, but other than a reassuring smile when she noticed Ada's attention, Louisa's face was unfathomable.

Ada had never envied her that skill more.

Sergeant Potter swung the door open, but Inspector Lambert helped them down with care.

For the first time, Millgarth Police Station's grim exterior struck helplessness into Ada.

Sergeant Potter pushed her towards the station with relish. 'Let's see what your little friend has to say about this.'

It took Ada a few seconds to realise who he meant. No one had described Davey as little since he was ten.

'I'm not sure little is the right word.' She pulled the calm words from deep beneath her fear.

Sergeant Potter shoved her with a little more force, and Millgarth came ever closer. Was Davey in there now? And Smith and Goodwin and all the other officers? How would they react to the sight of her in handcuffs?

Though their reaction would be the least of her problems if she were in prison. Sheer terror overtook her at the prospect, and she fought to tamper it down.

As they reached the entrance, Ada tried to summon Louisa's proud composure and walk in with her head held high.

There were no footsteps or voices behind her. Where was Louisa? She tried to turn to check, but the combination of cuffs and Sergeant Potter's grip unbalanced her, and she stumbled into the foyer, nearly falling to her knees. So much for a dignified entrance.

'Miss Chapman?' Young Constable Smith stared at her from behind the desk. The worst possible person to see her. He would tell this story till they both grew old.

Which I might not do. They hang murderesses.

No. Don't think like that.

'Afternoon, Bertie.' Ada's voice was chipper. She still drew from the well of calm dug deep beneath her fear.

'Are you cuffed?'

'She could be our murderess!' Sergeant Potter crowed.

That was too much. 'I'm not a murderess!'

I didn't do it! I didn't do it! I didn't do it! Mabel's denial made sense in that moment as Ada shared the horror she had once experienced.

'That's what they all say!' Sergeant Potter taunted.

But I didn't do it.

Ada clung to that fact. Mabel had turned to denial because it was all she had to protect herself, a shield from the horror she'd been forced to commit, but Ada had innocence.

That is no guarantee.

Sergeant Potter compelled her down one of the dull corridors she had walked so many times, but their grey walls were ominous now rather than dreary. She could paint a picture of a thousand terrors based on this corridor.

If I ever paint again.

At the door to the holding cell, Sergeant Potter whispered in her ear, 'You'll be with your friend Miss Spencer soon.' He uncuffed her and pushed her inside. The door slammed shut behind her, and she was alone.

Where had they taken Louisa?

Chapter Twenty-Two

Confinement

Ada called Louisa's name and thumped the door with her fist. The sound reverberated through the small cell. When she eventually gave up, her hand was throbbing. If Louisa were with her, she would tell Ada there was nothing to gain by breaking it.

She stood on her tiptoes, staring out the narrow-barred hole at the top, but there was only grey walls and ceiling. Was this her future? Cells with doors that were never opened, no matter how much she pleaded?

'Who's Louisa?' a voice asked.

Ada spun round. She hadn't even noticed the cell's other occupant, a woman in a patched brown dress who gave her a curious look. She was vaguely familiar; had Ada done a sketch of her?

'My friend,' she replied. 'She was just behind me.' She looked back at the door, then eyed the wooden bench with distaste. Unable to face sitting still, she chose to pace the small confines.

They must have taken Louisa to be questioned, and Ada bit down a hysterical laugh. Louisa – her prim, sensible, clever Louisa – being interviewed by the police. Well, they'd have no luck there, faced with her stubborn streak. Besides, she'd nothing to admit.

Unlike Ada.

No. No. No. Murder was a ridiculous charge. Inspector Lambert knew that. He was trying to scare her, and, damn him, he was succeeding.

He couldn't actually believe she'd slept with Mr Pearce. But why had Miss Armstrong told the police she had? Did the blighter really tell his mistress that? Had he manipulated her, same as his wife?

Miss Armstrong had been serious when she asked if Ada killed Mr Pearce. Whatever the bastard said, she believed Ada had reason to want him dead.

Will his manipulations cause me to be charged as a murderess? Am I gonna hang because of that twisted scoundrel's lies? Is that why Miss Armstrong told Mrs Mason she was sorry? For causing my death?

No. She wasn't going to die. Inspector Lambert didn't believe her to be a killer. He couldn't.

The second charge, though, perversion of the course of justice...was there a case for that? Would the information she withheld be enough for that charge to stick and send her to prison?

It's not a hanging offence, though. Or is it?

The other woman interrupted her thoughts. 'We've met, haven't we?'

Her words made the memory slide into place. Standing outside a house in Holbeck, visions of Miss Clarke's bloody death filling her mind when the late maid's sister arrived. The very woman she'd been looking for – and a person with a compelling reason to want Alexander Pearce dead.

'Mrs Parks? What're you doing here?' Ada paused to focus on her.

'The police arrested me.' Well, that was obvious enough, but Ada couldn't even resent the implied sarcasm as she'd asked a silly question. 'I'm guessing they arrested you, too. But didn't you say you're their sketch artist?'

'I am. Was.' Ada made the change with dull acceptance. That was the least of her problems now. What would life be like in prison for a woman known to have helped the police?

No. No. No. She wasn't going to prison. This was all a misunderstanding. It would all be cleared up. Her and Louisa would be out of here within an hour.

What the hell were they saying to Louisa? What the hell was Louisa saying to them?

She tried to calm her panicking thoughts. Louisa had the wits to answer questions without incriminating them both.

Unlike me.

She resumed pacing. How dare she even consider the possibility of Louisa implicating her when she was the fool who couldn't watch her words?

Mrs Parks' eyes followed her with keen interest. 'Why would they arrest you? What reason do you have to kill the swine?' She gasped. 'You didn't? Not you and him?'

'No. No, I bloody well didn't.' Ada's strides quickened. Was that what everyone would believe from now on? Maybe she should just tell them the damned truth.

I can't do that to Louisa.

Pacing no longer felt like enough. She wanted to kick and scream and punch the walls, but the police would think her mind gone if she did. The only place worse than prison was an asylum.

'You should sit down,' Mrs Parks said. 'You're making me tired just watching you.'

Ada shook her head and kept moving. To sit still would be akin to torture. Her hands twitched, and she wished she had cigarettes with her. If ever there was a situation where she needed to smoke, it was this one.

'Are you scared?' Mrs Parks asked.

'Yes,' Ada admitted. 'Are you?'

Mrs Parks nodded, her face wan.

'Why are you here?' Ada asked.

Mrs Parks sighed. 'I didn't tell them everything.'

Ada gave a huff of laughter; that made two of them. 'Your sister, I presume?'

'My nan told you how she died. I lied to the police about that, but they found out anyway.'

'Not from me. They learnt about Albion Place.'

Distant shouting from within the station interrupted them. Davey. From the few words Ada could decipher, he was calling something ridiculous. The shouting grew muffled, with more voices mixed in, and then silence.

Ada waited a few moments, expecting footsteps and Davey's face to appear in the slot in the door, but the gap remained empty. Inspector Lambert or Sergeant Potter must have ordered him to stay away.

'Your colleagues don't sound happy,' Mrs Parks said.

'I've been called a murderess; I'd like to think that didn't go down too well.'

Davey wouldn't believe that of her. He'd fight her corner.

Even though I withheld information from him, too.

And he'd been quick enough to believe Mabel a killer.

That's because she is.

Mabel, her laughter and joy in the world turned to cruel bitterness, rotting in the dankness of Armley Gaol.

Ada shivered. Would prison break her, too?

No. This was just a scare tactic. Inspector Lambert wouldn't imprison her unless he actually thought her a murderess.

What was the sentence for perverting the course of justice?

Would it apply to Louisa, too?

What were they saying to her right now?

'Murder?' Once more, Mrs Parks dragged Ada from her spiralling thoughts.

She needed to concentrate. Why had Mrs Parks been arrested? If Ada learnt that, maybe it would help, though how she didn't know. Still, it was something to do other than fret over Louisa getting questioned.

Mrs Parks continued, 'So they think you killed him?'

'I don't know what they think. All I know is it wasn't me, much as I don't blame whoever did it.' She paused. 'I presume they accused you as well?'

Mrs Parks nodded. 'Someone saw us, earlier that day, arguing about my sister's death, and now they'll use that to see me swing if they can't find the wife.'

'You were with him? The day he died?'

Mrs Parks looked affronted. 'It doesn't mean I killed him.'

Ada nodded, even as she marked it as suspicious. The police file said Mr Pearce had already been ill when he got home. In Louisa's neat notes, she'd written that Mrs Parks was not a serious contender because of a lack of means. This changed that.

Ada kept those thoughts to herself, saying as calmly as she could, 'I'm surprised he was willing to see you. Did he have much to say for himself?'

'He tried to charm me.' She scoffed. 'Like that would work.'

'Why did you want to see him? I'd have thought you'd be happy to never set eyes on him.'

'Needs must.' Mrs Parks' muttered.

'I can't think what need would be that great.'

'Then you've clearly never known hunger,' Mrs Parks snapped.

'I have. My family's had its hard times like any other. But what does hunger have to do with Mr Pearce?'

'Forget it. I don't know why I'm talking to you. Maybe you did kill him, and good on you, but I won't hang for your crime.'

Her sudden change startled Ada. What had caused it? Why would hunger force her to see Mr Pearce?

The penny dropped, and awful realisation washed over her.

'You needed money. For food and your kids and your nan.' The words came out in a hushed voice. Ada didn't want to say them, and she knew Mrs Parks didn't want to hear them, yet they tumbled out anyway as the terrible pieces came together. 'You were blackmailing him about your sister and the pills.'

Miss Clarke's death hadn't stained Mr Pearce's reputation, but if it became public knowledge that he supplied the pills, that would be a scandal even he couldn't step away from.

Mrs Parks turned to face the corner, and her response confirmed Ada was right. Yet if the police had one suspect already sitting in their cells, why arrest Ada? And Louisa?

Was this nothing more than punishment for not sharing her information? Inspector Lambert's way of proving he followed through on his threats?

But Louisa was hardly involved except for the unmentioned trip to the Mills brothers, and they'd been questioning her for hours. Or what felt like hours. How much time had passed? She glanced at her wrist, but there was only a fading red line from the handcuffs. Why did she never remember to wear a damn watch?

She tried to concentrate on the implication of what she'd learnt from Mrs Parks, but her mind always returned to Louisa.

When Constable Goodwin arrived with food, doing an excellent job of not catching Ada's eye, her worry only ramped up. The bowl of slop barely passed as edible. Ada ate a few mouthfuls before passing her portion to Mrs Parks and returning to her aimless walking.

It'd been after dinner when they were arrested; did the food mean it was now teatime? Maybe the police were taking this arrest more seriously than Ada initially thought. Was Louisa in genuine trouble? What if Louisa ended up in prison like Mabel because of her?

No. No. No. Ada was overreacting. If nothing else, Louisa had money. That always helped. Her father had been a ruthless lawyer, and there must be old friends who would defend his daughter. Or would they run away from what his daughter entangled herself in? What Ada entangled her in.

Ada was shaking so much she was forced to stop walking. Not trusting her legs, she sat on the cold tile floor. She struggled to breathe, her fear choking her. Mrs Parks crouched down beside her, but Ada barely registered her well-intended words of concern.

She would tell the police this was all her idea. That Louisa tried to stop her, and Ada begged her to keep quiet. The police would come for her next, and that was the song she would sing. She had to get Louisa out of here. That was what mattered. Louisa wasn't Mabel. She was innocent. And she wouldn't last long in a prison.

Ada sobbed into her hands, her imagination unleashed, the worst possible scenarios tormenting her. By the time the door creaked open and Louisa stepped in with her head held high, Ada was relieved just to see her alive. She scrambled to her feet, needing to hold Louisa close, and damn if anyone saw them, but Sergeant Potter shoved past Louisa and grabbed Ada's arm before they were anywhere near each other. Louisa mouthed something behind the sergeant's back, but he pulled Ada away before she had time to figure out what her partner was trying to say.

What had Louisa told them? What would Ada say to make sure she didn't contradict it?

Wouldn't it just be the perfect end to this whole mess if they both implicated themselves trying to protect the other?

Sergeant Potter's hand dug into her arm painfully, and she tried to yank it away. 'I can walk, thank you.' He only intensified his grip as he led her back down the dim corridor.

At least no one else was there to stare at her.

When they reached the closed door of the interview room, cold fear slid down her back.

Chapter Twenty-Three

A Choice

Sergeant Potter shoved Ada into the interview room where Inspector Lambert waited, his face passive. His deputy didn't follow her as the door clicked shut. It was just the two of them in the tiny miserable space, with its drab brown walls and worn table and chairs.

'Take a seat, Miss Chapman.'

Ada sat opposite him, smoothing down her dress as if she were at a dinner party and trying to hide her quivering hands. At least they hadn't handcuffed her this time. The ghost of the metal still dug into her skin.

Inspector Lambert watched her. She tried to gauge what was going on in his mind, studying his expression and posture, but came up blank. For the last couple of hours, she'd obsessed over what he must be thinking, but faced with him, she was uncertain of it all. She had no inkling what lay behind those stern eyes and severe mutton chops.

Ada focused on her breathing. She wouldn't unravel like in the cell; she needed to appear unafraid. Or would it be better to break down and appeal to his chivalrous tendencies? All that time to think, and she still didn't know what she would say.

Whatever gets Louisa out of here.

But what would that be?

Inspector Lambert cleared his throat. 'You read Mr Pearce's file whilst I was out of my office.' A statement, not a question.

'Yes.'

'And using the information from that file, you visited Miss Clarke's address, where you met her grandmother and sister. The same sister we now have in our holding cell.'

Ada nodded, not trusting her voice. Her hand reached for her marked cheek – a nervous tick – but she shoved it back under her skirts.

Inspector Lambert continued, 'There you learnt Miss Clarke didn't die due to consumption, but because she took abortive substances. Her sister also told you Mr Pearce had an affair with a Black actress named Eliza Armstrong. You then visited Miss Armstrong at the City Palace of Varieties, and in her dressing room, you saw a boat belonging to Gallant Pearce. The next day, I summoned you here to the station, and what did you tell me about all this?'

He had her, and he knew it. Hopelessness infused every inch of her. She was done for. They would throw her in Armley Gaol.

Then save Louisa.

'Nothing, sir.'

'Nothing,' he agreed. 'And then I, in my ignorance, sent you across town chasing a police lead. What did you tell me you found there?'

'A girl covered in lip rouge and some old women who didn't look like Mrs Mills.' That, at least, was a version of the truth.

'Nothing, Miss Chapman. You told me nothing. Now, is Clara Pearce at Albion House?'

'Not that I know of, sir.'

'I'm sure you can appreciate why I'm struggling to believe you. Why lie? Why go scurrying around town for a man you barely knew? Unless he meant more to you than you've admitted. Eliza Armstrong claims you also had an affair with Alexander Pearce. That's motive. And you live next door; that's opportunity. There are many ways you could have got poison into that wine bottle. How did you do it?'

'I didn't.' Ada tried to say it with force, but it came out more like a sob.

'There's been various speculation. My personal theory is that maid of yours.'

'Sophie?' Ada gasped. 'She 'as nowt t' do with any of this.'

'She's very loyal, isn't she? More to Miss Knight than to you, but I think Miss Knight cares about you greatly. One of you gives the maid the poison; she gives it to Mrs Mills – who has her own reasons to hate the man – and into his drink it goes.' The words were ludicrous, and yet he made them sound so plausible.

Whether or not he believed the accusation, Ada had to make him see sense. 'I didn't sleep with Mr Pearce. I didn't kill him. And don't you have a witness who saw Mrs Pearce buying hyoscine? I overheard the constables talking about it yesterday.' Red hot shame flooded her as the words left her mouth. But for all her defence of Mrs Pearce, if it were a choice of who would swing for this crime, Ada wouldn't sacrifice herself or Louisa or Sophie. 'You're talking nonsense.'

Sarah Bell

Inspector Lambert's expression didn't change. Could he not frown or smile or sigh? Ada almost wished Sergeant Potter were here; at least she could tell what the evil bastard was thinking. The inspector continued to watch her with cold eyes as if his silence alone could draw all her secrets out.

Just remain calm. I can't let him trick me. Yet her body betrayed her; her heart thumped, her stomach ached with fear, and anxiety flooded her veins and made her shake.

Calm. She forced her wringing hands to a stop, but it made no difference to the rest.

'You're scared, Miss Chapman. What are you afraid of?'

'Being arrested for a murder I didn't commit?' Too sarcastic, it would do her no favours. *Damn. Damn. Damn.*

'This is not a joking matter, Miss Chapman.'

Why had she wished he would frown? It only increased the leadened doom in her stomach.

'You do know what the sentence for murder is?' he asked.

The snap and the creak sounded in her mind, and she flinched.

'I'll take that as a yes.' His voice was softer now, gentler. Was that a good sign? 'If you are not our killer, tell me why you have been interfering in this case.'

Perversion of the course of justice was a better accusation than murder. If she must go to prison, let it be for that.

Would Louisa visit her? Or would her visits dry up? Just like Ada's to Mabel. She'd be all alone, and the full extent of what she'd left Mabel to suffer washed over her. Guilt mixed with her anxiety till she wanted to rip out her stomach to rid herself of the feeling.

It'd be fitting, really. A punishment that fits the crime, if not the crime I'll be sentenced for. Ada clamped her hands to her mouth to stifle the hysterical giggle that threatened to erupt from there.

'Miss Chapman?' Inspector Lambert prompted.

Ada searched for composure. The important thing wasn't if Louisa visited; it was that she wasn't in gaol alongside her.

So, Ada clutched that goal close and resumed talking. 'I've been silly. I'll admit that, sir, and I've let you down. But I'm not a murderess, and Louisa and Sophie had nothing to do with all this. Sophie informed you straight away – on Louisa's orders – both times there was suspicious activity next door.'

'Miss Knight sang a different song.'

'Louisa's trying to protect me.'

'That's a big risk to take for a...*companion*.' He said the word with heavy emphasis. How much did he know?

That was one truth that wouldn't help them.

She'd have to lie.

Forgive me, Louisa.

'She's lonely. The only friend she had before she hired me was a terrifying old woman. Her father was a man who treated affection like a disease. Me and Sophie, we're her employees, but also the only friends she has in the world. Other than us, the only people she knows are ones I've introduced her to. She's scared to be alone again, and who could blame her for that? But I've done enough damage. To her and to everyone else: I've risked Davey's career, I've abused your trust, and all because I thought I was smarter than the police. I won't let an innocent woman take the blame for my crimes because I'm one of the few people she has in her life.'

Ada hated the words. Wanted to take them back, to denounce them immediately. But they could save Louisa, and so she let them and their implications hang in the air.

Inspector Lambert was silent.

Her own words echoed through her head. *My crimes. My crimes.*

Dear Lord, she was a fool.

Better me than Louisa.

Inspector Lambert still didn't respond. Was her gamble for nothing? What was he thinking? What axe was about to fall on her head?

Or noose.

'I may have withheld information, but I'm not a killer!' she shouted into the silence. She needed him to respond, to know what hers and Louisa's fate would be.

'No. You're not.'

Ada's chest unclamped just a little. She stared at him, trying to regulate her breath.

Not a killer. He doesn't think me a killer. I won't hang.

'Then why act like you think I am?' Because shouting at a police inspector would certainly help her case.

'Because, as you said, you're withholding information. Tell me everything, Miss Chapman, and you and Miss Knight will walk out of this station free women. You might even still have a job.'

She snorted. 'You'd really keep me on the books?'

'Depends whether you prove I can trust you. Tell me everything, and you both walk out of here – back to your lives – and we brush all this aside as a terrible misunderstanding. The pair of you can walk free within the hour.'

It would keep Louisa from prison. It might send Mrs Pearce or Miss Armstrong there.

'Sounds like you know most of it by now,' Ada hedged.

'Tell me anyway.'

Easy choice.

She told him everything.

Chapter Twenty-Four

The Aftermath

The cell door swung open to reveal that the awful sergeant was back. Louisa searched for Ada beside him, and her heart sank at the empty space. The police could not have taken Ada away. They did not have enough to prosecute, and if they tried, she would hire the best lawyer she could find.

'Where's Ada?'

Sergeant Potter grinned, and she fought the impulse to shudder. 'Wouldn't you like to know? Come with me, you little bluestocking.' He tried to grab her arm as he had earlier, but she stepped out of his reach and glared at him. He appeared to reconsider, bowing mockingly at the open doorway.

Again, really? Do these fools truly think I will speak this time?

Louisa marched with dignity, head held high, as she followed the sergeant. The police would get the same results from her as before. Sergeant Potter could threaten, Inspector Lambert try to outsmart her, and the constables glare, but she would not say a word. She knew her rights.

Her certainty was shaken when they bypassed the interview room. Sergeant Potter led her to the foyer, where

Ada waited beside Inspector Lambert. Her partner gave her a quick small smile with no real happiness behind it, and her concern only increased. What new ploy was this?

A man in a smart suit stood at the front desk. Mr Connolly, her lawyer and an old friend of her father's. That was fast. Her earlier confidence returned, and she took the final few steps towards him with renewed assurance.

'Ah, Miss Knight,' he greeted her, and they shook hands. 'I came to secure your release, but it would appear I am not needed. You are free to go, and I should be on my way. You know where to reach me should you need any further counsel.'

Louisa's understanding of the situation disappeared as quickly as it arrived, leaving her scrambling to follow the implications of his words. 'I am free to go?' Why would they let her go if Mr Connolly had not yet had the chance to secure her release?

Inspector Lambert answered her question. 'Yes, you are, on the condition you stay away from any active investigations.' His tone was grave and his face stern. Louisa felt a sense of déjà vu.

Louisa nodded. 'Yes, sir. And Ada?'

'Me too.' Ada briefly met her eye before looking away. Her face was red, her birthmark barely distinguishable in the violent flush that had overtaken her cheeks. If they were to be set free, why did Ada look so furious?

Louisa bit back any more questions. This was not the time to argue but to get her and Ada as far away from the station as possible. She said diplomatic goodbyes to Inspector Lambert and Mr Connolly and strode towards the exit, her nerves taut. At any moment, she expected someone to stop her, for the inspector to call them back or for Sergeant Potter to block her path, but no one did. She concentrated on Ada's footsteps, refusing to look back.

Outside on the street, she turned to face Ada and laughed. Louder and higher than merited, but she could not stop. All the stress of the last few hours, hidden behind a calm facade, burst out of her until her stomach hurt with mirth, and she leant against the wall to remain upright.

Ada did not match her giddiness. She looked no happier at being outside the station than she had inside, and Louisa sobered.

'Ada, what's wrong?' Sharp breaths punctuated her speech.

'Um, I...' Ada shook her head and sighed.

Louisa was about to ask what happened in her interview when Mr Connolly exited the station. Louisa stood up straight again, away from the wall, and gave him a polite nod.

'I am glad this ended well, Miss Knight. Good day.' He tipped his hat at her and walked away.

'If Mr Connolly didn't get us released, who did?'

'I did,' Ada admitted in a quiet voice. 'I told Inspector Lambert everything. I broke my promise to Mrs Mason and made all we've done these last few days pointless. But I...I was scared, Louisa.' Ada's voice broke, and it tugged at Louisa's heart.

She pulled Ada into a hug, whispering small comforts in her ear. How awful must the situation have been for her? She had seen one lover sent to jail. Had those memories taunted her? Had she feared for Louisa? And Inspector Lambert knew her, no doubt making it easy to manipulate her and gain her trust.

Ada continued in the same shaky whisper. 'If Mrs Pearce is at Albion House, they'll find her now. I told him my suspicions about Mrs Thornton. That she cares more about protecting the women under her protection than about the law. The perfect person to hide Mrs Pearce. He said he's going to get a warrant. What if they find her and she hangs? It'll be my fault. I let Mabel down. Now I've let Mrs Pearce down. And I've let you down. I've let everyone down.'

'No. No. You have not.' Louisa held her a little tighter, but again she had no words to make it all right. She could not change what had happened. Not the loss of Mabel or the police's trickery.

'I was so scared,' Ada repeated between sobs.

'So was I,' Louisa admitted. She had not realised how much until it was over.

Ada's hand encircled Louisa's wrist, her thumb stroking the pressure point. They would have to separate soon. They were in the middle of the street, in broad daylight, outside a police station, but Louisa allowed herself the comfort for a moment longer. They were both safe and together, and she luxuriated in that contentment, pushing the outside world away. A moment. Just a moment for the two of them.

They could not ignore the rest of the world forever, and Louisa pulled away. She kept her focus on Ada, refusing to notice any passers-by or their reactions.

Ada wiped at her eyes. 'What did you say?' she asked. 'You were gone for hours!'

'Because I refused to say anything, Ada.'

Ada scrunched up her face. 'You can do that?'

'Yes. I invoked my right to silence and to counsel.'

'Oh.' Ada sounded so lost in that one noise, and Louisa wanted to hold her close again and make it all go away for just one moment more.

But reality had to be faced.

'It does not matter,' Louisa told her. 'I know this kind of legalese because my father taught me and–'

'And I'm just a common labourer's daughter?' Ada snapped. Red was creeping across her cheeks again.

'That is not what I meant.'

Ada turned away, scuffing her shoe against the ground, and exclaimed, 'Jesus Christ, I want a cig!'

Louisa bit back a bark of laughter, moving her hand to cover her mouth, because for all she hated swearing, she could not condemn blasphemy, and Ada knew it.

'I've got one, miss!' A teenage boy dressed up as a police officer tried to rush up the pavement and search his pockets at the same time. Constable Smith, Louisa assumed, based on Ada's description. The officer walking behind him in a more sensible manner was Constable Goodwin.

Ada took the cigarette with a muttered thanks and a tight smile. She leaned close so he could light it, and the boy blushed. Louisa would have to tell her that later, to warn her to tread carefully.

'I see they've released the two of you,' Constable Goodwin said.

'I couldn't believe they'd arrested you,' Constable Smith cut in, talking to Ada. 'Course, I didn't believe a word of it. As if a clever woman like you would ever have gone near a dastardly man like that Pearce. I knew that actress was a liar.'

'Yes, apparently Miss Armstrong wants me strung up as a murderess.' Ada spoke with a false cheer that did nothing to hide her fury.

A brief mental image of Ada's neck in a noose, one that Louisa had fought to keep at bay all afternoon, struck. An accompanying wave of grief and anger threatened to overwhelm her. The cold, chilling thought came to her unbidden – *Miss Armstrong must pay for her actions* – and she tried to silence it. Ada was here. Alive. No harm done.

Constable Smith was still talking. 'Still, to think you'd killed him when we all know it was his wife. Did Wilkinson tell you I found a key piece of evidence?'

Constable Goodwin sighed. 'Here we go. He finds one clue, and we never hear the end of it.'

'It helped, didn't it? Confirmed he didn't do himself in?'

That caught Louisa's attention. 'Why would you have thought he took his own life?' She had never even considered that option.

'Because of the fingerprints. Oh, miss!' Constable Smith turned to Ada. 'I never got to tell you–'

'That's enough, Smith. You do realise it's not considered good practice to tell recently-released suspects key information?' Constable Goodwin turned back to her and Ada. 'No offence, misses, it's not that I think you were involved, but I wouldn't want you getting into any more trouble.'

Louisa forced a smile. 'We understand, Constable. We should be going, Ada?'

Ada threw the cigarette end to the ground and crushed it

under her shoe, which Louisa took as agreement. She bade a polite goodbye to the two constables.

Ada muttered a 'bye,' and they walked away.

Louisa did not dare say anything more until the police station was a safe distance behind them, but her mind was not quiet. Miss Armstrong's accusation was in the forefront, alongside the fact they were due at the Varieties to meet Mrs Mason soon. Was that still a good idea? The original reason for the visit had been to give Louisa and Ada a chance to ask Miss Armstrong about the missing boys, but that was now unlikely to be the main topic of conversation. Louisa did not trust herself to be in a room with the woman and keep calm, and Ada even less so.

The talkative constable's slip-up intrigued her, too. Ada had mentioned a fingerprint analysis when she looked at the police's file. They'd been checking whose prints were on the hyoscine bottle found in the Pearces' wine cellar.

Then there was the woman in the holding cell, Mrs Parks. She had told Louisa little other than her name, but it was one Louisa also recognised from Ada's snooping. Why was Miss Clarke's sister under arrest?

As they neared Vicar Lane and their tram stop home, Louisa slowed her pace.

Ada sent her an inquisitive look.

'That constable's sweet on you.' Not the most important thing she had learnt today, but the easier option, just to start the conversation.

'Bertie Smith? Nah!' Ada's tone sounded amused rather than sullen, and Louisa considered that a start. Much as she understood and shared Ada's anger, encouraging her to stew in it would do no good.

'He turned red as a beetroot when you leant close to him.'

'He'd do that if any woman leant close to him. But I'll find a way to drop a few subtle hints I've no interest next time I'm at the station.' She made a little huffing noise. 'If I'm ever invited back, that is. Inspector Lambert said I might keep my job if I co-operated.' Her voice turned a touch hysterical, and there was no amusement in the trill of laughter that followed. 'I'm not sure he meant it, though. He tricked me, and it worked.'

So much for not letting her stew. There was no avoiding the discussion any longer, and Louisa checked her wristwatch. If they chose to go to the Varieties, they did not have time to go home first. They would need to decide.

'We are due to be at the Varieties in half an hour. If you still want to go.'

'Yes.' Ada's voice was steel. 'I have questions for Eliza Armstrong.'

Chapter Twenty-Five

A Conspiracy of Women

The nearer they got to the music hall, the more Louisa's reservations grew. If the police saw them anywhere near Miss Armstrong, they'd be back in Millgarth's cells before sunset. Yet there was no rationalising with Ada's seething anger, and Louisa did not want to walk away either.

She had been so certain of Mrs Pearce's guilt, so dismissive of any other possibility, and now doubts pulled at her. If someone went to prison for this crime, should it not be the right person? The police had arrested Ada and suspected her of murder; did that not show some sloppiness in their procedure?

And if the police found Stephen Cartwright, would they be sending him back to the loving arms of a murderess? A crime of passion was still a crime.

Ada was not the only one with questions for Eliza Armstrong.

'Buy a ticket, miss?' A skinny boy tried to hand Louisa a leaflet.

'No, thank you.' She waved it away.

'Wait, I know you!' The boy pointed at Ada. 'If you're looking for Miss Armstrong again, she ain't 'ere. She's left, she 'as.'

'Left?' Ada barked, and the boy took a step back.

'Aye, she's left. What's it to you?'

'I need to talk to her.' Ada's tone was still harsh, and the boy frowned.

'You were a lot nicer last time.' He crossed his arms and glared at her petulantly.

'Well, I'm having a bad day, kid.'

Since Ada's usual skill with children had disintegrated, Louisa addressed the boy before he could retort. 'Do you know where she went?'

'She didn't say. You could ask Miss Jain. She might know. I could take you t' 'er.'

Ada raised an eyebrow. 'For another two shillings?'

'Seems fair, miss.'

Ada shook her head, but the slight upturn of her lips made it a fond gesture.

Louisa replied, 'I need to find my friend first.' Best not to leave Mrs Mason waiting, and she would also want to know about Miss Armstrong. 'But then, yes, I would like to speak with Miss Jain.'

Mrs Mason stood outside the Varieties with her husband, a short Black man in a faded blue suit. Beside them, people milled around, waiting for the doors to open. Louisa greeted the pair with as much warmth as she could generate. Then without preamble, she told them what the flyer boy had said.

'Maybe she's found Stephen!' Mrs Mason's eyes glittered with hope.

'Maybe she's on the run,' Ada spat.

Mrs Mason's face darkened as quickly as it had lit up.

Her husband asked, 'Because of all this noise with your

neighbour?'

'Do the police think Eliza was involved? Did you hear something at the station?'

'Yes, we did. Do you know why we've been at the station?'

Mrs Mason's eyed Ada inquisitively. 'You work there?'

'Because we were arrested!'

A nearby group of theatre-goers turned to stare.

'Ada!' Louisa hissed.

'Maybe this isn't the best place for this conversation?' Mrs Mason suggested.

'Arrested?' Mr Mason said. 'Since when did peelers arrest their own?'

'Since your friend told them I was having an affair with the evil dead bastard.'

A shocked gasp from the crowd. Louisa hissed Ada's name again, feeling the burning stares on the back of her neck.

Mr Mason looked puzzled. 'But I thought...' He wiggled his finger between the two of them. 'You two were, you know...'

Louisa's heart sped up. He knew? Did he care?

'Arthur!' Mrs Mason hissed, similar to Louisa earlier.

Louisa wanted to ask them more, to know for certain, but this was not the time or place. She forced herself to continue as if there had been no interruption. 'The boy with the leaflets said he could take us to speak with Miss Armstrong's acting partner, Miss Jain. I believe you've both met her?'

'Yes. She was always friendly to us,' Mrs Mason replied.

Ada snorted.

'Yes, Miss Chapman, from your story, she was less polite to you, but she was trying to protect her friend.'

And most likely still will. Even so, if Miss Jain had news on either the boys' whereabouts or the reasoning behind Miss Armstrong's accusation, Louisa wanted to hear it.

Mrs Mason looked thoughtful. 'Perhaps it would be better for me and Arthur to speak with her alone. She might be more willing to talk to us.'

'Are you going to ask why her friend had me arrested?'

'We can if you insist.'

'I'd rather find out for myself.'

'I'm not sure that is a good idea.' Mrs Mason paused. 'To be blunt, you are clearly angry, and with good reason, but you and Miss Jain shouting at each other is not going to help the situation.'

'Damnit,' Ada muttered. 'Damnit, you're right. Why am I cursed to be surrounded by sensible people?'

Louisa was not sure if that was a joke and whether she should be offended.

Mr Mason laughed. 'I know the feeling.'

His wife shook her head but also smiled. She addressed Louisa, 'We'll meet you out here in half an hour, say?'

'Maybe not here.' If the police also came looking for Miss Armstrong, it would be better if they were not found loitering outside her place of work. 'We'll meet you round the corner near the arcades?'

The Masons agreed, and Ada nodded, though her frown implied she was no happier about the situation.

Lands Lane was near empty, with only a few men coming

and going from the public houses. The rain had held off today, but it was still cool for July.

Louisa sat on a bench, and Ada joined, her expression far away. Louisa took the moment to reconsider all she had learnt that day. An idea was beginning to take shape in her mind, but she kept getting distracted by Ada, who wiggled in her seat, crossing and uncrossing her arms and legs. Louisa did not ask if she was all right. Better to try and distract her.

'Did Mrs Parks tell you anything?'

That stilled Ada's restless movements. Her tone was softer, her anger subdued when she answered. 'She saw Mr Pearce the day he died.'

'So, they arrested her for his murder, then? As well as arresting you, and speaking to Miss Armstrong, and looking for Mrs Pearce. What do they think this is, a conspiracy of women?'

Ada gave a huff of bitter laughter.

Louisa stored the fact away to consider how it lined up with the day's other pieces of information. Her idea was already reforming.

The Masons returned after only ten minutes, with smiles on their faces.

'Miss Jain said Eliza has gone to find Stephen,' Mrs Mason announced joyfully. 'She had a letter from him. He's going to one of the ports; she didn't tell Miss Jain which, but she did say that Stephen told her to find him next to the biggest ship possible, like the *Titanic*. Miss Jain also mentioned seeing an old white woman talking to her backstage, if that means anything to you?'

Mrs Mills? But then again, she was not the only person to

fit that description. Still, it would be an almighty coincidence.

A conspiracy of women. Louisa shook her head, not willing to voice her suspicions yet.

Ada opened, then closed her mouth. She must have decided to follow Louisa's lead, and Louisa needed time to stop and consider the options. Her fingers itched for pen and paper.

Mrs Mason continued, 'And a constable has been round, asking questions. Miss Jain described him as a tall, plain officer.'

'Davey. So that's where they sent him off to,' Ada muttered.

Mr Mason took up his wife's story. 'Whoever he was, he didn't find much. Miss Armstrong was already gone. She could be with the boys even now.'

'So, it all ends happily then.' Ada's voice was laced with sarcasm. 'Unless her lover's wife hangs for a murder she might have committed. Or I hang for it!'

'I don't think Eliza killed Mr Pearce.' Mrs Mason spoke evenly.

'Eliza? A murderer? Nah,' her husband chimed in.

'You said so yourself,' Mrs Mason reminded Ada.

'Before she got me arrested.'

'Perhaps Eliza was scared. Her former lover dead, her nephew missing, and the police asking her questions...it would be enough to scare anyone.'

'Anyone,' Ada repeated in a whisper and then said no more.

Her earlier tearful words re-played in Louisa's head: *'I was scared.'* For all Mr Mason's relaxed commentary on their relationship, Louisa dared not take her hand.

'Thank you for your help,' Mrs Mason said. 'But Eliza stands more chance of finding Stephen on her own now.'

'And Gallant?' Louisa asked. 'We discovered proof the boys are together.'

'Eliza will see him taken to the authorities and returned to his remaining family. Whatever accusations she may have made and why, I am sure she would be grateful for your efforts in trying to find her nephew.'

So that was it. It was done.

After awkward goodbyes, the two couples headed in opposite directions. Louisa and Ada's journey home was quiet, and a profound sense of relief washed over Louisa as she stepped out of the cab and looked upon her home. Her fingers traced the top of the gate with a reverent touch.

Sophie rushed down the footpath. 'What happened, ma'am? I was so worried. At first, I thought it was because...' She dropped her voice. 'Because of the same reason I was fired.'

'It is not illegal,' Louisa whispered. 'Not for women. I have told you that.'

'I know, I know. Did Mr Connolly get you out? I called him. Was that the right thing to do? I found 'is name int' documents in your study. I didn't think you'd mind, given circumstances–'

'Yes. Yes, you did the right thing, Sophie. I thank you. It was clever thinking.'

The maid beamed. 'I'm so glad you're both home, ma'am. Shall I go make a pot of tea? And you'll be wanting food.'

'That would be lovely, thank you, Sophie.'

The maid bustled back into the house; Louisa half-expected her to start skipping.

She removed her outerwear and entered the sitting room. Ada followed, throwing herself onto the sofa with such force, Louisa winced.

'So, it's over then?' Ada said into the silence. 'Miss Armstrong has gone to find the boy. If Mrs Pearce is at Albion House, the police will find her. If not, well, then we know no more than they do. It's over. I told them everything.' Ada spat the last words.

Louisa sat next to her, but the touch of her hand did nothing to relax Ada, who turned to her with a fretful face. 'Do you think Mrs Pearce will hang? Or will she be charged with manslaughter like Mabel?'

'If she gave him the poison, it would depend on how and why.'

'If?' Ada repeated.

Louisa did not answer immediately, leaning over to the coffee table for her notebook. All her well-thought-out logic was laid out on its pages. Mrs Pearce was the only sensible suspect. But she had learnt so much more since she'd written these notes. Her desire for the answer to be simple and clichéd had blinded her. She had not wanted this to need their assistance.

She contemplated her next words. How to voice the ideas forming in her mind? Would it be better to say nothing? After all, maybe she was wrong. She had been before.

She should tell Ada, though. Then they could decide what to do next.

'What if you were right, Ada? What if there is a chance

Mrs Pearce is innocent?'

'Are you serious?' Ada's green eyes flashed, the full force of her simmering anger hitting Louisa. 'Now you tell me I might be right? When it doesn't matter because I've done exactly what the police wanted and could be the reason a woman dies? Where was this support earlier?'

Louisa fought to remain calm. 'Matters have changed since then. Think about it, Ada. Think about what–'

'Oh! Don't use that voice with me!' Ada jumped to her feet and glared down at Louisa. 'That's all you've to say? Matters have changed?'

'That might have been badly expressed, but–'

'Do you even care? I tried to save you, and what did you do? Nothing! You did nothing to save me or yourself or anyone. And you're proud of it! I can see it.'

'Why would I not be?' Louisa's calm slipped away. Ada might have a right to be angry, but that did not mean she got to shout at Louisa for not sharing her mistakes.

She also stood so Ada could no longer look down on her. 'I did the sensible thing in the circumstances, and you are angry because I did not create some dramatic scene? I did the best thing for both of us.'

'And I'm just a fool? I'm the one who got us out of the station!'

'Mr Connolly was there. We would have gotten out of there soon enough.'

Ada shook her head, staring at her in disbelief. 'You just don't care.'

'Of course, I care, Ada. How can you question that?'

'Do you, though? Do you actually want *me* here? Or do

you just want *someone?* Anyone. As long as you're not alone.'

Her accusation robbed Louisa of any reply. All her old fears came bubbling back to the surface and cemented with her shock and anger. For Ada - the very person she was scared would leave one day - had callously turned that fact back against her.

'I'm sorry,' Ada said hastily. 'That was cruel. I didn't mean it.' She reached for Louisa's hand, but Louisa stepped away.

'I think you did.'

They stared at each other. An apology hovered on Louisa's lips, and she saw one on Ada's face, too, but then her partner's face hardened. 'Fine.' Ada stormed out of the room, slamming the door, followed by the stomp of her feet on the stairs.

Louisa picked her notebook off the sofa. Let Ada have her tantrum. She would show her what she meant.

With renewed determination, she went back to the hallway. She was putting her hat on when Sophie appeared with the tea tray. 'Are you heading back out already, ma'am?'

'I have a quick errand to run.'

'Most of the shops will be shut.'

'I am just off to the chemists; they are usually open late. I will be back soon. I think Miss Chapman will have gone to her painting studio if you could take the tea upstairs.'

Louisa was out the door before the maid could say more. She had questions that needed answers, and she would rely on what she trusted most: science and logic.

Chapter Twenty-Six

It All Comes Together

A collection of sketches laid propped against the window, a cold cup of tea and a saucer of cigarette butts beside them on the sill. The full cast of those involved in this drama stared back at Ada. The pictures were far from her best work, but she'd needed to draw, to move her hands and expunge her anger and frustration onto the paper. To concentrate on something other than her cruel words to Louisa, her stupidity in falling for Inspector Lambert's manipulations, and the fact that even now, Leeds City Police could be marching into Albion House.

From the middle of the row of sketches, the portrait of Mrs Thornton judged her. It was not an expression Ada had seen the woman wear in real life but instead how she imagined she would react if she learnt of Ada's part in getting Albion Place raided by the police. Ada's guilt manifested into pencil and paper.

First in the line-up, on the far left, was Mrs Pearce, the catalyst of this whole mess. Ada's pencil had made her neighbour fragile and scared, and she no longer remembered if that was an accurate representation or her imagination. Or more guilt.

The picture of Gallant and Stephen could be any two

small, cowering boys. She might've done them a disservice in that portrayal. They'd survived, and if Miss Jain spoke true, they might have even made it out of the city and got a message to Miss Armstrong. Did Gallant Pearce also get a message to his mother? Was she, too, long gone from the city?

Her gaze flickered to the sketch of Mrs Mills. Miss Jain had seen an old white woman at the Varieties. Had it been Mrs Mills? Why would she be there? On Mrs Pearce's behalf? It was hard to imagine the actress working with her lover's wife, but they did share a grievance. Had they planned his death? If so, Ada should stay the hell away and let events play out. A plotted murder was not the same as Mabel and her desperate attempt to escape Mr Shaw's clutches.

The thought did nothing to ease her guilt, and the next two sketches didn't help: poor dead Miss Clarke and her sister, Mrs Parks. Though Ada had long wanted to capture Miss Clarke's beauty on paper, what she'd drawn was more haunting than she'd intended. She couldn't stare at it for too long without a deep sadness sinking over her. In contrast, she'd drawn Mrs Parks with anger etched in every pencil stroke. What had Mrs Parks done the day she met Mr Pearce to blackmail him?

And last of all, Miss Armstrong. The last work was bland and uninspiring, an amateur attempt at portraiture. The complexity of Ada's emotions, as they jumped between anger, confusion, and sympathy, had created a jumble of heavy lines and shaky shading. She didn't know what to make of the woman whose words caused her brief arrest. Ada had no reason to protect her, but upon reflection, she could summon no joy when she pictured her behind bars.

Why had Miss Armstrong lied to the police? A cover-up? Sheer anger? Or did she not think it a lie? Staring at a poorly-drawn sketch wouldn't provide the answer, and Ada turned away with a heavy sigh.

On the unused bed, she'd propped up two old portraits against the wall: Louisa and Mabel. The two loves of her life. She couldn't save one, and in trying to save the other, she'd only made the situation worse. She slammed them down. There was no new picture of Louisa amongst the sketches on the windowsill. The hurt in Louisa's eyes earlier wasn't an expression Ada wanted committed to paper.

She needed to apologise. However angry she might have been, that didn't excuse her behaviour. She'd turned her deepest fear into a weapon of spite, but it was a double-edged sword.

Even if Louisa had changed her mind about Mrs Pearce's guilt, it didn't matter anymore. Ada made certain of that back at Millgarth. She should tell Louisa to forget the whole business. That the most important thing was to make sure neither of them ever sat opposite Inspector Lambert in that interview room again.

How ironic. Their roles were reversed, and now Ada was the one advising caution.

Yet, it would also be deliciously ironic if, after all his tricks, they solved this where Inspector Lambert couldn't.

And if Mrs Pearce didn't do this, as Louisa suggested, how could Ada step aside and let her hang?

Guilt squirmed through her once more. She'd been willing to do just that when she thought it'd save Louisa. And she would again. No questions asked.

Footsteps in the hallway had announced Louisa's return a couple of hours ago. It was time to stop hiding. She would apologise and tell Louisa she'd been right days ago; they should have stayed the hell away.

Her mind set, Ada hurried to Louisa's study. She knocked on the door and half-expected a well-deserved re-buff, preparing herself to march in anyway, but Louisa called, 'Come in.'

Ada gave her no time to speak. 'The first thing I need to say is I'm sorry and...what the hell's going on in here?' Her apology was waylaid as she observed the odd assortment of mess that littered Louisa's desk. She had never seen it in any state but perfect order before, as if the ghost of Louisa's father would allow no less.

Amongst the debris stood several bottles of red and white wine in various stages of fullness, their contents spread between what appeared to be every piece of glassware in the house. There were wine glasses as expected, but Ada also spotted tumblers, snifters, and pint glasses. Some of them she suspected hadn't seen the light of day since before Louisa's father died. Mixed in amongst them were an equally strange array of objects – several medicine bottles, a dish of pills, a cluster of ripped-out notebook pages, and a bowl filled with the remnants of a meal mashed up in a childish manner that certainly wasn't how Louisa ate.

'Apology accepted.'

Louisa's words reminded Ada why she came here in the first place, and she jerked her head round to her partner, who wasn't quite managing to keep a straight face.

Ada's own lips quirked at the sight, but she needed to be

serious for what she had to say. 'That came out wrong. What I meant to say is I should never have said those awful things. They're not true. It was a horrible thing to say, and I need you to know it's not true.'

'There was some truth,' Louisa said bitterly. She cast her eyes away from Ada and towards her bookshelf. 'I've no family. The majority of our friends are people I know through you. I can cope with my own company much better than some but, without you, I would be lonely. There's no denying it.'

'It was still cruel of me to say.'

'Yes, it was.'

That stung, and Ada winced. She always said how she appreciated that Louisa didn't mince her words, but it didn't help take the edge off that particular truth.

Louisa continued in a softer voice, 'But the blame is mine to share if you think you are just anyone. You are not just anyone, Ada. You think I would let just *anyone* waltz into my life and turn it upside down?'

'No. You're far too stubborn for that.' Not the best thing to say in an apology, but Louisa laughed, and tendrils of hope curled around Ada's heart.

'I am, indeed.' A small smile played at Louisa's lips, but then she frowned. 'You were angry. I understand that. Inspector Lambert used your fear, holding the threat of what happened to Mabel over your head, making you believe I was at risk. Anyone would be angry in those circumstances.'

'I still took my anger out on the wrong person.'

'Yes, you did. But none of us are without our limitations. We have both been...*not our best* for this whole debacle. For ourselves or each other.'

Ada took a step towards her, holding out her hand. 'So, we learn from this?'

Louisa took it and squeezed. 'You know how fond I am of learning.'

Another old joke. If Louisa taught Ada facts and history and fascinating things she had never known, then she told Ada that what she learnt from her in return was kindness and friendship and love.

They shared a smile. Ada wanted to hug her, to kiss her, to ask in what way she could best show her affection, what would bring Louisa joy?

But the debris still cluttered Louisa's desk, and Ada had to ask.

'Speaking of learning...' She gestured to the mess.

'What the hell?' Louisa quoted with a teasing smile. 'I raided our local chemists and grocers and, in doing so, have done my reputation no favours.'

'Pills and wine are not the wisest items to be seen buying.'

'Especially not these pills.'

That drew Ada up short. She picked up the dish. The pills were small cream circles that could've been anything, but logically there was only one option. 'Louisa? Are these what I think they are? How did you get them?'

'I went to the chemists and hinted that I was with child.' Louisa remained blasé as if the words she'd just uttered were a perfectly typical thing for her to say.

'You told old Mr Thompson you're pregnant?' Ada's voice rose several octaves in disbelief. Try as she might, she couldn't imagine such a scene. Not Louisa saying it or Mr

Thompson believing her.

'Not in as many words. Such matters must be handled with subtlety. He told me to purchase something else and meet him round the side entrance. Which gave me a good excuse to buy this.' She held up one of the bottles and passed it to Ada, who studied the label.

'Hyoscine? Should I be worried for my safety or my libido?' Ada laughed, but Louisa frowned, and she hurried to add, 'Sorry, that was in poor taste. But why do you have this?'

'I might know who and what killed Mr Pearce.' Shocking words delivered with complete calm.

Ada gaped at her. 'Truly?' Surprise gave way to excitement. She'd solved this. Brilliant, clever Louisa had solved this.

'I am not certain of all of it – it is a working hypothesis at this point – but I think I know.' Her voice dropped to a soft plea. 'I just do not know what to do with the information.'

'Tell me what you think, and we can decide.'

'Is it for us to decide?' There was no conviction to Louisa's argument.

'It shouldn't be, no, but...'

'But we have to make a choice. Morality or legality?'

Ada's stomach plummeted. That wasn't a promising question. 'Tell me what you've found, Louisa, and then we can talk it through together.'

Louisa nodded and reached for what remained of her notebook.

Chapter Twenty-Seven

A Terrible Idea

Once Louisa finished her explanation, she rushed to add, 'As I said, it is uncertain. There are still a lot of variables. Eliza Armstrong, for one. And Mrs Pearce's intentions for another. I cannot even say for definite that she was involved.'

Ada chewed her bottom lip. 'Are you going to tell the police this?'

She had been considering that very question when Ada interrupted. If her suspicions were right, then informing the police might send two women to prison – and potentially the noose – but neither of them would be Ada. Yet, in letting her go, Inspector Lambert had made it clear he did not believe the allegations he had levied against her. Ada was not at risk. What was there to gain by informing the police but more grief?

Justice for a murdered man? The maintenance of law and order?

Louisa shook her head as if the action could dispel her father's admonishments and the unbending morals he drilled into her. 'I see no reason to inform them yet. They have people to advise them on such matters; they do not need my conjectures. All it will achieve is another lecture about interfering.'

Ada's face relaxed, but Louisa's father's voice only got louder. If she closed her eyes, it could be twenty years ago, when she had sat cross-legged on the floor as her father talked, and she struggled to keep up. Striving to understand his words, so she could make a clever reply, and he would grace her with the twitch of his lips that was not quite a smile, and she would know he was proud of her.

A quiet knock on the door drew her attention, and she seized onto the distraction. She was not that girl anymore, but a woman grown. This was her household now. How her father would have hated it. Hated her. But she did not have to live up to his expectations anymore.

'Come in, Sophie.'

The maid stepped into the room hesitantly, with the taut anxious expression on her face that was a harbinger of bad news.

'I went to see if Miss Chapman wanted some food bringing up. I thought she was still in her studio, and well...I saw this.' Sophie held up a sketch of a woman Louisa did not recognise.

'Mrs Thornton,' Ada said. 'The woman from Albion House. What about her, Sophie?'

'I saw her, miss. Talking to Mrs Mills, the day she disappeared, and I think it was her I saw at their house last year, the lady talking to Mrs Pearce, though Mrs Pearce didn't look happy about whatever she was saying.'

Ada gasped, and Louisa's stomach jolted. 'Are you sure, Sophie?'

'Yes, ma'am.' Sophie nodded so vigorously, her cap wobbled.

'How did she talk?' Ada asked.

'Posh, like Miss Knight.'

'It was her.'

'What does it mean, miss? Do you know where Mrs Mills is?'

'Yes, and I've sent the wolves to her door.' The bitterness in Ada's voice was unmistakeable, but its target was harder to determine.

'Unless Mrs Mills and Mrs Pearce are already gone.' Louisa tried to be optimistic for Ada's sake, internally trying to coordinate this new information with her theory. 'Disappeared with Miss Armstrong.'

'Where would they go?' Sophie's brow furrowed.

'As far away from here as possible.'

'To a port,' Ada added. 'To a big ship like the *Titanic*.'

'To America?' Sophie said in awe. 'With Mrs Pearce? Should we tell the police?'

Louisa hesitated, both Ada and Sophie's stares scolding her.

If her theory was right, Mrs Pearce might have played a part in her husband's death, but her intentions were murkier. Science could not give her a window into a woman's mind and heart.

She's still a killer. Her and the other woman. Her father's voice resounded in her head, and her answer stalled on her tongue.

Ada spoke into the silence. 'Not yet, Sophie. Can you promise not to tell the police unless we ask you?'

Sophie nodded. 'You think I'd side with the police? After they arrested the pair of you?'

Louisa smiled at her affront. 'Thank you, Sophie. As for

what we choose to do next... There are still too many questions, too many variables.'

'I have an idea,' Ada said. 'A terrible idea. You're going to hate it. I hate it. If you say no, I'll probably kiss you in relief.'

The corner of Louisa's mouth quirked. 'I'll bear that in mind. Tell me your terrible idea.'

'We go to Albion House. We confront Mrs Thornton. We find out if Mrs Pearce is still there or not, and if not, then we find out where she went. We can learn for certain if your theory is right, and if it is...'

Let her run. Ada's earlier words hovered unspoken, and anxiety prickled under Louisa's skin. It went against every lesson she was ever taught. Every principle she thought she had.

'And if I am wrong?'

'We've still found her. If it turns out it was murder, cold and calculated, then we tell the police. At least we will know for sure that we did the right thing.'

The spectre of Mabel danced between them. How many times must Ada have questioned the morality of her actions?

Yet, there was a certain logic to Ada's idea. Once she was in procession of all the facts – facts only Mrs Pearce could give her – then Louisa could decide the right course of action.

That relied on them finding her, though.

Louisa proceeded with caution. 'Either way, we are getting ahead of ourselves. How do you intend to get inside Albion Place? The police will be watching it if they have not already got a warrant.'

Ada grimaced. 'This is the part you won't like. Someone will need to go in disguise, like a down-and-out woman in need of the home's shelter. Mrs Thornton will recognise me, as will the police. Plus, I don't exactly blend in.' She made a gesture towards her bright hair and birthmark.

Dread crept over Louisa. 'You were right; this is a terrible idea.'

'I'll do it,' Sophie blurted out quickly. Her hands twisted her apron again. Nothing about her expression or posture said she wanted to do this.

'I would not ask that of you, Sophie.'

'I know, ma'am. However, I'm offering to. It makes the most sense. Miss Chapman's right: they'll recognise her. And no offence, ma'am, but I don't think you'd do a very convincing job. I should be able to, though. I could've ended up in a place like that anyway if it hadn't been for you.'

Sophie was right, but the idea still did not sit well with Louisa. She hired Sophie to do the housework, not sneak past police officers. Besides, for all Sophie's brave words, she was clearly terrified.

'Thank you for offering, Sophie, but it is not necessary. Even if this plan works, what will we do if Mrs Pearce is not there anymore, as we suspect? I doubt Mrs Thornton will just tell us where she has gone.' A reasonable piece of logic and she hated herself for it, even as guilty relief snuck its way through her veins.

Ada was stroking the edge of her birthmark, as she tended to do when she was deep in thought. Louisa focused on her partner's fingers, forcing her father's voice to the recesses of her mind.

I am not that girl anymore. I am the woman Ada helped me to become.

Ada was chewing her lip again, too, and Louisa knew what she would say before she said it. 'I have another idea.'

'Is it another terrible idea?' Louisa tried to keep her tone light even as dread uncoiled its tendrils once more.

'It is, but it might just work. We will need Sophie's help, though.'

'I want to do this, ma'am. I want to find Mrs Mills. And Mrs Pearce might be quite rude at times, but that doesn't mean she should hang. I heard them arguing once. I was speaking to Mrs Mills at the side door, and then Mr Pearce started shouting, and Mrs Pearce was sobbing. Mrs Mills told me to leave and made me promise not to say owt, which is why I didn't, but I wanted to. I was so scared he'd hit her.' Sophie sniffed.

'Hit her?' Ada demanded. 'Mrs Mills said he never hurt her, not with fists anyway.'

'She told me the same when I saw her next, but what I heard Mr Pearce say was, "Why do you make me hurt you?" What kind of awful question is that? I admit I didn't like his wife very much, but no one deserves to have such mean things said to them and from someone who was supposed to love them. I want to help find her. Please, miss. Let me help.'

Louisa blinked away the image in her mind, the scene Sophie described. What did her father's unquestionable law have to say about the years of psychological torture Mrs Pearce had endured?

Nothing. Look the other way and pretend it is not happening. Not my business.

Cold determination settled around her like a cloak.

'Then let's find her.'

Chapter Twenty-Eight

The Trap Ensnares

Ada stood in front of Inspector Lambert's desk with Louisa and Sophie like naughty school children called before the headmaster. She forced herself to stand still and not squirm under his suspicious gaze.

This was her choice. She was the one doing the trickery this time. Still, whenever those grey eyes focused on her, she was certain her deception screamed at him, evident in every blink and twitch of her hands. If ever she needed to keep a blank face, it was now. She sought to mimic Louisa and appear poised but doubted her impression was convincing. Especially not to the man who'd played her so damn well yesterday.

'Umm...' Sophie's hesitation gave Ada a good excuse to look away from the inspector.

Louisa spoke in her kindest voice. 'Tell the inspector what you told us, Sophie.'

For all her boldness yesterday evening, Sophie was shrinking away from Inspector Lambert's gaze, and Ada regretted having to ask this of her. She had already done so much for them, including her superbly executed sneaking into Albion Place.

'I, um, I saw that woman,' Sophie stammered. 'The one in

Miss Chapman's picture.' She pointed at the sketch of Mrs Thornton on Inspector Lambert's desk. 'At the Pearce house. She was talking with Mrs Mills.'

'This was the last time you saw Mrs Mills?' Inspector Lambert asked.

Sophie nodded.

He turned to Ada, pointing to the sketch. 'This is Mrs Thornton? The woman who runs Albion House. The Good Samaritan with no Christian faith in God or man?'

Ada cringed to hear that particular description thrown back at her but kept her voice steady, 'Yes, sir.'

'May I keep this, Miss Chapman?' She nodded, and he moved it into a file. 'Thank you for sharing this information. I am glad you have learnt your lesson in that regard.'

Yesterday's fire reignited in Ada's heart. She bit her tongue hard to prevent herself from replying, focusing on the pain rather than her fury.

Inspector Lambert stood. 'Now you must excuse me, as this gives me fresh work to do. Miss Chapman, you know your way out.' He gestured towards the door, and all three women said polite goodbyes.

As they walked down the corridor, Sophie opened her mouth to speak, and Ada shook her head. Not yet. Louisa made the same gesture, and the girl remained quiet.

As they stepped into the foyer, Ada's attention jumped to the front desk. Part of her plan relied on who was there. It was Davey, as she'd thought it should be on a Friday, but the tightness in her chest only increased. She may have lied successfully to Inspector Lambert – or so she hoped – but Davey always knew.

Ada waved to catch his attention, and he called a greeting.

'I will meet you outside,' Louisa said in an undertone and guided the still anxious-looking Sophie to the entrance.

When Ada reached him, Davey gave a jerk of his head in the general direction of Inspector Lambert's office. 'What was all that about?'

She explained about the portrait of Mrs Thornton and Sophie, ending with, 'I imagine you'll be going back to Albion House soon.'

Davey raised his eyebrows. 'I'm surprised you told us. Considering three days ago, there was nothing of interest there.'

'Davey...' But what more was there for her to say? She'd lied to him.

He waved a hand, batting away any explanation or apology, and dropped his voice to a whisper. 'I sat in that cell with Mabel, too. And now, I understand why you wanted to go there. But they're not the same person, Ada. Saving one won't save the other.'

'I know that.' She'd felt no guilt lying to Inspector Lambert, only nerves. But, with Davey, both emotions fought for superiority. A part of her wished he'd call her out for lying, so she'd have to tell him the truth, but he only frowned at her.

She continued, 'I've learnt my lesson.'

Davey raised his eyebrows again.

'I spent most of yesterday afternoon in a holding cell. Is it really that surprising I've had a change of heart?'

His expression softened. 'I still can't believe that. I didn't know it was going to happen, I promise. The inspector made sure to keep me away from the station. Had me searching for your friend, Eliza Armstrong.'

'She's not my friend.' Ada's affront wasn't entirely an act. She might not want the woman to hang, but she still had plenty of questions for Miss Armstrong, should they find her.

'Yes, they told me what she said about you and Mr Pearce. I nearly choked on my tea.'

Ada laughed, and the moment of honest hilarity was a welcome relief. 'That's the most sensible reaction I've heard yet.'

'May be the only time you've ever called me sensible.'

'First and last.'

He chuckled.

Ada saw her chance. 'Davey, will you call us? After you've been to Albion House? I need to know how this all ends.'

He hesitated, and Ada thought her plan was finished, but then he nodded. 'All right. I'll be in touch.'

'Thank you.' It came out more emotional than she had intended, almost a sob, and his eyes widened. Ada said a hasty goodbye. Guilt threatened to consume her, even as relief danced through her veins. If he asked any more questions, her whole plan would come spilling out. So, she fled from her oldest friend.

As she exited the station, it crossed her mind that if this all went wrong, the next time she saw him, they would no longer be friends, and guilt tightened its hold on her throat.

Ada paused in the vestibule. She could go back and tell him everything. As he said, he'd been inside that prison room, too. She would make him understand. He'd help.

But if he didn't, it might cost two women their lives.

Once Ada started talking, she wouldn't stop. It wouldn't just be her plan she revealed but Louisa's theory as well. She'd be naming two women as potential killers to a police officer.

She had to stick to the plan. Her terrible ridiculous plan that might just lead them to the truth.

Ada walked down Millgarth's steps and found Louisa and Sophie waiting further down the pavement. The maid was no longer fidgeting; Louisa must have found a way to calm her nerves.

'Davey said he would call,' Ada told them.

'What now, ma'am?'

'We go home and wait,' Louisa answered.

On their sitting room floor, Ada sat with her sketchpad and pencils, drawing a picture for the Brontë commission she'd nearly forgotten. Her concentration kept slipping, however, and Top Withens ended up like a child's rendering of a house.

Louisa's constant switching between a novel and her notebook told Ada she was just as agitated. Sophie had taken herself off to the kitchen, where the occasional clatter implied she, too, was filled with restless energy.

The phone rang after Ada had balled up the world's worst portrait of Emily Brontë and thrown it into the empty fireplace. Both of them tensed at the shrill tone, then Ada jumped out of her seat and clattered into the hallway. She almost dropped the handset in her eagerness and shouted over the operator, 'Yes, yes, I accept.' A series of clicks, followed by static, and then the hiss of a connected line.

'Hello?' she said a little breathlessly.

'Did you run to the phone? Also, you know you're supposed to say which number I've reached.'

'Davey,' Ada said tersely, twisting the cord in her fingers. 'What's happening?'

To her left, Louisa hovered by the doorway, listening.

'We have Mrs Thornton in custody. She admitted to harbouring Mrs Pearce, though she claims she didn't know who she was. Apparently, she doesn't read the papers, and you need to work on your sketching ability.' Even through the crackling phone line, Davey's scepticism was plain. 'She says Mrs Pearce claimed she needed to leave the country to get herself safe from a bad situation and was debating whether to go to Hull, as the nearest large port, or Southampton, where she'd be less likely to be recognised. To hear Mrs Thornton tell it, the suspect never told her which port she'd decided on.'

'So, you don't know where she's gone?' Ada tried to keep her voice even. It sounded like Mrs Thornton had done exactly as Sophie – coached by Louisa and Ada – told her to.

'I didn't say that. Goodwin spoke with Thomas Mills and his family, given that Sophie's evidence implicated them, too. His wife admitted her mother-in-law was with them this morning. She said the older Mrs Mills was meeting her mistress on a train to Hull.'

'So, she's on the move? She decided on Hull?' Ada tried her best to sound confused, even as excitement coursed through her veins.

'Looks that way. It could all be a decoy, but Inspector Lambert and the dragon–' Ada snorted, despite the seriousness of the conversation. 'They're going to Hull, anyway, to check. And we've sent a telegram down to Southampton, just in case. If it ain't a trick, this'll all be over soon.'

'Maybe.'

'You don't sound convinced. And...Ada?'

'Yes?'

'Promise me you won't go to Hull.'

'All right. I promise I won't go to Hull.' Ada shot a look at Louisa, who tilted her head ever so slightly to indicate she understood.

'And you haven't crossed your fingers?' Davey continued.

'I haven't crossed my fingers.'

Louisa smothered a laugh, but the familiar sensation of guilt curdled in Ada's stomach.

She wasn't technically lying, but she was certainly misleading him. They were so close to answers, though, and preventing a friend from getting a little hurt wasn't worth risking two women's lives.

'You'll let us know if you find her in Hull?'

You won't.

'Yes. Talk to you soon. Goodbye.'

'Goodbye.' The line clicked off.

'So not Hull then?' Louisa smiled, and Ada matched it. The last remnants of guilt washed away with giddy excitement. Was it possible her terrible plan had worked?

'And not Southampton,' Ada added. 'If Mrs Thornton went along with our suggestion and left a false trail.'

'Let's assume she did. And let's assume they would go to the biggest nearby port that isn't Hull and head in the opposite direction.'

'A lot of assumptions,' Ada said. 'I know how you feel about assumptions.'

'I will have to live with them. How do you feel about a trip to Liverpool?'

Chapter Twenty-Nine

Dockside Disclosures

Louisa had expected Liverpool's docks to be both sprawling and hectic, but that did not make the reality any less overwhelming.

Salt and smoke fought for dominance in the air. A mishmash of boats lined the waterfront, from the smallest fishing boats to the giant passenger liners, stretching out beyond the edge of her vision. People from all walks of life thronged the pathways: upper-class passengers with their luggage-laden servants, steerage passengers clutching suitcases and carpet bags tightly, sailors loading and unloading cargo, and dockworkers tying up the rigging. Such a multitude led to a cacophony of noise – hellos, goodbyes, orders and scolding – and it pressed in on Louisa as she and Ada struggled through the mass. She reached out for the comfort of Ada's hand. It was unlikely anyone would notice amongst so much teeming humanity, and their excuse could be that they did not want to lose each other.

It was to the shadows of the colossal passenger liners, the ones that 'looked like the *Titanic*', that Louisa and Ada headed. Louisa led the way, head craned up to keep the bright red funnels in sight. With no knowledge of the layout of the docks, there was nothing for it but to continue walking in their direction.

The closer they got, the more convinced Louisa became that they had misconstrued the whole situation. That she was chasing ghosts once more.

They slowly edged nearer to the largest ship until the name painted on its stern was readable: RMS *Lusitania*. It must have just arrived, gangplanks lowered and passengers disembarking. If the Pearces, Miss Armstrong, and Stephen were here, how would they ever find them? She scanned the bustling crowd with a sinking heart. They had set themselves up for failure.

'Keep going,' Ada shouted in her ear over the noise. 'They'll be somewhere less busy.'

Louisa weaved through the crowds of people, studying every face she passed. She neared the bow of the ship, out of breath and with aching feet, when Ada gasped and tugged her towards two figures half-hidden in the ship's shadow. As they came closer, arguing voices drifted their way, and a jolt of recognition hit Louisa.

She stopped a few feet away, dragging Ada to a halt with her, and studied the figures before them. One was Clara Pearce, wearing a drab cotton day dress and a once-white cap that definitely were not her own, yet looking healthier than she had in some time. Widowhood suited her. Or no longer unknowingly consuming hyoscine suited her. Or both.

The woman with her must be Eliza Armstrong. But where were the boys? Gallant and Stephen were nowhere in sight.

Ada set off again towards the pair, and Louisa did the same, holding her hand a little tighter. The other two women were so engrossed in their whispered discussion they did not notice the approaching couple. The pair stopped half a yard away, and Ada called a cheery 'Good day!'

The women's heads jerked round. Eliza Armstrong's face twisted with comical horror, but Mrs Pearce frowned. 'I know you.' Her confusion was evident in her voice.

Miss Armstrong smoothed her face into a genial mask. 'Miss Chapman, what a pleasant surprise.' Her surprise sounded anything but pleasurable. 'Are you here to have us arrested? Though that's not a sketch artist's duty, last I checked.'

'You're my neighbours!' Mrs Pearce had pieced together who they were, but she did not sound any less confused for doing so.

'We are, yes.' Louisa turned to Miss Armstrong 'and that depends.'

She frowned and studied Louisa with critical eyes. 'On what?'

'The police aren't here,' Ada cut in. 'They're in Hull, thanks to Mrs Thornton and Mrs Mills.'

'I do not follow.' Mrs Pearce looked between the women, puzzled. 'What is happening? How do you know? About Mrs Thornton and Mrs Mills? And...Hull?'

To their right, a porter dropped a suitcase and swore loudly. Mrs Pearce jumped and stepped backwards away from the noise, eyes wide.

'Maybe we should have this conversation elsewhere?' Louisa suggested.

'No!' both women exclaimed.

'It has to be here,' Miss Armstrong stated firmly.

They are still waiting for the boys.

'You were saying something about Hull, Miss Chapman,' she added.

'It was our idea.' Ada did not quite hide the smugness from her voice. 'To get the police off your tail.'

'Why would you do that?' It was Mrs Pearce who asked, but Louisa noticed Miss Armstrong's rapt attention.

'Um...' Ada hesitated. Louisa knew her reason for being here, the face Ada saw when she looked upon Mrs Pearce, but how could she ever put that into words Mrs Pearce would understand?

So, Louisa answered for her. 'Because I think you were right. Your husband was poisoning you.'

Mrs Pearce's face went slack, and her legs wobbled underneath her. She grabbed hold of Miss Armstrong's arm for support. 'He was? I thought I was being paranoid. I accused him, and he was so indignant, he took my glass and drank the whole thing to prove me wrong. Why would he do that if he had poisoned it?'

'Because he knew it wasn't enough to hurt him. Then he finished his own, unknowing that the two of you had shared an idea: how to stop an unfaithful spouse.' Louisa scrutinised Mrs Pearce's reaction, searching for any sign that confirmed her suspicion.

Mrs Pearce shook her head so violently strands of brown hair fell from under her cap. 'No. No. I...I never meant to kill him. The chemist said it would do no harm.'

Louisa fought to remain calm, even as her mind processed the ramifications of Mrs Pearce's confession. The decision she had to make.

'He said it would do no harm!' Mrs Pearce wailed.

Facts. Louisa could process facts. 'In small quantities, hyoscine is harmless. In fact, it can even have health benefits, but two doses combined have the potential to be fatal, particularly if one of them is larger than recommended.'

'Not his! It must have been the one in my glass. I could taste it. This horrible bitter taste. At first, I thought he had bought bad wine, but I did not dare to tell him. He considers himself a wine connoisseur, always has a new one for me to try from this or that region.'

Considered, but Louisa kept her correction unspoken.

Was this the truth or the act of a woman desperately trying to avoid justice?

Beside her, Ada said, 'Do you know why he did it? If you'll excuse the bluntness, I find it odd that a man of his appetite would want to drug his wife to lower hers.'

'Oh God,' Mrs Pearce gasped. 'Henry. He never forgave me for Henry.'

'His cousin,' Ada interjected.

Mrs Pearce nodded. 'He always thought there was someone else after that. Made all these ridiculous accusations. I would call him a hypocrite, and he would call me one back, and I...' Tears ran down her cheeks, and Miss Armstrong whispered words of comfort.

'Projection,' Louisa commented, as much to herself as anyone else. 'Thinking you capable of the same immorality as him.'

'It was just the once. The whole foolish affair did not even last a month. I could not do it. Henry spoke of love, of running off together, and I knew I never could. I had my son to think of. It never should have happened to begin with, but he had always been nice, ever since I first met Alex, and he shared my anger about the affairs.'

Eliza Armstrong flinched, and Mrs Pearce gave her a reassuring smile. 'Alex tricked you, too, I realise that now, and Henry was long before that. Gallant was barely out of skirts. My Lord, I cannot even remember the woman's name – the one who triggered my liaison with Henry. I did not want an affair of my own; I just wanted Alex to stop. But he never did. That is why I turned to the hyoscine, after that maid. I knew she was too pretty to hire. I knew what would happen, but Alex insisted, and if I said no, he would only find a way to...' Her words caught in her throat, and she shook her head as if she could shake away the memories. 'The girl was a silly flirty ditz, but she did not deserve to die like that. Do you know how she died if you have spoken to Mrs Thornton?'

Louisa nodded. There was a moment of silence, and Louisa knew they were all picturing the same thing: Miss Clarke's last desperate moments on this earth. Mrs Pearce was right. However foolish the girl had been, she did not deserve to die that way. But life was not fair, and people did not get what they deserve. Why should Clara Pearce be any exception?

Because there was a chance to make a small part of the world – just a few lives – less miserable.

What of the family of a dead man? His parents, his siblings. Should they not be given closure?

The mutual remembrance ended, and Mrs Pearce continued softly, 'She offered for us to go with her – Mrs Thornton, I mean – after the girl's death. She came to the house about a week later and said she would take us somewhere safe, away from Alex. I should have said yes, but I said no like a good wife. I told myself we were in no danger, that it was not Alex's fault and the girl was to blame, that she'd brought it on herself. Silly foolish lies. Was he poisoning me even then?' Her voice had turned shrill. 'Had he been poisoning me ever since Henry?'

'I could not say,' Louisa admitted, though she had her suspicions.

'I think we can all take a guess,' Miss Armstrong spat as if she had read Louisa's thoughts. 'I'm sorry, I don't mean to be callous, but we both know what tricks he was capable of. I don't think he wanted you dead, though.'

'Who knows what he wanted; I certainly never did. I thought I did, as did you, but he was so good at making me doubt myself. And look how that ended. He poisoned me, and that poor girl, and then I poisoned him and –'

A loud gasp from nearby interrupted her. The four women turned to find its source, which came rocketing into their midst. A small boy with stained, travel-worn clothes and a dirty face hurled himself at Mrs Pearce, fists flying. In a reedy voice, he screeched, 'You killed him! You killed Papa! How could you? I hate you. I hope they hang you. You killed him! You killed him!'

Mrs Pearce knelt, trying to capture his hands and shush him.

Louisa turned away, not wanting to eavesdrop on such a private moment. Instead, she scanned the crowds around them to check if the scene had caught anyone's attention. One man gave them a strange look and then kept walking, but no one else paid them any heed. Everyone had a place to get to or work to do.

When she turned back, Miss Armstrong was also crouched beside the boy, trying to calm him. 'Gallant, do you remember me? Your father's friend.'

'You're not a friend,' he shouted. 'Did you help? Did you help kill my papa? Stephen never should have told you where we were.'

Miss Armstrong glanced in the direction Gallant had appeared from, where another dirty and weary-looking boy hung back, a muck-stained plaster cast on his arm, his face identifiable from Ada's sketch. Stephen Cartwright. He smiled at his aunt, who smiled back. The moment of recognition ignited something within him, and he sprang forward and ran into her arms.

Miss Armstrong started crying, and Louisa looked away again. Next to her, Mrs Pearce still tried to calm her sobbing son. Tear tracks streaked his grimy face. His mother wiped them away with her thumbs, and the boy leant into her touch. The tiniest tilt of his head. That said he still needed her, no matter how angry his words were.

Louisa made a spur-of-the-moment decision. 'Your mother did not kill him. Your father's death was an accident. He drank something he should not have.'

'How?' Gallant's face scrunched up in confusion.

'He, um...he...'

'He drank some wine with something nasty in it,' Ada supplied.

'He was poisoning your ma, and the silly bugger drank 'is own poison. I told you, didn't I? You said your ma was ill, and I said it was your nasty piece of work da that were doing it.' For all he spoke with cocksure confidence, Stephen still clung to Miss Armstrong's skirts. If nothing else, at least Louisa would have good news to give Mrs Mason when she next saw her.

Gallant turned a scandalised face on his friend. 'No. It's not true!'

'I've told you: your da was bad news.'

Smart boy, Louisa smiled in approval.

Doubt crept into Gallant's face. 'Is it true?' he asked his mother.

She hesitated, then nodded. It broke the boy, who crumpled into her skirts, sobbing afresh.

The rest of the group stepped away.

'So much for not drawing attention t' ourselves,' Miss Armstrong muttered. Her eyes darted around the dockside.

Louisa copied the motion. There were a few glances their way, quickly averted.

'He's been all torn up about his da,' Stephen told his aunt.

'Can't blame him,' Ada said.

'Who are you?' Stephen asked. 'Wait, are you the neighbour wit' birthmark?'

'Yes?' Ada squeaked, hand fluttering to her cheek.

Louisa shared her confusion, and it must have been just as plain in her own expression.

'The one he talked about?' Stephen demanded.

'What'd he say?' Ada aimed the question more at Miss Armstrong than Stephen.

'I owe you an apology, Miss Chapman.'

'What d'you do, Auntie Eliza?'

'Why does your nephew know who I am? And why did you tell the police I...well, you know what you told them.'

'What did you tell 'em?' Stephen piped up, looking at his aunt with curious eyes.

Louisa glanced at the Pearces, where Gallant appeared to have settled. 'Your friend seems calmer now. Maybe we should go check on him.'

'Yes, go check on Gallant, Stephen,' his aunt ordered.

The boy muttered something that sounded suspiciously like 'adults,' but he followed Louisa back towards Mrs Pearce and her son. They paused a short distance away. She had wanted to draw Stephen away from the conversation between Ada and Miss Armstrong, but she did not want to interrupt the Pearces' reunion quite yet.

'Where were you planning to go?' she asked Stephen. 'On the ships? I presume you got the money for tickets from selling whatever you stole from Gallant's house, but how exactly did you intend to convince a shipping company to allow two unaccompanied minors on-board?'

'Smart one, aren't you, miss? But we weren't going t' be alone, were we? I sent a letter t' my auntie. We're off t' America. We can start a new life there.'

'I am not sure that new life will be quite what it is sold as. Different country, same problems.'

'Ain't no one gonna try to arrest us for murder, though. What will happen to Gally's ma? Did she off his da?'

'No.'

'Are you lying?'

'Not quite.'

'If the police found her, will they say she offed him?'

'Probably.'

'Are you gonna tell 'em?

Mrs Pearce had not intended for her husband to die. He drank his own poison and hers. Then, there were the other drugs found in his system. The ones mentioned in the police report that Ada did not remember the names of. Louisa, however, had a good idea of what they were and how they got there.

Louisa had already lied to Mrs Pearce's son about her role in his father's death. How could she now try to have his mother arrested?

'Do you think I should tell the police?' Why was she asking this child for his opinion?

'Nah, miss. Old bleeder deserved it.'

'You knew him, did you not? Through his connection with your aunt. A strange circumstance. And how did you come to know Gallant?' She could not resist asking the questions that so bugged her.

'He said he was a widower. Auntie Eliza saw 'im with Gally one day, and he spun some tale about his dead wife. This weren't long after my uncle died, and my auntie was right made up to find someone t' talk with. He bribed Gally with toys and sweets and money to not tell 'is ma or say owt to Auntie Eliza. There was this really nice boat set; Gally gave me one of 'em. His bleeding da told his wife he was taking Gally out on boys' trips when actually he was coming t' see Auntie Eliza. So, my auntie started having me round more often, so Gally would've someone t' play with when they went off. Course, Gally didn't tell me all this till now, or I'd have been straight t' my auntie. Wanna know the really sad bit, miss?'

'There is a sadder part to all this?'

'I don't think it was the toys or sweets or any of the bribes that kept im quiet. He just enjoyed spending time with 'is da. He liked 'em sharing a secret. And now 'is da's gone, just like mine.' He scuffed the muddy cobbles with his shoes.

Stephen's words struck a too familiar cord, and Louisa turned to look at the Pearces once more.

'He needs his ma. I'd do owt t' bring mine back.'

And Louisa would do anything to have met hers. She felt the old ache building inside her.

She had come here for the truth, and she believed she had it. Now for the part she had been hiding from – what to do with that information? She should run and find the nearest constable. It was what her father would expect her to do. The principles he taught her to abide by.

But Ada had introduced her to a different set of principles. She glanced back at where her partner spoke with Miss Armstrong. Hopefully, Ada was gaining the answers she needed. The explanation she deserved. With that done, they would have all the information they came for. There was nothing left for them to do here.

Except what is right and lawful. And moral. Morality or legality? Letting a killer walk free is neither. Louisa closed her eyes, focusing on the noise of the port to block out her father's voice. Shouts and steam whistles and seagulls' screeches.

'Miss? You all right?'

She opened her eyes again and looked down. Stephen was watching her, bemused.

Am I really going to listen to the advice of some common child instead of that of my father?

'Miss? Are you ill?'

Louisa never got to answer as Gallant Pearce came running over, a bundle of energy and words. 'Mama's coming with us!' His face was bright. His mother must have explained away her involvement in his father's death.

Mrs Pearce moved to Louisa's side, speaking quietly so the boys would not hear. 'Whatever you told my son, you think me a murderess, do you not?'

'It was manslaughter.'

'That's life imprisonment, still.'

'It would be, yes.'

'You can find a constable quicker than I can leave this city. My life is in the hands of a woman I barely know.'

'You did not care to know me.'

'No,' she admitted. 'I did not.'

'But I did not care to know you, either. Perhaps if I had, I would have seen the horrors lurking behind the idyllic surface of your home.'

'Horrors is a strong word.'

Louisa could have said many things. She could have reminded Mrs Pearce of pleading on her knees for forgiveness. Of Mr Pearce's affairs, and Miss Clarke's death, and that his son was so starved of paternal affection, he had been willingly bribed. But who would that help?

'I suppose so,' she agreed.

'I must confess, I still do not understand why you came all this way. Your companion works for the police, yet she speaks of misleading them. Why would she do that? Why are you here, Miss Knight?'

'Mrs Mason, who is a friend of Miss Armstrong's, asked me to find Stephen.' That did not answer her first question and was a half-truth at best, but Louisa would not even try and explain the rest.

'Well, you found more than Stephen.'

What I should find is the nearest police officer.

Louisa did not believe in an afterlife, yet she still felt her father's judgement every second she hesitated.

Yet, if she did as he wished, Ada would never forgive her.

Mrs Pearce sighed. 'I am tired of living in suspense, waiting to be caught. I beg you, Miss Knight, tell me: will I be leaving this dock with my son or in handcuffs?'

Chapter Thirty

An Infuriating Explanation

Ada seethed as Miss Armstrong explained how Mr Pearce had teased her about his neighbour's new companion. 'The pretty young girl with the birthmark' who was making eyes at him.

'And you believed him?' Ada demanded.

'He spoke of how kind you were. How he thought you'd pinned your hopes on the lonely widower next door - since no one could know about us - and it upset him to have to let you down.' She snorted. 'I don't think he ever cared about who he hurt. He was just trying to make me jealous.'

'Yet, you mourn for him.' Harsh, but with Miss Armstrong standing in front of her, the simmering anger from yesterday was brought to a boil.

Miss Armstrong gave a sad smile. 'I mourn a version of him that never existed. I've been in mourning for Alex since long before he died.'

It was hard for Ada to maintain her malice in the face of such plain sadness. 'I'm sorry. He was a bastard of the highest order. No one deserves the way he treated you.'

'Even people who tell the police you slept with him?' Was Miss Armstrong seriously joking about this now? Despite herself, Ada smiled. The whole chain of events was too ridiculous to do anything else.

Miss Armstrong matched it with a tentative quirk of her lips.

Ada's next question might ruin the moment of accord, but she had to ask. 'Did you actually believe I had an affair with him?'

Miss Armstrong's smile dropped. 'No. You were so baffled, I knew it wasn't true. But the police had so many questions, and I couldn't sit in a cell when I should be looking for Stephen, so I thought...' She gave a slight shrug, spreading her hands out in a 'what-else-could-I-do' gesture. 'Let the police waste their time investigating an affair that never happened. I didn't know you were trying to help find Stephen at that point.'

A fresh spark of fury dissipated Ada's equilibrium. 'What if I'd gone to prison?'

Miss Armstrong shook her head. 'I don't give the police much credit, but you are one of theirs. I'd like to think they'd hesitate before sending you down.'

She was right. Inspector Lambert had scared the truth out of her, but from the other side of a police cell, Ada doubted he ever intended to send her to prison. Would he have offered the same leniency to a stranger? Particularly one of Miss Armstrong's skin colour?

Had she not done the same when faced with the threat of arrest? In that interview room, she had not cared if Mrs Pearce or Miss Armstrong were imprisoned or hanged as long as it wasn't her or Louisa.

'You were right,' Ada said.

'And I'm glad of it. There was a point where I thought I'd

misjudged because that police inspector, he believed me far too quickly.'

'Really?' The word came out as a shrill demand.

'I thought he'd argue, deny it, call me names and a liar, but none of that. He was angrier about your visit to me. He was furious about that, asking me all sorts of questions, but when I said you'd had an affair with Alex, he just believed me. Wrote it down all calm.'

Ada gave a huff of amusement. Now she understood. 'Would it make any sense if I said I think he both believed you and didn't?'

Miss Armstrong scrunched up her nose. 'Not really, no.'

'I don't reckon he thought I had an affair, but he had to act like it could be true until I proved otherwise. And teach me a damn lesson whilst he was at it. I think you're right, however; it was the interfering that angered him. That's what earnt me my time in a cell.'

'You got out, though.'

Unless Inspector Lambert finds out we came here. She'd thrown concern to the wind, determined to outsmart the man who'd outsmarted her and rectify the words he'd drawn out of her at the station. In doing so, she'd ignored the fact she might walk herself – and Louisa – into a cell in Armley Gaol. It was too late to turn back now. She said none of this to Miss Armstrong, only a taut, 'I did.'

'Still, I'm sorry my actions hurt you, especially when you and your friend were trying to find my nephew.'

'I'm not sure how much help we were. You'd have made it here together, anyway. Can I ask...how did you come to be here with Mrs Pearce?'

Miss Armstrong smiled. 'It would've surprised me, too, if you'd told me last week where I would be today and who I would be with. Is it true? What your friend told Mrs Pearce? They were poisoning each other?'

Ada nodded. 'As far as we can tell. There are...other complications.'

Miss Armstrong sent her an inquisitive look.

'Another woman he wronged. The point is no one can say exactly what – or who – killed him. Maybe it was the hyoscine he'd put in his wife's glass that tipped the whole situation to its fatal conclusion.' A phrase she borrowed from Louisa's explanation.

'Or maybe not. I doubt your police colleagues would see it that way, but I must confess I prefer it. A fitting end. He killed the man I loved a long time ago.' Miss Armstrong's eyes glazed, but before Ada could say anything, she continued with forced cheeriness. 'But that doesn't answer your question about how I came to be here. Clara – Mrs Pearce – knew the boys had been close; Gallant told her everything after I caused a scene at their house. After he ran away, she sent her maid to beg me to ask Stephen if he'd seen him, but–'

'Stephen was already missing.'

'Yes. He told me Gallant had found him in the hospital - by the sounds of it, that boy could put your investigative abilities to shame - but he was scared to come to me for help. Worried I'd hand his friend over to the police. They planned to run away together, but he decided to send me a letter at the last moment. He's a good boy for all his rough edges. So, when the maid came by again yesterday morning, I had news to share with her. The boys must've had a tougher time getting here – Stephen's letter said they'd be here last night. It gave us plenty of time to talk, myself and Clara, to piece together all of Alex's lies. We have a lot in common, though society would have us be enemies.' She gave a tight smile. 'Now that I've answered your question, I have to ask: will you tell the police you found us?'

Ada shook her head. 'I wanted answers, but I don't want to see anyone hang or imprisoned.'

'You'll just let us walk away? Even Clara?' Miss Armstrong sounded sceptical.

'Yes. I have my reasons.' Ada didn't elaborate even though Miss Armstrong had been open with her. It had been hard enough to tell Louisa. Instead, she asked, 'What will you do now? I doubt you'll be able to return to Leeds.'

Miss Armstrong gave a slight humourless chuckle. 'Now there's the question. Stephen mentioned America in his letter. He called it where people go for a new life, but I think it'd be best to convince him that's a poor idea. This country's far from perfect, but I doubt America will be an improvement for me. I haven't decided where we will go, and perhaps it'd be better for us both if you don't know.'

'I can't disagree with that.' The police had broken her easily enough once.

'What will you tell your police colleagues?'

'I was never here.'

'And your friend?'

Ada hesitated. Louisa had come this far. Would her sense of righteousness, her father's belief in the law, now tie her hands? What would happen to them, should they take different turns at this crossroad? Ada didn't want to walk a different path from Louisa, but if they disagreed, she couldn't follow her. Not this time.

'I can't speak for her.'

'Then I shall find out.' Miss Armstrong moved to where the others stood, and Ada followed. 'We should go,' she said to Mrs Pearce.

Ada watched Louisa's face with growing trepidation. Her actions now would decide so many futures, including Ada's, and she would do the right thing. The question was whether they would agree on what that was.

A coin spinning in the air, which side up would it fall?

Heads or tails?

Legality or morality?

'We should go, too,' Ada prompted, and Louisa turned to face her. So often, Ada struggled to understand what was happening behind those hazel eyes, but this time she saw the conclusion forming there, the determination setting in. Then Louisa smiled, the soft sweet private smile only for Ada, and she knew her decision and why.

'Yes, we should. We would not want to miss the train home. Goodbye, Mrs Pearce, Miss Armstrong, and good luck.'

'Good luck,' Ada echoed, her heart soaring.

The group parted ways, splintering off in opposite directions back into the crowd. Ada moved closer to Louisa, wrapping her arm round hers and taking her hand. The docks were too busy for anyone to notice or care.

There were a lot of things to say, but they were for later. For now, Ada relished the freedom from the obligation she'd given herself.

They would go home and back to their lives. Back to re-decorating and painting and studying. To soft kisses, secret smiles, and nights where Louisa asked to take her upstairs, and Ada knew it was for no other reason than because she wanted to show her affection.

It was over. Another woman wouldn't be sentenced because a man had no self-control. A happy ending. This time, at least, there was a happy ending. The thought of Mabel still stuck in Armley Gaol clouded her joy, but there was nothing she could do about that.

There is one thing I could do.

The thought stuck with her throughout waiting on the platform and boarding their train. There was one small change she could make to the end of Mabel's story.

'You're quiet,' Louisa commented as the train made it out of the city and chugged past farmers' fields. 'What are you thinking?'

'About Mabel.' She'd promised herself she would keep no more secrets from Louisa. 'And about you. What changed your mind? Why did you let Mrs Pearce go?'

'It was the right thing to do.' A simple answer, but Ada understood it. Still, she needed to know.

'Was it because of me?'

'Not because of you alone. I am far too stubborn for that.'

Normally, Ada would've laughed, but she was too tense to do anything but focus on the words she had to say next. They came out in a garbled rush. 'I should start visiting Mabel again.'

Louisa didn't even flinch. Using her handbag to shield

them from view, she interlinked their hands, and Ada relaxed a little. Her last doubt vanished as Louisa said, 'I think you should. It is also the right thing to do.'

The decision made, they lapsed back into silent contemplation of the passing greenery. The conversation was over, the entire situation was over, and she had made a resolution about Mabel. Ada rode a cloud of giddy relief the rest of the way home.

Chapter Thirty-One

The Final Piece

Louisa had not considered whether the elderly Mrs Clarke and her granddaughter were religious when she suggested they make this visit on a Sunday morning. They had given it a week since returning from Liverpool, going about their day-to-day lives in the hope of avoiding further suspicion.

She tried to gauge from the outside if anyone was home, but there were no tell-tale signs either way. Their house was as Ada had described it, faded door and rotten window frames.

'Shall we knock?' Ada said. She held a parcel in her hands, clutching it so tight, her knuckles were white.

Louisa nodded and rapped the wood with her fist. It took a while for someone to answer, and Louisa had decided they must be church-goers after all when the door swung open.

'Oh, hello.' Mrs Parks frowned, her uncertainty written across her face.

'May we come in?' Ada asked.

'I, um...sure.' Mrs Parks did not sound at all sure, but she stepped aside to allow them to pass.

The sitting room was the dusty mausoleum Louisa had feared her home would become after her father's death. A shrunken woman sat at a chipped dining table, and two young girls sat on the floor playing with homemade woollen dollies. All three turned intrigued eyes on their guests.

'Look, Nana, we have visitors.'

Mrs Clarke peered at them. She clicked her fingers at Ada. 'I remember you. You came asking about my Susie. Betty said the police arrested you, too. Huh. Can't trust those peelers, eh? Like my Betty would hurt a fly, eh dear?'

'They took Mummy away,' one girl sniffed.

Mrs Parks shushed her daughter. If Louisa had not already had her suspicions, she would not have noticed the tightening at the corners of her mouth.

'At least these are better circumstances than the last time we saw each other,' she said to Ada. 'But what brings you back here? We've told you all there is to know about Susie'

'I wanted to bring you this.' Ada handed over the parcel.

The two girls abandoned their toys and inched closer, curiosity ablaze in their eyes.

When Mrs Parks tugged at the strings, it opened to reveal a framed portrait of Miss Clarke. Ada had been working on it throughout the week.

'It's not my best work,' Ada said apologetically.

Mrs Clarke still took it from her granddaughter with fervent hands. 'Susie,' she whispered. 'My Susie. How did you...'

'That's Auntie Susie?' the younger girl asked, trying to clamber onto her great-grandmother's knee.

'It looks just like her!' the older girl exclaimed. She turned to Ada with a look of pure admiration on her face.

'Miss Chapman's a sketch artist.' Mrs Parks turned to Ada. 'I'm surprised you remember her in such detail.'

'She was a memorable woman.'

A sad smile graced Mrs Parks' face. 'Thank you.' She gestured at the table. 'Please stay for tea.'

Ada looked frightened at the prospect. 'That's very kind, but I'm afraid we need to go. I just wanted to deliver that for you.'

Louisa hesitated. Had Ada forgotten there was another reason for their visit? But then Mrs Parks moved to follow them, stepping out alongside them and closing the door. 'Is this the end of it all then?'

'The case has gone cold,' Ada said. 'The warrant for Mrs Pearce is outstanding, but there is every reason to suspect she and Gallant are out of the country. The police can't look for her forever. You're safe now.'

'Safe?' Fear flashed in Mrs Parks' eyes.

'The police don't have enough to prosecute you.'

'You got lucky,' Louisa added. 'No one in the public house saw you put the pills in Mr Pearce's food.'

She shook her head, muttering denials, but then asked tearfully, 'Is that what killed him? I never meant for him to die. I was just so angry. He was so unbothered by Susie's death and his part in it. That's why I had them, to make him face what he did. You know what he said to me? That he was going to the water closet, and he hoped when he came back, I would be calmer and able to be more rational.'

Louisa raised her eyebrows. Mr Pearce always managed to lower her opinion of him one notch more.

'I'd have thrown them in his food, too,' Ada muttered.

'I thought they would make him a little ill. I didn't think they would kill a man, not the way they can kill women.'

'They most likely would not have, had he not also drunk

hyoscine later that night. Two doses of it. One he put in his wife's drink, the other she put in his. What killed him is impossible to determine.'

That was the reason they had decided to tell Mrs Parks the truth. She would not have to live with the guilt that her actions alone had killed him.

'We're taking the view it was the poison he contributed that tipped the scale,' Ada said.

'I...I like that idea.' Mrs Parks gave a watery smile. 'It's justice for Susie.'

A wave of grim satisfaction overtook Louisa. It only further confirmed she had made the right decision. Seeing Mrs Pearce and Mrs Parks imprisoned would have been a failure of the law. It would not have been a satisfactory conclusion, even if it were the legal one. Three children would have grown up without parents. Mr Pearce had cost enough people their happiness whilst alive; why should he inflict further misery in death?

'Do the police know? About the pills?' Mrs Parks asked.

'No,' Ada reassured her. 'And they won't either.'

She sagged with relief, muttering her thanks to them and God. Louisa and Ada gave her one last reassurance and said their goodbyes.

There was one more place they needed to go.

Ada kept up a string of chatter as they walked to the tram stop. She was clearly only doing it to hide her nerves, but it would be churlish to say so.

'The new table and chairs are being delivered on Tuesday,' Ada told her.

'Good. I cannot wait to see how they look.'

The plans to re-decorate the dining room were in full motion now. Louisa had left any lingering wish to cling onto her father's home on Liverpool's docks beside the RMS *Lusitania*.

Ada switched topics unexpectedly. 'Did I tell you they've let Mrs Mills go? There's no need to ask Mr Connolly to look at their case.'

'Yes. You mentioned it over dinner yesterday. How everyone at the station believes she must have gotten the money for bail and a lawyer from Mrs Pearce, but they cannot prove it. Daniel Mills hired him, and his mother is holding to her story they paid with family savings.'

'Oh, right, yes, course I did.' Ada shook her head. 'Sorry. I'm distracted.'

Louisa stepped a little closer to whisper in her ear. 'I will not lie and tell you this will be easy, but you can do it.'

'I have to. It's the one thing I can do for Mabel. But thank you for being so understanding.'

'You do not have to thank me.' How could she not be understanding? What was the alternative? To demand a woman be left alone to rot in jail? It was not an ideal situation, but life was never ideal. On that, at least, Louisa still agreed with her father.

As they reached the empty tram stop, Louisa resumed their earlier conversation. 'No other news from the station, then?'

Ada shook her head. 'Only that everyone continues to be frustrated that they got outsmarted by a housemaid and a female do-gooder. Mrs Thornton, in particular, still stings. That she so obviously lied through her teeth, and they can't prove a word of it wrong.' A slight smirk crept across Ada's mouth. 'Other than that, I think everyone is on strict no-telling-Miss-Chapman-more-than-absolutely-necessary orders. Inspector Lambert suspects me and you and...Davey...'

Ada said his name like a sigh. Constable Wilkinson had conveniently forgotten to report a call from the train station, saying that two women matching their description had been spotted, but he had made his resentment at having to do so clear, cold-shouldering Ada ever since.

'They cannot brood on their failure forever,' Louisa told her with a reassuring smile.

'I know. Still, I wonder if I'd be better quitting, but then...'

But then who will interfere next time?

For inevitably, there was going to be a next time. The unease that coiled around Louisa's heart was no less than it had been two weeks ago, but she could no longer argue against intervention. The unquestionable law of her father's lectures was a thing of the past.

The tram arrived, and in the more public setting of its car, they returned to lighter topics. The conversation halted as they reached their stop and exited into the shadows of the imposing walls of Armley Gaol.

'Maybe this is a terrible idea.' Ada took a step backwards, away from the prison.

Louisa caught her arm to stop her from walking into the road. 'Your last terrible idea turned out alright.'

Ada gave a breathy little laugh, but then she nodded; her face set in a determined expression. 'I know you said not to thank you but thank you anyway for accompanying me here.'

Louisa gave her a soft smile. 'Good luck. I will see you at home.'

'See you at home.' Head held high, Ada marched towards the prison as love pulled at Louisa's heart.

Maybe the visit would go well. Maybe it would not. Either way, Ada would come home. Life would go on. It would be different and challenging, but were not all things worth having worth fighting for?

Acknowledgements

I owe many thanks to my friends and family for their overwhelming support and encouragement for me and this book (when I finally told them about it!). I don't think I can ever fully express my gratitude and love for you all.

To my mum and dad, for everything.

Specific to this book, for fostering my love of reading, for supporting my writing (even when I was being odd and refusing to talk about it), and always encouraging me.

To Nathan, who – in true younger sibling style – insisted he was included in the acknowledgments.

To Nicole, Emily and Michael, for being generally lovely, and, in particular, for their advice, bolstering, and letting me spam the group chat with writing memes.

To Becky and Iram, for always supporting me, through high school, adult life and publishing.

To my editor, Charlie Knight, for being wonderful throughout the entire process and bringing my wayward punctuation under control.

To the critquers at Scribophile, whose advice helped me to polish the early drafts of this novel and steered it in the right direction.

To the writing community on Twitter, which introduced me to so many amazing fellow authors to share this journey with.

And, finally, my thanks to you, the reader. I hope you enjoyed joining Louisa and Ada on their story as much as I enjoyed writing it.

Sarah Bell

About the Author

Sarah Bell is a queer indie author from Leeds, England. She has enjoyed reading and writing since she was a child and loves the chance to lose herself in other worlds and times. Outside of fiction, her interests include history and language. Not too surprisingly then, she has a degree in History & English from the University of Huddersfield. *The Murder Next Door* is her debut novel.

Stay up to date with her writing news on:

Twitter and Instagram (@sarahbellwrites)

And her website (sarahbellwrites.com)

Lightning Source UK Ltd.
Milton Keynes UK
UKHW011914010522
402309UK00004B/64